Amely Bölte, Theodore Johnson

Madame de Staël

An historical novel

Amely Bölte, Theodore Johnson

Madame de Staël
An historical novel

ISBN/EAN: 9783337028671

Printed in Europe, USA, Canada, Australia, Japan

Cover: Foto ©Andreas Hilbeck / pixelio.de

More available books at **www.hansebooks.com**

MADAME DE STAËL:

AN HISTORICAL NOVEL.

BY

AMELY BÖLTE.

TRANSLATED FROM THE GERMAN

BY THEODORE JOHNSON.

———

NEW YORK:

G. P. PUTNAM & SONS, PUBLISHERS,

ASSOCIATION BUILDING, 23D STREET.

CONTENTS.

BOOK I.

BOOK II.

BOOK III.

MADAME DE STAEL

BOOK I.

CHAPTER I.

THE DEATH OF LOUIS XV.

Natura la fece e poi ruppe la stampa. It was a dull, close, overcast day. A drizzling rain thickened the atmosphere and enwrapped everything in a gray shroud. The first verdure of May was sprouting, and the magnificent shade-trees in the gardens of the Tuileries raised their heads more proudly as leaf after leaf shot forth from their branches and hourly imparted a more and more attractive appearance to them.

To-day, however, no one feasted his eyes on the fresh verdure; not an idler wended his way hither; not a warm sunbeam stole down from the overcast sky to kiss away the moisture from the young leaflets.

The streets of Paris were deserted; only pressing necessity could induce any one to leave the shelter of his roof. Curiosity, generally so imperious a mistress, raised its voice but feebly in the face of the storm raging without, and only a few persons ventured into the streets to inquire after the health of Louis the Fifteenth, who was so dangerously sick at Versailles that prayers for the salvation of his soul had already ascended to heaven in all the churches of the capital.

All France was anxiously looking forward to the moment when death would free the country from a King who had brought it to the brink of ruin; and when the news that Louis the Fifteenth was dead, came at last, the people set no bounds to their rejoicings. All requirements of propriety were disregarded; the very laws were powerless in the face of this universal exultation; and the Parisians laughed, when, outwardly at least, they should have mourned.

"THE KING'S GRANARY IS FOR RENT!"

Such was the inscription which a wit had written in large letters on the entrance of the Halles, and all passers-by stood still to enjoy the joke.

His successor, it was hoped, would not embark in corn speculations, so injurious to the welfare of the people; the prices of grain would fall, and bread would be cheap; the people looked forward to the future with bright anticipations of better days.

Madame Du Barry had departed; there was no longer a *Parc aux cerfs;* virtue and innocence were no longer in danger of falling victims to arbitrariness, and law and order were to prevail once more. Heartfelt joy reigned everywhere.

While such and similar thoughts engrossed the minds of the people; while the rich as well as the poor hopefully looked forward to the future; while all France, as if freed from a heavy burden, drew a deep breath of relief, Louis the Sixteenth ascended a throne which rested on foundations undermined by Voltaire and the philosophers of the eighteenth century, when it had need of the strongest props; and these the unfortunate King was not to find during the whole of his eventful reign.

The multitude was unable to penetrate the critical condition of the country; individuals, misled by appearances, kept only their personal circumstances in view; and the public consists of such individuals.

Only thinkers, philosophers, and statesmen, gravely examined the true state of affairs, and weighed its effects upon the future of the country. The results of their investigations were disheartening in the extreme, and added greatly to their apprehensions.

Among those who inquired in this manner into the condition of France, at the death of Louis the Fifteenth, there was a foreigner who, by means of adroit commercial speculations, had succeeded in amassing a considerable fortune in the course of a few years. To be better able to carry on these speculations, he had familiarized himself with the financial condition and resources of the state; and this knowledge taught him how to weigh the present with calmness and penetration, and to inquire what steps should be taken in order to fill the depleted treasury. Little did he imagine, in adding figure to figure, how closely every cipher he wrote was to be connected with his own fortunes. What was now to him a mere pastime to while away his leisure hours, what he hastily jotted down in order to test his own financial ability, was to attract one day the attention of all Europe, and to become the turning-point of his career.

The foreigner whom we see engaged in these calculations at the accession of Louis the Sixteenth, was still in the prime of life. He was a native of Geneva, where the Necker family lived in somewhat reduced circumstances. Educated for the mercantile career, he had gone to Paris at an early age and obtained a situation at the counting-house of Thellusson, the banker; afterwards he was also appointed Consul of Switzerland—an office neither important nor lucrative.

Young Necker, however, had already known how to provide for himself in a different manner. He was a born financier, and circumstances greatly favored his speculations. He
was not long in amassing considerable wealth, and married
Mademoiselle Curchod, a beautiful young country-woman of
his.

This young lady was the daughter of a Swiss preacher, a
strict Calvinist, and possessed no other fortune than the excellent education which her father himself had given to her. She
was a most accomplished woman, and possessed scientific
knowledge such as young ladies seldom acquire. Brought up
like a boy, she was perfectly able to meet the grave demands
of a life requiring her to provide for herself.

For a time she was at the head of a small school in her
native country; she then had an opportunity of going to
Paris as companion to a wealthy lady, and here she became
acquainted with young Necker, whom she soon learned to love
with all her heart. So she was overjoyed when he proposed to
her, and she entered his house as the happiest of wives.

A new world arose before her in the brilliant capital of
France. But what a world it was! Brought up in the austere principles peculiar to the Calvinists of the small republic
of Geneva, she wished beyond measure to see what Parisian society permitted itself, and how much those who wished to belong
to the *Bon-Ton* had to permit themselves; and she then began
to reflect on the course she had to pursue in order to assimilate herself to the peculiarities of this strange society.

Ignorant of Parisian manners, she possessed few of the attractions peculiar to fashionable French ladies. Neither her bearing nor her way of expressing herself indicated a woman
brought up in the highly refined sphere of Parisian society.
Her toilet was wanting in elegance, her bearing in pleasing, and

her politeness in winning grace; in short, her mind and manners were too much those of a learned woman to appear to great advantage.

But, in return, modesty, candor, and kind-heartedness distinguished her in the most favorable manner.

A moral education and thorough instruction had fully developed the noble gifts of her heart and mind. Her sentiments were pure and faultless; but she did not know how to express them in attractive words.

Method and regularity were the rules of her duties. Everything about her was measured and systematic; even in jesting she rarely exceeded certain bounds, and used the language and tone of a school-mistress even in her *salon*.

She was pained to notice how her bearing and manners were at variance with those of other ladies of her age; and yet she was unable to bring about the change for which she longed. She was anxious to please others, in order to please her husband the better. She trembled at the thought that his eyes might discover what was wanting in her. She, therefore, took the utmost pains to be amiable, kind, and chatty, in order that he, too, might find her so; unfortunately, however, she was unable to conceal these studied efforts from the eyes of others, and so they were not appreciated.

Their wealth was constantly on the increase; they moved into a very fine house, and desired to extend the circle of their acquaintances. Necker himself was not the man to form a brilliant circle of friends. Educated for the mercantile career, he was deficient in general culture. Accustomed to the mysterious operations of the banking business, and absorbed in the calculations of commercial speculations, he knew but little of the world, held intercourse with very few friends, had no time for reading books, and was but superficially informed of what-

soever was foreign to his business. Prudence and self-love,
therefore, caused him to be reserved in conversation, and he
avoided expressing his views whenever topics with which
he was not familiar were alluded to. This reserve of his was
looked upon as pride, although it was but prudence that counseled him to keep silence whenever he knew his knowledge to
be deficient.

Madame Necker was desirous of offering to her husband,
after his grave labors at his counting-house were over, the recreation of a pleasant social circle in her *salon.* Her tastes caused
her to look upon *savants* and artists as the persons best fitted
for this purpose; but to attract men of this class was by no
means easy. It is true, a young and beautiful lady has many
opportunities of getting acquainted with distinguished men,
but such acquaintances rarely ripen into the sort of dignified intimacy which she was desirous to bring about; and the
stiff and pedantic manners of the young daughter of Switzerland seemed to add greatly to the difficulties of such an undertaking.

She had hitherto had but one friend, Thomas, the academician, whose acquaintance she had formed at the house of her
protectress, shortly after her arrival in Paris. The bearing
and manners of M. Thomas were no less formal than her own,
and so she felt particularly attracted toward him. One day
she confessed to him the plan she had conceived, and the difficulties she would have to meet in carrying it into effect.

That she wished to exert a refining and ennobling influence on her husband, and to elevate his mind by bringing
him in contact with distinguished men, met with his cordial
approbation, and he promised to assist her to the best of his
ability.

Whenever he was invited to Necker's house, he begged permission to bring a friend with him, and soon visitors were no longer wanting to the house.

Madame Necker was overjoyed, although she took good care not to betray her exultation. She was too distrustful of her tact to permit herself a word, a remark, a smile, that was not the result of deliberation, but appeared on her lips on the spur of the moment.

She resolved to strain every nerve in order to render her house as attractive as possible to the most eminent men; but it was not for her own sake that she took this resolution. She wished to see her husband play a brilliant *role;* she wished to impart to him, by means of this social circle, a nimbus which was to deceive him as to his own talents, and to make an author and *litterateur* of the banker. In this respect she was an excellent Lady Macbeth.

She never tired of praising and encouraging him. To all he said and did, she added comments surrounding even his most insignificant actions with a radiant halo. She wanted others to respect, revere, and love him as she loved him, and she was indefatigable in her efforts to convert the world to her own opinion.

Necker did not interfere with her. He silently accepted her homage, and allowed his beautiful young wife to erect altars to him. It is so sweet to be praised. Madame Necker knew the secret of making her wedded life a happy one, and turned her knowledge to good account. Her husband, upon whom all her thoughts and feelings were concentrated, could no longer do without her, and she promoted his happiness in every possible manner.

She taught him to believe in himself, and to find in his mind faculties whose existence he had never suspected up to this time; she convinced him that he was endowed with all kinds

of talents, and that it depended only on himself to turn them
to account; and the future proved the power of her love and
confidence.

Necker's bearing toward his guests was stiff and reserved.
His wife noticed it, and tried to make amends for his conduct
by redoubling her own politeness. The conversation with their
visitors being left to her alone, it was often very difficult for
her to prevent unpleasant pauses; and whenever the conversation in her *salon* flagged, her uneasiness and anxious air betrayed the painful impression it made upon her mind.

Necker, however, seemed to notice neither her confusion nor
her generous efforts; and it was this circumstance that comforted her when, in her despondency, she was ready to charge
herself with being deficient in talent and vivacity to throw the
kindling spark into the midst of her guests.

Her caution always prevented her from uttering rash remarks.

She had given birth to a daughter a year after their wedding.
The young wife looked anxiously at her husband; she was
fearful lest a daughter should be unwelcome to him—" God has
given her to us," he said; and with an air of fervent gratitude
he pressed the little creature to his heart.

She was to remain their only child.

Cherished and petted, she grew up a chubby, healthy child,
with whom her father liked to play as soon as the grave labors
of the day were over.

His accounts grew more and more extensive, his calculations more and more intricate and exhausting; and, therefore,
as soon as he had closed his books, he delighted in the innocent
prattle of his child.

The millions which he had amassed by this time rendered it
incumbent on him to be very careful in the investments which

he made, and, as a matter of course, in his financial operations he never lost sight of the political horizon.   When Louis the Fifteenth died, the welfare of France was already indirectly connected with that of Necker; and as he now, at the accession of the new sovereign, examined the political and financial condition of the State once more, self-interest was a leading motive of his, and he found that his fortunes, in a great measure, were linked with the fate of France.

1*

CHAPTER II.

NECKER'S SALON.

FOR some time past, Madame Necker had received at her house every Friday a small circle of friends, among whom there were some of the most eminent men of that period. To-day, for the first time, her *salon* had remained deserted, and she now turned her eyes toward the door, hoping that some guests might still enter the room.

Bright flames were blazing in the large fire-place, despite the vernal verdure in which nature was already clad. Close to the fire, his hands folded at his back, stood M. Necker, engaged in an animated conversation with Baron Grimm, whose effeminate features, painted cheeks, and courtly deportment contrasted singularly with the short, heavy-set, and common-looking figure of the honest Genevan. They were speaking of a topic which engrossed to-day the thoughts of all Parisians. The news of the death of King Louis the Fifteenth had reached their ears, too, and both commented gravely on the condition of poor France at the close of this long and calamitous reign, which Frederick the Great had jocularly called the reign of the three cotillons.*

Madame Necker participated, to-day, but very little in the conversation; nay, contrary to her habit, she scarcely seemed to listen to it attentively. She sat leaning back in her large comfortable easy-chair and played with her fan, now opening it, now closing it, and now screening her eyes with it from the

---

* "Memoires de la Du Barry." Vol. II., p. 42. "Memoires de Madame Necker de Saussure."

flames in the fire-place. The expression of her face showed plainly that she was absorbed in reflections which carried her far away from what was passing around her.

At her side, on a small wooden footstool, sat her only child, a little girl of eight, cutting all sorts of figures out of a sheet of paper. She had placed her stool in such a manner that the back of the easy-chair covered her almost entirely, and concealed her from the eyes of her from whom, it seemed, she wished to hide what she was doing. A smile of satisfaction lit up the features of the child. While her full, fresh cheeks crimsoned still more, she suddenly jumped up from her seat, and exclaimed joyously, " Oh! look at this, Papa! It looks just like the little Abbe Raynal, does it not? You would have recognized him, I am sure, even if I had not told you whom it is intended to represent?"

Necker turned kindly to the little girl; all bitterness and gravity disappeared from his features as he seized the paper figure and said, " Indeed, my dear Germaine, this is a very pretty little figure, and, although it does not resemble our friend, it resembles the bad class of men to whom he belongs, and who are even worse than he. Would to God we had those gentlemen as much in our power as I now hold this paper image."

These words attracted Madame Necker's attention. She had raised herself, so that her exceedingly tall hair-dress, which was adorned with plumes and bows, towered over the back of her easy-chair. She exclaimed in a warning, reproachful tone, " Germaine, how impertinent you are! How could you interrupt the very interesting conversation of the gentlemen in such an absurd manner?"

" Never mind her," said M. Necker. " She wanted some one to share her joy, and so she went of course to her father."

The little girl fixed her large, black eyes with a grateful

expression on M. Necker, and then quietly sat down again. She knew that this was the best way of soothing her angry mother.

At this moment, the door of the *salon* opened, and several guests entered without being announced. One of them, a corpulent little man with a light-colored wig and blue eyes lying deep in their sockets, hastened with a quick step through the room, bowed to Madame Necker, and seizing little Germaine's hands, squeezed them heartily, and imprinted a kiss on the forehead of the child, who seemed to be accustomed to this affectionate salute.

"How late!" exclaimed M. Necker, as soon as the new-comer turned to him. "I thought already you had been called to Versailles, my dear Raynal, to assist in relieving the conscience of the dying King."

"The King would have rued it, for I should have refused him absolution," exclaimed Raynal, laughing. "Their majesties know already whom to apply to under such circumstances. But, although I was not called to Versailles, I have been hard at work all day for the King in order to be able to give full particulars of his death in to-morrow's issue of my paper. His death was very tragic, almost too tragic for a simple mortal. Providence might have dispatched two poor sinners with what it inflicted upon him alone. But things that have happened cannot be altered. He has enjoyed the good things that fell to his share, and I do not envy them to him."

"What did you ascertain about him?" inquired M. Necker.

"Little or much, as you please. It was very difficult to obtain authentic news about his condition. Madame Helvetius, the Abbe Morellet, and some other friends of mine, went to dine at Sevres, where they would be closer to the source of news; for the couriers, who were hourly dispatched from Versailles, halted there in order to change horses. I was requested to accompany them, and should have done so had I not thought that the trip would take too much of my valuable time. And then they were not very successful. Mademoiselle Espinasse, who was also there, met me an hour ago, and did not know much more about it than I. I congratulated her on our having at last been delivered from the reign of the King's mistresses; but she shook her head and replied with a very gloomy air, ' My dear Abbe, the future may have worse things in store for us.' *   I laughed at her fears. ' You must have a very lively imagination to think such things likely,' I replied to her. A man could not have made that remark. The poor lady takes too gloomy a view of the new era that is dawning upon us."

" And the view you take of it is too rose-colored," said Necker, laughing.

" Well, perhaps it is ; but then the course of my own life certainly justifies me in taking such a view of the future. Imagine the life I led at St. Sulpice's, where I had to read a mass for eight sous at six o'clock in the morning in midwinter, in order not to starve to death. What would have become of me but for my hopes in the future? . Tell me, my dear friend Necker, if any man could have borne such a life without the firm conviction that better days awaited him? Hope is the most essential element of my life."

" Well, well, my dear Raynal," replied Necker, gravely but good-humoredly. " I believe you found some other means than hope to render your condition less intolerable."

" What if I did ? Necessity has no law," said Raynal, shrugging his shoulders.

" It seems to me, that is not exactly in consonance with Christian principles," replied Necker, laughing.

---

* " Memoires de l'Abbe Morellet," p. 25.   Raynal, Biographie Universelle.

" He who falls into the water must not ask what hand is to
save him from drowning," said the Abbe, merrily. "As the
living acted so niggardly toward me, I had to apply to the
dead; and it was this, I suppose, that you intended to allude
to; for the rest, it was a mere trifle, that sum of sixty francs,
for which I permitted such a sinner to be buried in consecrated
ground. Do you not think so, too?"

"To be sure, it was very little," replied Necker, to whom
this conversation with the Abbe seemed to afford pleasure;
"and yet it was enough to bring about your removal."

" That was the best effect it had; for since then, I am sure
I have become another man," replied the Abbe, with an air of
self-satisfaction. "Had they not removed me, and thereby deprived the church of one of its best pillars, I should not have
become editor of the *Mercure de France*, nor written my *History of Philosophy*. So the world should thank the church for
restoring me to it that I might glorify our enlightened age.
But the world is ungrateful; it does not appreciate its great
men until they are dead, and sometimes not even then. Look
at your free Switzerland; what has it done for its heroes?
What monuments immortalize the intrepid soldiers that fought
at Morgarten, or the names of Walter Furst and Tell? '*Et tu
Brute*,' I might say to you in this respect, and I do not believe
you could find a word to defend yourself."

"If I could not, my wife certainly could," replied Necker,
laughing. "She will intrepidly defend the honor of her native
country. Let us allow her to enjoy this little triumph, which I
gladly leave to her."

Madame Necker did not hear this remark. The tall, grave
gentleman who had entered with the Abbe Raynal, after bowing
to the lady of the house, had stood still beside her chair and
entered into conversation with her.

"I had already abandoned the hope of seeing you here to-night, Thomas," said Madame Necker to him in an undertone.

"It would have been the first time when I should have voluntarily renounced the pleasure of being in your society," replied the gentleman, in the singularly emphatic tone in which he uttered every word.

A smile of satisfaction overspread the cold features of Madame Necker at these words; but it was not long in disappearing and giving place to her habitual polite expression. She replied in a very calm tone:

"I know how to appreciate your kindness toward me, my dear Thomas. However, it was but natural for me to suppose that the curiosity which impelled so many persons to-day to leave the city, and go to meet the couriers, had induced you to do so too, especially as Madame Geoffrin accompanied that party to Sevres. The greater is the pleasure which your arrival affords me. I suppose you did not dine at Sevres, then?"

"Of course not," exclaimed Thomas, gravely. "It was nothing to me to hear the news of the King's death an hour sooner or later; and I look upon the death of a man—especially a man upon whom such a terrible responsibility rests as upon this King—as such a grave matter that I cannot treat it as a subject fit for frivolous conversation."

"You express my own sentiments," replied Madame Necker, approvingly. "In my own mind, too, the King's death has given rise to very grave reflections. Louis the Fifteenth brought France to the verge of ruin. How is his successor to save it? Nothing but a miracle, it seems to me, could do that; and miracles, unfortunately, do not happen any longer."

"Let us hope for the best," replied Thomas, gravely. If France has declined in some respects, it has made immense progress in others. The sphere of science has expanded wonderfully, and the country abounds in gifted men, whose works rank with the best productions of any age. Posterity will look back with astonishment upon our glorious achievements ; and our contemporaries render already, well-deserved homage to the authors of our great Encyclopedia. We must not lose sight of this, my esteemed friend ; we must not shut our eyes to the bright sides of our age, which bears so many great and promising germs in its bosom."

"But, in return, it robs us of something vital and essential—of our faith in the hand of God in history. Science cannot indemnify the people for what philosophy took from it; for it does not enter the hearts—it does not reach the lower strata of human society. We should not deceive ourselves on this head, my excellent friend."

"Science may be popularized, and it will be," replied Thomas, emphatically. "The fruits which civilization matures are destined for everybody. Let us await their ripening. Nations become what their governments want to make them, and ultimately must make of them. Rousseau did not write his *Contrat Social* and *Emile* in vain. The Government will see that poverty and anarchy are two social Titans that can be resisted most successfully by giving schools to the people."

A loud burst of merriment behind them interrupted them at this moment. Little Germaine had crept close up to the corpulent Abbe and fastened a long strip of paper to his wig. Whenever the vivacious little man, in his conversation with M. Necker, moved his head, the strip of paper danced on his black coat, and caused the mischievous girl to burst into loud laughter.

Madame Necker did not see immediately what had happened ; she heard only the merry laughter of her child, and exclaimed in a grave, warning tone, "Germaine !"

The little girl paused immediately, and concealed herself behind her father.

"Excuse my daughter's impertinent jest, Abbe," said Madame Necker now; and rose to remove the paper from his wig. "The air of France seems to produce singular effects. In my native country no child would dare to jest in this manner with a grave gentleman. I do not call to mind a single time when even the idea of doing such a thing has occurred to me in my childhood. Hence, I am at a loss to understand how my daughter can permit herself such jests; salutary exhortations are not wanting to her, and I try to educate her in such a manner as to awaken her mind, and fill her with admiration for the gifted men whom she is fortunate enough to see at her father's house. So it is not my fault, if her conduct is not in keeping with the pains I am taking with her education."

"Wisdom does not come prematurely," said M. Necker, looking kindly at his child, whose large, radiant black eyes gazed up to him confidingly. "You expect too much of her. Her thoroughly healthy nature revenges itself by such little jests, for which our dear Abbe will not be angry with his young friend."

Raynal held out his hand to the child, who seized it and warmly pressed it to her lips.

Madame Necker shook her head disapprovingly. "That constantly overflowing heart of hers!" she said in such a low voice that only Thomas heard her words; "How is it ever to learn prudence? My child's character refutes what Rousseau says about the rights of nature. If I should fail in compelling her now, already, to regulate with her head the pulsations of her impetuous heart, her unbridled passions might make her one day very miserable. You appreciate my efforts in this direction, do you not? You have written such an able history of our sex; you have shown so strikingly what we were at all times, and, again, what we should be; and so urgently recommended to us moderation in all things. Would to God I could teach my child to realize the ideal which you have depicted to us."

"In order to do so, she has only to imitate the example you set to her," replied Thomas in a measured tone, strangely at variance with the meaning of his words, which did not escape the ear for which they were destined.

CHAPTER III.

THE VISIT TO THE SICK-ROOM.

A serious malady had confined Madame Necker for several weeks to her bed; and when she was out of danger, her recovery proceeded but very slowly. With great impatience she looked forward to every new day, hoping it would at length bring her the strength which she needed so urgently to attend to her domestic duties as heretofore. She was aware that her husband missed her very much; she knew that her friends painfully felt her absence; and still her physician admonished her to be quiet and patient; still he demanded that she should take upon herself no other task and duty than that of taking care of her health.

Madame Necker sighed at these demands. She had constantly enjoyed the best of health, and could now scarcely bear to be seen by anybody in her present state of weakness.

Sickness had rendered her naturally delicate complexion almost transparent; her clear blue eyes seemed to have grown larger, and the outlines of her handsome features had become more marked and angular. Stretched out on a *chaise longue*, her head resting on her small white hand, she thoughtfully gazed into vacancy.

Suddenly the door opened softly, and Necker, first looking cautiously into the room in order to see if she was asleep, stepped in.

"How are you, my dear?" he asked, tenderly.

"I am better," she replied, kindly. "You shall not miss me much longer."

"Hush, hush," he said deprecatingly. "I do not mean that. But you yourself need no longer to lead such a solitary life. We are at liberty to divert you—I and your other friends. Thomas is down stairs; may he come up?"

"I believe it will not hurt me to see him."

"Very well, I shall send him to you. He can tell you plenty of news."

"Oh, that is not what I care for. Above all things, I long to know what you, my friend, are doing. You are silent."

Necker, smiling, pressed his finger to his lips.

"Then I am not to learn yet what the King wanted of you? If he offered you an office, and if you accepted his offer? Oh, it is very hard for a wife not to be able to stand by her husband's side at the very time when fate at length bestows on him the position due to his merits, and a career in which he is able to turn his talents to account, opens before him. How glad I should have been to share all this with you just now! I should have cheered you in your grave labors, and comforted you in your struggle with the difficulties with which your path is beset. And now I am lying here, not only helpless, but in need of help. When I call to mind how much you have done for me, how I owe all my happiness to you alone, and how greatly I shall always be indebted to you, it is mortifying to me in the extreme to be unable to show you how faithful and affectionate a wife you possess in me. Do not pay any attention to what the doctor says, Necker. Pray, do not heed him! Speak to me, confide in me! Where could you find anybody worthier of your confidence? Do not go with your cares to strangers; do not accustom yourself to confide to others what I alone should know."

" See, see how greatly my mere presence excites you," gently said M. Necker, laying his hand, as if soothingly, on the high and beautiful forehead of his wife. " Have patience for a few days yet, and you shall know all ; you shall share my cares as formerly, and I hope my joys too. In the meantime, I am taking pains to pursue a course worthy of you, dearest. I hope you will approve it."

" Necker !" exclaimed his wife, gazing at him with a touching expression of tenderness, while she drew his hand from her forehead, and pressed it to her lips. " I do not deserve so much kindness. So you are content with what has happened to you recently ? "

" I am as content as a man who is going to perform important duties should be. But where is Germaine ? Marmontel is waiting for her in the *salon*."

" She is in her room. It is so difficult for her to be as quiet as I have to ask her to be ; so I sent her to her own room. I grieve very often, Necker, to see that my education does not bear the fruits which I expected. I am quite unable to overcome the child's impulsive nature."

" Pray do not even attempt to do so, dearest. Your daughter is her father's image ; I recognize myself daily more and more in her ; so you would pay me a very sorry compliment by telling me that you dislike the peculiarities of her nature. Every tree has a bark of its own. Just give her full liberty, and you will live to see the day when she will bear the most splendid fruits. But this is likewise a point on which we shall no longer converse."

He imprinted a kiss on her forehead and left the room.

A few minutes afterward, Thomas came in. He saluted his fair friend gravely, pressed her hand respectfully to his lips, and moved a chair to her side.

"How long it is since we have met," said Madame Necker. "I was already prepared to set out on my last journey. But God has been merciful enough to postpone it for the present."

"M. Necker requested me to cheer you; to divert you by telling you some entertaining news, and to avoid any serious conversation. Permit me to fulfill his wish that it may be vouchsafed to me to pay frequent visits to your sick-room. It was very painful for me, during the last few weeks, to feel that I had no right to offer you services which my sympathy prompted me to render to you. Grant me now at least the comfort of being the first who may devote himself to your entertainment," said Thomas, in a mild and, withal, grave tone.

There was a pause. For the first time in her life, Madame Necker was at a loss for a reply. In her confusion, she played with the sky-blue blanket that had been wrapped around her feet, and leaned her head on her hand.

"Did you deliver any speeches at the Academy while I was sick?" she asked, after a while.

"None of any importance," he replied, "I was too deeply afflicted at the loss of Madame Geoffrin; and however earnestly I strove to compose myself, I was unable to concentrate my mind on a subject that was not so dear to my heart. So I have left it to time to accomplish what my will was unable to do, and meanwhile confined myself to working at the pages which D'Alembert, the Abbe Morellet, and I are going to devote to her memory."

"Will you permit me to read them?"

"It will afford me the greatest pleasure to lay them at your feet as soon as they are printed."

"The death of our lamented friend will leave a considerable gap in our circle, particularly as we have lost Mademoiselle D'Espinasse, whose wit and amiability we admired so much.

Who is now to lead our conversation as she used to do? Her loss is irreparable; and I have been told she died in such a terrible state of mind!"

"It is but too true. They say that she had bestowed her affections on a gentleman who did not love her."

"I am at a loss to understand how any lady, of genuine sensibility, can do so. Perhaps the malicious world charges her falsely with this inexcusable weakness."

"No, I believe the charge is true. It can be substantiated. For the rest, this was not the first time when her heart led her astray in this manner. I have been assured that she bestowed her affections on other gentlemen, too, who refused to have anything to do with her."

"Impossible!" exclaimed Madame Necker, in surprise.

"Why should it be impossible?" asked Thomas. "The same thing happens so often to us men, that we can understand very well how a lady may rashly fall in love with us."

"And the news that you were going to tell me?" said Madame Necker, in order to turn the conversation into another channel.

"I have plenty of news to tell you; only I must reflect where I had better begin. Gluck and Piccini are still waging their musical war; and inasmuch as our young Queen Marie Antoinette is of course very fond of German music, and intent on bringing about its triumph, intrigues and all sorts of manœuvres to gain over adherents to either side, are not wanting. At the Academy, in the coffee-houses, and at the literary soirées, everybody speaks of this subject. A great many persons are afraid of inviting guests, lest they should quarrel about Gluck and Piccini, whose 'musical war' has greatly disturbed the harmony of our social life. Everybody is expected to side either with Gluck or Piccini, and is judged accordingly. Our friend Marmontel has declared in favor of Piccini, and has ever since been on the *qui vive*. The best thing one can do is to avoid the subject entirely; for the exasperation of the two parties has already reached the highest pitch, especially since the performance of *Armide*."

"I am very sorry to hear it. Such difficulties, even after the cause has disappeared, leave a great deal of irritation in the hearts of the contending parties. Now tell me something more pleasant."

"Let me speak, then, of Voltaire, whose wit is as keen and inexhaustible as ever. He is very anxious to go to Paris, and hopes that his friends will encourage him to undertake the journey. Louis the Sixteenth will not prevent him."

"At his age! He is soon going to celebrate his eighty-fourth birth-day."

"Nevertheless, he is still as vigorous as a young man. In a very short space of time he recently wrote three pamphlets and completed two tragedies. He is intent on having his *Irene* and *Alexis* performed in Paris. The other day, at Ferney, he read them to his friends until 2 o'clock in the morning; he then went to bed and rose at nine as well and wide-awake as ever. What do you say to that?"

"It is wonderful, like the hale old man."

"Let me read to you now an article which he sent us the other day for publication in the *Courier de l'Europe*. The very style shows that Voltaire wrote it:

"'Louis the Fifteenth one evening took supper with a few intimate friends at Trianon; they conversed about hunting; and gunpowder having been mentioned, one of the guests said it was a composition of saltpetre, sulphur, and charcoal. The Duke de la Valliere asserted that good artillery powder consisted of one part sulphur, as much charcoal, and five parts saltpetre, dissolved in well-filtered, well-evaporated and well-crystalized nitre.'

" ' How ludicrous it is,' said the Duke de Nivernois, ' that we should daily shoot grouse in the park at Versailles, and sometimes kill men or be killed in the same manner, without knowing the material with which it is done.'

" ' Oh, that is not so very wonderful,' replied Madame de Pompadour; 'I do not know either how the rouge with which I paint my cheeks is made, and I should be in a tempest of perplexity were I to explain how the silken stockings which I wear on my feet are made.'

" ' What a pity it is,' said the Duke de la Valliere, ' that his Majesty the King confiscated the *Dictionnaire Encyclopcdique*, for which we had paid one hundred *Louis d'ors ;* it contained answers to all our queries.'

" The King defended the confiscation. He had been informed that the twenty-one folio volumes which were to be found on the dressing-table of every lady, contained many things highly dangerous to the State; so he had resolved to examine the book before permitting any one to read it.

" Toward the close of the supper he ordered a page to fetch a copy of the dangerous work; three footmen carried the twenty-one large volumes into the room.

" They looked for the article on gunpowder and found that the Duke de la Valliere had been right. Madame de Pompadour read the article on rouge, and found that the Parisian paint contained cochineal; and that used by the ladies of Madrid, saffron.

" She found how her stockings were woven, and the ingenious process filled her with the utmost astonishment.

" ' What a beautiful book !' she exclaimed; ' Sire, you confiscated this encyclopedia of the most useful knowledge, only

2

in order to possess it alone, and to become the only *Savant* in
your kingdom.'

"All of the guests wished to examine the volumes; they
pounced on them, as the sons of Lycomedes did on the riches
of Ulysses. They found everything in the book; those who
had lawsuits pending could see already what the judgment
would be. The King found in them an enumeration of all the
prerogatives of his crown. 'In truth,' he said, 'I am at a
loss to understand how the ministers could tell me that this
was a dangerous book.'

"'They did so only because it is an excellent work,' replied
.the Duke de Nivernois. 'They would not have raised their
voices against a trashy or indifferent book. When ladies de-
cry one of their sex, you may be sure that she is more beautiful or brilliant than her adversaries.'

"Meanwhile the guests continued turning over the volumes,
and Count C. said in a loud voice: 'It was fortunate for you,
Sire, that during your reign there were men who possessed so
much knowledge and handed it down to posterity. These
volumes contain everything, from the manufacture of guns
down to the art of making pins, from the greatest down to
the most insignificant things. You ought to be thankful to
God for causing men to be born in your kingdom to render
such services to humanity. The other nations will have to
buy or re-print this encyclopedia. Deprive me of all my estates, Sire, but pray leave me my encyclopedia.'

"'But I have been told,' replied the King, 'that this useful
and excellent work is full of errors.'

"'Sire,' said Count C., 'there were on your supper-table
to-night two bad dishes which we did not touch; nevertheless
we had an excellent supper. Did you want us to throw the
whole repast out of the window on account of those two dishes?'

"The King acknowledged the force of this argument. The books were restored to their owners. Thus closed this pleasant day.

"But envy and ignorance would not put up with their discomfiture; these two immortal sisters continued their hue and cry, their cabals, their persecutions; ignorance is never at a loss for means when it is determined to fight.

" What was the consequence?

" The work prohibited in France had four large editions abroad, and yielded its publishers the enormous profit of eighteen hundred thousand dollars."

" Excellent!" said Madame Necker, when Thomas had concluded, and put the journal containing Voltaire's article into his pocket; " and you read it so as to add to its impressiveness."

" You are kind enough to praise what my position requires me to possess."

" Did Turgot really resign his portfolio? Who is his successor? "

" I do not know, or rather, I am not at liberty to tell you," replied Thomas, smiling. " Your physician does not want anybody to talk politics with you, because your nerves cannot bear it yet; so an academician has been sent to you. Science does not excite, it soothes."

" Something has happened, I know it," replied Madame Necker, excitedly. " The King sent for Necker. I remember it distinctly; I know that it is not a mere fancy of mine; I know that he dressed for the purpose of appearing before his majesty. But that is all I am able to call to mind, and no one will tell me the result of the audience. Dear Thomas, do you not know of a way to restore my health at the earliest moment, that my friends need no longer conceal from me what I long so intensely to learn? "

"Indeed I am happy enough to be able to serve you in this respect," he replied, playfully. "There has recently arrived in our city a stranger—Mesmer is his name—who influences his patients by touching them with the tip of his finger, or, if they prefer, by means of the notes of his harmonica, and gives them or frees them from any disease they please.* This gentleman has already created a great sensation in Germany. What injures him here is the fact that he displays so little wit and imagination. Even a doctor like him can no longer succeed in Paris without possessing remarkable accomplishments."

"But what is his wonderful power based on?" asked Madame Necker. "If he should not experiment on me in a manner injurious to my health, I should gladly permit him to cure me in his singular way."

"His opinion is that there is yet an unknown element influencing and affecting our nerves; according to this principle there is also a reciprocal action between organic as well as inorganic bodies. There is also a power of attraction, similar to that of the magnet, between different human beings. It is this animal magnetism, whose mysterious effects he has discovered, that he now uses in curing diseases. What principles he follows in this respect he will explain to you personally when he tests his art in your own case. Let me mention, however, that he has found in Paris many persons on whom he is unable to produce any effect, and I am afraid he will make the same discovery in your case."

"What makes you think so? Why is Paris so unfavorable to his cures?"

"Because the currents of life are too violent and impetuous here; we Parisians do not easily yield to our emotions, and do

* "Correspondance Litteraire de Grimm et Diderot." B. iv., p. 218.

not suffer ourselves very often to be carried away by our imagination."

" And you think Dr. Mesmer's whole art rests on nothing but that?"

" I am satisfied of it. Besides, Prince Gonzaga has arrived with his wife, Corilla, the celebrated improvisatrice, who was crowned in Rome. You may imagine the sensation which she is creating in society. All fashionable ladies and gentlemen are flocking to her; all are desirous to form her acquaintance and hear her; our friend Marmontel is one of her most enthusiastic admirers."

" I hope she will remain for some time in Paris; for I should like to take my daughter to one of her performances. I wish to make Germaine acquainted with distinguished ladies, that she may imitate the example which they set to her. If we have no goal before us, the path which we pursue often seems to us so long and dreary; mere duty possesses too few attractions for the singular character of my child."

" You wish to educate your daughter so as to make a famous lady of her. Is not thirst for fame a passion, too?"

" You will admit at all events that it is a noble one."

" But withal a very dangerous one; for it lives more than any other on the applause of the multitude."

" At all events, I am anxious to prevent her imitating the example of the Parisian women, who love with their heads and think with their hearts. You know it was the Neapolitan Embassador who said this of us." *

" I remember; but I do not believe that he included you."

Madame Necker blushed slightly.

" And how is our friend Rousseau? Have you seen him recently?"

---

* "Grimm's Memoirs." B. iv.

"He is not in Paris; he is at Ermenonville, and I have been told that he has become quite a hypochondriac. There is a report that his confessions are about to be published in Holland; but he himself denies it, and says if the report is correct, somebody must have purloined his manuscript. Doctor le Begue de Presle, his intimate friend, rode out the other day to his house in the country. When he inquired for Rousseau, the philosopher crawled out of his cellar. Le Begue de Presle reproved him for not leaving such little domestic duties at his age to Madame Rousseau. "Oh," he replied, "when she goes down to the cellar, she does not come back."

"Poor man! I wish we could render him some assistance and add to his comfort. But he rejects all offers."

"And what is worse, such offers irritate him and often make him seriously angry. So we have to leave him alone."

"But will posterity not condemn us for it? People at a distance do not see the difficulties obstructing our path."

"There are too many proofs in existence to justify our course. But the hour during which I was allowed to stay with you has expired. I will not exceed it, lest the physician should forbid me to visit you again."

He bowed and left the room. Madame Necker looked thoughtfully after him.

CHAPTER IV.

THE FESTIVAL.

M. NECKER wished to celebrate the recovery of his wife by giving a brilliant festival, which was to take place on the day when she would first resume her place in the midst of her social circle, and which was to show her in a touching manner how dear she was to her family and to her acquaintances. All had taken pains to contrive some little surprise and attention for her; above all, Germaine could hardly await the hour when her mother would enter the festooned *salon* where her daughter was to wish her joy of her recovery. Dressed in white, her dark hair adorned with roses, she had been there for an hour already, counting the minutes up to the moment when her mother would make her appearance. In her hand she held a sheet of paper, on which she fixed her dark eyes every now and then, as if trying to engrave the words written on it once more upon her memory. Marmontel, Grimm, and Thomas were engaged in an animated conversation in one of the window-niches. They had been invited to take.dinner with the family, while the other guests were not to make their appearance till a later hour.

M. Necker had gone to his wife's room in order to conduct her to the *salon*. He had likewise prepared for her a little surprise, which he now wished to communicate to her alone. He entered her room with a solemn air; but no sooner had his eyes fallen on her, than he forgot what he had intended to say to

her, and silently stood still before her. For the first time since
her sickness she was richly dressed, and had chosen for her
costume a color which she had never worn before. Crimson
satin sits well on blondes only when their complexion is faultless. The almost transparent paleness of her skin, caused by
her long confinement in the sick-room, now produced the most
favorable effect; at the same time her fine blue eyes beamed so
brightly, and she looked so serene and animated in the blissful
consciousness that her former position at the head of her domestic and social circle would be restored to her, that her appearance made a most fascinating impression.

"How beautiful you are!" said M. Necker, at last, gazing at
the tall, queenly form of his charming wife. "Sickness has
certainly not impaired your charms."

She laid both hands on his shoulders, and gazed tenderly into
his eyes.

"Beauty and charms will pass away very, very soon; for this
reason, my dearest friend, pray do not love in me only that
which is perishable, but also that which connects us for all time
to come. I must be the friend of your soul, an echo of your
better self, if I am to look forward to the future with courage
and confidence."

"You are to me all that, as sure as I live," said Necker,
gravely. "You have but one fault, and that is, that you will
never allow us to exercise the sweet privilege of forgiveness
toward you, too.* He who now and then has need of our indulgence, thereby endears himself to us."

"That is a harsh remark, my friend. Then I should have to
be less perfect in order to please you still better? How easy it
would be for me to play such a game! But suppose I should

* "Notice sur le Caractere et les Ecrits de Madame de Stael." Vol. I.,
p. 20.

make this first little deviation from the true path, how difficult it would be for me to retrace my steps! I know myself. I am unable to take a light-hearted view of life; what I am, I am with all my heart. Let me, then, belong to virtue, and devote myself with all my heart to it and to you. Believe me, my friend, it will be none the worse for you."

"As if I did not know that, my dearest wife. Besides, my censure was half a jest. But pray be seated now, and, to show you how much I have missed you, let me relate to you how much fate has suddenly elevated me, and what I have been obliged to undertake and perform without your advice. The King has sent for me, and intrusted the Finance Department to me."

"I guessed it, I guessed it," exclaimed Madame Necker, jubilantly.

"All France, nay, the whole world, has now fixed its eyes on me, and calls upon me to save this country. I am as sensible of the burden of my responsibility as any man can be; and it added greatly to the gloom with which my solicitude for you filled me during your sickness. It was a sad, sad time for me. Thank God, the gloom has cleared away, and daylight surrounds me once more."

"And what did you propose to the King? What changes have you made?" excitedly exclaimed Madame Necker, seizing her husband's hand, and holding it between both of hers.

"I see that even now this intelligence excites you greatly; I was right, therefore, in withholding it from you," said M. Necker, gravely. "Now you shall know all that has happened; only let us not allude to it any more to-day. Enjoy yourself to-day, dearest; rejoice in the knowledge that your ambitious plans concerning me have been realized, and that a vast field where I am able to prove whether or not I really

2*

possess the talents which you attribute to me, has been opened to me." •

"Tell me only one thing: Is the King content with you? How does he treat you? How does he behave himself?"

"Exceedingly well. I am a foreigner and Protestant; I had not yet filled any office here except representing little Switzerland in this city; so great prejudices had to be overcome."

"The greater the honor that awaits you."

"The more difficult, also, my position, dearest. But, thank God, I have hitherto been exceedingly successful. All the world is praising me. The public credit is gaining strength, the financial condition of the country is daily improving, every new decree eradicates old abuses, and we are fighting with fire and sword the abominable practice which, for centuries past, have prevailed in the administration of France. I have established a new system of administration in Berry, which has created a great sensation. All Paris is full of it. You will now hear people talk a great deal about your husband. But you must expect, too, to hear many of them comment unfavorably on the course I am pursuing. There is no light without shade; and the brighter the sun shines, the darker is the shadow."

"I am speechless, Necker, speechless for joy! To see your merits fully recognized was my fondest wish."

"I am only afraid that public opinion may desert me sooner or later. It is so fickle, and cannot be relied upon at all."

"It will not desert genuine merits, like yours, my friend."

"It is not faithful to them either, dearest. But pray accompany me now to the *salon*. Our friends await you, and we have already tried too long their impatient desire to greet you."

He offered his arm to his wife. She accompanied him slowly and thoughtfully.

: At the door of the *salon* Necker stood still. Immediately the folding-doors opened as if by a magician's wand, and under a charming canopy of blooming shrubbery, Germaine stood before her mother, handed her a bouquet of the most beautiful roses, and sung the following verses, which Marmontel had written for her, to an air from Figaro's " Wedding: "

Moi qui goûtais la vie avec délire,
Dans un instant j'ai connu le malheur.
Belle maman, témoin de ta douleur,
J'ai dit: Pour moi la vie est un supplice.

En me donnant la plus digne des mères,
Ciel! tu m'as fait le plus beau des présents;
Daigne veiller sur ses jours bienfaisants,
Ou tes faveurs me seront trop amères.

Oui, je crains moins la douleur pour moi-même,
A tous ses traits je suis prête à m'offrir.
Les plus grands maux c'est ceux qu'on voit souffr?
A des parents qu'on révère et qu'on aime.

De mille maux l'essaim nous accompagne,
Mais, sont-ils faits pour un être accompli?
Ah! d'un objet de vertus si rempli
Que la santé soit au moins la compagne.

Dans les hameaux ou nous dit qu'elle habite
Et qu'elle suit la douce obscurité;
De la nature en sa simplicité,
Jamais maman n'a passée la limite.   ·

De leurs esprits l'essence est impassible;
Ma mère a droit à cet heureux destin.
Ciel! n'as tu pas réuni dans son sein
Un esprit pur avec un cœur sensible.

Un Dieu touché de mon humble prière
A fait cesser le mal qui m'accablait.
Dans ce moment, hélas! il me semblait
Qu'un jour nouveau me rendait la lumière.

J'ai reconnu combien mon âme est tendre;
A quelque chose ainsi malheur est bon.
Dieu! gardez-moi de pareille leçon.
Je n'aurais pas la force de la prendre.

M. Necker had added the following verse to Marmontel's
poem:

> De mon papa voyez l'amour extrême;
> Rien, m'a-t-il dit, ne peut nous désunir,
> Un seul instant pourrait tout me ravir.
> Ah! par pitié, prenez soin de vous même.

Madame Necker had listened attentively to her daughter's
song, fixing her beautiful eyes now on her child, and now on
her husband and the friends assembled in the background.
She now bent over her daughter, imprinted a kiss on her forehead, and whispered, "God bless you, my Germaine!" She
then held out both hands to her guests, and welcomed them in
a few cordial and polite words. Marmontel, whose warm
heart would always overflow, pressed her white hand affectionately to his lips, and said, with tears in his eyes, "God be
praised for restoring you to us! After so many terrible losses,
this blow would not have found me strong enough to survive
it. Since our dear Geoffrin and Mademoiselle de l'Espinasse
have left us for evermore, fate could not take you from us likewise!"

"Let us not speak of such sad subjects to-day, but let us rejoice, my dear Marmontel," said Necker. "Come! I have just
been informed that dinner is ready. Let us go to the table,
and in a glass of generous Rhenish wine, drink to oblivion of
the past and enjoyment of the present. Thomas, give your
arm to my wife; you, Marmontel, will offer yours to your little
bride Germaine, and I shall follow with Baron Grimm, who is
as tenderly devoted to me as if I were his mistress."

The distinguished gentleman to whom Necker had just
alluded, smiled. "At all events, my dear Necker, I am a very
faithful lover of yours; and for this reason, I am sure, you will
forgive me for being neither handsome nor young."

"You are a regular cupid; you have bandaged your eyes,

and I follow your example. Friendship must be no more keen-sighted than love."

Both of them, laughing, took their seats at the dinner-table, and the host saw to it that his guests did not engage in a grave conversation to-day. Madame Necker entered readily upon all jests, and suffered to pass many a sally which she otherwise would have frowned down.

"Our friend Raynal is not here yet," said M. Necker. "Unfortunately he could not be here as early as he desired, inasmuch as he intended to accompany hither a few guests whose appearance was to afford an agreeable surprise to my wife. I hope we shall afterwards find him in the *salon*."

No sooner had he uttered these words than Raynal, without being announced, entered the room, and without further ceremony seated himself on his vacant chair at the small dinner-table.

"Pray, do not let me disturb you," he exclaimed. "My friends will quietly wait in the *salon* till I return to them. In the meantime I may chat a little with you, and enjoy what has been left."

"It is very amiable of you, my dear Abbe, to bring distinguished guests to our festival, and I am very grateful to you," said Madame Necker, politely. "Nevertheless, I am already happy enough to be again in the midst of my old, tried friends, and it was scarcely necessary to add strangers to our circle."

"I believe you will not be dissatisfied with me," said Raynal, smiling.

"Will you not tell me at least what guests I shall have to welcome in the *salon?*"

"If you insist on it, of course; at all events, you would have found it out in the course of a few minutes. Mesmer is here, and his celebrated clairvoyant too."

"You are jesting," exclaimed Madame Necker, in surprise.

"No, no, I am in dead earnest. I heard you were very anxious to witness one of her very singular performances, and so I thought I would add to the interest of to-day's festival by bringing those two persons to your house. Prepare to make the most wonderful discoveries in the world of spirits, to penetrate to-night all that hitherto was concealed from man both in heaven and on earth, and to see the future revealed to your eyes. Prepare, prepare!"

"You were right, indeed, my dear Abbe; nothing could be more agreeable to me than to meet this celebrated man. How does he look? Describe him to me."

"He is a short, light-haired gentleman, whose appearance does not indicate by any means the divine knowledge of which he is possessed; but still waters are deep."

While this conversation was going on in the dining-room, Dr. Mesmer, absorbed in profound reflections, sat in Madame Necker's salon, and caused his eyes to wander abstractedly from one object to another. His companion, a pale young girl with raven hair and the unmistakable appearance of a morbid condition of her nervous system, was pacing the room in great agitation. Finally she stood still in front of a corner-table on which lay Madame Necker's fan and a small memorandum-book. She opened the former, held it to the light, and admired its Chinese workmanship; she then turned her attention to the small memorandum-book. She took out the pencil which held the ivory cover together, and turned over the leaves. In order to read what was written on them, she had to step closer to the window. She found on one page the following words, written in a neat lady's hand: "To-day, on my birthday, I must express to each of my friends in a different manner how grateful I am for the sympathy manifested

toward me.* Besides, I have to allude particularly to what
has happened in the last two months, that they may perceive
that my sickness did not prevent me from taking the liveliest
interest in their welfare." Now followed the names of the
friends, with hints as to the remarks that might be made to
them in the course of the conversation. The young lady read
everything with close attention, and, while she was doing so,
a very peculiar smile played round her lips. She was absorbed in this occupation a long time, and did not lay down
the memorandum-book until a noise at the door indicated the
entrance of new guests. Madame Necker had just returned
from the dining-room, with the gentlemen and her little
daughter, who remained at her mother's side. She turned, in
the first place, to Dr. Mesmer, whom she bade welcome in a
few flattering words; then, quickly taking her fan and the
memorandum-book, which she had laid on the table before
going to the dining-room, she went to his young companion.
"Dr. Mesmer will be kind enough to show us, in connection
with you, Mademoiselle, the importance of the discoveries
which he has made," she said to the girl, who, bowing, replied
very humbly, "I am happy, Madame, to be called upon to
serve the light of truth, and I rejoice at the opportunity which
has been given to me thereby to meet one of the most
accomplished ladies of France."

At this moment Prince Gonzaga was announced. He entered the room with his wife, the celebrated Corilla. Madame
Necker now turned to these new guests, whom she received
almost awkwardly, in consequence of the too great pains she
took to appear perfectly at ease. The elegance with which a
native Parisienne moves in her *salon*, is not acquired, but innate,
despite all her efforts and preparations. Madame Necker was

* "Memoires de Morellet."

frequently unable to strike the right key. The appearance of the improvisatrice, moreover, made a profound impression on her. The beautiful Princess wore a heavy dress of white satin, made in the Greek fashion, and fastened at the waist only with a golden belt; a tasteful wreath of green leaves adorned her curly black hair; she wore no gloves on her full, white arms, but had adorned them only with plain golden bracelets. A sweet smile played round her beautiful lips when she kindly thanked Madame Necker for the invitation tendered to her and her husband. "Oh! I should thank you with all my heart for accepting it," replied Madame Necker, "and my friend Marmontel, who was kind enough to act as mediator between us, may rely on my fervent gratitude. Permit me, Princess, to present to you my little daughter, who is so astonished at what she has heard of your wonderful talent, that she cannot sleep at night. Germaine, kiss the hand of the Princess."

Corilla gracefully held out her hand to Germaine, who pressed it to her cherry lips. "How beautiful you are!" she then exclaimed, gazing up to the Princess with radiant eyes. "Ah! if I could be like you, how well I should please my parents. Even though I learn a great deal, I shall never be able to make so fascinating an impression."

"Child, child, how wildly you talk!" said Madame Necker, soothingly.

"Do not blame your little daughter," said Corilla, kindly laying her beautiful hand on the child's head. "She still yields to her impressions; how beautiful that is, and how soon we unlearn it when we have entered the grave school of life. When our illusions have vanished, our wishes disappear likewise, and our days creep along with intolerable slowness. May that time be remote from her!"

"And from you, too," interposed Marmontel. "The little

god must not allow your torch to sink very soon, either, Princess."

" A poet like you should versify that idea on the spot," remarked Prince Gonzaga.

" If the presence of your esteemed consort did not make me bashful, it would afford me pleasure to comply with your wish ; but, as it is,—"

He shrugged his shoulders, smilingly.

" If that prevents you, I shall withdraw," said Corilla, preparing to walk away.

" No, no, Princess, I did not mean that. Even though you should pass an unfavorable opinion on my feeble talent, I shall try to do what I can." And he began :

> L'amour est un enfant qui vit d'illusion,
> La triste verite detruit la passion ;
> Il veut qu'on le seduise, et non pas qu'on l'eclaire.
> Voila de son bandeau la cause et le mystere.

" Excellent ! " exclaimed the Prince and Corilla, with one accord ; and the other guests joined in their praise. Meanwhile, several new guests had arrived ; groups were chatting here and there, and several persons were introduced to the distinguished strangers. Germaine, however, did not remain to-day, as usual, at her mother's side. She clung to the beautiful Corilla; she followed her as if perfectly fascinated, and did not tire of expressing her intense admiration for her. The expression of her countenance indicated that she was animated with the fervent longing to become similar to this lady, and that the child's mind ambitiously thirsted for such homage, praise, and admiration as were bestowed upon Corilla.

Such moments oftentimes leave profound echoes in the soul, and we may take it for granted that Madame de Stael's *Corinne* arose already on this evening in the gifted mind of Germaine Necker.

Madame Necker had meanwhile entered into a conversation with Thomas, while Mesmer, on the other side of the room, was bringing the young lady, who had accompanied him to Necker's house, into a magnetic sleep. All looked in eager expectation, and conversation was soon hushed. Profound silence reigned in the room.

Suddenly, Mesmer bent down to the girl's ear and asked her to tell him what engrossed the thoughts of the lady of the house.

"She is dissatisfied with herself, inasmuch as she did not succeed in telling her guests all the polite things which she had prepared to say to them."

"And what prevented her from so doing?" asked Mesmer.

"Circumstances."

"Can you tell me what she intended to say, or what she did say?"

"I will try." And slowly, and making long pauses, as if trying to call everything to mind, she repeated every word Madame Necker had uttered, adding to it what she had intended to tell her guests, but what circumstances had prevented her from saying.

Her audience were greatly surprised at this communication. Thomas looked wonderingly at his beautiful, pale friend. "Is it true, then, what she says?" he asked in a low voice. "Did this person really divine your most secret thoughts without your having furnished her the key to them?"

"I do not know her at all; this is the first time that I have seen her in my life, and I know no more of her than she does of me," replied Madame Necker, in a low voice, trembling with emotion. "I am astonished beyond measure. What she says is a perfect enigma to me. Should the abnormal state of her nervous system really impart to her soul the power of discerning objects not perceptible by the senses, and of seeing into the inmost recesses of the human mind?"

"Such a power would frighten me," replied Thomas, gravely. "Nor could it do any good. How dreadful it would be for us to be unable to keep our thoughts to ourselves, and to have a secret and silent witness even to what we thought we could conceal from all eyes. Not to be alone with one's self—the idea would drive me mad."

"All you have to do is not to think of it, and the invisible witness is no longer present," said Raynal, good-humoredly. "Our neighbor Bacon, you know, says, 'Whoever is delighted with solitude is either a wild beast or a god;' and inasmuch as most men combine in their nature a little of either, an unknown companion would not be so very bad for them in lonely hours. Only we ought also to possess the power of calling up this invisible friend; in that event nothing would be wanting to our happiness. But let me try now if the young lady is able to divine my thoughts, too."

So saying, he stepped close up to Mesmer and whispered something in his ear.

There was a pause of eager expectation.

Finally, the clairvoyant began in a slow, solemn tone:

"The Abbe Raynal is thinking of the humorous article which he intends publishing to-morrow about Dr. Mesmer and me in the *Cour'er de Paris.*"

"By the Eternal, she has hit it!" exclaimed Raynal, in surprise, "I did think of that. Now, Marmontel, try your luck likewise. Let us hear from the lips of the clairvoyant what is passing in the heart of our poet."

Mesmer spoke to the clairvoyant. In a few minutes she replied:

"M. Marmontel is delighted with the beautiful verses which

he improvised on the blindness of the god of love, and by which he thinks he proved to the celebrated Corilla that he, too, might travel as an improvisator."

All fixed their eyes on Marmontel, who averted his head in great confusion, and vainly tried to smile as serenely as he had done before.

"She hit it again," said Raynal, maliciously. "But suppose we should now try to read in the heart of my little friend here, too?" he added, turning to Germaine Necker, and seizing her hand. "It seems to me this will be the best way for me to ascertain whether or not she really intends to become my little wife."

The little girl laughed. "Just ask her!" she said to him in a low voice. "I should like to hear what she will say about me."

Raynal complied with her wish. Her eyes now hung anxiously upon the lips of the clairvoyant.

"Germaine Necker," she said, "longs intently to be admired like the Princess Gonzaga. She thirsts for fame; she is envious of beauty; hence, happiness will always flee her, and an early grave will give her glowing heart that peace which she will never find in life."

"Enough!" cried Necker, advancing a step with a menacing air. "This is growing too serious for a mere jest. Let us hear no more of it!"

So saying, he folded his child to his breast as if to protect her from all the woe threatening her.

Thomas offered his arm to Madame Necker, who was afraid she might faint away, and conducted her into the adjoining room. All the guests left the house. Mesmer alone remained with his clairvoyant, who awoke now quickly and walked away with him.

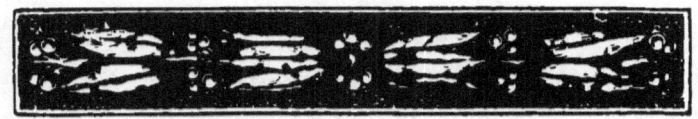

CHAPTER V.

THE February sun shed its feeble rays on the earth, and illuminated with its pale light the gloomy streets of the old city of Paris. M. Necker had worked in the Department of Finance, and was now on his way home at an unusually early hour; so his wife did not yet look for his return. She sat in her boudoir, where no one was permitted to disturb her in the morning, engaged in instructing her daughter, when the quick footsteps of a gentleman fell on her ears. She looked in surprise toward the door in order to see who it was that dared to enter here so impetuously, when it was thrust open, and Necker's short and heavy-set figure appeared in it. His wife looked at him inquiringly, with a glance whose anxious expression seemed to spy for some disagreeable cause of his appearance; but his smile and the serene expression of his countenance soon calmed her fears. He said to her, merrily:

"Voltaire has arrived! Despite his advanced age, he has ventured to undertake the journey to Paris. The whole city is in commotion in consequence of his unexpected arrival. He has not been here for twenty-seven years past. The appearance of a ghost, a prophet, an apostle, could not have excited more astonishment * than his arrival did. He is welcomed like a miracle, and eclipses everything else, the rumors of an impending war, the court gossip, the quarrels of the clergy,

---

* "Correspondance de Grimm et Diderot, en 1778."

and even the great struggle between the adherents of Gluck
and Piccini.   The pride of the Encyclopedists bows to the
Patriarch of Ferney ; the Sorbonne trembles before him; the
parliament does not venture to speak; literature proudly raises
its head; and all Paris is on its legs to pay homage to its idol,   .
who is admired and revered as no hero of the whole century
ever was."

   " So he is really here ! " exclaimed Madame Necker, in joyous surprise.   " There was a good deal of talk about his com-
·ing for some time past.   He was said to be anxious to return to
Paris, and longed for an invitation.   Well, I am particularly
glad of it for our daughter's sake; for this is no doubt his last
journey, and she will have an opportunity to get acquainted
with the illustrious man before he is taken from us and from
mankind."

   " He performed the journey from Ferney to Paris, despite
the cold weather, in five days.   That is a good deal for a man
of eighty-four.   But although, to all appearance, he enjoys the
best of health, he insists all the time that he is very sick," said
M. Necker.   " Whenever anybody congratulates him on his vigorous and healthy appearance, he flies into a towering passion."

   " I shall take good care, then, not to compliment him on it,"
replied Madame Necker.   " I am glad that you cautioned me
in time.   But tell me now also where he stays, and if you think
I had better call on him."

   " He alighted at the house of the Marquis de Villette.   I
have been told that the Marquis has given the poet a cabinet
resembling the boudoir of a goddess of love.   You had better
call on him this very day.   It is early enough for it yet, and
you know he is so restless and mobile that we must seize him
as soon as possible if we wish to prevent him from slipping
entirely from our hands."

"It seems, Necker, you do not wish to accompany me to him?"

"I am unfortunately unable to do so," he replied, regretfully. "I had already to interrupt some very important business in order to inform you of Voltaire's arrival. Times are too grave. The welfare of France and my honor are at stake. If I am unable to prove to the world that I am exceedingly well-qualified for the position which the King has intrusted to me, both he and I will be severely censured, and both of us lose our game. At so grave a moment I must leave the joys of social life to you alone. But Voltaire may possibly consent to dine with us. In that event, I should be exceedingly glad to meet him again and converse with him."

"I shall invite him in your name," replied Madame Necker. "I am sure he will receive you very kindly, inasmuch as it was you who originated the idea of erecting a statue to him, the expense to be collected by subscription."

"And what a letter he wrote to me in reply! Who ever traced such a portrait of himself as Voltaire did on that occasion!"

"Never mind; the idea nevertheless flattered his vanity, and you may be sure that he will receive you the more kindly for that matter," replied Necker, stepping toward the door. "For the rest, his presence here is certain to give rise to many amusing scenes; for the clergy have determined to profit by his arrival in order to save his soul. The priests are vieing with one another in this respect; all of them are desirous of immortalizing their names by converting the Patriarch of Ferney. One of them was already foolish enough to steal this morning into his room while Voltaire was still in bed; and, kneeling down before him, the priest shouted excitedly, "In the name of God, listen to me! I am your scapegoat; I am destined to take upon me the guilt of your life; but now confess your sins to me without delay, and beware of letting this opportunity pass without profiting by it;." etc., etc.

"Our poet happened to be in very good humor; so he asked the priest, very calmly, who had sent him on this errand? "Who but the living God," replied the priest. "Well, then, reverend father," said Voltaire, quite seriously, "pray let me see your credentials." This very simple and natural question perplexed the poor man so much that Voltaire finally took pity on his confusion and tried to soothe him by speaking very kindly and gently to him. He dismissed the priest with the assurance that he would confess to him if he should come to him at a more convenient time. From such a beginning we may infer the steps which the reverend gentlemen will take in order to bring about the salvation of the Patriarch."

"Their impertinence evidently knows no bounds," exclaimed Madame Necker.

"Well, he will know how to defend himself; no one gets the better of him so very easily," said M. Necker, leaving the room.

As soon as he had closed the door after him, Madame Necker rang the bell, ordered her carriage, and told her lady's-maid to dress her.

"Have you already reflected about the answer you are going to give Voltaire in case he should vouchsafe a few kind words to you?" asked Madame Necker of her daughter, when she had finished her toilet.

Germaine hesitated. She stood before the looking-glass and tried to arrange the small round rose-colored bonnet which was fastened to her tall hair-dress, and which caused the full, florid face of the young girl to appear in the most unfavorable light. When her mother now stepped to her and bent her delicate, white face down to her, the contrast was most strik-ing, and the girl burst into tears.

"What is the matter, my dear child?" asked Madame Necker, fixing her clear eyes wonderingly on her daughter.

"I think I am so homely, mother," replied Germaine. "You told me I should be handsomer when I had grown taller. But look now for yourself. My head already reaches up to your chin; I am no longer a little girl, and yet I am as fat and awk-ward and common-looking as if I had been born in a peasant's hut. I wonder what is the cause of it!"

"You are tall for your age, Germaine; but still you look like a child. Your face is that of a child. I had already in my thirteenth year such full, round cheeks as you have now."

"Why do I not resemble you, mother? Why is my com-plexion not as white and delicate as yours? You are so beau-tiful and fascinating, Voltaire will be surprised to see that your daughter bears no resemblance whatever to you."

"He will take little notice of your appearance, my dear child, if your mind shows him that you have already acquired considerable knowledge for a girl of your age, and even know how to appreciate his extraordinary talents. Voltaire himself was never handsome; on the contrary, he was exceedingly ill-favored; but his great mind caused everybody to forget that he was not good-looking. So it depends on you to do likewise. Follow me now, and do not yield to such foolish despondency."

Germaine breathed on her handkerchief, pressed it to her eyes, and accompanied her mother to the carriage.

The house of the Marquis de Villette lay at no great dis-tance from Necker's residence; it was on the corner of the Rue Baune and the quay bearing Voltaire's name, and almost directly opposite the Pavilion de Flore, on the left wing of the Tuileries, which Louis the Sixteenth inhabited.

3

Madame Necker ordered her footman to inquire if Voltaire was at home and received visitors. Having received an answer in the affirmative, she alighted, and caused the porter to conduct her through the *entre-sol* to the first floor, where he pointed out to her a narrow, dark corridor, at the end of which was a small door leading to the room occupied by Voltaire.

She rapped at this door, and the poet himself made his appearance immediately, and asked her to come in.

"You must forgive me, Madame Necker, for receiving you in this *trou de rien*," he said to her, politely; "but the sons of the Muses generally have not where to lay their heads; happy, therefore, he to whom even such a shelter as this is vouchsafed."

Madame Necker was scarcely able to conceal her surprise when she looked about "the boudoir of the goddess of love," which, in fact, was but very scantily furnished.

"Where you are, your surroundings are not noticed," she then replied, with her most winning smile. "The thought of meeting you again made me so happy, that I undertook to penetrate to you without my husband, whom official duties unfortunately prevented from accompanying me, and thus fulfilling the fondest wish of his heart."

"Yes, yes, I know he is engaged in cleaning the Augean stables of French finances, and with his good intentions is paving himself a very pretty road to hell," replied Voltaire, laughing. "I never was so wise or mad as to undertake to sweep before the doors of other people, so I do not understand anything about the pleasure derived from such a course. It must be very pleasant, though, inasmuch as so very many persons pursue it. M. Necker is content, I suppose."

"He hopes that his efforts will be successful; and as long as there is hope, he will courageously walk his thorny path—"

"And sow tares! Ha! ha! ha!"

"I trust not," said Madame Necker, smiling. "But, instead of sneering at the cause which keeps my poor husband away from you, you ought to pity him."

"God forbid that I should commit such a sin against the welfare of this kingdom!" exclaimed Voltaire, pathetically. "But pray sit down! It makes no difference what parts we play on this great stage of life, for, no matter what we may do, the last act always remains a bloody one. However, a good digestion helps us to surmount and accomplish a great deal, provided we keep our eyes fixed on the aim we have marked out for us, and constantly bear in mind that nothing is so important for us as to amuse ourselves and enjoy good health.* For, as I said before, '*Le dernier acte est toujours sanglant.*' † I have always taken pains to live in consonance with these views, and if I have, nevertheless, to submit to the execution of my death-warrant, it is, at all events, no fault of mine."

"Your health is so good that we need not look for that dreadful event for a long time yet," remarked Madame Necker, forgetful of her determination not to speak to him about his appearance.

"That is a mistake which you share with a good many other persons, Madame," replied Voltaire, in a tone of irritation. "This *trou de rien* admits too little sunshine to reveal to your eye the vestiges which time has left on my face, and my poor body is wrapped up in so much clothing that I can scarcely find it myself. Little, of course, can be said of my appearance, as long as people have to take pains to discover anything of me save my voice."

* "Voltaire, Correspondance," Vol. V.: "*Tout est egal dans ce monde pourvu qu'on se porte bien et qu'on s'amuse.*"
† Ibid. Vol. III.

" I hope you will remain for some time in our midst," said Madame Necker, in order to turn the conversation to another subject, and to soothe his irritation.

" A man who may daily look for his dissolution is not at liberty to speak of coming days, Madame. I hope, however, death will grant me time enough to obtain a passport for my soul, lest it should have to stand, bare and naked like a beggar, at the gates of eternity."

" Your century will stand up for you," said Madame Necker, politely.

" Yes, yes, we know that. *Apres nous le deluge.* When I am no longer there to take care of Voltaire, the man, he will be thrown on the first dung-hill, as food for the dogs. I must try to prevent that. So I will confess and obtain absolution. I will become a free-mason, and, at the eleventh hour, take my seat in the Academy. After these three points have been settled, I do not believe that St. Peter can any longer shut the gates of heaven against me." He burst into laughter.

" At all events, you make light of the matter," said Madame Necker. May I hope that, notwithstanding these important occupations, you will find time to dine with us? My husband urgently invites you to do so."

" Your wishes are orders to me, Madame, especially when they are in consonance with mine," said Voltaire, jumping up restlessly ; for his nervous, excitable nature did not permit him to remain long on the same spot. " I shall, moreover, be glad to avail myself of this opportunity, in order to recommend my remains to M. Necker. The priests would be capable of putting me, like a scare-crow, into a corn-field."

" No, they shall not !" exclaimed Germaine Necker, jumping up and pressing the hands of the poet to her lips, while tears streamed from her eyes. " No, they shall not ! My father will never permit it; and, if he did, I should bury you with my own hands, and plant roses on your grave!"

"I like young folks animated with such sentiments," cried Voltaire, his small, sunken eyes glistening with pleasure. "It did me good to hear that! Madame Necker, the words which your daughter uttered just now do honor to the education which you have given to her. If your daughter continues in the same path, she will one day receive a letter of acknowledgment, such as M. Necker recently addressed in the King's name to a brave, kind-hearted sailor.* The letter will state: ' She has buried Voltaire, for which she receives our most gracious thanks; she has buried him with his big, long wig, his lace cuffs, and all his fine clothes, and deprived us of the sad sight of a body which will not be of much account until doomsday; and it will be a long, long time yet before the trumpet resounds.' Such will be the acknowledgments, Mademoiselle, which will be bestowed upon you if you take care of my remains, and help me to change into a chrysalis like any other butterfly. But accept now already the acknowledgments of your most obedient Voltaire, for the kind intentions you have manifested toward him."

"My daughter shares my admiration for you," said Madame Necker, coming to the assistance of her daughter, who seized in silent confusion the hand which Voltaire held out to her. "It cannot surprise you that she should be quite carried away by the impression which the sight of such an eminent man as you must make upon so young a mind."

---

* By order of the King, Necker wrote the following to a sailor: " Excellent man! The intendant informed me day before yesterday of the courageous deed which you performed on the 31st of August, and communicated the intelligence yesterday to the King. His Majesty instructs me to express to you his satisfaction at your conduct, and to order you one thousand francs and a pension of three hundred francs. Continue assisting others whenever you can, and pray for our good King, who loves and rewards kind-hearted men. (Signed) NECKER, Minister of Finance."

" You make me proud, Madame, proud and withal sad ; for what prospects open before me when I gaze into the radiant black eyes of your daughter, and am immediately to abandon the hopes to which they give rise ! Oh, whimsical fortune ! Why did you cause this young heart to throb for me only to sacrifice itself, like an Indian widow, on my grave ! Why did you cause me to find this young half at a moment when my old half is to cease sighing and cooing ? What a son-in-law I should have been to you, Madame ! Forgive me if nature no longer enables me to aspire to the happiness of wedded life."

" I certainly regret it both in my own interest and in that of France," replied Madame Necker, still in the same tone, which she did not allow to be disturbed by any of Voltaire's singular sallies ; " but how loth we shall be to lose a name which our lips have so long uttered with the most intense admiration, and which our ears never can nor will hear without experiencing the proudest joy at belonging to the same country as its eminent bearer."

So saying, she rose and prepared to leave.

" As soon as my ' Irene ' has been performed, I shall call on you," said Voltaire, rubbing his hands gleefully. " I have to superintend the rehearsals that the actors may learn to play their parts in a satisfactory manner."

" We are looking forward to the first performance with the liveliest interest," replied Madame Necker.

" That is just what I am afraid of. People forget that I have grown old, and still demand of me very remarkable works. That is exceedingly unjust."

" Your genius, as we have known for a long time past, never grows old ; at all events, you have never yet proved the contrary to us," said Madame Necker, smiling.

" I am going to do so as sure as my name is Voltaire ; just

wait for the first performance of my tragedy," replied Voltaire, laughing, and offering her his arm in order to conduct her through the dark corridor. "Although beautiful eyes illuminate the darkest night," he remarked to her, in the corridor, "your blue stars could not light up this Orcus even in the daytime. One must be accustomed to darkness in order to be able to see here."

He bowed deeply and retired, while the outer door closed behind the ladies, who entered their carriage again, and drove toward the Bois de Boulogne.

CHAPTER VI.

THE FIRST LAUREL-WREATH.

CARNIVAL had never been merrier in Paris than in 1778. There was an endless round of gay festivities, and motley crowds of masks filled the streets. The court participated in the amusements as far as etiquette permitted; and even the princes of the royal family, as well as the young queen herself, permitted themselves many a liberty, and perpetrated many a jest, which they could not have done under ordinary circumstances.

Madame Necker kept entirely aloof from this whirl of pleasure. Much as her husband's new position had elevated her in social life, she took no pains whatever to turn it to account in this respect. She contented herself with the knowledge that the name which she bore was mentioned everywhere with respect and gratitude, and she shared the joy with which this filled her heart, with those friends of her house who were especially devoted to her husband, and among whom Grimm was his most ardent admirer. He never tired of eulogizing Necker, and expressed incessantly his joy at seeing him labor so enthusiastically and indefatigably for the welfare of France.

A friend whose heartfelt sympathies follow us in the path of glory without a tinge of envy rising in his soul, what a rare boon! It was vouchsafed to Necker, who derived comfort and strength from it in the stormiest days of his eventful career.

While her husband, owing to his official duties, could devote but little attention to his family, Madame Necker devoted as much time as she could spare to the education of her daughter; and she took especial pains to impart to her that practical view of human life which she hoped would soften the impetuosity of her feelings, and keep her in the narrow path of prudence and propriety. For this purpose she had renounced all pleasures of social life, and devoted herself with all her heart to the establishment of a hospital at St. Sulpice, where Germaine, as soon as it would be completed, should see all kinds of suffering, and even look death in the face. She hoped much, nay everything, from these practical lessons which her child was to receive, and she left nothing undone in order to render them as impressive as possible.

Germaine, therefore, remained alone much oftener than formerly, and her lively mind caused her to engage in various occupations in order to while away her time. Dolls had never been the companions of her early years, She had grown up with books, and the only mechanical knowledge she had acquired had been to wield the pen. So she now stuck to her old friend. She read and wrote, and often recited aloud what she had penned. Her days passed in this manner. Madame Necker did not interfere with her. She considered these occupations exceedingly useful; she thought them conducive to her mental development, and hoped they would lead her to serious reflections. An education whose ultimate object was not self-education seemed to her entirely fruitless.

One day the Abbe Raynal surprised the young girl standing before the looking-glass in the *salon*, and reciting something in a loud voice. She had commenced writing a drama, and was now rehearsing the *role* of the heroine.

"All alone!" he said to her. "I thought there were two persons in this room. What are you doing here?"

3*

Germaine became greatly confused, and concealed her manuscript in her hand.

"I hope you do not want to conceal anything from your old friend?" he said kindly. "Just let me see what you were reciting. If it is your own work, so much the better. In that event my advice might be useful to you."

The last words seemed to overcome the timidity of the young girl. So she gathered all her courage and handed the paper to the Abbe.

"Ah!" he exclaimed, as soon as he had glanced at it, "A regular manuscript! A complete drama! Say, my young friend, suppose you let me take it home and peruse it carefully. Perhaps we might prepare a very pleasant little surprise with it to your mother on her birthday."

"Ah, I wish we could do that," exclaimed Germaine, crimsoning with joy. "It would make me so happy if she should praise me!"

"But are you doing anything for which she censures you?" asked the Abbe.

"Yes, she does, although I always take pains to show her how dearly I love her. For this reason I am so sorry that I did not marry Mr. Gibbon."

"What! The fat Englishman?" asked Raynal, in surprise.

"Yes, the fat Englishman! It does not matter how he looks, provided my parents like him; and both of them were so fond of him, and missed him so much when he returned to his native country. Had I quickly made up my mind to marry him, he would have remained with them for ever. But this did not occur to me until he was gone," she added, in a low voice.

The Abbe burst into a fit of laughter.

"No, no, my young friend, that need not weigh down your conscience," he said, kindly patting her cheek. "Your parents do not ask such a sacrifice of you, and, besides, you have to grow a little older in order to be able to make it. But tell me now if your mother will soon be here, or if I must lay on your little shoulders all I have to communicate to her."

"She has gone to St. Sulpice, and will not be back until dinner."

"Well, then, listen to me. 'Irene' will be performed to-morrow night; but there will be such a throng that your mother must be at the theater half an hour earlier than usual if she wants to witness the ceremonies in honor of the poet, which are to precede the performance. I have just seen Voltaire, and am, therefore, well-informed of everything. Marmontel detained me a long time on my way to your house; otherwise I should have been here an hour ago. He had in his pocket a letter from Voltaire, which he insisted on reading to me. The sarcastic old gentleman writes him in it that but for his 'Belisaire' the whole literature of our century would present a pitiful appearance; and Marmontel believes every word of it, and feels highly flattered by it. You know the work; he presented you a copy of it, beautifully bound; and I am sure, if he had not written it, you might have done it just as well."

"I do not find it as easy to write a book as I thought it was before I tried to do so," replied Germaine, very gravely.

"A very true and sensible remark, my young friend," said Raynal, approvingly. "You are daily growing more and more sagacious, and make me quite proud of you."

Germaine cast a grateful glance at him.

"I am so glad to hear you praise me," she said, "and feel then doubly anxious to deserve your good opinion."

"I shall always do so when you look so kindly at me," said Raynal, affectionately. "We old men like to be kindly treated by young folks. We have need of them, while they can do without us."

"I do not think we can," replied Germaine. "We have to learn a great deal from you."

"It is true, that would be the right course; but very few young folks deem it prudent to pursue it. They scout the good advice of old men as entirely superfluous, and so we finally learn to keep silence. Such is the course of the world, my child."

"At all events, my dear Abbe, you shall find that I do not pursue it," warmly exclaimed Germaine, taking his hands between both of hers. "You must tell me all that I should know; for you are my best friend."

"And you are likewise my best little friend," replied the old gentleman. Taking her head between his hands, he imprinted a kiss on her forehead, and, nodding to her a parting greeting in the door, hastened from the room.

As soon as the door had closed after him, Germaine fetched pen and ink, and wrote down what he had requested her to tell her mother. The excitable state of her mind, which was easily carried away by all sorts of impressions, caused her to forget quickly what had fallen on her ear without producing a deeper effect upon her; for this reason her mother had taught her to jot down all such little items. As soon as she had done so, she took up a book and read until her mother's return.

M. Necker had determined to give himself a holiday, and accompany his wife and daughter to the theater in order to witness the sixth performance of "Irene." The tragedy had been played five times, and the poet had been unable to be present at any of these representations. The rehearsals had greatly exhausted him; he had been taken sick in consequence, and he had recovered only a day or two since. All Paris was now desirous of celebrating his recovery. It had been arranged that he was to attend the first sitting of the Academy, and thence repair to the theater. Madame Necker had been informed by her friends of the hour when he would start, and had secured for herself and Germaine a window close to the Louvre, where they could see the illustrious poet pass by. M. Necker intended to go to the Academy, and afterwards join his wife and daughter, and accompany them to the theater. Both of them anxiously looked forward to the moment when Voltaire's carriage would slowly drive through the crowded streets. All stores were closed to-day, all laborers had ceased working, and not a Parisian *gamin* had remained at home.

The large, open carriage had been at the door for some time already, when Voltaire, leaning on the arm of the Marquis de Villette, made his appearance. Immediately, all caps were thrown into the air, and deafening acclamations burst forth.

The poet looked greatly exhausted; but he had not neglected dressing in consonance with the celebration of the day. He wore his very large and long wig, which he used to comb every morning himself, and which had covered his head for forty years past; his crimson-velvet coat was trimmed and lined with the magnificent ermine which the Empress of Russia had presented to him several years ago; and his lace cuffs were perhaps still longer than usual, and made of the most exquisite point d'Alençon.

The carriage moved slowly down the narrow street toward the Louvre. Here all gates, and every accessible point were densely crowded with enthusiastic spectators, whose cheers grew perfectly deafening as soon as they caught sight of him. The members of the Academy came to meet him in the anteroom—an honor which they had hitherto not paid to any of their colleagues. He was conducted to the President's chair, and unanimously requested to take it.

Voltaire gratefully received all these marks of homage, and listened attentively to a eulogy which d'Alembert delivered on Boileau.

When the sitting was over, many friends of his greeted him, and among them Necker also stepped up to him and cordially held out his hand to him.

"You have put me to your triumphal car to-day," he said, smilingly. "You appear everywhere as a triumpher, as the Cæsar of our century."

" I cannot complain, since you, my Cato, have risen for me," replied Voltaire, quickly; for other friends already thronged around him.

When he left the old Louvre, his passage to the Tuileries really resembled a triumphal procession. A vast concourse of people filled the large court of the Princes; no less crowded with spectators was the high terrace of the garden, where a galaxy of the most beautiful ladies had assembled, and waved their handkerchiefs to their favorite poet. When his carriage drew near, the enthusiasm of the crowd knew no bounds; all wished to see him and pay him homage, and many persons even tried to cling to the wheels of the carriage, in order to catch a glimpse of the illustrious man.

As soon as Voltaire had taken his seat at the theater, between Madame de Villette and Madame Denis, his niece, M. Brizan appeared with a laurel-wreath, which Madame de Villette placed on the poet's head. Voltaire, however, immediately took off the wreath, and the deafening shouts and cheers of the audience could not prevail on him to adorn himself with it again.

All the ladies had risen at his entrance, and Madame Necker and her daughter had not failed to follow their example.

" How happy Voltaire must be to-day," whispered Germaine to her mother. " I should like to be crowned likewise! But I am afraid it is impossible."

The theater, meanwhile, became more and more crowded; even the corridors were filled to their utmost capacity; all wished to see the poet, and the spectators in the pit were almost suffocated by the heavy pressure from without. The royal box was occupied by the court, Marie Antoinette and her ladies honoring by their presence the Sophocles of the eighteenth century. The blue, silver-embroidered dress of the Queen, the ostrich plumes and diamonds on her tall toupet, added to the charming appearance of her majesty; and well did she deserve the general admiration that was bestowed on her, as she bent with a sweet smile over the railing of her box in order to greet the poet.

Such was the excitement reigning in the vast audience, that more than twenty minutes elapsed before the actors were able to obtain a hearing. At length, however, the audience became more quiet, and listened to the play.

"Irene" was never performed with greater perfection than to-night, and the most rapturous applause rewarded the actors.

At the close of the performance, there were fresh bursts of applause, and the poet was called before the curtain. Voltaire stepped forward and bowed his thanks to the audience. At the same moment, there rose in the middle of the stage, as if by a magician's wand, a pedestal, surmounted by the poet's bust, and all the actors surrounded it in order to wreath and crown it. Voltaire's name burst from all lips, and every kind of praise, every expression of admiration which the human heart is able to conceive. Here, at least, envy had to be silent.

Madame Vestris now came forward and addressed the following lines to the illustrious man:

Aux yeux de Paris enchanté,
Reçois en ce jour un hommage
Que confirmera d'âge en âge
La sevère postérité.
Non, tu n'as pas besoin d'atteindre au noir rivage
Pour jouir de l'honneur de l'immortalité.
Voltaire, reçois la couronne
Que l'on vient de te présenter ;
Il est beau de la mériter
Quand c'est la France qui la donne.

These lines were in keeping with the feelings of the audience ; they were vociferously encored, and she was obliged to repeat them again and again, until the audience knew them by heart.

Voltaire's appearance indicated that he was greatly exhausted. At his age it is very difficult to bear up under such intense excitement, and his pale face betrayed the pains he took in order to keep erect. His glistening eyes, however, and the almost melancholy expression of his lips, showed that he was by no means insensible to the enthusiastic homage paid to him.

Upon stepping out into the passage, he found all the ladies ranged into two lines, and Voltaire had to walk between them to his carriage. At the door he was again detained. The crowd shouted, "Torches! Torches! We all want to see him!" He was scarcely able to reach his carriage. His impetuous admirers then jumped on the steps in order to kiss his hand. The coachman was requested to drive slowly, that the people might be able to escort it ; and amidst shouts of " *Vive Voltaire!* " and, "He has written *Oedipe*, *Merope*, and *Zaire*," the crowd accompanied him, as far as the Pont Royal.

Voltaire, who, as we said before, was greatly exhausted, leaned back in a corner of the carriage and had closed his eyes. Overpowered by the impressions of the eventful day, he was no longer able to withstand them. "It is too much!" he said in a low voice, and held his hand before his eyes.

When he reached the house of the Marquis de Villette, he

found that another carriage had already arrived there before him. It now gave place to his, and as soon as he alighted, two ladies appeared before him.

"Permit my daughter to present her laurel-wreath, too, to you, Voltaire," said M. Necker to the poet, while Germaine -bent her knee, and presented the wreath to him. "She has witnessed to-day scenes which she will never forget; for such moments remain isolated; they never recur."

"They never recur," gently said Voltaire, drawing the young girl to him, and imprinting a paternal kiss on her forehead. "They never recur!" he added, faintly; "so give no more wreaths to me. Let her keep this wreath who presented it to me."

So saying, he placed the laurel-wreath on the head of the young girl, who uttered a low cry when she saw herself crowned in this manner. Trembling with happiness, she intended to seize Voltaire's hand; but the poet had turned even paler than before, and was about to sink to the ground. M. Necker quickly hastened to him, supported him with his strong arms, and, assisted by the footman, carried Voltaire into the house and to his room.

Madame Necker had meanwhile entered the carriage with her daughter, and quietly awaited the return of her husband. Germaine still wore the laurel-wreath on her head, and her eyes beamed strangely.

"You may consider this event a presage," began her mother, "that fate intends to open to your mind a more extensive and conspicuous sphere than is usually granted to our sex. A great many opportunities are presented to you to cultivate your mind; all you have to do is to imitate the example which these illustrious persons set you, and if you are courageous and energetic enough to aspire to the highest goal, you will be certain to reach it.

Germaine looked at her mother inquiringly, and heaved a deep sigh. "Yes, if I were a boy!" she said, despondingly.

"Why, my child?" asked Madame Necker, in surprise.

"It would then be so easy for me to enter the path of fame; for all I should have to do would be to walk in the footsteps of illustrious men. But a girl is unable to do so. I am at a loss to know what goal I am to mark out for me. Tell me, mamma, the name of the lady whom you would like me best to resemble?"

Madame Necker was unable to answer this question immediately.

"I do not want you to resemble any of those whom you have met. I want you to ascend to an eminence which no woman has reached before you. At all events, I want you to make the attempt."

"But it is so very difficult to aspire to a degree of perfection which one has never seen."

"You may imagine it."

"Yes, like that of Corilla and Voltaire; but I shall never be like them." She sighed. "Do you not think, mamma, I might imitate Madame de Genlis? She writes so very beautifully!"

"That is not enough; one must, besides, be entitled to personal respect and admiration. The woman must never be separated from the poetess, my child."

"But is that so in her case?"

"You shall make her acquaintance, and then judge for yourself; but until then do not question me any more about her."

At this moment M. Necker stepped from the house. This put an end to the conversation between mother and daughter. They quickly drove home, and Germaine Necker hastened to her room and hung the laurel-wreath over her bed, where sweet dreams soon hovered around her.

CHAPTER VII.

A VISIT TO ROUSSEAU.

GERMAINE NECKER passed a very restless and dreamy night. At daybreak she awoke, and hastened to seat herself at her small writing-table, in order to work at the manuscript which the Abbe had sent back to her, with a note, in which he advised her to subject it to a revision.

The cracking of whips and sound of jingling bells interrupted her in this occupation. She rose and hastened to the window. Snow covered all the roofs, and the streets too were shrouded in it. Despite the lateness of the season, the young Queen Marie Antoinette was once more able to enjoy the favorite amusement of her native country, and to astonish the inhabitants of Paris by a brilliant sleigh-ride. The magnificent cavalcade was just drawing near, and Germaine Necker opened the window lest any part of the gorgeous spectacle should escape her.

The cavalcade was headed by a sleigh shaped like a large bee-hive, and supported by two winged genii; the beautiful queen was seated in it. The bracing air flushed her cheeks; she glanced around merrily, and smiled whenever she saw a gay face among the lookers-on in the streets.

Her proudly erect head was covered with a bonnet surmounted by three large ostrich plumes; and a blue-velvet cloak lined and trimmed with ermine was wrapped round her shoulders. The sleigh was also lined with blue velvet, and on the outside covered with draperies of the same material, beautifully embroidered with gold.

Two splendid white horses drew this fairy-like equipage; their bits were made of solid gold, and their harness was decorated with blue velvet and golden bells.

Germaine Necker had never seen anything like it; as if spellbound, she fixed her eyes on the beautiful Queen; and uttering a cry of delight, she dropped the window and clapped her hands.

But already the next sleigh attracted her attention. It was that of the Queen's brother-in-law, the Count d'Artois.

Rose-red and silver were the colors which he had chosen, and his sleigh looked like a huge shell, while he himself wore a black-velvet coat, richly trimmed with fur, and a Carret-cap of the same material. The slender young man presented a most prepossessing appearance in his tasteful costume, and many a beautiful lady glanced furtively after him.

Now followed the courtiers of the Queen and Prince; but, although they likewise displayed much splendor, their sleighs were eclipsed by those which had preceded them, and so they attracted less attention than those of Marie Antoinette and the Count d'Artois.

Germaine Necker now closed her window, and hastened to the fire-place in order to warm her fingers. She was greatly surprised to see that her mother, who had been standing behind her for some time already, was in the room.

"Such a sleigh-ride is a very pleasant amusement, is it not?" said Madame Necker, gazing into her daughter's eyes. "Still I deplore the short-sightedness of the Queen, who indulges in this expensive pleasure at a time when the lower classes suffer so much from want and cold."

"I am sure the Queen is not aware of it," replied Germaine. "She looks so good and kind-hearted."

" She is good and kind-hearted, my daughter; but it is very
wrong of her to arrange expensive sleigh-rides at a time when
so many people are crying for bread. Can they be blamed for
being exasperated on witnessing such displays of extravagance
on the part of the court? We should never present our own
affluence in such a manner to the eyes of those who are on the
brink of starvation. Your excellent father is now a member
of the royal cabinet, and straining every nerve in order to bal-
ance the expenditures and revenues of the State. In the meantime, he has intrusted me with the management of his own
fortune, and honored me in the most flattering manner by the
confidence which he reposes in me. I attach the more importance to it as I had no dower to bring to your father. My
knowledge, my education, were the only property I possessed
when I came to Paris. Here your father offered me his hand,
and I deemed myself only too happy to share the lot of so noble and excellent a man. It is no more than right and just that
I should now take the utmost pains to prove to him that I am
not entirely unworthy of the love and happiness which he has
bestowed on me. I have repeatedly told you all this already,
my daughter," said Madame Necker; " still I believe I cannot
reiterate it too often, in order to impress you duly with the
value of a good education, the only treasure which I had to
offer to my husband."

" But you were beautiful, too, mother," said Germaine.

Madame Necker blushed at this remark.

" That is a mere matter of taste," she replied; " even though
your father, at first perhaps, paid some attention to my appearance, he has long since ceased attaching any importance to
it. Believe me, my child, love, as well as friendship, in order
to be lasting, needs intellectual harmony, and rests firmly only
on a basis of mutual respect."

" But respect, mother, is so cold, and admiration so warm!"

Madame Necker knit her brow slightly, and contracted her shapely mouth. After a brief pause of reflection, she replied:

" You must not compare the delicate and refined conduct of my friends with the noisy acclamation with which Voltaire is greeted everywhere. The multitude, moreover, as history proves, is exceedingly fickle. Genuine merit never hankers after its applause; it is far above such vanities. See, my daughter, there is at this moment in our city a man whose merits far surpass those of a Voltaire, and yet he sits alone in his garret, thinking and writing for immortality."

" You allude to Rousseau, mother!" exclaimed Germaine, warmly.

" I do, indeed, my child. And this will show you what a heart this great man possesses. Read this letter which he has written. It is addressed to his aged nurse. Thomas brought it to me; you may keep it, and learn from it how beautiful it is to be grateful for benefits that have been conferred on us."

Germaine seized the letter hastily, opened it and read as follows:

"MONTMORENCY, July 2, 1761.

" Your letter, dear Jacobine, has reached me, and gladdened my heart at a moment when I was unable to answer it.

" I avail myself now of an undisturbed moment to thank you for your remembrance and for your love, which always will be dear to me. For my part, I have never ceased remembering and loving you.

" In times of suffering I have often said to myself that, if my dear Jacobine had not nursed me so carefully in my childhood, I should have suffered less in later years.

" Believe me, I shall never cease taking the most affectionate interest in your health and happiness, and that it will always

gladden my heart to hear from yourself that you are well and
in good spirits.

"God bless you, my dear, good Jacobine!

"I do not write anything about my own health, in order not
to grieve you; may the good God preserve yours, and grant
you all the blessings for which you long.

"Your faithful Jean Jacques, who embraces you with all his
heart.   "ROUSSEAU."

"How kind! How cordial!" exclaimed Germaine, profoundly moved, when she had read the letter.

"These simple words are so very beautiful because of the
noble feelings which they express. And now go and dress, my
child, in order to accompany me to Rousseau."

"To Rousseau!" exclaimed Germaine, as if she hardly
trusted her ears. "You are jesting, mother!"

"I am in dead earnest. I wish to give you an opportunity
to satisfy yourself that genuine merit does not always need
the pomp and noise of popular applause. For some time past
I have already tried to find a pretext for paying him a visit;
for he is greatly averse to amusing inquisitive idlers. In order
to be admitted by him, we will appear in the simple costume
of my native country; I am sure we may permit ourselves
this little stratagem. I shall send my maid to you immediately,
in order to assist you in dressing. Go now and put your papers
into your bureau."

So saying she left the room. Germaine still remained for
some minutes in the same attitude, looking, as if absently, after
her mother. It was not until then that it occurred to her that
she had to make haste. She carefully folded up Rousseau's
letter, and pressed it reverentially to her lips before putting it
into a small case which contained other precious relics of the

same description; she then gathered up the leaves of her manuscript and put it likewise into the bureau.

Madame Necker had not ordered her own carriage, in order not to endanger her incognito. There were hackney-coaches at the corner of the street; she beckoned to one of them, and entered it with her daughter. She ordered the coachman to drive her to the Rue Platriere, without designating the number of the house. Upon reaching that street, she told him to halt, and tried to find the house where the celebrated man lived.

A narrow back-door led them into a dark hall, where they were scarcely able to discover the staircase. They ascended it slowly.

" I hope we shall find him at home," whispered Germaine to her mother; I should be so sorry if he were absent."

" Do not get excited," replied her mother. " Above all things, do not let him see that you know who he is."

When they reached the fifth floor, Madame Necker stood still. Here lived the author of "Nouvelle Heloise." She looked about for the door that might lead to the poet's room. Already she stretched out her hand toward a bell before her, when she suddenly heard somebody sing.

She listened.

It was a male voice, neither sonorous nor agreeable, and somewhat tremulous; but the intonation was perfectly correct. It seemed to be a very melancholy air, which he sang repeatedly; finally all was silent.

Madame Necker now rapped at the door, but so softly that the sound scarcely fell on her own ears.

She waited a while for an answer from within. But as none was given, she courageously rang the bell.

Footsteps resounded within; he approached; and the door opened.

Germaine, trembling with suspense, seized her mother's arm.

A man appeared now in the half-open door; when he perceived the two ladies, he politely took off his cap and bowed to them.

"Is this the room of a certain M. Rousseau, who copies music?" inquired Madame Necker, in an indifferent tone.

"Yes, Madame," replied the man. "I am Rousseau. What do you want of me?"

"I have been told that you are an excellent copyist, sir, and yet charge only reasonable prices; I would request you, therefore, to copy some pieces for me."

"Pray come in," replied Rousseau, politely.

Madame Necker and Germaine now followed him through a dark and narrow ante-chamber into his sitting-room. Here he invited Madame Necker to seat herself in an arm-chair, and placed another for Germaine beside it.

"My costume, M. Rousseau, shows you that I am not a permanent resident of Paris; it would, therefore, be very agreeable to me if you could serve me immediately."

"I have little to do at the present time, Madame; it will, therefore, afford me pleasure to work for you immediately. What is it that you wish me to copy?"

Madame Necker now handed him a roll of music, which she had hitherto held in her hand.

Rousseau took it, and requested her to keep her seat, and to permit him to put on his cap again, while he would glance over the music. He then sat down at the table close to them and unfolded the roll.

Madame Necker profited by this moment to look about the room.

Three old arm-chairs, several other rickety chairs, and a

4

writing-table, formed all the furniture which it contained. On the table lay several books, some sheet-music and dried plants. Over the fire-place hung an old silver watch. A cat was sleeping close to the fire. A dozen views of Switzerland and several coarse copperplates adorned the walls. Among the copperplates she noticed a portrait of Frederick the Great, and, on looking closer at it, she found that Rousseau had written on the margin the words, "He thinks like a philosopher, and acts like a king." *

Germaine had constantly followed her mother's glance, and both of them now fixed their eyes on the poet's figure. His form was by no means imposing. He was of medium height, and had a broad, arched chest. His features might be called regular, but they did not, by any means, indicate that he was a man of genius. His eyes, which he now fixed on the music, and now on his fair visitors, were small, round, and restless. His shaggy eyebrows imparted to them a harsh and gloomy expression, which was softened again by his exceedingly shapely and attractive mouth. His smile was so melancholy, and withal so sweet, that it lit up his features with a wondrous charm, and irresistibly attracted his visitors toward him.

His dress consisted of a cotton cap, which did not look very neat, and was adorned with a ribbon which formerly had been as red as fire. He wore a flannel waistcoat under his furred coat, dark-brown pantaloons, gray stockings, and old, worn-out shoes.

Rousseau had meanwhile looked over the music. He had found among the pieces an air from "Le Devin du village," which had aroused his distrust, and he now turned with a searching glance to Madame Necker.

"Do you know the composer of this air, Madame?" he asked, sharply.

---

* "Il pense en philosophe et se conduit en roi.

"I do," she replied, calmly. "His name is too well known that I should not have heard it; but I have never seen him. He has composed very pretty songs, and written excellent books. Are you acquainted with him, or is he, perhaps, even a relative of yours?"

Rousseau was about to make a reply, but he suddenly interrupted himself. He was probably afraid of uttering half a falsehood by evading the truth, and so he preferred keeping silence. Instead of answering Madame Necker's question, he smiled significantly.

"We mothers are greatly indebted to M. Rousseau," added Madame Necker. "He has procured us the right of nursing our babes at our own breasts, and thereby secured us the performance of one of our noblest duties. This is a gain which we shall never be able to extol enough."

Rousseau cast on Madame Necker a glance reflecting his whole soul. At the same time, a heavenly smile lit up his features. She perceived that she had hit the spot where he was most perceptible of flattery.

In the meantime, a woman about forty years old had entered the room. She bowed with studied politeness to the ladies, and, without uttering a word, seated herself on the other side of the table at which Rousseau had just sat.

It was Theresa, Rousseau's factotum, who played at the same time the *role* of mistress and servant.

Madame Necker felt no sympathy for her, and she had to take pains to conceal the unpleasant impression which Theresa's appearance made upon her.

To resume the conversation, she asked now how much Rousseau would charge her for copying the music.

"Six sous a page, Madame," replied Rousseau. "That is the usual price."

"Shall I pay you something in advance?" she asked, politely. "You have to purchase music-paper."

"Thank God, Madame, I am able to do so," replied Rousseau, smiling at her kindness. "I am in better circumstances than you seem to think; for I receive a small pension, and—"

"And you might have a much larger income," interposed Theresa, "if you collected what the opera owes you." So saying, she shrugged her shoulders peevishly.

Rousseau made no reply. He seemed not to be courageous enough to enter into a quarrel with his housekeeper. Since her entrance, his bearing and expression had undergone a marked change, and a certain depression seemed to have seized him. He restlessly moved to and fro on his chair; finally he rose, and begged permission to leave the room for a few moments.

No sooner had he withdrawn than Theresa said:

"Madame, pray excuse M. Rousseau; I am sorry to say that he is sick."

Madame Necker replied, there was no need to add any excuses to those of M. Rousseau.

"Have you need of me, M. Rousseau?" she now shouted in a loud voice, no doubt to display her solicitude for him in the presence of the strangers.

"No, no!" he replied, re-entering the sitting-room.

"Madame," he said, turning to his visitors, "pray intrust your music to other hands; for I regret to say that I feel too unwell to work for you as rapidly and promptly as you desire, inasmuch as your sojourn in Paris, perhaps, will not be of long duration."

Madame Necker replied that her departure was not yet near at hand, and although she would like to have the music at an early day, she would submit to a brief delay rather than intrust it to other hands which might prove to be less skillful.

With these words she rose in order to leave the room. Rousseau politely accompanied her to the door, where she took leave of Theresa by coldly nodding to her.

She went down stairs with her daughter in silence, and beckoned to the coachman to come up. No sooner had the coach door closed behind them, than Germaine buried her face in her hands and burst into low sobs.

"Poor, poor man!" she lamented. "He is going to copy the music at six sous a page! That breaks my heart! Father must give me money for him, and I will take it to him. I will give him all I have, my dresses, my jewels—all, all! I do not want to sit any longer on soft chairs when Rousseau has in his room only such hard and uncomfortable ones. Oh, this is too dreadful! The King ought not to suffer it!"

Her mother allowed her to continue in this manner for some time; she then interrupted her.

"Now compose yourself, Germaine," she said, calmly. "I foresaw that the circumstances of Jean Jacques Rousseau would make a deep impression on you, and I am glad that you did not give the reins to your emotions in his presence. But your lamentations are wasted. How can we assist him who rejects all offers of assistance? It is his greatness to reject all that is offered to him, and accept nothing but the fruits of his labors. If he would accept any assistance, many a great King would deem it a glorious privilege to become the benefactor of Rousseau. But the author of 'Emile' and the 'Contrat Social' will not hear of it; nor can he do so without incurring distrust and suspicion."

"And so he suffers all kinds of privations," exclaimed Germaine, mournfully. "How melancholy and unhappy he looked! Ah, never, never, shall I forget this visit to Rousseau!"

CHAPTER VIII.

THE FIRST POEM.

The sun shed its most scorching rays upon earth. The inhabitants of Paris fled from the oppressive heat; the streets were deserted, and the fine old shade-trees in the garden of the Tuileries scarcely afforded them sufficient protection from the torrid sunshine. Even the most industrious artisans ceased working to-day.

The court was at Versailles; the young Queen whiled away her time at her little dairy-farm, while Louis the Sixteenth was occupied in his favorite pastime, the trade of a locksmith. On a day when nobody was at work, Necker, too, could permit himself a brief relaxation, and he did so the more willingly as Nature was still decked in a thousand charms.

During the present year he had not had many opportunities of visiting his small villa at St. Ouen, where formerly he had passed every Sunday in the midst of his friends. He now merrily invited some of his intimate acquaintances to share with him for a few days the pleasures of rural life, and they willingly accepted his invitation. He himself, accompanied by Grimm and Raynal, preceded them to St. Ouen in order to surprise his wife and daughter by his unexpected arrival.

Madame Necker was not very fond of rural solitude. She regarded as wasted every minute that did not add to her knowledge. Hence nothing but a sense of duty had induced her to precede her husband to the villa, in order to superintend the pieparations for a little family festival, with which he was to be surprised to-morrow.

She was standing at the window, and gazing up to the sky adorned with all the gorgeous tints of a magnificent sunset. She was surprised that her husband should tarry so long, and, pressing her high white forehead against the window-pane, she listened if the sound of coach-wheels was not yet audible in the distance.

Thomas, who had accompanied her to St. Ouen, in order to assist her in the preparations for the festival, entered the room at this moment. Pale and grave as usual, he approached with a slow, measured step, and placed himself by her side.

At this moment, the merry, clear voice of Germaine, who was in the garden, fell on their ears, and soon after they saw her running after a young girl of the same age, who seemed to be intent on concealing herself from Germaine.

"She is so old already, and yet she likes to play like a little child," said Madame Necker, disapprovingly.

"Her heart is still very young, although her mind has arrived at an almost precocious maturity. I am glad that you have followed my advice and given young M'lle Huber as a companion to her. I never saw Germaine so happy as on the day when you presented the young girl to her."

"It is unfortunately but too true, my friend!" said Madame Necker, sighing.

"Unfortunately? How so?" asked Thomas, wonderingly.

"Let me confess," replied Madame Necker, with half a smile, "that I was jealous of my own child on that day. I have educated her for myself. I have devoted myself entirely to her education, and must see now that she turns from me, and prefers the little stranger's company to mine."

"You are jealous?" asked Thomas, in surprise, as if he had

not heard anything but this word. "If you can yield to jealousy on this occasion, what would you feel in my place?"

Madame Necker blushed, and averted her face.

"Shall we go down to the garden?" she asked.

"You are dressed too airily; you have changed your *toilette* for the arrival of your husband," said Thomas, looking at her dress, which sat charmingly on her. The transparent dress of white gauze veiled her beautiful neck and full white arms but very imperfectly, and her tall slender form seemed even more delicate in the airy costume which she wore. He gazed at her admiringly. "A genuine queen of the Anglo-Saxons," he exclaimed. "How beautiful you are to-day."

Instead of making a reply, Madame Necker turned, rang the bell, and ordered the servant to bring in lights. At the same moment Germaine rushed into the room. But as soon as she caught sight of her mother, she slackened her step, and assumed a stiff attitude.

"A cloud of dust is drawing near—it must be he!" she exclaimed, with beaming eyes.

"Who? You should always mention the names of the persons to whom you refer," said her mother.

"I spoke of my father. Whom else could I have referred to? For three long, long days I have not seen him, and, if he brings guests with him, as I expect he will, how little time he will be able to devote to me even to-night!" she exclaimed in a mournful tone, and burst into tears.

"Germaine!" cried Madame Necker, disapprovingly. "You shed tears again! Must you weep, then, on all joyful occasions? My poor, poor child! What will remain to you for grief in case it should knock at your door?" *

---

* M'lle Huber said of Germaine Necker, "Ce qui l'amusait était ce qui la faisait pleurer."

"Nothing can grieve me more," continued the young girl, " than to be so indifferent to my noble father that he hardly misses me when I am far from him ! "

" But is not such the case with me, too ? Did I not leave him in order to pass these days with you at St. Ouen ? and will he now be able to devote all his time to me ? You are a foolish child, Germaine."

" Ah, I am very, very unhappy ! I should like to be every-thing to him, and I am but his child. But you are the wife of his heart ; he chose you ! "

" Hush, hush, I do not want to hear any more of these fool-ish complaints," said Madame Necker, coldly and sternly. " Go to your room and calm yourself, so as to be able to re-ceive our guests becomingly. What would your friend Raynal say if he should see you now ? "

The girl, sighing, left the room.

" It is very singular," remarked Thomas, when the door had closed after her, " that Germaine should be so passionate and impetuous in her affections. And then this jealousy of her own mother ! "

" I do not know myself how so unnatural a feeling can have arisen in her heart," replied Madame Necker, covering her eyes with her beautiful white hand in order to conceal her grief from Thomas' view. "I am often at a loss how to coun-teract this jealousy. She always draws comparisons between herself and me, and they generally result in adding to her de-pression. Hence I am taking pains to impress her with a sense of the superiority of her education. I constantly urge her to strive for fame and discard vanity ; but just when I hope to have led her into the right path, there happens such an out-burst, and overthrows my whole structure."

" May be to-morrow's festival will produce a salutary effect
4*

upon her; for praise will not be wanting to her," said Thomas, consolingly.

"That is what I thought, too; the trouble is only that her own father does not think very highly of literary women, and believes that only such of them as possess very marked talents should lay their productions before the public. It remains to be seen whether or not he will consider his daughter sufficiently gifted."

"Why should he not?" asked Thomas, smiling. "Do you not know that paternal love likes to adorn its darlings with very beautiful plumes?"

"But its eyes are not bandaged like those of the little god of love," replied Madame Necker, jocularly. "And as I see that my daughter has magnificent eyes, but an ugly snub-nose and thick negro lips, so her father may think that, with a great deal of mind and an extraordinary imagination, she is wanting in plastic diction, and prevented by her restless and passionate temper from making up by earnest application for what nature has refused to her. If such should be his opinion, he will not encourage, but restrain her, and thus destroy my last hope.",

"Yes, if such should be his opinion," said Thomas. "But let us wait and see. In that event I can only say to him with Pope, 'True ease in writing comes from art, not chance,' and ask him to wait until she acquires the skill in which he thinks her to be deficient."

"Do so. Meanwhile your courage will sustain me. Let us wait and see."

"Provided it does not last too long," exclaimed Raynal, who entered the room at this moment and overheard the last words. "It is very pleasant to wait for one of your epicurean suppers, which always indemnify us for curbing our impatience, so richly that my old mouth waters at the mere thought of them.

But as a general thing I am not very fond of this theory of waiting. It proved most effective in Roman history, when Fabius Cunctator avoided a pitched battle and hemmed in his enemies. But now-a-days; ahem!· Franklin did not wait; he swam like a duck across the immense ocean, and accomplished his purpose. Had he remained at home, he would not have obtained anything from us."

"He was not indebted for his success to his eloquence," said Thomas, sneeringly.

"God knows he was not. It seemed almost as though the American Embassador was mute, so little had he to say. However, he is doing now a great deal better. Since France has declared for the Colonies, his tongue has been loosened. I met him the other day at a dinner-party, and was amiable enough to address him as follows: 'I must confess to you, sir, that America presents a truly grand spectacle.' 'Yes,' replied the taciturn doctor from Philadelphia; 'but the spectators refuse to pay for it.' Let me ask you if that was not a very sharp answer?"

All laughed.

"Did you hear that he is courting the widow of Helvetius?" asked Madame Necker.

"I did, indeed," replied Raynal. "And he is in dead earnest about it; he is head and ears in love with her, and wants to marry her."

"Oh, I suppose that is a mere supposition," said Madame Necker.

"But a well-grounded one. We men are sometimes likewise keen-sighted in this respect. Believe me, if it depended on him, he would take this charming widow to America. But she loves her independence, and is afraid of the sea."

"Whom are you speaking of? Of Madame Helvetius?"

asked Grimm, entering the room. " In that event, I can tell you something that will amuse you. Franklin has proposed to her, and been rejected. He goes home in high dudgeon, and writes the following letter. Hear! hear!" So saying, he took a paper from his pocket and read :

" I returned last night to my house greatly dejected at your determination not to marry again, in honor of your late lamented husband. In my despondency, I threw myself on my bed, and dreamed that I was dead, and walking in the Elysian Fields. I was asked there whom I wished to see. 'Conduct me to the philosophers,' I replied. 'There are two of them close by ; they are on very friendly terms.' 'Who are they ?' 'Socrates and Helvetius.' 'I feel the highest respect for both of them, but I should prefer to see Helvetius first, because I am somewhat familiar with French, while I do not know a word of Greek.' He received me very politely, and assured me that he had long since known me by name. He then inquired very anxiously about the state of religion, liberty, and government in France. 'You do not ask me at all about your dear friend, Madame Helvetius? And yet she loves you so dearly! It is only an hour since she told me so.' 'Ah, you remind me of the days of past happiness; but those who wish to be happy here, must not call them to mind. At first my thoughts always were with her. I then took another wife, who bears a passable resemblance to her; it is true, she is not as beautiful as my widow, but she possesses a great deal of mind and common sense, and loves me so dearly that she does not long for anything else than to please me. She has just left me to fetch some nectar and ambrosia for my supper. Stay here, sir, in order to get acquainted with her.' 'I see that the fidelity of your first wife far surpasses yours, inasmuch as she rejects all proposals. I myself loved her madly; but nothing

could prevail on her to desist from her purpose, and marry me.'
'I am sorry for you,' he said, 'for she is a very good and amiable woman. But do the Abbes, Laroche and M——, not sometimes call on her yet?' 'They do, indeed, for she has re-
tained all her old friends.' 'You should´have tried to gain
M—— over to your side by means of some *café à la crême;*
perhaps you would then have been more successful, for he is as
able a speaker as St. Thomas was, and knows so well how to
argue a point that no one is able to refute him; you might
have also caused the other Abbe, Laroche, to oppose your suit,
by presenting him with a fine edition of the Classics; perhaps
this would have been still better, for I always noticed that she
liked to do the reverse of what he advised to her.' At this
moment the new Madame Helvetius, in whom I recognized
immediately my old American friend, Mrs. Franklin, made
her appearance. I requested her to follow me, but she replied coldly, 'I have been a good wife to you for forty-
nine years and four months, and thought that that would
satisfy you. Now I have formed this new acquaintance,
which is to last eternally.' Vexed at this refusal of my
Eurydice, I immediately resolved not to stay any longer with
these ungrateful shades, and to return to this world of sunshine and to you. Here I am now. Let us avenge our wrongs
together."

"A capital letter!" exclaimed Raynal. "But confess, it is
merely a jest of yours or a mystification."

"Neither the one nor the other. Still waters are deep. You
see now how cleverly Franklin revenges himself on the lady
who rejected his suit, but lends a willing ear to the tender sighs
of others."

Necker had meanwhile entered the room, and cast a significant glance on Grimm.

"The letter will afford a great deal of pleasure to your sovereign, the Empress of Russia," he said.

"That is the reason why I copied it," replied Grimm, gravely.

"What does my young friend think of it?" asked Raynal, turning to Germaine, who clung to her father's arm. "I have to speak with her privately as soon as we have tasted M. Necker's nectar, which I shall relish after the dust on the road and the heat of the day, no less than poor Helvetius did that which his Hebe presented to him."

"At bottom, that letter is somewhat impious, and, above all, decidedly immoral," said Madame Necker, emphatically.

"If we keep in mind the object for which it was written, I think you are mistaken," said M. Necker, merrily. "We cannot do without jests. For the rest, opinions differ greatly as to what is moral. For my part, I say, *La morale est la nature des choses.*"

Germaine raised her radiant eyes to her father's face, and pressed his arm to her side, in order to show that she understood him, and approved what he said. Madame Necker noticed it. A slight cloud passed over her features, and, interrupting the conversation, she rose and requested the guests to follow her.

Additional guests arrived next morning, and the little villa was soon filled to its utmost capacity.

Germaine Necker was invisible. She sat with M'lle Huber in a shady bosquet of the garden, studying her *role ;* for she intended to play herself the heroine in her drama to-day. A small stage had been erected in a pavilion ; and Raynal, who was likewise to appear in the drama, accompanied her now thither, in order to rehearse the whole once more.

In the afternoon the guests were informed of the entertainment which was in store for them, and all hastened to the pavilion. Germaine was behind the scenes when the specta-tors entered, and she looked anxiously through a hole in the curtain in order to see the air with which her father looked forward to the performance.

It had been resolved not to inform M. Necker that Germaine had written the play; this could be concealed from him the more easily, as he did not question anybody on this point. His daughter was to appear in the play, and he thought that was the surprise prepared for him.

A large bill at the door informed the guests that "Les Incon-venients de la Vie de Paris" was the title of the play.

The curtain rose, and on the stage appeared a mother, who had two daughters. One of them had grown up in rural retire-ment, while the other had enjoyed all the advantages of a city education.

The mother prefers the latter; she praises her cultivated mind, her graceful bearing, her social talents, and neglects and slights the former on all occasions.

Adversity now knocks at her door. In consequence of a lawsuit she loses her whole fortune; she is obliged to reduce her expenses very largely, and even suffers painful privations. The elegant city girl is unable to adapt herself to these circum-stances; she complains loudly of the fickleness of fate, and vents her spite upon her mother.

The simple country girl, on the other hand, redoubles her tenderness, and becomes the stay and comfort of her whole family.

The scenes of this little drama were very skillfully connected; the characters were exceedingly well developed; and the inter-est was kept up from beginning to end. Loud applause re-warded the actors, and Marmontel was even so deeply moved that he drew his handkerchief from his pocket in order to dry his tears.*

Germaine was applauded most enthusiastically, and, at the close of the performance, called before the curtain. When she made her appearance, flowers and wreaths were showered upon her, and a thousand encomiums bestowed on her. Her heart, however, longed only for her father's applause, and she awaited, tremblingly, the first word which he would utter.

M. Necker now beckoned to her to come to him, and folded her to his heart. "She has performed her *role* exceedingly well," he said to Grimm.

"More than that," interposed Raynal; "she has not only played, but also written exceedingly well. Neither of us, my dear Necker, would have been able at her age to write such a drama."

"It is your own composition, then?" asked her father, in surprise.

She made no reply. He fixed his keen eyes searchingly on her face.

"Yes, it is true," he said, coldly, disengaging himself from her arms; "my only child is an authoress."

At these words Germaine fainted away.

---

* "Correspondance Littéraire." Vol. iv., p. 290.

CHAPTER IX.

DR. TRONCHIN.

SEVERAL months had elapsed since " Les Inconvenients de la Vie de Paris" had been performed at St. Ouen. A severe illness had confined Germaine Necker to her bed, and when she rose to-day for the first time, she had grown taller, and her complexion had almost turned pale. A smile of satisfaction overspread her features when she looked at her face in the mirror, and discovered that she was no longer as red as formerly. She thought she looked now a great deal more like her mother than before.

She leaned back in the *chaise longue*, and gazed into the flickering flames in her fire-place.

At this moment her father entered the room. She uttered a feeble, "Ah!" when she saw him, and, quickly raising herself up, she intended to hasten toward him; but he signed to her to keep her seat.

"Do not stir, my child!" he said, emphatically, taking a chair in order to seat himself by her side. "You are much better, and will not be long in recovering entirely; but you must still be very cautious. Beware of overtaxing your strength. At your age you have still a long future before you, and will soon make up for what you have missed."

"Mother thinks I must not be too indolent."

"Not too indolent, but a little of it can do no harm. You are, moreover, my only child, my only joy, my whole happiness. Why should you exert your strength if you feel no inclination to do so; and such must be the case now when you are still so very feeble."

" I am not desirous of distinguishing myself, since I know that you disapprove it," she said, her quivering lips betraying her profound emotion.

" We should not speak of it now," said her father, in a grave, but gentle tone, seizing her right hand. " But I shall soothe you, perhaps, more effectually by coming to an understanding with you on this point, than by allowing you to brood over it. It grieved you to hear me disapprove the road to fame which you have entered already at so early an age. Ah, my child, the path which you desire to pursue is a very thorny one, for it exposes you defenselessly to the shafts of obloquy and slander. Publicity is to a man a stimulus rousing dormant powers; but on a woman it inflicts wounds which oftentimes never heal again. A man may bid defiance to the world; a woman must listen to her soft admonitions, and proceed very cautiously. Now, as there is nothing to me dearer on earth than the happiness and tranquility of my child, it wrung my heart to find her so unexpectedly in a path where I should have preferred not to see her at all. But since you have entered it, it does not matter. If you feel inclined to commit your thoughts and feelings to paper, and have them examined and criticized by others, do so. I shall not hinder and disturb you; for all I care for, is to make you happy. Only remain truthful and good, my dear daughter, and you will always please me." *

" My dear, dear father ! " whispered Germaine, deeply moved, pressing his hand to her lips. " How shall I render myself worthy of your love ? "

---

* " Madame Necker de Saussure."   P. 22.

"By being happy, my child. Let me read in your eyes that the life which I have given to you is a boon to you; let me feel that you repose the most implicit confidence in me, and that you feel convinced that your joy is my joy, that your grief finds an echo in my breast, and that I am your first and best friend. Will you do so, Germaine, and can you do so?"

"How should I not," she exclaimed, rapturously, "my own, my dearest father!"

Her father averted his face in order to conceal from her the tears which filled his eyes, and left the room.

Germaine remained in profound emotion. She pressed her hand firmly to her impetuously throbbing breast, and looked about as if intoxicated with rapture. So happy, so blissful, she had never felt before; so sweet and enchanting had life never seemed to her.

Finally, she folded her hands on her breast, and muttered a prayer, in which she thanked God for the happiness which he had vouchsafed to her. Her father loved her, he loved her better than anything else on earth; oh, it was almost too much happiness!

Exhausted as she was, her eyes closed, and she fell into a gentle slumber. A blissful smile played round her lips, and dreams hovered around her, such as she had never dreamed before. Her lips moved, she called in her sleep for her father, and when she awoke, she prayed, "Forgive me, my God, if I should love him better than Thee!"

Dr. Tronchin found her pulse next morning somewhat irregular, and whole condition slightly worse; but she assured him she never felt better. But he refused to believe it, and said that only the utmost mental tranquility would lead to her recovery, while any strong excitement might even endanger her life.

Madame Necker knit her brow as she heard this. "My daughter cannot lead the life of a prisoner at her father's house," she said; "nor can her mind rest here entirely. She would, moreover, be unable to bear the tedium of such an idleness."

"And yet she must bear it," replied Dr. Tronchin, sternly; "for it is the only medicine which I can prescribe to her, and we do not care if the patient relishes the medicine, if only it is efficacious. Mademoiselle Necker must live in the country, and pass the whole day in the open air, if possible in the midst of cows and sheep. Pen and ink she will leave at home, and books too. Man is created to live with nature, and not with paper."

"I see you have read Rousseau's 'Emile,'" said Madame Necker, somewhat sarcastically.

"As may be expected of every cultivated man," replied Dr. Tronchin, calmly. "But I did more than that: I allowed the work to convince me."

"Many things look well in theory, but turn out to be worthless in practice," replied Madame Necker, bitterly; perhaps for the first time she was unable to master the irritation which the doctor's words had caused her. "Our sex dislikes man in his original state; it is not until he has cultivated his mind that we appreciate him as a companion. Hence, the higher the aims which a woman strives to reach, the more it is necessary for a man to elevate his moral and intellectual ideal. I had conceived grand, far-reaching plans in regard to my daughter; your fiat has thwarted all of them, and restored my child to mediocrity. If she must cease adding to her knowledge, she must likewise renounce all prospects of fame and distinction. All the time and pains which I bestowed upon her education have been wasted."

"But, Madame, said Dr. Tronchin, smiling, "you may be sure

that your daughter will turn to account the talents with which nature has endowed her, and that my cure will not impair them. Her mind will grow healthier and stronger with her body."

"That is rank materialism," exclaimed Madame Necker, in dismay. "Such principles will certainly ruin France. If you make man a mere living machine, without rendering the mind, which is to ripen for eternity, independent of the body, he will become the sport of his passions; for what would govern him? I shudder at the thought of the abyss on the brink of which we are standing. First comes Gall with his phrenology, as if the soul were something palpable; he is preceded by Mesmer, who idolizes the nervous system; and the kind-hearted Lavater finally discerns our whole character from the features of our face. It is always the body and nothing but the body in which our *Savants* try to find the key to the soul, instead of listening to the Bible, which says, that the flesh is the seat of all sins. How far we are still from the light of truth if we continue in this path."

"It remains to be seen if it is the wrong one," replied Tronchin, smiling. "Enthusiasm for an ideal world is more suitable to the minds of beautiful ladies than positive intercourse with reality. Psychology, and not physiology, is their science; for they would hardly be able to make a thorough diagnosis. Love is their theme, and ours—necessity."

"All physicians do not occupy your stand-point."

"I know it," replied Dr. Tronchin, smiling. "Since Molière betrayed so many of our secrets, we have had to resort to various methods; the faith of the public in our old system was shaken more and more, and so we had to try to prop it here and there. Thank God, such props are not wanting to us, and their number is daily on the increase. Men want to be deceived; they want to be cured by a method which they do not understand, and use remedies of whose properties they are entirely ignorant. One of these methods is magnetism, of which delicate ladies are so fond because it is such a very nice titillation of the senses."

"You forget that you are speaking to a lady," said Madame Necker, gravely.

"But to a lady who stands far above her sex. 'La femme à Thomas'* cannot be an ordinary woman. You have no time to brood over little ailments; the management of a large fortune, the education of your daughter, the establishment of a hospital, the exigencies of social life—all these occupy you so much that you never afford me the pleasure of treating you unless exhaustion overpowers you, and compels me to exclaim, 'stop!' So you cannot take umbrage at my censuring your sex for not thinking and acting like you."

This handsome compliment did not fail to make an agreeable impression on Madame Necker, who replied in a kinder tone:

"If women in general are not what they should be, it is owing to their education, doctor. For what I am, I am solely indebted to my father's solicitude."

"You insist on being a production of art, and on making a Pygmalion of every schoolmaster," said Dr. Tronchin, smiling, and taking his hat.

Mother and daughter sat a while in silence opposite to one another, when they were alone.

"You seem to be vexed," began Germaine, finally. "I hope it is not in consequence of anything that I have done?"

Madame Necker did not reply immediately. She seemed to be at a loss for an answer. Finally, she said, coldly:

---

* When Thomas had written his "History of Woman," Madame Necker was greeted at the Italian Opera with the words "Voilà la femme à Thomas!"

" I have noticed that you hesitate in your conversation with your father, whenever I enter the room. Have you something to communicate to him that you wish to conceal from me ? "

" Oh! no," replied Germaine, blushing.

" Why, then, are you silent in my presence, or rather, why do you break off a conversation which seems to afford you pleasure, and begin to speak of other things as soon as I join you ? "

" Because—" replied Germaine, hesitatingly, " Because—you are more rigorous than father, and do not relish the thousand little witticisms by which I try to amuse him. I am always so glad to see him laugh ; for after the severe labors which his official duties impose upon him, it is a real blessing to him. At all events, he tells me so. I do not like to jest in your presence, because you have always been averse to it, and often called it an intellectual vagabond life. Now, inasmuch as I do in the presence of my dear father things which are not in consonance with your wishes, but please him, I am silent as soon as you join us, in order not to grieve you."

" So your father likes your jests and witticisms," said Madame Necker, slowly ; and for the first time her pure and noble heart was filled with a feeling of bitterness, which was the more painful as it concerned her own husband, her own daughter—two beings to whom she was devoted with all her heart.

She left Germaine, locked herself in her room, and—wept. Since she had given her hand to Necker, these were her first tears. She was fearful she might henceforth no longer occupy the first place in her husband's heart ; and how was she to retain this place when she saw that her daughter, by means entirely different from those which she had employed, succeeded in amusing and pleasing him ? To meet her on the same ground, and dispute the victory with her there, was entirely out of the question.

She had hoped that her husband would love her in her daughter,* and she had, therefore, taken so many pains to give her an excellent education, in order to see herself rejuvenated in her. And now this bitter disappointment!

"She must leave Paris," she said, after reflecting a long time. "Let her go to St. Ouen, as Dr. Tronchin advises; but I shall stay here with my husband and try to regain his affections. He is mine, and shall remain mine. Germaine has yet all her life before her, and all paths are open to her; but I have nothing to expect and nothing to lose in this world, save his love. It is my most precious treasure, and I shall risk everything in order to keep it."

---

* "Madame Necker de Saussure." P. 23.

CHAPTER X.

THE VILLA AT ST. OUEN.

THE vernal sun shed its bright rays on the earth and greeted the sprouting corn.

Germaine Necker was walking, with a quick step, through the alleys of the garden, holding in her hand a book bound in blue cloth. The noonday rays fell vertically upon her bare head without her feeling their intense heat. She seemed so thoroughly absorbed in what she was reading, that she was perfectly inaccessible to all outward influences. Her beautiful hands and arms, which her mother had always covered so carefully that her daughter might retain this charm, were exposed to the scorching rays of the sun. She seemed to have forgotten herself entirely.

Her sojourn in the country had greatly strengthened her health. She was unusually tall for a girl who had just reached her sixteenth year, and her strong and well-developed limbs caused her to look at a distance much older than she really was. Her firm step, her deep voice, the steady glance of her eyes, which girlish bashfulness did not cause her to drop, deprived her of the sweet charms of her age; but her wonderful talents made up for what was wanting to her in this respect. Her black hair hung loosely on her shoulders, while she lifted her large dark eyes eloquently toward Heaven, and burst into loud exclamations of delight.

"Yes, I am happy beyond measure," she said, "to have such

5

a father! In examining the annals of all periods of history, I cannot find a name which I should like to compare with his.

"This great report is not a book, it is a deed. In giving the people an insight into the financial condition of poor France, he tells it that it is of age.

"Let Count d'Artois whisper to his friends that this *conte bleu* is an absurdity which the citizen of Geneva has permitted himself in his impudence; let him and his boon companions deride it as much as they please; they are unable to lessen the importance of the great achievement.

"This book utters the weighty words: '*Le peuple est souverain!*' The people will insist on its rights, and demand a reasonable degree of liberty. My father's *Compte Rendu* will give rise to a revolution in France.*

"How fortunate that I live at this momentous time! The eyes of all France will be fixed on my father; and I am his daughter, and may bask in his glory.

"How I long to express the admiration with which his great deed fills me! But he is far away, and when I see him I shall not be courageous enough to give vent to the feelings of my heart. I write to him, but only anonymously. He must learn what I feel, even without knowing that these are my feelings.

"The old gardener and his son are working yonder at the asparagus beds as quietly as if nothing had happened; and yet this book makes men of them. Shall I inform them that they are no longer the slaves of a despot, but citizens of a State in whose burdens they participate, and to whose government they should pay due attention?"

She hastened off in the direction where the two men were at work. At the approach of their young mistress, they took off their caps respectfully. All the servants and peasants loved

---

* D'Alembert.

her; for she was very charitable. The poor and suffering always found her willing to listen to their complaints, and her sympathy did them often as much good as her money. All of them knew that she had a very kind and generous heart, and all liked to confide their cares and sorrows to her, because she always listened to them with that solicitude and attention which, for the moment, seemed to make the sufferer's condition her own.

Hence, all her wishes were executed by these people with utmost readiness, and the gardeners now ceased-working in order to listen to her attentively.

"I just wished to tell you," she began, "that a new era dawns upon France. My father has written this book, in which he sets forth the revenues and expenditures of the State. All of you may read it, and see whether or not the King judiciously spends the money which you intrust to him. All of you will henceforth participate in the government; you are now citizens of a powerful State; the rights of man are recognized in France, and the voice of the people will be heard. Are you not glad of it?"

"If you, Mademoiselle, say that we may be glad, we are glad. M. Necker is the benefactor of us all," replied the old man. "But for him, France would be lost. But I cannot read the book, inasmuch as I have never learned to read. But my son there, he can read."

The young man had listened to her words attentively, and, to all appearance, more intelligently than his father. His eyes sparkled, and the expression of his face showed plainly that he would like to do something else than digging in the garden.

"I read the newspapers," he said, "and have already heard something about it at the village inn. To be sure, if our institutions could be made similar to those of North America, I should be exceedingly glad; but for my old father here, I should have long since gone to America and helped the people there to fight the soldiers of the King of England. The people there lead a very different kind of life. They have their daily bread, and pay few or no taxes. They know what they are working for."

"Our institutions will never become as democratic as those of North America," replied M'lle Necker, surprised at a demand which far exceeded her wishes; "we must keep our good King. But we may lessen the expenditures of the State, and thereby relieve the burdens of the people. You see, that is the object which my father is trying to attain."

"I know it," replied the young man, "we talked of it last night at the village inn."

M'lle Necker was exceedingly anxious to hear what these people said about her father when they sat together in the evening. She had his glory so much at heart that she wished to follow it everywhere.

At this moment her companion, M'lle Huber, joined her, and requested her to go into the house, where luncheon was ready.

"I cannot eat," exclaimed M'lle Necker, shaking her head. "I am as if intoxicated with happiness, and looking for men who will share it with me, and to whom I may express what I feel."

"You may talk to me during luncheon as much as you please," said her young friend, trying to draw her away.

"And preach to deaf ears. Have you not told me time and again that household affairs and a new bonnet interest you a great deal more than all the teachings of Montesquieu?"

"Of course they do. But for your sake I shall listen to you, and try to understand what you say. But tell me now what important event has happened."

"I referred to this book. Look at the old oak yonder. It
took it a thousand years to grow to its present size, and no
one tells us now what hand put into the earth the acorn from
which sprang that mighty tree. The beginning was so small,
and the end is so vast. Such will be the case with this *Compte
Rendu*, too. The consequences of this first step are incalculable; no one is able to say whither will lead the path which
this book indicates to us. A new era is dawning upon us in
consequence; the seeds have been sown, and we see them
sprouting; but we are as yet unable to divine who will be the
reapers. Oh, I admire my father so much! He is a great,
great man."

"You attach so much importance to this book containing so
many figures!" exclaimed her friend, doubtingly. "I am afraid
your filial love sees a little more in that book than there is really in it. But come into the house now."

"I will follow you if you will promise me to lend me your
pen for half an hour. I have to write an anonymous letter."

"I shall not render you any assistance for that purpose.
Madame Necker would never forgive me if she should find it
out," said M'lle Huber.

"Never fear," exclaimed Germaine, laughing. "It is no love-
letter; I only want to write to my father, and he must not
know the hand-writing."

"But do you think, then, that he does not know my hand-
writing?"

"In truth, I did not think of that. Very well, let us go then
to our pastor; he shall copy the letter."

M'lle Huber was already accustomed to the singular whims
of her friend, and whenever they did not conflict with the instructions given her by Madame Necker, she yielded to them
willingly. So the young girls went in the course of the after-

noon to the village, in order to call on the clergyman who was to copy the enthusiastic letter of Necker's daughter. They found the aged man in his room, and sat down opposite to him while he entered upon the task which was not quite easy for him.

"I know of somebody that would do it still better than I," he said, putting his spectacles on his nose. " He is the son of the forester who lives at the end of the large meadow. He writes a splendid hand."

"Let us go to him, then," exclaimed M'lle Necker, jumping up in order to carry her intention into effect.

"I do not think that it would be becoming for us to do so," said M'lle Huber, disapprovingly.

"Your constant stickling for such trifling matters of etiquette," said Germaine, stamping the floor indignantly, "annoys me greatly. It is just because I was brought up amidst such narrow-minded views that my whole nature now revolts against them, and I shall follow my *premier mouvement* at any cost. My first impulse comes from God, it can never mislead me; our after-thoughts arise from human teachings, and are, therefore, in consonance with the usages of society, and they are not our highest moral law. I shall go."

"I shall accompany you, my daughter," said the pastor. " M'lle Huber will then consider less objectionable a step which I have suggested to you."

They found the young forester reposing from an excursion into the forest, whence he had just returned. Upon hearing what distinguished visitors wished to see him, he quickly arranged his dress and appeared before his guests. M'lle Necker was evidently surprised at his fine-looking figure and prepossessing manners, which rendered him more similar to a courtier than to a man in his humble circumstances. Never concealing her emotions, she quickly betrayed the impression which he had made on her.

The pastor meanwhile addressed him, and explained to him the cause of their visit.

"Your request makes me very happy," he said, "and I should comply with it with still greater pleasure if you would permit me to deliver the letter to M. Necker in person. I admire your eminent father so ardently that I should be proud to make his acquaintance."

"But he must not find out who addressed that letter to him," exclaimed Germaine, warmly.

"Of course not. I shall tell him that a stranger gave it to me. Is that in consonance with your wishes?"

"It is, it is. But tell me now if, during your sojourn in Paris, you cannot find out what people think of my father there, how his *Compte Rendu* was received, and if the Parisians are able to appreciate how bold he was in laying it before the government, and in calling upon all France, nay, upon the whole world, to witness his honesty."

"If you wish it, I shall visit the most popular coffee-houses and listen to the conversation of the guests," replied the young man. "If you have any further commissions to give me, I am at your service."

"When will you have copied the letter? And when may I look for your return from Paris?" exclaimed Germaine.

"You must not allow me for this purpose a too limited time, Mademoiselle, inasmuch as I do not know when M. Necker will admit me. But you may depend on it, I shall make as much haste as possible in order to fulfill your wishes," he said, casting an enthusiastic glance at Necker's daughter.

"Then we may go," said the pastor.

On their way home he said to them, "Mademoiselle Huber,

all that has occurred on this occasion was in strict accordance with propriety, was it not?"

"Because you were present," replied M'lle Huber. "But the young forester intends to call on us at St. Ouen."

"His visit will probably do us no harm," said Germaine, sarcastically.

The girls now walked slowly in the cool evening air along the path which never was entirely deserted; when they soon after entered the high-road, they met a poor woman who carried her babe and a heavy bundle of faggots.

"How can you carry such a heavy load?" said M'lle Necker to her. "You should have left your babe at home."

"It would have cried itself to death," replied the woman. "We poor folks, Mademoiselle, are happiest in this world if we are alone; for we cannot pay sufficient attention to them without running the risk of starving to death."

"But then such a baby is a great joy, and you know whom you are toiling for. Let me carry your little daughter for a moment; it will relieve your burden."

"A lady like you cannot do that," cried the woman, in dismay, and evidently fearful lest Germaine should let the child fall to the ground.

But Germaine, laughing, held it up in her strong arms, and showed how easy it was for her to carry the little one.

"What if anybody should meet us here and see you with the dirty child," said M'lle Huber, glancing along the road.

"In that event I should throw the little creature into the ditch and jump after it, in order to hide my disgrace," cried Germaine, laughing. "It is a vain endeavor," she then added, "to attempt surrounding my heart with a coat of mail. It insists on throbbing, and it shall throb. Falsehood, deception, and a thousand vices endangering our character, are suffered to exist without let or hinderance; but when we yield to the impulses of our heart, when we feel genuine sympathy, and, giving vent to it, say to anybody, 'I like you,' then an outcry is raised as if we had committed a crime. Is not that too stupid and silly?"

"As you represent it, it is indeed."

"As if I represented it otherwise than it really is! Do you think I did not notice the expression of your countenance when you thought that I conversed with the forester as if he were my equal? As Necker's daughter, you wanted me to treat him haughtily, and look upon him as an obsequious footman, whom we reward very liberally with a gracious smile and a gold piece. That was what your code of propriety told you. Mine told me a very different thing. A man whose forehead nature has stamped with nobility, is my equal. I am a pupil of Rousseau. I did not vainly visit that proud man in his humble garret, where he lived as independently as a sovereign prince. I did not vainly read his 'Contrat Social,' while other girls played with their dolls. Inasmuch as I did not grow up and was not educated like other girls, I cannot now be like other girls. My good woman, did you nurse your babe at your own breast?" she asked now, the remembrance of Rousseau having suggested this idea to her.

"I did, Mademoiselle; where else should I have obtained the milk? I shall continue nursing it in the same manner until it is over a year old."

"A very sad reason, indeed; but still you suckle the babe," said Germaine.

At this moment a heavy hand was laid on her shoulder. She turned and saw that Marmontel stood behind her.

"For God's sake where do you come from?" exclaimed M'lle Necker. "You seem to have sprung from the earth."

5*

"I tried to rent a villa for my family at St. Brise, found a very good one, and, inasmuch as there was no opportunity for me to return to Paris, I walked over to St. Ouen, in order to throw myself on your hospitality until to-morrow morning."

"We shall try to entertain you as hospitably as possible," exclaimed Germaine, joyfully; "but, in return, you must tell me as much as you can about Paris."

"As soon as you have satisfied my curiosity in regard to this child," he replied, smiling, and looking at the dirty little creature, which she held up with tender solicitude.

"Well, I found it here on the road, where I met that poor woman, who groaned under a two-fold burden."

"That does honor to your heart, Germaine," he said, kindly. "But here is the gate of your garden. What are you going to do with the child?"

She hesitated. She would have liked to accompany the poor woman to her home; but Marmontel was tired, and she could not ask this sacrifice of him.

"Wait a moment here, my good woman," she said; "I shall immediately send a servant, who will carry your child home. I myself, unfortunately, cannot accompany you any longer."

So saying, she gave her the babe, and furtively slipped a piece of money into her hand.

"Oh! I am able to carry the child home. I thank you a thousand times. God bless you!" said the woman, walking away with a radiant face.

Marmontel now offered his arm to Germaine, who walked in very good humor by his side through the shady alleys of the garden.

"What are you doing here," he asked. "Are you writing another drama?"

"Oh! no. Dr. Tronchin has forbidden it. I am only al-

lowed to read, and, moreover, only for certain hours. But now
I am again quite well and strong, and I hope he will now permit me again to write. I have extracted a great many passages
from Montesquieu; I have read again Voltaire's ' Les Nations,'
and my dear Rousseau's ' Contrat Social,' and filled my poor
head with some sensible ideas about political economy. But
ah, my dear friend, I used to amuse myself so exceedingly
well when I read Ann Radcliffe's novels, ' The Mysteries of
Udolpho,' and those other beautiful books which caused me to
shudder so pleasantly, and, after nightfall, to look in dismay
into every corner, in order to see if there might not be a ghost
or some horrible monster threatening me with its fiery eyes.
I am quite sorry every now and then that I can no longer
indulge in such agreeable dreams. Sir Charles Grandison and
Clarissa, they are different characters; they love with all their
hearts. The new Heloise belongs to this class; but for these
heroes we look in the world, and not in twilight hours, as if
they were ghosts."

"You will not be long in discovering those heroes there,"
replied Marmontel, laughing. "Suitors will not be wanting to
Necker's daughter."

"Who are attracted by my father's fame and fortune, but not
by his daughter!" she exclaimed, vehemently. "But I want
to be courted for my own sake: I want to be loved, and shall
give my whole heart in return. I dislike all that is cold,
studied, and measured. Love must touch me like an electric
spark, and, like a flash of lightning, strike me and the man who
is to belong to me. Do you not think so too, my dear Marmontel?"

"Our imagination sometimes misleads us in this respect, my
dear Germaine, and we afterwards find that reality does not
correspond to our expectations. Human life is full of illusions,

and these illusions form our happiness. For when they cease, there is but little that remains to us."

They now entered the house. Germaine hastened first to the porter, in order to whisper to him that as soon as the young forester made his appearance, no matter what time it might be, he should take the young man to her room, and inform her of his arrival. She then returned to Marmontel.

"You have spoken with me on all sorts of topics, and not said a word about my father's great achievement. What is the reason?" she said to him.

"I did not know if you had been informed of the appearance of this *conte bleu*," he said, jocularly; "for it is a very dangerous book, whose author, if he had lived during the reign of Louis the Thirteenth or Louis the Fourteenth, would no doubt have been hung, while at this juncture he will only be beheaded."

"You are jesting," said Germaine, turning pale.

"I am jesting to a certain degree," replied Marmontel. "To be sure, they will not literally cut off his head, but only figuratively. The court party will overthrow him."

"Should it really be able to do so?" asked Germaine, anxiously.

"It is. Your father's downfall is certain to take place."

This reply caused her to look with increased impatience for the return of her messenger from the capital, who did not arrive till the following evening.

CHAPTER XI.

NECKER sat thoughtfully, and his head leaning on his hand, at his writing-table, and forgot that hour after hour elapsed. The King had rejected his request to give him, beside the office of a cabinet minister, at length also the rank due to his office; and after this refusal, nothing remained for him but to offer his resignation.

The old nobility were decidedly averse to tolerating the Genevan commoner in the cabinet. These aristocrats did not object to the fearful abuses and frauds by which the treasury was constantly plundered; but they felt highly offended at the sudden elevation of a man who accepted no salary, had no favorites, was proof against bribery, who was the embodiment of honesty, and whose only fault was that he did not bear a name illustrious in the history of France.

Necker deeply felt the cruel injustice of this treatment and the marked ingratitude of the King. He had at court enemies who disliked his economy intensely; Marie Antoinette was opposed to the minister who always spoke of retrenchments; and the Count d'Artois hated him, since he had refused to pay his debts any longer. The French court had so long been accustomed to the greatest extravagance, that it was at a loss to know how it happened that the public treasury was no longer as well filled as formerly, when the sums drawn from it were by no means as large as those spent by the predecessors of

Louis the Sixteenth. It was disagreeable to the court to hear
that the State was on the brink of ruin, and unable to discharge
its obligations; and it hated the man who had disturbed the
amusements of Versailles by such gloomy pictures of the future.

Necker had longed for the glory of extricating his adopted
country from its terrible difficulties, and devoted himself with
all his heart to this great task. He was now to stop half-way,
and leave his office at the very moment when, by publishing
his *Compte Rendu*, he had made such an important step forward.

He now regretted having placed himself in a position which
compelled him to offer his resignation. Why should he have
hankered after the outward rank of a position which he filled
in reality? Why yield to the petty pride which revolted at
such a slight which he could well afford to despise?

Suddenly the low rustling of a lady's dress fell on his ears,
and his wife entered by the door which had only been ajar.

She looked at him inquiringly with her clear blue eyes, and,
when she noticed the cloud on his forehead, she stepped close
up to him, laid her right hand on his shoulder, while with her
left she tried to smooth his face, and said, " So thoughtful, my
dear Necker ! "

Instead of replying to her, he laid his head, as if wearily, on
the partner of his joys and sorrows, and tenderly pressed her
delicate white hand to his lips.

" There are several acquaintances in the *salon*. Will you
not salute them ? " she asked, gently.

" I cannot see anybody to-day," he replied, in a voice tremulous with emotion. " Go back to them and excuse me. I am
unwell."

" Bodily unwell, too ? "

" Yes The mind does not leave the body untouched ; both of them generally suffer together."

" And you wish to conceal from me what weighs you down ? " she asked, in a tone of mingled surprise and vexation.

" It would probably be the first time when you did not share what concerns me, my faithful wife. I tried to conceal it from you merely for a time ; but as I am unable to do so any longer, let me tell you that I have been dismissed."

His wife uttered a cry, and Necker, as if overcome by its sound, sank upon a chair and buried his face in his hands.

He wept.

Immovable like a rock, he had hitherto stood before his wife in all relations of life; his deep emotion, therefore, made an overpowering impression upon her. Bursting likewise into tears, she knelt before his chair, drew his hands gently from his face, pressed them to her lips, and buried her own face in them. She uttered not a word, in order to give him time to master his grief; when she finally thought that he had calmed sufficiently to relieve his mind by speaking to her, she begged him to tell her the reason why the King had dismissed him.

" At my own request ! " he replied. This answer re-assured her greatly. It was only repentance that was gnawing at him now, and tormenting his heart with the bitter reproach that he had sacrificed the welfare of France to his wounded pride.

" We shall go to-morrow to St. Ouen, to our daughter," said Necker, as soon as he had composed himself. " Society and remembrance of my lost position are now exceedingly painful to me. So you will do me a favor by inviting as few guests as possible."

" Nothing is sweeter to me than to live with you and for you," replied his wife, tenderly. " But, my dear Necker, it seems to me the whole matter is not yet settled. You have offered your resignation to the King, but his answer has not yet arrived."

"It can only be such as I expect. Otherwise he would have to grant my former request, which he can no longer do. So pray prepare everything for our departure."

"Above all, let me request our guests to excuse you and me for to-day. I likewise feel unable to pass my time in idle conversation; the more so, as I know that you are here sad and alone."

She left him in order to issue the necessary orders, and then returned to her husband.

"If it is agreeable to you, we shall go to the country this very day," she said to him.

"Why?" he asked, sharply.

"The evening is so beautiful, I should like to enjoy it with you in the open air. I have ordered the carriage; it is ready now. Come!"

She rose. He fixed his eyes on her. She dropped her's in order to avoid his glance.

"You have the King's reply!" he said at length, quickly, as if it was difficult for him to utter the words.

Averting her face, she handed him a letter. He seized it, broke the seal, glanced over the contents, and exclaimed, "I am ready. Let us go." And he followed her hastily to the carriage.

Germaine Necker did not look for this sudden arrival of her parents. The young forester had reported to her that the Parisians were extolling her father; that both the rich and the poor were reading the *Compte Rendu* with the utmost enthusiasm; that even the ladies at the Queen's court were studying this book, and that every one was speaking only of the revenues and expenditures of the State. She was overjoyed at her father's success, and could not hear enough about it. The young man had to hasten daily to the city and bring her news from it. He had to buy for her all the papers and political pamphlets of the day; every word concerning her father was important to her.

Her room was full of these papers, which she did not permit anybody to touch; and as she herself took no pleasure in arranging them, there was soon scarcely room enough left for her to move in the boudoir. M'lle Huber laughed at this chaos, which was so little in consonance with her taste; but Germaine did not pay any attention to her jests, and left everything as before.

Every now and then some of the many papers which she received contained attacks upon her father, and the indignation with which they filled her was indescribable. His opponents in the press called him the Genevan charlatan, compared him with Mesmer, derided his arrogance, and caricatured him in every possible way. He had unfortunately been imprudent enough to allude in his work to the great merits of his wife, and to extol her virtues in a manner which caused a great many persons to smile. His adversaries knew how to turn this to account. The young forester had at first hesitated to buy such papers and pamphlets, too, for M'lle Necker; but when she became aware of their existence in consequence of some allusions which she had found in the other papers, she insisted on getting them, too.

She had just received another package of papers, etc.; among them was a caricature, headed, "The Hero of the Deficit," and representing her father, who was just about to open the door of the royal cabinet, but Count d'Artois, saying, "No more 'Contes bleus,'" prevented him from so doing. She tore the caricature into a thousand pieces, trampled on them, and flnally threw them out of the window. She then sat down on the floor and burst into loud sobs. M'lle Huber heard these sobs, and hastened to her in order to console her. But her words were utterly wasted.

The whole nature of the young girl revolted at the ignominy so unjustly heaped on her father; she could not bear the idea that his eminent services were to be requited in this shameful manner; and as she had not yet learned to conceal her grief, she freely gave vent to her feelings.

Exhausted by this powerful agitation, she had finally fallen into a slumber, which her friend took care not to disturb. The roll of a carriage, however, the noise of voices, the opening and closing of doors, woke her up before long. For a moment she listened attentively; she then jumped up and hastened down stairs.

When she crossed the hall, Marmontel had just entered the door, breathlessly.

"Your poor father!" he exclaimed, holding out his hand to her. "Come, we must try to comfort him. He has not deserved such base ingratitude."

"Oh, it is the basest ingratitude!" she cried, thinking only of her caricatures. "Ah, Marmontel, you do not know how it grieves me!"

"Hush, hush! You must not now show that you grieve, but receive your father with a smiling face, as if nothing had happened."

They entered the *salon*.

Necker, deeply moved, folded his beloved daughter to his heart. He felt as if he must now seek for two-fold indemnification in her love for the injustice which had been done to him, and he pressed her long and silently to his breast. It was not till then that he greeted his friend, who, having accidentally learned what had occurred, had hastened to St. Ouen in order to condole with him.

Shortly after, Necker's brother made his appearance. He had intended to visit him in Paris, and, being informed of his sudden departure, and suspecting that some untoward event had happened, had followed him to St. Ouen.

The small circle sat together in moody silence. No one cared to allude to the subject which weighed down all hearts, and yet this silence was exceedingly disagreeable to all of them.

Marmontel finally entered into a conversation with Germaine, inasmuch as, owing to her ignorance of her father's removal, she seemed to be most inclined to turn her thoughts toward other subjects.

"Are you aware, my young friend, that our poor M. Raynal is going to be exiled from Paris on account of the new edition of his 'History of India?'"

"Indeed!" she exclaimed, in surprise. "It is true, I read several allusions to the probability of the book being prohibited; but I did not see anywhere that the personal liberty of the author was endangered."

"Well, it is not. He will leave Paris quietly until the storm blows over; but his book will be publicly burned to-morrow by the executioner on the steps of the archepiscopal palace."

"That sounds awful!" exclaimed the young girl, to whom her lively imagination depicted the ceremony. "I should like to see it."

"Do not wish for it; it would afford you but little pleasure. Such acts remind us of the times of the Inquisition, and are unworthy of an enlightened age."

"I wonder why the King permits such things," asked Germaine, in surprise. "If I were in his place I should be fearful lest they should detract from my glory."

· "Louis the Sixteenth does not think of his glory, for he is a King. He is a good man, but never will be a great ruler. It is true, he reads a great many historical works, especially histories of England, but he never derives any salutary lessons from them. His surroundings probably exercise a most injurious influence over him. A court cannot exist without parasites; nobody else would consent to wear the livery of princes and become their humble and obsequious servant. These court parasites cannot work, inasmuch as they are of noble birth; they are born servants of the King; they serve him because he supports them."

"Why do not these noblemen remain on their estates," exclaimed Germaine, "or serve in the army as the Condés, Montmorencys, and so many others have done recently, since Lafayette opened them the way to the New World?"

"Yes, if they had estates, my dear Germaine! Originally the noblemen were vassals of the King, who supported the throne with their means and strength. But this relationship has undergone a very marked change since that time. There are at this juncture, perhaps, eighty thousand noble families in France, a number which has grown so large in consequence of the eleven thousand offices with which titles of nobility are connected. Besides, our kings granted patents of nobility nearly every day, and during the War of Succession they were sold for two thousand dollars each. Among all these noble families there are only about one thousand whose names are as old as the monarchy, and familiar to our ears by the remembrance of glorious deeds. These great names, however, were not always handed down to the descendants with the great qualities of their ancestors, and prodigal grandsons squandered their fortunes, so that there remain to the latter now-a-days but two ways to escape starvation, namely, either to serve as parasites at court, or to marry the daughter of a rich plebeian."

" But I believe the writings of Rousseau and Voltaire, and the American War of Independence, will impart more dignity to nobility of the mind, so that it will eclipse that of birth," exclaimed Germaine.

" I doubt it," replied Marmontel. " It is so pleasant to be something without possessing any merits."

" And so unpleasant to see great merits ignored because one's name is Necker and not Condé."

" There you are perfectly right," he said, laughing.

At this moment the footman entered and told Germaine that the young forester was in her room.

The young girl crimsoned at these words, and glanced timidly at her father. M. Necker, leaning his head on his hand, had thus far sat in seeming apathy, and not listened to the conversation; but now he raised himself up, and fixing his eyes inquiringly on his daughter, he said :

" What forester is it who is at this hour in my daughter's room ? "

Germaine was in a tempest of perplexity. She turned alternately red and pale, and panted for breath. At length, she gathered courage enough to stammer, "It is my messenger. I send him often to the city to purchase books and papers for me."

" Which you could not get from your father ? "

" Perhaps you would dislike to send them to me; at all events, you never sent them to me."

" Because you never asked me to do so, and I could not anticipate that you took interest in such things. What kind of papers did he purchase for you ? "

" You will find all of them in my room," said Germaine, in a low voice.

"And your messenger, too. Come then, my child; let me see both of them," he said, rising, taking his daughter's hand, and conducting her out of the room. Those who remained in the *salon* looked after them in silence.

Father and daughter ascended the staircase slowly.

The passage up-stairs was dark; the return of the parents not having been expected, the upper part of the house had not yet been lighted. In M'lle Necker's room, however, burned two wax candles, whose light enabled M. Necker to recognize the bearer of the anonymous letter immediately.

"Ah!" he said to himself. "That is what I suspected. Have you not yet found out for me, young man, who wrote that letter to me," he said to the forester.

"Not yet, Monsieur," replied the young man, bowing in confusion.

"And what is the news which you bring to my daughter to-day from Paris?" he went on to ask.

"Very painful news, which I need not communicate to her, since Monsieur himself is here," he replied, in a very respectful tone.

"So the rumor of my removal was already generally known?" he asked in surprise, and not suspecting that Germaine was as yet entirely ignorant of it.

"Your removal!" she screamed, and sank senseless to the ground.

A gloomy silence reigned next morning in the streets of Paris. It was Sunday, but no one thought of pleasure and amusements.

Like wildfire spread the dreadful tidings that Necker had been dismissed. Only gloomy faces were to be seen on the promenades and in the coffee-houses. No jests, no witticisms, to which the Parisians are generally always accessible, were able to cheer up the multitude. All believed to have lost their protector in Necker, and saw both themselves and France threatened with hunger and distress.

As far as the eye reached, the road to St. Ouen was covered with carriages.

The Archbishop of Paris, followed by the Dukes of Orleans and Chartres, and all the eminent men of the country, hastened thither in order to tell Necker that they disapproved the step which the King had taken.

Necker, pale, but composed, received these manifestations of sympathy. Self-love always suffers a little when it hears the language of compassion assume the tone of sympathy.

Germaine was not present. She stood with M'lle Huber on the roof of the house, and looked at the endless number of carriages which arrived and left. Her eyes were still swollen from the tears which she had shed, and around her lips was quivering the grief which had struck her heart; but the sympathy manifested for her father did her good.

CHAPTER XII.

LOUIS PHILIPPE'S GOVERNESS.

MADAME DE GENLIS sat in an elegantly furnished boudoir, and was playing a voluntary on her harp. Through the half-open window penetrated to her the fragrant odors of hyacinths and stock gilly-flowers, wafted to her by the gentle breeze which played in the foliage of the trees, and moderated the heat of the day.

For a moment she then leaned back in her comfortable easy-chair, and allowed the instrument to rest in her arms. Her eyes wandered thoughtfully and dreamily about the room, and at last she fixed them on the large painting hanging on the wall opposite to her, and representing her aunt, Madame de Montesson, who had succeeded in becoming the wife of the Duke of Orleans, and having her niece appointed governess of his grandsons.

"What has she gained by it, after all?" she said to herself in a low voice, as she called to mind all these relations which, in many respects, were so painful to her. "The Bourbons refuse to recognize her; she must submit to the humiliation of not being permitted anywhere to appear as his legitimate wife; what good does it do her that she is his wife before God, if men treat her as though she were not? What is to her an honor which no one sees, no one respects, no one admits?"

A sigh escaped her breast as these thoughts crossed her mind.

Madame de Genlis was still a very handsome woman. She possessed a cultivated mind, and her gracefulness lent a charm to her every movement; but all these attractions were insufficient to procure her that position in the world for which she longed. She had no fortune; her husband squandered more money than his income amounted to; and to protect herself from want, she had entered upon a calling which imposed many privations upon her. She had written books which had been favorably received. To live in brilliant style at the capital and receive at her house the most eminent men of the age, would have satisfied her ambitious heart; instead of this, her vanity was unable to achieve a higher triumph than that of obtaining the title of governess, which made her ridiculous in the eyes of a great many people.

Toward the close of the eighteenth century there were not so many authoresses as talented ladies, whose standing in society and at home, and the intercourse with eminent men, gave them an influence which often enabled them to sway public opinion. There was no need for them to write anything in order to obtain the recognition for which they strove; for the *salon* was the arena where they were able to display the charms of their mind, and acquire influence even in the political world.

At that time the gentlemen never separated from the ladies in society; the conversation at parties always was general, and the interests of both sexes were identical. All took particular pains to acquire elegance of diction; the gentlemen, in order to entertain the ladies agreeably; and the ladies, in order to add to the charm of their words. All made verses, and a favorite amusement was to trace word-portraits, and to let the other guests guess the person who was meant.

At a later time, when political affairs overshadowed all other

interests, a change took place in this respect; grave debates
seemed no longer suitable to the ears of ladies, and the *salon*
was too narrow a field for the unbridled hatred of the contending parties. With this change, manners, nay, costumes, underwent a marked transformation, and social refinement disappeared.

It was Louis the Sixteenth who founded the first club, after
an English model, and caused newspapers and pamphlets to be
purchased for general use. Little did he suspect at that time
that such a club, a society of men meeting regularly at a certain
place, would be formed against him a few years afterward under
the name of Jacobins, and demand his execution.

France at that time made immense steps in the development
of intellectual culture, and Europe looked at her with astonishment and admiration. Frederick the Great sent to Paris for
the ornaments of his court, and Catherine of Russia became the
generous protectress of French *savants*. Nearly all princes vied
with each other in taking poets or eminent scholars under
their protection; and the representatives of intelligence, thus
honored and distinguished, deemed it a priceless boon that
they had been sent into the world endowed with the imperish-
able treasure of mental ability.

Society granted the ladies full liberty to admire talents and
wreathe laurels to them, but it disliked to see their beautiful
hands grasp at such crowns of their own. For them there
was but one kind of glory to exist: that of loving and winning
love. Only the rose was to bloom for them, only its buds were
to be plucked by them.

Marriage was a mere family compact; it gave the wife a position in society; it was looked upon as one of the obligations
which man takes upon himself with his existence. Love was
not allowed to have any influence at the conclusion of this

compact, inasmuch as that might have led to a subversion of civil order. The parents or relatives made the choice, and if man and wife liked one another, it was a lucky accident.

Madame de Genlis had been married in this manner, and so, without grieving too much, submitted to circumstances which separated her from her husband.

She lived with her pupils at Chateau Belle Chasse, which had been arranged for her in princely style, and where every comfort of wealth and luxury was offered to her; nevertheless, she felt the sacrifices which her position imposed upon her, and she sighed for the gay life of the capital. Hence, he who visited her in her solitude, and entertained her with news from the capital, was twice welcome to her.

A *valet de chambre*, dressed in the fashion of that period, with powdered hair, and large lace cuffs, now entered the room, and informed her that a carriage was visible in the long poplar alley leading to the chateau.

She rose, stepped before the looking-glass, and cast a searching glance at her slender and delicate form. She then put her harp aside, and prepared to go to meet her guests in the ante-room.

By the doors of the hall, which had been thrown wide open in order to admit the ladies with their hoop-skirts and their bonnets fastened to the high hair-dress, there entered with a slow measured step Madame Necker, followed by her daughter, and allowed herself to be ceremoniously embraced by Madame de Genlis. Germaine followed her mother's example. Madame de Genlis then conducted them to her boudoir, where all three of them seated themselves.

"How amiable you are to visit me here," said Madame de Genlis, very politely. "I should have gladly called on you first; but the duties of my position unfortunately prevented

me from so doing. How long it is since we met last! M'lle.
Necker has meanwhile grown up and become so tall and
strong that I should have hardly recognized her. The air in
the country evidently agrees with her. And now you live entirely at St. Ouen, as the Duke told me. You have renounced
the pleasures of the capital."

"Say, rather, that I have never known them," said Madame
Necker, smiling. "A pleasant domestic circle always was
the goal of my wishes, and as these were more than fulfilled,
and in great part thwarted, I submitted to the change as to a
duty, rather than a favor of fate."

"Thank God, it has relieved you again of this burden," remarked Madame de Genlis, somewhat maliciously.

"If I consulted only my own interest, I should certainly say,
thank God," replied Madame Necker, with her usual calmness;
"but the welfare of the whole French people was at stake, and
my wishes could not but be disregarded."

"That you, although you are foreigners, take such a lively
interest in our welfare, certainly entitles you to our gratitude,"
said Madame de Genlis, politely, but with a sarcastic smile
playing round her lips. " But you are aware how vain men
are; and so many imagine to be able to manage the affairs of
the country very creditably, nay, they assert even that only a
native of France, and, moreover, a Frenchman belonging to
the old nobility, is able to do so. Love of country and loyalty
must have been handed down from age to age, and be closely
interwoven with the interests of him who wishes to serve his
country efficiently. Only a foreigner could have been capable
of committing the indiscretion to publish a statement of our
financial condition. This is what is said at court; that the
Duke of Orleans dissents from these views, I am sure he has
told you repeatedly, and proved to you very recently."

" Is it possible," exclaimed Germaine, excitedly, " that anybody on earth should call my father's great deed an indiscretion ? "

" You must pardon my daughter," interposed Madame
Necker, " if she smarts under every word of censure uttered
against M. Necker."

" I pardon it not only, but approve it," replied Madame de
Genlis. " Mademoiselle Necker is still very young; she is only
just entering upon real life, and is as yet ignorant of human
nature. She has hitherto seen only one side of everything,
and forgets that it still remains for her to view the other. This
is a sweet privilege of youth. Ardent devotion to the present,
to friends, to great ideas, passes away with it, and our sighs do
not bring back anything. I congratulate you, M'lle Necker,
upon possessing a father on whom your filial love may bestow
such warm admiration. May you retain this sweet privilege
a long time !"

Germaine rose and pressed the hand of Madame de Genlis
to her lips. " You are as talented as you are amiable !" she
exclaimed. " You do not know how ardently I admire you,
and how urgently I have begged my mother to take me to
you."

" Indeed !" replied Madame de Genlis, responding by an
affable smile to this warm effusion. " I am very glad of it.
If my writings interest young folks and win for me the affections of hearts still susceptible of the beautiful and good, my
toils are amply rewarded. I have just finished a little play,
which will perhaps also please you."

" What is its title ?" asked Germaine. " How inexhaustible
your imagination is, and how inventive your mind ! Nature
has lavished its choicest gifts on you, and you know how to
turn them to account. But tell me now, what is the title of

your play; what is its subject; and for what purpose did you write it?"

"You propound to me a great many questions at the same time," said Madame de Genlis, smiling; "let me begin, then, with the first. The title is *Zélie ou l'Ingénue;* and the subject, like that of all my writings, is destined to instruct young folks. Women should become authoresses only when, in doing so, they try to attain an object far above the mere gratification of our vanity. I myself determined to publish my writings only after a severe inward struggle, and, despite all the reasons which induced me to take this step, I have to call them often to mind in order not to rue it."

These words were uttered for the purpose of making an impression on Madame Necker, but they deceived only Germaine.

"Ah! How lamentable the lot of our sex is!" she exclaimed, mournfully. "We are told that we are born only to perform the narrow duties which husbands and children impose on us, and are always to obey. My father has often praised, in my presence, the happiness of stupid persons, and even commended writing a work entitled *Le bonheur des sots.*"

"What, has he had time to spare for such things?" asked Madame de Genlis, in surprise.

"He knows, like you, how to work for twenty-four hours every day," replied Madame Necker, smiling. "But to return to your latest work,—would you take umbrage, or smile at my desire to be the first to get acquainted with its contents?"

"It will afford me great pleasure to read the play to you," replied Madame de Genlis, kindly. "It is always agreeable to an author to hear the opinion of able critics, before his work is submitted to the public. Then it cannot be changed any more, but must remain as it is."

Madame de Genlis then took from her writing-table a manu-script written in a very neat hand, and read the play to her guests in a very impressive manner. Her voice was clear and sonorous, and the tact with which she varied her tone, and never exceeded the bounds of good taste, rendered her recita-tion exceedingly attractive and entertaining. Germaine burst repeatedly into loud exclamations of admiration, and when Madame de Genlis concluded, Necker's daughter sank, with streaming eyes, at her feet, pressed the hands of the authoress to her lips, and assured her she had passed with her one of the most beautiful hours of her life.

Madame de Genlis, raising her up and imprinting a kiss on her forehead, thanked her for her warm applause, and said, " I hope you and your dear mother will take with you from Belle Chasse such impressions as will cause you to repeat your visit."

" Your presence here is a sufficient inducement for us to do so," said Madame Necker; "and if we deny ourselves the pleasure of visiting you frequently, it is because modesty pre vents us from molesting you too often."

" That is a virtue by which, I hope, you will not punish me," replied Madame de Genlis, who felt her superiority as a conversationalist too well not to display it before her guest. " Perhaps you will allow me to show you the chateau and the gardens; that is to say, if it does not weary you, Madame Necker, for you look feeble."

" I regret to say that I am in feeble health ; nevertheless, I must not use this as a pretext to evade the disagreeable duties of my position; how much less, then, should I deny myself to-day a pleasure which your kindness offers to me," replied Madame Necker.

Madame de Genlis found this answer stiff and pedantic.

" She cannot get rid of the tone of a governess," she said to herself; "no intercourse with the world will change her."
" You spoil me by your great kindness," she replied, smilingly.
" I am now hardly courageous enough to serve you as a guide, fearful as I am lest your trouble should not be repaid."

" Ah! a portrait of the Duke!" exclaimed Germaine, standing still before the full-length portrait of a man in full uniform.

" You know him?" asked Madame de Genlis.

" Only by his resemblance to our good King."

" He is not like him, though, either in his appearance or character. Louis the Sixteenth is not as good a man as he is said to be. His first thought always springs from the impulses of evil passions, and only the second is good-natured. This may become very dangerous to a king; for scarcely drops the first syllable from his lips, when the obsequious zeal of a courtier carries it already into execution. A king must first think, and then act; that is what I teach my princes."

" I think you are perfectly right," said Madame Necker.

" Then I must dissent alone from your opinion, and venture to assert that all that is great and beautiful has been done on the spur of the moment," exclaimed Germaine, glowingly.
" If we are always to calculate and reason, what is to become of the pulsations of a warm heart? Poor human nature! they would like to deprive you of all your rights, and, in return, build altars to reason. Love from reason is no worse than hatred from reason. I do not want any feeling, standing under the scepter of this cold master; I do not want the tear which reason weeps, any more than the grief to which it sets bounds. I do not want the joy which is manifested in accordance with mathematical calculations, nor the word of love which they dictate to the lips. You passions all that agitate

the human breast, I invoke you! Is it not to be dead to be without you? . . . . "

" For God's sake, Germaine! . . . . " exclaimed Madame Necker, in a low voice.

" Pray do not interrupt her," interposed Madame de Genlis. " I like to hear the utterance of sentiments which, in this slippery sphere, fall but very rarely on my ears. Propriety has suppressed much that is natural and innocent, and good manners do not permit other things to be uttered. Add to it the cloistral seclusion in which our young girls grow up. They are utterly inexperienced at the time when they enter life, and love and passion are words which have no meaning for them. Such, however, is not the case with M'lle Necker. At her cradle sat the encyclopedists, and philosophers added zest to her play. Having become a governess, it is of course interesting for me to see the results of an educational system so different from our own. I had always been told that M'lle Necker was wondrously gifted, and I have now obtained with great pleasure the conviction that those reports were perfectly true."

" My daughter is very young, Madame, and although she often still allows herself to be swayed by her feelings, and is somewhat rash in her opinions, years and the world will teach her to cool down and master her emotions."

" I am afraid not, Mamma. 'Suppress nature, and it will come back at the gallop,' says Fénélon. Never, never shall I place myself on a footing of equality with trained human natures; never shall my lips utter sentiments which my heart does not feel. I am my father's daughter. I shall strive to be as truthful as he is, and my heart shall be as open as his life. Hypocrisy and falsehood shall never stain my character."

" Excellent as these principles are, M'lle Necker, it is very

· 6 ·

difficult to adhere to them in life," replied Madame de Genlis, smiling. "Society compels us only to deviate from truth, and we must be false in a certain sense in order to succeed in this world. As a foreigner, however, you encounter in this direction fewer difficulties than we descendants of an ancient name."

"For God's sake, Madame, do not call me a foreigner," cried Germaine, excitedly; "I am a child of this soil with all my heart, and cannot bear being thus declared *hors la loi*. No place on earth would indemnify me for Paris, and *la rue du Bac* is an earthly paradise. In France alone is to be found that conversational sprightliness and wit, of which no other people on earth can boast. All new discoveries in the realm of science hasten to us in order to be put to the test, before mankind accepts them. How many of them did we see here within the last twenty years! Gall, Mesmer, Saint Germain, and Cagliostro, the balloon and the lightning-rod, Gluck and Piccini, all were anxious to exhibit their new discoveries to us. In truth, I would rather live in a Parisian garret on a hundred louis d'ors a year, than dispose of millions in any other country.* Paris offers us an incessant stimulus to mental activity; not a day elapses but that brings forth something new, while stagnation reigns everywhere else. And what is a life without progress, but death?"

Madame de Genlis smiled.

"It is very flattering to my country that you desire to look upon it as your own," she said; "and, perhaps, we may soon be happy enough to consider you wholly ours; for your esteemed father, no doubt, will not hesitate to grant an independent establishment to his only daughter. What with his social position and fortune, the choice of a husband cannot be difficult to him."

---

* Her own words.

"We do not think of separating from our daughter," interposed Madame Necker.

"I do not think it a separation when you are able to see one another every day, and it will be the easier for you to live close together, as your religion compels you to give the preference to a young man struggling for an independent position in life; for thus far no heir of a great name, as far as I know, has adopted the faith of Calvin. However, it may remain for M'lle Necker's gifted mind to bring about such a miracle, and I shall certainly not grudge her this triumph either."

"My daughter has learned to respect the religious faith of others, and will take no pains to bring over any proselytes to her own; least of all will she try to convert members of the old nobility of France, with which neither my husband nor I desire to connect her."

"I beg your pardon, then," said Madame de Genlis, apologetically, "if I have entertained for you wishes which would be but natural in your place."

At this moment the footman announced that Madame Necker's carriage was at the door.

The ladies parted in the most polite and cordial manner. Madame de Genlis accompanied her guests as far as the outer door, and embraced both of them amid the most flattering assurances of the pleasure which their visit had caused to her. Then, uttering a "Thank God!" she returned to her room and wrote in her diary: "These Neckers are the most intolerable persons I have ever met with—full of pride and arrogance; and the daughter especially, is utterly unable to set bounds to her extravagant utterances; despite her intense admiration for me, she displeased me exceedingly, and I shall take pains to depict in a novel the consequences of an education such as she has received. I advised the mother cautiously, to marry her to some brewer or baker, and I hope she understood what I meant; at all events, she left immediately."

Madame Necker meanwhile sat by her daughter's side, struggling for composure. Her feebleness added to her irritability, and a wound that is constantly torn open afresh, finally smarts at the slightest touch. Incessant pains were taken to revenge her husband's position upon her and her daughter, and this was not the first time when she had been cautioned against dreaming of a connection with the old nobility of France. The ill-will dictating such hints, could not but mortify her, inasmuch as it was so utterly undeserved.

Germaine cast an anxious glance at her mother's pale face, without suspecting, however, what had given rise to this pallor. She had not noticed the drift of Madame de Genlis' remarks, and, much gratified at the conversation she had had with her, gazed up to the sky glowing with the purple tints of the setting sun. She began to hum a song, and finally, forgetful of the place where she was, she sang in a loud and deep voice. Her mother's warning voice restored her presence of mind to her. She laughed loudly at what she had done. "It was too ludicrous, indeed!" she exclaimed. "How fortunate that my voice did not cause our horses to run away! May I seat myself on the box beside the coachman?" she asked, after a while. "The evening is so very fine."

Madame Necker told her it would be unbecoming.

"Can we not drive by way of Saint Brice," Germaine began soon again. "I should like to know when Piccini will come to Marmontel, that I may take my singing-lessons there."

"You may send a messenger thither to-morrow and ask for a written reply," replied her mother.

"Always no, and always no," hummed Germaine.

"And if it were 'always yes,' I soon should not know what you might not ask for," said her mother, frowningly.

"I know it, and can tell you if you like to know it, too: beauty, and a handsome husband!" exclaimed Germaine, laughing.

"Hush, for God's sake, hush!" cried Madame Necker, in dismay. "It is dreadful for me to hear such words from the lips of my daughter."

"My father would laugh with me at such jests," replied Germaine, gently. "Forgive me if I vexed you. It is impossible for me to be such as you want me to be."

Madame Necker made no reply to this remark. She had leaned back in the corner of the carriage and closed her eyes; her restless neighbor, therefore, was confined to her own thoughts until they reached St. Ouen.

BOOK II.

CHAPTER I.

A VISIT TO MARMONTEL.

M. NECKER's villa was close to St. Brice, which could be easily reached on foot from St. Ouen. Since Marmontel and his young wife had taken up their abode there, Germaine often wended her way thither, greatly rejoicing in the diversion which these visits afforded to her, and of which she had so much need.

Madame Marmontel had chosen her husband from inclination, but without knowing much about him. During a visit which she and her mother had paid to Paris, M'lle de Montigny had seen the poet at the house of her uncle, the Abbe Morellet, and her relatives had immediately proposed a match between them.

Already over fifty years of age, somewhat corpulent, and by no means prepossessing, Marmontel had little to offer to the young girl beyond his illustrious name, which, coupled with the prospect of a brilliant life in Paris, had no doubt captivated her youthful imagination. And so she had become his wife.

The feeble health of their child had now induced her to remove to the country, and in her loneliness she was always exceedingly glad to be visited by her young neighbor, who created a new life around her from the rich cornucopia of her gifted mind. Marmontel, too, was fond of her. Little as Marmontel liked her father—perhaps, only because that grave and practical man looked upon the tasks of the poet as child's play, and smiled condescendingly upon them—a condescension against which Marmontel's proud spirit rebelled—he highly esteemed Necker's wife. Madame Necker always treated the guests of her house with great consideration, and, above all, she took pains not to wound their little vanity, a point which oftener than is commonly believed puts an end to both friendships and enmities.

Germaine had grown up under his eyes. He loved her as a daughter, and gladly forgave her any imprudence, even when she offended him personally. They were on the most intimate terms, and it was because of the jests which she was at liberty to permit herself with him that she liked so much to be in his company, and greatly preferred him to her friends Thomas and Raynal.

It was a bright, sunny day when Germaine, accompanied by a footman, set out for St. Brice. The birds sang so merrily, the fields were so green, the sky was so blue, all nature laughed at her so benignantly that she was soon in the best of spirits, and had to laugh with her surroundings.

Madame Marmontel sat at the door of her little villa, holding her youngest child on her knees, while another played in the grass at her feet. She embraced Germaine tenderly, and offered her a chair by her side; but M'lle Necker, throwing down her bonnet and shawl, seated herself with the child in the grass, and laughed and jested with the little creature as if she herself were still a child.

"Dear Germaine," said Madame Marmontel, "you overheat

yourself; you are already crimson. Come, leave the little boy and rest."

"Do not disturb me. I must give the reins to my spirit," she replied, laughing. "You do not know how the quiet life at our house weighs me down. I need exercise and excitement. I must see new and stirring scenes, in order to feel well. All around me is now mute and still. As long as my father governed France, I had so much to hope, fear, and expect; every new morning could bring fresh successes, fresh crises, and I passed many a sleepless night in expectation of the morning and of the newspapers. Now they do not contain anything that I care to read. Everything seems to be dead."

"But you do not lead a very lonely life; there are constantly guests at your house, and your father's friends visit you almost every day."

"So they do. But they have grown old—much too old for me. I have need of a fresh, merry life, and that cannot be found at our house. Those who visit us stand already with one foot in the grave."

"You are jesting!" exclaimed Madame Marmontel, laughing.

"I am jesting in dead earnest," cried Germaine, springing to her feet, and striding up and down the small lawn. "I am jesting like a man who feels the rope already at his throat, and does not care to put his head into the noose. My jests are bitter, bitter earnest. Just look at the nice young gentlemen, my dear Adele, by whom I am surrounded. There is my dear Grimm, who, for the rest, is not grim-looking at all; he is a handsome young sexagenarian, and always has his head full of the reports by which he wants to entertain his august friends at the north pole. I cannot jest with him, for a courtier is not at liberty to laugh; it would injure his rouge. Then there is d'Alembert, poor faithful soul! who still sheds tears for his

late lamented M'lle Espinasse; with him I can only weep, for
he longs to follow her into the grave, into the still, cool
grave. Diderot has suffered for a long time past from an incurable disease. Our faithful Thomas is by far too good for
this earth; he writes now-a-days only funeral orations; he
judges only the dead; he sits, grave, stiff, and taciturn, like a god
of Hades, before my mother, and says every now and then,
' Virtue is beautiful, for you are its priestess.' "

" Germaine, Germaine!" exclaimed Madame Marmontel, reproachfully, yet laughing merrily at the exuberant humor of
the young girl.

" Then there is Raynal," continued Germaine, without allowing herself to be disturbed by the exhortation. " He is a new
Messiah, a preacher in the wilderness, but he only wants to
subvert everything, and not rebuild anything. What is bad, is
bad; and when he is asked how a change for the better is to be
brought about, he shrugs his shoulders. Now, I am utterly
averse to such teachings. I want to enjoy life and be happy.
I want to hope, wish, and share the aspirations of humanity,
which only youth can do; for it has a future; it will see the
seeds ripening into fruit, and so it scatters them broadcast and
with joyful courage."

" You must marry," exclaimed Madame Marmontel. " Look
at my children; they are the right kind of seeds. Here I find
hope, a future, and all that you long for." She held her babe
up to her.

Germaine patted the child's cheeks, and then, glancing
archly at the mother, said, " You wish to convert me to a faith
which is as old as the world; but it will not stand the test in
this respect. I wish to exist first for myself, and then only for
others. Was I not also a child? And now that I am grown
up, the world shall first pay me what it owes me; I want to

help to raise the wings of our times that they may carry me along in their flight; I want to join in their aspirations, and have my name mentioned whenever they call for deeds. Our lot is to share the joys and sorrows of humanity. To shirk this lot is to impoverish one's self, and narrow one's heart instead of expanding it. All honor to the duties of maternity; but I want to perform, in the first place, the duties of humanity, and not until then those of maternity."

"So excited, my young friend;" exclaimed at this moment a voice behind her, and Marmontel, holding out his hand to her, stepped forward. His round face glistened, owing to the heat of the day; his wig was somewhat displaced, and his whole figure presented an exceedingly ludicrous appearance. Quickly passing from earnest to jest, Germaine stooped, picked up her bonnet, put it on the poet's head, and burst into loud laughter. Marmontel entered into the jest, and made a graceful obeisance.

"But what do I see?" cried Germaine, suddenly. "These buttons on your waistcoat, each of which is as large as a green frog, are splendid! Let me look at them closely! In truth, Ovid's "Metamorphosis!" What, you dare to exhibit them publicly during the reign of so virtuous a King as Louis the Sixteenth, while Rome banished the poet from its walls? Law and justice, are you then empty words! And you, my most austere poet, why did you choose these voluptuous pictures when others wear the Roman Emperors on their buttons, and cause their children to count political history on their fingers by looking at the bright metal. As you insisted on adopting that fashion, I should in your place have tried to combine some secret little pedagogical object with it."

"A poet is not at liberty to be so practical," exclaimed Marmontel, laughing. "We must know how to lose our heads every day! How should they, then, at last sit so firmly on our bodies? But now pray inform me of the advantage which you derive from the Babylonian tower on your head, beside its height?"

"The advantage of not being overlooked so easily," she said, laughing.

"Very good," exclaimed Marmontel. "You always are quick at repartee. Even though I should now place myself between you and the sun, you would not be totally eclipsed."

"Because I would then borrow fresh light from you," she said, archly.

"Hush, hush! No personalities; otherwise my little wife will be jealous."

"Never fear. Holding the future, as she does on her knees, she can do without the past."

"That was a malicious remark, Germaine," exclaimed the young wife, threatening her with her finger.

At this moment the conversation was interrupted by the appearance of a young man, who fastened his horse to the garden-gate, and then walked down the short path toward them with a quick step and proud air. All of them fixed their eyes upon him.

Marmontel was too near-sighted to recognize the new comer until he was quite close to them ; but he then hastened toward the stranger with the liveliest joy, and replied as follows to his polite greeting :

"What, M. de Narbonne, you here at my humble home? May I inquire to what I am indebted for the pleasure of seeing you in this rural solitude?

"I had unfortunately to disturb the tranquillity of your Tusculum on purpose," replied M. de Narbonne, bowing to the ladies, and then casting at Marmontel a glance which contained the mute request to introduce him to the ladies.

"My wife," said Marmontel, " and our neighbor, M'lle

Necker, who has honored us with her visit. M. de Narbonne," he then added, "Cavalier of Honor to the Princess Adelaide and Colonel of the Piedmont Regiment. Pray take a seat."

Upon hearing the name Necker, the young man had cast at Germaine an inquiring glance, which had not escaped her. She was likewise unable to conceal her surprise at so unexpectedly meeting here this young nobleman, who was praised everywhere in Paris on account of his prepossessing appearance, his ability, knowledge, and winning manners. She fixed her dark radiant eyes searchingly upon him; but when their glances met, she dropped her eyes, and a deep blush mantled her cheeks.

"Marshal de Duras," began M. de Narbonne again, "has sent me to you, M. Marmontel, in order to request you to favor him with a new production of your dramatic muse. He desires to have it performed at Fontainebleau during the visit of the Grand-Duke of Russia. Besides, he would like to surprise our Queen with a new opera of whose origin she would be ignorant; and if it is to afford pleasure to her, it must have been written by you. May I be the bearer of a reply in the affirmative?"

"It will, of course, afford me particular pleasure to comply with the Marshal's request; however, I cannot tell yet when it will be possible for me to do so," said Marmontel, bowing politely. "I am still at work upon a new opera jointly with Piccini, who, for this reason, stays with me here at St. Brice; as soon as we have finished our work, I shall lay it before the Marshal. We hope it will be successful; but we may be mistaken. Authors often overrate their works."

"You never can do so," replied Narbonne, with the exquisite politeness peculiar to that period. "May I inquire what title the opera will bear?"

"'Dido' will be the title."

"A very promising title. And how soon might the Marshal look for a communication from you regarding the completion of the work?"

"Pray tell him that I shall think of it, and soon inform him of everything, in a personal interview. Assure him, furthermore, of my devotedness, and of the pleasure which it affords me to serve him."

"So my mission has not been unsuccessful, and I may be glad that it remains for me to convey so favorable a reply to the Marshal," replied M. de Narbonne, politely. "My good star seems to have guided me hither; for the desire which I have entertained for a long time past, to be introduced to the family of M. Necker, has now, at least in part, been fulfilled." Permit me, Mademoiselle, to tell you that I revere and admire your eminent father, and shall be proud to be allowed to present my respects to him personally."

As he said so, Germaine raised her dark eyes again, while a sunbeam of joy illuminated her face.

"You gladden my heart by honoring my father," she replied. "Every word of praise which you bestow on him, enters my heart."

"In that case I am afraid you will find me doubly eloquent," replied M. de Narbonne, with a winning smile; "for although I have never before been so happy as to meet with the daughter of the illustrious Necker, I have heard a great deal about her for a long time past."

Germaine looked in surprise at the young man. The graceful ease of his replies, coupled with the polished manners which constant intercourse with the best society imparts to us, was very different from the stiff and pedantic style reigning at the house of her parents. It made a very agreeable impression upon her, and she longed to join in the same tone.

" We have a common acquaintance who has often mentioned
your name to me," she said.

" You refer to Condorcet, the enthusiastic lover of liberty ?
He must have been chary of my praise; for he blamed me for
not going to America when the flower of our nobility emigrated
thither in order to fight for a cause which did not concern us
much."

" If the cause did not concern us much, the idea did," interposed Marmontel.

" For this idea I could kindle my enthusiasm just as well in
France, for there reigns so much republicanism in our midst that
we need not look for it elsewhere.* Our country needs our
best strength in order to rise from her decline. What your
father has done for us in this respect, M'lle Necker, is by far more
praiseworthy than all the fighting in the other hemisphere, by
which Lafayette, Ségur, and Montmorency wish to dazzle us
without being useful to us."

" I do not know, M. de Narbonne, if I can subscribe to this
opinion," said Germaine, while her eyes, following the flight of
her ideas, forgot her surroundings and glowed enthusiastically.
" History knows no instance of the subjects of an absolute
monarch being permitted to participate in a struggle for liberty,
and of being regarded at home as heroes that cannot be admired
too ardently. If we did not blindly rush forward to the future,
these heroes would have been beheaded as traitors to a principle constituting the basis of monarchial States. But we do not
see the abyss on whose verge we are walking. As the inhabitants of Troy shut their ears to Laocoon's words, so no pre-
monitory symptoms are heeded here, and we hope and wish
on, and play with the danger, until, growing far beyond
our strength, it will swallow up everything that stands in

* Narbonne's own words.

its way. We ourselves call the wrath of heaven down on our heads."

"Then we are agreed," replied Narbonne, who, while she was speaking, did not avert his eyes from her beaming face. "When I say there is republicanism enough in France, I refer to views such as you and I entertain, M'lle Necker; an ardent longing for reforms, for institutions which empower the people to participate in the government of the country, and tie the hand of the head of the State, when it whimsically tries to cut the thread of the life of the country, and wants to decide thoughtlessly upon the fate of millions. To strive for the attainment of this object, one need not fight in America in order to conquer for others those rights which we should first gain for ourselves. Is not that your opinion, too?"

He looked at her inquiringly. Instead of a reply, tears slowly rolled down her cheeks. The "you" and "I" of his words had produced a wonderful effect upon her. She did not feel that sympathy for the aspirations of the people for more liberal institutions, which he believed to find in her; her views on this subject had been quickened by the study of history and of Montesquieu's "Esprit des Loi;" but they still slumbered in her mind without her having found an aim in regard to which she might have tried to carry them into effect. His words had, all of a sudden, pointed out to her such an aim. She was not to indulge in dreams of liberty for nations which she knew only by name, but to help to achieve this liberty for the soil on which she lived, was her vocation.

The steadfast gaze which he now fixed on her confused her.

"Your words have deeply moved me, M. de Narbonne," she said, timidly. "Pardon me for withholding my answer from you for a moment. It could not but surprise me to hear that

n young man of your rank and position tried to find such a
harmony between his own political opinions and mine. It
makes us so very happy to hear others utter what we have
scarcely yet ventured to confess to ourselves."

"And yet, such is the usual course in affairs of the heart,"
said Narbonne, with a significant glance ; " why should it not,
then, be thus with political views ? "

Germaine became nervous and uneasy. She rose and
quickly walked up and down the small garden ; and she then
resumed her seat. M. de Narbonne had followed her with his
eyes.

"Will you intercede in my behalf with your esteemed
father, when I beg leave of him to be introduced to him ?" he
said to her.

"That will be needless, M. de Narbonne ; your name recom-
mends you sufficiently."

"Possibly you may meet M. Necker here to-day, for he
usually comes here for his daughter," interposed Marmontel.

"You remind me in time that I ought to go home," exclaimed Germaine. My father promised to meet me half-way,
and told me to say to you, dear M. Marmontel, that it would
be very wholesome for you to accompany me that far, and bid
him good-evening. But, inasmuch as you have a guest, I will
at once relieve you of this obligation, but impose on you the
duty of indemnifying my father in the course of to-morrow."

"The guest will not allow himself to be used as a pretext
for depriving M. Marmontel of the agreeable duty of accompanying M'lle Necker ; and if you will permit, he will himself
be so happy as to perform this part of his route in your company," said Narbonne.

"It is so easy to consent, when one gains either way," merrily said Germaine, rising from her seat.

7

They then set out.

M. de Narbonne led his horse by the bridle, and walked by Germaine's side. The conversation was at first monosyllabic, and referred to indifferent topics; gradually, however, Germaine's bashfulness wore off, as she yielded to the current of her own ideas.

The sun, resembling a vast ball of fire, stood in the western sky; dense clouds gathered before it, and emitted, every now and then, flashes of lightning; from the meadows arose humid vapors, and dissolved before the scudding clouds like fugitive shadows; the flowers sent forth their last perfumes, and closed their cups; nature breathed the tranquillity attendant upon the parting of daylight.

The dark eyes of the young girl beamed more gently as she gazed upon the peaceful scene around her. Powerful as were her emotions, the beauty of this tepid summer evening made a deep impression, while by her side walked a young man who seemed to her the incarnate ideal of all the dreams of her youth. Her eyes filled with tears; and yet she felt like laughing. She was unable to compose her mind, and did not understand herself amidst this chaos of conflicting emotions.

" So thoughtful? " asked M. de Narbonne, after a pause.

" I am gazing upon nature in its deceptive peace," she replied, as if absently. " Look at that cloud yonder; lightning rests in it as passion slumbers in the human soul. There is but an electric spark needed, but a word touching the right point, and our emotions exceed their limits, our will is unable to curb them any longer."

" I wish I could utter this word!" exclaimed Narbonne. But she took no notice of this remark, and, folding her hands on her breast, as if in prayer, she added:

" Creator of this beautiful nature, let your hand rest on me and protect me, for I am unable to do so myself. When happiness knocks at my door, I shall open it; for all I long for is happiness; but how it will come to me I do not know, and I am almost afraid of its appearance. It stands menacingly before my eyes like the cloud yonder with its hidden thunderstorm. Ah, I know it will crush me; and never, never will it be vouchsafed to me to walk as a light-hearted, merry child of the moment on earth. There is too much earnest in my soul, and, moreover, I always do what I regret a moment afterward."

She had uttered the last words in so low a tone that her companion had not understood them.

"You are speaking to the clouds of heaven," said M. de Narbonne, jocularly, "which are unable to reply to you, and meanwhile forget a son of earth who sighs for words from your lips."

"Pardon me," replied Germaine, perceiving her absence of mind; "I have grown up alone; I had no playmates; I am still so much alone that I could not but accustom myself to uttering my thoughts to myself, and listening to the sound of my own words. My mind is exceedingly active, and I long to communicate my thoughts to others."

"One should gain thereby if you would be kind enough to prefer human ears to the elements."

"You are sarcastic, M. de Narbonne, and, what is worse, I feel that I deserve your sarcasm."

"In this manner one will be able, without committing any indiscretion, to read in the inmost recesses of your heart," replied the young man, smiling.

"Unfortunately nothing will be easier than that," said Germaine, suddenly assuming a jocose tone, "for I am almost unable to keep any secrets of mine. It is my nature to divulge everything." *

---

* "C'est ma nature ainsi," a stereotyped phrase of Madame de Staël.

"But the little god forbids it; when he speaks, you will have to keep silence."

"I shall not submit to any such compulsion; I am too ardent a lover of liberty for that," she said, laughing.

"Ah, then, you misunderstand political liberty, as most people do. A free constitution necessitates the greatest self-control on the part of the individual. When one makes one's own laws, one is certainly not at liberty to break them. He who does not know how to obey, and wants to disobey the laws, is not fit for a liberal constitution."

"So I am proscribed from the very first, for I am—let me confess I am—utterly averse to such obedience."

"There will be a master who will teach you obedience, or do you know him already?"

"Poesy has made me acquainted with him," said Germaine, jestingly. "When I walk on the summits of life in pursuit of the beautiful and good, I divine the highest bliss, and call it love."

"And he who is to be its embodiment to you, has not yet appeared before your eyes?" asked M. de Narbonne, gazing into her eyes.

Germaine was about to answer this question, when M. Necker emerged from a by-path, and greeted the party with a joyous "Ah!" His daughter immediately took his arm, and, after Marmontel had exchanged a few words with him, she presented M. de Narbonne to him. There was nothing very polished or winning in Necker's manner, and toward young noblemen whose arrogance he knew, and whose condescending bearing offended him, he usually assumed an air of haughtiness which made him ridiculous. The contrast between his conduct and that of the courtly cavalier became then only the more striking. To-day, too, he assumed, as soon as he heard

Narbonne's name, an air which was to inform the nobleman that he stood before a man to whom he must bow. But this did not deter M. de Narbonne. Condorcet had familiarized him sufficiently with Necker's peculiarities, and his polished manners enabled him to soften the stiffness of the celebrated financier by his easy and winning grace. He made the most favorable impression upon Necker, who, at parting, expressed the wish to see him at his house at his earliest convenience.

While Germaine was now walking by her father's side in the constantly growing darkness, she felt as if her feet no longer touched the ground: so hopeful and light was her heart, so full of strange expectations was her head.

"How beautiful this day was!" she exclaimed, and related to her father what she had heard during her visit to Marmontel's house. Necker listened to her thoughtfully. The remarks of M. de Narbonne found an echo in his breast, and he desired to converse on this subject with the young nobleman, inasmuch as he occupied a stand-point from which many questions might be viewed in an entirely new light.

Germaine, however, did not allow him to dwell on this grave subject; she managed to turn the conversation toward less serious matters, and, by dint of a thousand jests and bright sallies, to make her father laugh merrily. Her satisfaction at his mirth added to her vivacity, and the result was that both of them tried to surpass one another in telling witty anecdotes.

They performed the short distance much sooner than they desired, and reached the villa where Madame Necker awaited them. Supper was ready, they sat down to it, and Madame Necker asked in a tone of ill-concealed vexation, how Germaine came to be so excited?

"I have passed a very happy afternoon," replied the young girl; but she then dropped her knife and fork and burst into

tears. The sudden return of her thoughts to M. de Narbonne
caused this painful emotion; she told herself that he was
already far away at this moment, had reached Paris, called
upon some of his friends, and no longer remembered his meeting with her who would have given everything to see him
again. All at once she felt so lonely, so deserted. Her mother
looked at her in surprise. This glance added to Germaine's
confusion. For the first time in her life she could not utter
what passed in her heart, and her frank and open nature suffered from this concealment which the opinion of others, and
not her own wishes, forced upon her. In an agony of grief
and perplexity, she jumped up and hastened out of the room.

Madame Necker sighed. "How silly she is!" she exclaimed.

"Never mind," said her husband, soothingly. "She has
reached an age when she herself does not know what she
wants, and when there awaken in her heart feelings which she
is unable to interpret. Leave her alone. She is like all other
girls."

"I never acted thus," said Madame Necker.

"Because nature had given you the character of a saint," replied her husband.

This reply pacified her.

CHAPTER II.

MARRIAGES DE CONVENANCE.

M'LLE NECKER stood on the balcony of her house and peered into the distance. Her elegant toilet indicated that she awaited visitors, and her face plainly expressed the impatience with which she looked forward to their arrival.

A dense cloud of dust on the road leading to Paris now indicated the approach of a carriage. At this discovery she was about to turn quickly and hasten back to the *salon*, when the sound of a man's step fell on her ears; she stood still in order to listen, but at the same moment M. de Narbonne came already to meet her.

"What?" she exclaimed, in surprise. "Have you wings? I did not see anybody arrive, and yet you are here? That looks like a miracle."

"Which I gladly perform in order to hasten to you," he replied, bowing politely.

"The compliment loses its value when I call to mind how long it is since we met last, M. de Narbonne."

"The days when I was not allowed to hasten to St. Ouen seem to me as many years, M'lle Necker."

"You were not allowed to come here because you did not want to do so?" she replied, in a slightly reproachful tone.

"Because I could not do so, you should say, M'lle Necker."

"And what was it that detained you in your beautiful Paris? if you do not consider this question impertinent."

"The festivities in which I had to participate. Lafayette, you are aware, has returned; he was received at court simultaneously with the Grand-Duke of Russia, the most singular juxtaposition that can be imagined. The representative of absolute despotism by the side of the champion of absolute liberty! All the ladies were in ecstacies about him, and envied his wife the privilege of possessing him. She found his plain brown dress and his unpowdered blonde hair perfectly charming, and looked rather contemptuously upon the gold-embroidered coats, the powdered wigs, the swords, shoes, and lace-cuffs. All of them wished to be introduced to him, and asked him about the toilets of the American ladies, which they, no doubt, intended to imitate in order to participate also in the glory which our soldiers have obtained in that war. Even my pious mistress, Madame Adelaide, is an ardent admirer of the heroic Lafayette."

"How I long to see him!" exclaimed Germaine. "How gladly I should have attended those festivities! Ah, I have to undergo so many privations here."

"He will no doubt call on M. Necker," replied Narbonne; "for what name could be more agreeable to Lafayette's ears than that of your distinguished father?"

"If we only lived again in Paris!" she exclaimed. "But now tell me quickly a little about the festivities. What toilets did the ladies wear? How did the queen look?"

"Very beautiful, of course,' said M. de Narbonne, laughing; "still I am unable to answer this question positively. I, too, was this time so wanting in gallantry as to have eyes only for the hero whose glory now fills all Paris."

"And yet you did not wish to share this glory?" asked Germaine.

"Because I have plenty of opportunities here to assist in

establishing a free constitution, and I am better able to work for it with my head than fight for it with my sword."

"So you still attend those lengthy lectures of M. Koch, in spite of all festivities."

"I never fail to do so, and am, besides, occupied in other useful studies. I read the German poets and philosophers. Do you not wish to learn that language, that we may read these authors together?"

"If it is worth while to do so."

"Let me assure you that it is. Charles the Fifth used to say that a man had as many souls as he spoke languages, and I know what he meant. With a new tongue we acquire also new views of life, and add to our mental development."

"Will you send me a teacher?"

"With great pleasure."

There was a pause. Germaine looked absently before her, while the young man fixed his eyes on her, searchingly.

At this moment a carriage drove into the court-yard.

"It is the Grand-Duke!" exclaimed Germaine. "I forgot to tell you that he had caused himself to be announced. Come to the *salon* that we may be present at his reception."

"I hoped to see you alone," replied M. de Narbonne. "We see plenty of celebrities in Paris, and need not come to St. Ouen for that purpose. Fate is not propitious to me." He left her in evident vexation.

Germaine's eyes filled with tears. He knew that his departure pained her, and yet he did not remain. Should he intend to torment her?

At this moment a servant entered the room in order to call her down stairs.

Since Louis the Sixteenth had dismissed Necker, several European princes had requested the distinguished financier to

7*

enter their service; and among them was also the Empress Catherine. It was in compliance with her wishes that the Grand-Duke visited him to-day, and repeated to him verbally how glad the Empress would be if he should make up his mind to devote his talents to Russia.

Necker received his august visitor in his plain brown dress, and with the stiff bearing which was intended to impart dignity to him, and listened gravely to the encomiums which the Grand-Duke lavished on him; but his wife was deeply moved by the homage which a great princess paid to her husband, whom she had never seen; she turned pale, and finally fainted away.* Germaine, who stood modestly by her mother's side, supported her and led her out of the room.

Necker excused the accident, which he attributed to the severe trials to which his position had subjected the delicate health of his wife. As usual, he bestowed upon her the warmest praise, a weakness from which he was unable to abstain, despite the sneers of the public.

Germaine meanwhile returned to her father, and stated that her mother was better; and the august visitor left soon after, with the promise that he would speedily repeat his visit.

When Necker was alone with his daughter, he paced the room thoughtfully. "It is sad," he exclaimed, "that we are appreciated so much better abroad than in the country where we have settled. France has no need of me. and yet I cannot turn my back on France."

"You are a celebrated man; all the world admires you. I should like to be honored as you are."

She leaned her head on her hand, and gazed sadly into the garden.

"It is made easy to you; you are my daughter," said Necker,

---

* "Memoirs of Madame d'Oberkirch."

fixing his keen eyes on her, searchingly. "Where you appear, you are treated with marked consideration because you bear my name."

She sighed. "We lead a very lonely life," she said.

"You long for more diversions? My circumstances, my poor child, do not now permit me to afford them to you; prudence requires me to live in retirement, and the feeble health of your mother does not allow her to take you into society; but patience, Germaine, patience! Fate may fulfill your wishes in another way."

Germaine understood what her father meant. She made no reply, but indulged in a reverie, in which M. de Narbonne played a leading part. To step by his side into the world, to bear a name which, even at court, was one of the best, to walk through life with this fine-looking, talented, and admired young man, seemed to her the most enviable happiness, which a word from him might bestow upon her.

Since she had got acquainted with him at Marmontel's house, he visited the villa of her parents almost daily, and was on very friendly terms with her father. She believed she read in his eyes that he was attached to her, but he had never yet uttered the word love in his *tête-a-têtes* with her. Oftentimes, when she expected that it would escape his lips, he sighed, rose and left her suddenly.

M. de Narbonne was ambitious; he had conceived bold plans in regard to his future; his proud spirit longed for appreciation, and he wished to become the most welcome guest in the most brilliant circles of the capital. Wealth alone would not enable him to attain his object. The old nobility looked rather disdainfully upon the Necker family, and ridiculed it on every occasion. And ridicule is an adversary which no one is able to withstand.

Germaine had no idea of it.. She knew only that she was the daughter of the illustrious Necker, to whom emperors and kings paid homage; she was rich, and longed for splendor and fame.

Our desires do not count the obstacles besetting our path.

Her hours passed away slowly and wearily until there dawned a new day that might lead the longed-for visitor to St. Ouen. Germaine sat again on the balcony, and was gazing upon the road; but the young nobleman did not make his appearance.

The visits of M. de Narbonne had become fewer and fewer. This seemed to bode no good to her ardent hopes. When he came back, Germaine met him in confusion, and dropped her eyes as if conscious of guilt. - She did not want to tell him how intensely she had longed for him, as long as he had stayed away without sufficient reason; and, in restraining the emotions to which his appearance gave rise in her heart, she looked upon herself as insincere, and could not find words wherewith to address him.

M. de Narbonne was absent, and did not stay long. Germaine was scarcely able to master her feelings while he remained with her; but when she heard the sound of the hoofs of his horse in the court-yard below, she burst into tears and hastened to her room, in order to weep alone over her disappointed hopes.

A business affair led him again more frequently to St. Ouen during the following week. He conferred with M. Necker as to the establishment of a new organ that was to advocate the financial views of the fallen statesman; hence, the cause of his coming was by no means gratifying to his daughter, but for that matter she greatly rejoiced over his visits. One evening he remained longer than usual. Marmontel and his wife had also arrived; Thomas, who was in feeble health, and appeared more rarely than formerly, had come quite unexpectedly; and some other guests from Paris had surprised the family with their visit at a late hour. Germaine was exceedingly merry. Her large eyes were radiant, while she took the liveliest part in the conversation. She sang a few songs in her fine sonorous voice, and then recited some passages from the works of the best poets. The applause lavished upon her gladdened her the more as it was bestowed upon her in the presence of the man whom she longed most to please by her talents.

The conversation then turned, as usual, to the affairs of the New World; and, in the first place, the question was asked what shape marriage would assume in a free state where all classes were equal, and where it would, therefore, be subject to other conditions than in the Old World.

While this question was discussed, Narbonne remarked that the French soldiers had found the ladies in the Colonies very beautiful.

"In that case," replied Marmontel, "I wonder why our heroes did not lose their hearts there."

"Perhaps they did," replied Narbonne, laughing. "But they will not make any confessions to us on that subject."

"I should think, if one of them had really fallen in love there, he would have probably married a beautiful Puritan girl and sent her home," remarked Madame Marmontel.

"The ladies in the Colonies are educated too austerely to play with their faith," said M. Thomas, gravely.

"You always forget, my learned friend," said Marmontel, laughing, "that the little god does not ascertain one's religion before he shoots his arrows. So the cause must be sought in another direction."

"I think it is quite obvious," said Narbonne. "Most of our young heroes belong to the first families of France, and have been brought up in the belief that marriage is a family obligation which they have to discharge in the face of past and coming generations. However frivolous they may be in other respects, in this matter they will always act with due deliberation, and lend a willing ear to the voice of prudence, which tells them that a union at variance with conventional etiquette is a blunder which makes them ridiculous in the eyes of the world. He who is ambitious enough to go to the New World in search of glory, will not destroy his achievements by introducing a nameless wife into the circle of our society, where she would never be treated as an equal and with due respect. No honorable man will wish to subject a wife who bears his name to such painful slights."

Germaine had listened attentively to Narbonne's words. While he was speaking, she turned now red, now pale; and when he paused, she sank senseless into her chair. M. Necker hastened to her immediately in order to restore her to consciousness. Her forehead was bathed with cold water, and she was not long in opening her eyes again. But she called to mind immediately what had wounded her heart so deeply, and her features indicated the intense grief which convulsively shook her whole frame. She begged leave to withdraw for a few moments; a walk through the garden would do her good.

As soon as she had left the room, M. de Narbonne set out for Paris; the little circle moved closer together, and the disturbance which had interrupted the conversation for a few minutes was speedily forgotten.

When Germaine shortly after re-entered the room with a soft step, and rejoined the circle, no one thought any longer of what had occurred.

M. Necker had to go early next morning to Paris, where he had promised to meet M. de Narbonne at the Café de Fois. In accordance with his habitual punctuality, he arrived there first.

As usual at such places, the news of the day was talked over, and among these topics was also the marriage projected between M. de Narbonne and the daughter of M. de Montholon, First President of the Parliament of Rome. The young lady had inherited a fortune of three hundred thousand livres a year from her mother's relatives in St. Domingo, and she was said to be highly accomplished, but not yet fourteen years of age.

Necker heard this intelligence with mingled feelings of surprise. He loved his daughter too dearly not to watch attentively all that concerned her; and so it had not escaped him how her gifted mind had captivated M. de Narbonne, and what hopes this had awakened in her heart. On the other hand, however, he could not find fault with the young man for preferring a union which offered him so many advantages. Prudence, therefore, commanded M. Necker not to betray the disappointment which this intelligence caused him.

As M. Necker in all relations of life always preferred a straight course, he now too went to meet his young friend with frank expression of countenance, and holding out his hand to him, said:

"I congratulate you with all my heart on the union into which you are about to enter, M. de Narbonne; it would, however, have been more agreeable to me to receive the news from your own lips than from those of strangers."

M. de Narbonne blushed deeply, and replied, in confusion:

"I must admit that I did wrong so far as this is concerned, and beg you to feel convinced that I much regretted not to be

able to make a confident of you. I am unfortunately not at
liberty to communicate to you the reasons which prevented
me from doing so; for they would show you how reluctantly
I took a step to which I consented, not from inclination, but
from regard to the wishes of my family."

"It is always honorable for us to listen to the voice of
reason, no matter what our motive may be," said Necker. He
then passed to other topics, and they parted in the most cordial manner.

On the way home, Necker reflected whether he should communicate to his daughter that Narbonne was about to be
married, or whether it would be better to leave it to time and
chance to make her acquainted with it. He had not yet determined which course to pursue, when Germaine came to
meet him at a great distance from his villa.

"Alone and on this deserted road?" exclaimed her father,
in surprise. "People will be surprised, I should think, to see
Necker's daughter here."

"I am guiltless of any moral wrong by coming to meet
you," she replied, apologetically.

"But that is no valid excuse, my daughter. We cannot return to the primeval forest. Nor would you like to do so; for
you are ambitious, and long to play a brilliant *role* in the world.
But you can never do so if you disregard the rules of conventional propriety in this manner."

"I deem it beneath my dignity to conform to such petty
rules, which my reason does not recognize."

"Because your pride does not allow you to do so," said
Necker, gravely.

"And yet these rules of conventional decorum have a value
which neither your father's fame nor his millions can supply to
you. They rule, and we are subject to them."

"I cannot deny that that is true in many respects," exclaimed Germaine, throwing back her head with an air of vexation, "but the more irresistibly I feel tempted to rebel against it."

"You would only suffer the more. This is unworthy of your intellect. I know that *you* will not find happiness in solitude; you love society, and long to play a brilliant part in it. Take pains, then, to please such persons as might promote your interests in that sphere. In yielding to every caprice, and violating conventional etiquette in a thousand little ways, you yourself obstruct the path which you long to pursue. No young man will dare to offer you his hand, lest you should compromise him. Our friend Narbonne, I understand, is going to marry a young lady, almost a child yet, who has just left the convent, where she learned to submit to the rules of conventional decorum."

"Are you in earnest?" asked Germaine, in surprise.

"In dead earnest."

"Do you know the girl whom he has preferred to me?"

"She is a girl of good family, wealthy, and willing to conform to his ideas of propriety," replied her father, sharply.

Germaine bowed her head and uttered not a word. A gnawing pain racked her heart; it tormented her the more as her eyes remained tearless.

When they reached St. Ouen, she was unable to leave the carriage; she was as if paralyzed, and had to be carried to her room. M. Necker sat at her bed and held her hands. For long hours she lay motionless, and it was not till long after midnight that at length her spasms gave way, and a flood of tears relieved her heart.

In her father she found her best and most affectionate comforter. The more his daughter suffered through the world,

the greater was the tenderness with which he treated her, and
he tried to indemnify her with his love. Madame Necker did
not comprehend his indulgence on this occasion. She was
disposed to be angry at what he excused; and what attracted
him to his child, removed her still more from Germaine, so
that mother and daughter seemed to be strangers.

Henceforth, Germaine no longer stepped out upon the balcony in order to survey the road leading to Paris. Her health
was impaired, profound melancholy had seized her, and she sat
for hours with a book in her hand without reading a line in it.

Narbonne came to St. Ouen as usual, and was received as if
nothing had happened. At his first visit, Germaine was not
in the room, and he dared not inquire after her. When he
came the next time, he found her alone. She reposed on a
chaise longue, the window was open, and the fragrant odor of
the flowers penetrated to her. When he entered the room,
she rose and held out her hand to him.

"I am glad to see you again," she said, kindly. "I hope
the new ties which bind you will not cause you to forget your
old friends."

He pressed her hand to his lips, and said with deep emotion:

"I shall know how to be worthy of your friendship."

He then seated himself by her side, and uttered not a word
for a long time.

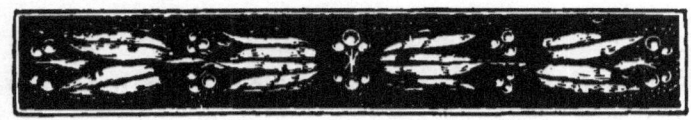

CHAPTER III.

Two young cavaliers, whose prepossessing appearance and proud bearing attracted the attention of most of the passers-by, walked one morning arm-in-arm through the galleries of the Palais Royal. They were engaged in an animated conversation, and paid no attention to what was going on around them; finally they entered the restaurant of the famous Février, whose culinary skill was far-famed at that time.

No sooner had they seated themselves at a small table in a distant corner of the room, than a tall, slender gentleman, round whose finely chiseled lips played a gracious smile, passed by the window, recognized the two cavaliers, and, uttering an "Ah!" of surprise, entered the room and approached them.

The younger of the two cavaliers had jumped up and hastened to meet him. "Condorcet, is it you?" he exclaimed, holding out his hands to him. "How glad I am to meet you this very day! My heart is so full of the New World that I was almost disposed to forget our old institutions, until, now that I have returned to France, they began to weigh me down as heavily as before. Ah! Condorcet, when I call to mind the enchanting dreams in which you indulged, and which carried my youthful imagination to the highest pitch of enthusiasm, my heart still throbs proudly and exultingly. And now that I have helped a foreign nation to conquer what we in France are not even permitted to long for in our dreams, I stand again on my native soil, and am at a loss to know what to do."

"Patience, Vicomte, patience! you will certainly find your place here, too," replied Condorcet, with a smile, slightly tinged with sarcasm. "Permit me, however, to pay my respects to M. de Narbonne, before requesting you to gladden my heart by relating to me events from which a member of the renowned Academy is as remote as the prince of hell is 'from the fields of the blessed."

"Why did you not follow us?" said the young hero of the American war. "Why did you stick to your old folios, and hold intercourse with dust and mould while we were drinking from the cup of life?"

"In order not to get intoxicated, Vicomte," replied Condorcet, laughing. "In order not to awake as you have now awaked. In order not to feel with still greater bitterness how difficult it is to endure the thraldom of traditions which we have inherited simultaneously with original sin."

"As usual, your colors are somewhat too gloomy," interposed M. de Narbonne, smiling. "Permit me to reply that our condition is by no means as hopeless as you represent it. In my opinion, there was no need for us to fight in another hemisphere for rights which we may obtain here, provided we are earnestly determined to do so. There is in France republicanism enough to convert our country, if not into a Republic, at least into a constitutional State; and that is the object which we should strive to attain. I remained at home in order to serve my country in this direction. To be sure, this sacrifice which I made, met with a very sorry reward. Young Ségur was preferred to me, because he fought in the Colonies; and the defender of the rights of rebels, although scarcely out of his teens, was sent to St. Petersburg in order to officiate there as the representative of royal prerogatives. In such a singular manner diplomacy plays with its own interests."

"Ségur was preferred to you, owing to his father's influence," replied Condorcet. "As Minister of War, he has a great deal of influence over the King· and those who know how to profit by the most favorable moment, are always able to manage his Majesty."

"It was not owing to that influence alone, but also to the charm surrounding these champions of liberty," replied Narbonne, gravely. "In the years of their absence from France, they have assumed a bearing which we both admire and envy. What makes us drop our eyes reverentially, seems no longer imposing to them; they look every man, no matter what his rank may be, boldly and joyously in the face, and their air indicates that they consider themselves his equals. This boldness charms us. Mankind always submitted to courage; he who wants to rule, has only to assume an air of independence, and he has already won half a victory. The prince of the royal family, the most ancient nobility, are bowing to heroes who mercilessly trample their prerogatives under foot. They are ashamed of their titles and dignities in the presence of a Lafayette, who has gained a civic crown, and donned the plain dress of a commoner, which our powdered and richly-attired courtiers contemplate with unfeigned astonishment. A hermit could scarcely look more plainly dressed in their midst than the victors of Yorktown."

"The picture you have just drawn is applicable to me, too," interposed Montmorency, crimsoning and glancing at his black dress. "In the last few years I have become so thoroughly accustomed to the comfort of wearing my hair in its natural state, and of dressing in a plain coat, that at my age I think I am no longer fitted for the stiff court costume."

"Of course, when one is twenty-five years old, and has seen the New World, one is no longer a child," replied Condorcet, with a smiling glance at Montmorency.

"I do not care if you laugh at my youth," exclaimed the young man, merrily. "I am not ashamed of it. Besides, it is an evil which improves every day. And now, when the present leaves so many wishes unfulfilled, my eye has need of this far-extending view of the future, lest I should despair of my country. I say to myself daily, "What we have not yet achieved, we may obtain hereafter. I am young enough to live and see the day when my beautiful France will likewise raise liberty-poles, and erect altars to the rights of man."

"In order to immolate on them the descendants of the ancient house of Montmorency," interposed Condorcet. "Ah, Vicomte, you do not suspect what a storm you conjure up by your enthusiasm over your own head! To mould one's own destiny is more difficult than you believe; to be indebted only to one's own merits for honor, fame, and popularity, is a task requiring extraordinary strength."

"But imparting strength, too," exclaimed the young man, enthusiastically. "Young as I am, I am able to feel how the sense of our worth grows with the deeds which we have performed. I do not want to feed any more on the glory of my ancestors, allow myself to be honored because they bore the same name before me, date my merits from the tombs, and exclaim, "Look at the dust which was once called Montmorency; and I swear by God and all the saints that no Montmorency shall henceforth do so any more!"

"Vicomte," replied Condorcet, gazing at the young man with an expression of growing satisfaction; "you have learned a great deal in a very short time; yes, I must confess that you have learned more than I thought a Montmorency would ever comprehend. Here is my hand! We must be friends. The dreams with which you charged me before are neither buried nor forgotten. There are other men who dream with me, and with them you shall now get acquainted. We have not stood still since you did not see us. The torch which you caused to illuminate another hemisphere has shed its rays as far as France. There are even now in France as many men as there are subjects. And that we have likewise already learned to pay homage to merit without regard to the ancestors of him whom we honor, is shown by Necker's great popularity."

"Whose downfall the court party brought about because he did not belong to an ancient family," interrupted the young man, warmly.

"You must not judge too rashly," replied Condorcet, calmly. "It is true, he lost his office, but not his influence. It was because the people idolized him that the nobility hated and feared Necker, and the King treated him so respectfully and leniently. Do you not perceive the immense progress which this fact indicates? What would it have been under another King of a Minister of Finance bold enough to dictate wise economy to the King and his court? He would at least have been hung."

"At least," repeated M. de Montmorency, "what else might have happened to him? But you are right. That this man, who deserved to be a citizen of the United States, was not deprived of his life and liberty, is a great homage paid to public opinion."

"Such as France never knew before," said Condorcet; "and on this ground we must build; we must strive to add to the power of this voice, in order to bring about through it the triumph of true humanity. Do you see now that we have something to do here too, and will you lend us your assistance?"

"Condorcet, I embrace you for the spark which you have thrown into my soul," exclaimed the young man, folding him to his heart. "Now I suddenly behold the dawn of a new day through the gloom that precedes it. Where is Necker? Take me to him; he is the only man in France whose acquaintance I long to make."

"Before calling on him, read his *Compte Rendu*, in order to familiarize yourself with his views. Besides, he would hardly forgive you for overlooking in America the appearance of his great book."

"What a clever sarcasm!" exclaimed Narbonne, laughing.

"Then you must not look for an enthusiastic devotion to mere ideas in this financier, who, with all the respectability of his character and incorruptible honesty, is intent only on restoring the equilibrium of the budget, and pursues the same course in regard to every virtue and right. Everything in life must receive what is due to it, and no more; for, if he gave too much here, there would remain too little there; if he gave both hands to one friend, he could not hold out a third to another; if he spoke too warm a word here, there might arise in consequence a deficit in his heart, by which somebody else might have to suffer. In short, M. Necker takes pains to resemble the good God as much as possible. Not a scintilla of blame could be adduced against him. There is in his infallibility something humiliating for other mortals to whom some human weaknesses still cling, and the consequence is that he is esteemed and admired, but shunned by most people."

"He never made that impression on me," interposed Narbonne, quickly. "I see him almost daily, and constantly become more attached to him. It is so seldom that we meet a man, who, entirely free from self-interest, serves and promotes the good only for its own sake."

"Is that so?" replied Condorcet, eyeing the speaker with a significant smile. "In that case I strike my sails, M. de Narbonne, and leave it to my young friend to form his own opinions at his interviews with the celebrated financier. But let me previously whisper a little warning into his ear. Necker has a daughter. The young lady, Vicomte, might succeed in misleading your opinion of her father, as she has already done with others. In that case I need not expect that you will indorse what I have said about Necker."

This remark rather disconcerted M. de Narbonne; however, he was not long in regaining his composure.

"You never liked Necker, Condorcet," he said, with seeming equanimity. "His system of economy did not agree with your nature; you looked upon this thrifty management of our finances as rather undignified; you regarded his views as too sober, and found fault with the rough common sense of the Genevan *parvenu*. Oh, I remember it all very well. Your opinion has misled me, and I hesitated a long time to get acquainted with the illustrious Necker, until finally an accident brought me in contact with him."

"And showed you that I had misrepresented Necker. I suppose these words were wanting to what you said just now?"

"They were, indeed. I discovered how unjust it is to judge others by comparing them with ourselves. Believe me, Condorcet, it does not matter much in the long run by what route we arrive at the goal, provided this goal is worth the pains we have taken to reach it. When a man devotes his life to the welfare of humanity, we do not find fault with him if he chooses a stony path leading to that aim. I wish you would become more intimately acquainted with Necker, in order to get a better opinion of him."

8

"I certainly do him justice," replied Condorcet. "Maurepas, the old minister, called him '*l'épine;*' but I have christened him '*le génie male*,' which certainly does not displease him; for he believes in himself as in another Saviour, and his wife and daughter encourage him in this lamentable infatuation."

"Why lamentable?" interrupted Narbonne. "He who does not believe in himself will hardly ever obtain much influence over others. The great Washington, no doubt, never had a poor opinion of himself, and he is the only man with whom Necker can be compared."

"As regards disinterestedness, I admit you are right," replied Condorcet. But otherwise, a certain modesty always graces the truly great man. However, let us not quarrel about it. However great his merits may be, they are only those of an individual, mortal like all of us. The really important service which he has rendered to our country, is the victory which he caused public opinion to achieve over the State and Church. The people has learned, and the King has not forgotten, that these thousands of voices which cheered and applauded him have a powerful sound; and this power, tested as it has been on this occasion, promises us a great deal."

"But we still have need of Necker in order to obtain it," said Narbonne. "He was courageous enough to utter what we thought, and this courage entitles him to our admiration."

"Which I am ready and willing to render to him," said Condorcet, smiling. "Only I do not want to make a demi-god of him. He is, moreover, already too prosperous. Wealth, honor, and fame, all the blessings of this earth have been bestowed upon him; and, besides, fate placed in his daughter the most gifted creature on earth by his side. * She possesses all those qualities which are wanting to her father—imagination,

_____

* "Memoirs de Condorcet."

fervor, and enthusiasm—a genius embracing heaven and earth. Carried and lifted up by her, Necker would be capable of surpassing himself. These remarks about Necker's daughter show you, M. de Narbonne, that I can be just, and, as a general thing, it is difficult for us men to be so in regard to women," he added, smilingly.

"M'lle Necker does not know that you admire her so ardently," replied Narbonne, "and she is unfortunately too affectionate a daughter to forgive you for preferring her to her father. You must get acquainted with her, Montmorency. She likes to give the reins to her ardent imagination, and, if you like, will dream the most beautiful dreams with you."

"To tell you the truth, Narbonne, I should like better to form the acquaintance of her father, and become his friend," replied the young man. "I must cling in my life-path to a great and noble character that would give to my being a certain stability, and prevent it from going astray too often. I have entirely unlearned in the New World to feel at ease in female circles. To flirt and chat with women reminds me of the court of Sardanapalus. The welfare of my country and the happiness of millions—they are the stars to which I intend to devote my strength; where they beam on me, there is my happiness."

"You have returned to us with a joyous and hopeful heart, my young Brutus," said Condorcet, with his peculiar smile, which now, however, was not free from an expression of heartfelt emotion as he fixed his eyes on the fine intellectual face of the young man. "Thank God that you are still able to entertain such sentiments. May you retain your noble enthusiasm and courage for many years to come! I should dislike to make you prematurely sober and prudent; but I think the acquaintance of our old financier will do you no harm; for under his wings, as under those of an old hen, gather all his young political sympathizers, and his house is the rendezvous of half the world."

"I was told that he lived in retirement at St. Ouen!"

"The road to that place is open to everybody, and, besides, he may return any day to his post."

"We shall see him to-night at 'Figaro's Wedding,'" said Narbonne. "I shall then take you to his box."

Necker had of late been often at the theatre, in order to divert his daughter. He felt that her life by the side of her sick mother, and her father, who was mostly very busy, was by far too austere for a young girl, and he was fearful lest her loneliness should add to her proneness to melancholy, and cause her to live in a world of dreams, which estranged her more and more from reality. So he often prevailed on her to read scientific works; and since she had met with the bitter disappointment which Narbonne's marriage with another girl had caused to her, he took pains to occupy himself a great deal with her, and watched her with the most affectionate solicitude.

Count de Montmorency was not long in ingratiating himself with Necker, upon whom his prepossessing appearance and frank and open bearing made a very favorable impression. This favorable opinion was much enhanced when Montmorency, in the course of his frequent visits, assumed a tone of reverence, mingled with familiarity and confidence, which imparted something filial to his relationship with the experienced statesman, and which was very agreeable to Necker. Necker's wife, too, was charmed with the unaffected courtesy of the young aristocrat, and treated him with great distinction.

'Germaine did not indicate in any manner that he had made a particular impression on her. Inasmuch as M. de Montmorency bestowed upon her only such attentions as were necessary and unavoidable, and did not seek her company, she had little reason to feel flattered at his conduct, and often shunned his presence intentionally.

She now wrote a great deal, and what she wrote seemed to engross all her thoughts.

As it was Necker's habit, whenever an idea which he wished to communicate to others occurred to him, to hasten to the *salon* in order to inform his wife or his daughter of it, and disliked to see that his sudden appearance interrupted them in their occupations, his wife had accustomed herself to write standing. As soon as the door opened, she quietly laid down her pen and feigned to be entirely unoccupied.

Germaine had learned from her mother to conform to these little peculiarities of her father. Her writing-desk stood on the mantel-piece, and she quickly set down there whatever she wished to remember.

In the forenoon they were generally alone. The nervous sufferings of her mother could be relieved only by warm baths, and the use of them occupied the forenoon. Madame Necker, moreover, now liked to be alone. The death of her friend Thomas had afflicted her heart deeply, and for a long time she was unable to recover from this terrible blow. The loss of her faithful old friend, to whom she could confide everything that occupied her mind, caused a most painful gap in her life, and the idea of her own death engrossed all her thoughts.

M. de Narbonne presented his young wife to the Necker family. "I know that she cannot become a companion of yours," he said to Germaine; "but still I wished to make you acquainted with her, for she admires you sincerely."

There was no need of this appeal. Germaine embraced her tenderly; and looked with mournful sympathy at the young creature, who in her presence seemed more child-like than ever.

"I wonder if she suspects how much reason I have to envy her," she said to herself.

At a late hour one evening, Narbonne and Montmorency called upon Necker in order to converse with him on the latest political events, and especially on the financial operations of Minister Calonne, which had created the greatest sensation throughout France. Inasmuch as there were no other guests, Necker remained with his young friends in the *salon*, where they chatted in the presence of his daughter about the political condition of France. Germaine soon took a lively part in the conversation; and M. de Montmorency, who had never before heard her discuss such grave subjects, was surprised to see that she surpassed her father by her brilliant eloquence, and the profound views which she took of every question. He involuntarily grew silent, while his eyes and ears hung upon her lips. Narbonne noticed it.

"Did you find it out now?" he whispered to him, casting a significant glance on Germaine, who overheard his words.

"Find out what?" she asked, blushing.

"Your extraordinary abilities," said Narbonne.

"Alas!" she replied, sighing. "They are of no use to a woman. Men love in us only ordinary qualities."

CHAPTER IV.

A DISAPPOINTMENT.

NECKER's daughter sat to-day again on the balcony of her father's villa, and gazed out upon the road. A solitary horseman came in sight; he recognized her already at a distance, and indicated by his salutation that he looked for a cordial welcome. Her eyes followed him as he threw the reins of his horse to the groom in the court-yard below, and then hastily ascended the staircase.

"I have occupied myself with you, M. de Montmorency," laying down a manuscript. "Your diary has interested me exceedingly. I have seen the great Washington with your eyes, and fought with you for a great cause. How even this echo of glorious deeds expands our soul!"

"History records such deeds everywhere," replied the young man, seating himself by her side; "but, it is true, our individual feelings heighten or lessen the impression which they make upon us. We, for instance, have bowed for centuries to the will of a single man, and paid homage to the merit of ancient names; it is then an entirely new phase for us to co-operate with a nation which has renounced all traditions, and obeys only its own will. Who knows but people may long one day as intensely for our monarchial institutions as we are now tired of them."

"Impossible!" cried Germaine, vehemently. "Those who, like myself, suffer in consequence of these prejudices, and have to sacrifice to them the happiness of their whole youth, cannot conceive such an idea."

Montmorency looked at her in surprise, and, withal, inquiringly. She grew confused.

"You bear an old name; hence you do not comprehend what I mean," she said. "Your position was assigned to you at your very birth; that of my father was a work of time, and due to his surpassing merits. These cannot be handed down from father to child. So I have to obtain a position in society by my own efforts. How am I to proceed in doing so?"

"A lady obtains a position in society through her husband," exclaimed M. de Montmorency.

"Not every man is courageous enough to demand for his wife the place that is due to her," replied Germaine, gravely; "and several events have shown but very recently how intolerant the most aristocratic circles of society are. Marriage is to be a strictly conventional matter, and love is to be utterly disregarded, lest new blood should mingle with that of the old families."

M. de Montmorency was about to reply, but he suddenly stopped short and paced the room uneasily and irresolutely. He then seated himself opposite to Germaine, took up his diary, and said: "Did you read it through?"

This question showed her that he wished to change the subject of conversation, and she helped him to do so.

Since that evening on which her gifted mind had first surprised him so greatly, he had taken pains to get better acquainted with her, and had often conversed with her alone. Both of them were of an age when such *tête-à-têtes* easily led to greater familiarity. What they felt and thought was reflected in each other's souls, and every agreement in this direction led to new communications.

Necker watched with grave eyes this growing familiarity, which, as yet, bore only the name of friendship. If any man at court was capable of rising above the prevailing prejudices, and of becoming Necker's son-in-law, this courage might be looked for in the young cavalier who had made such heavy sacrifices to the cause of liberty. So he determined to wait and see what would happen.

Both of them now went down to the garden, where they met Necker, who had just returned from a walk.

"My daughter caused me to take my walk alone to-day, because she awaited you," said Necker, after saluting his young friend. "I might become jealous of you; for, to tell you the truth, I am quite spoiled in this respect," he added, jestingly.

At these words, Germaine clung affectionately to his arm.

"My dear, kind father!" she exclaimed, tenderly. "You will always hold the first place in my heart. Who could love me as you love me? Your wishes, your will, always will be my supreme law, and never shall I seek for a happiness that you do not approve."

"Thus speaks a dutiful daughter!" said Necker, jocularly. "Sons are not always so obedient, M. de Montmorency. The young men of our times begin to pursue a course solely dictated by their own judgment."

"I do not approve these innovations," said the young man, gravely. "The freer a state, the greater must be the deference paid to parents and superiors. Never should I be capable of taking a step at which my mother would take umbrage. She has watched over my childhood with so much solicitude, that I certainly owe her this consideration now that she has grown old. No matter how difficult it may be for me to sacrifice my dearest wishes to her peculiar notions, I am satisfied that my

8*

own conscience will amply reward me in course of time for the struggle which I am undergoing now."

He paused and looked thoughtfully before him. Germaine leaned her head on her father's breast. Something told her that these words decided her fate.

All three of them returned in silence to the house.

Visitors had arrived in the meantime. While Germaine devoted herself to the guests, she noticed that M. de Montmorency fixed his eyes on her with a certain mournful tenderness.

Henceforth his conduct toward her grew even more cordial, and he visited her even more frequently than before; but at the same time he blamed her frankly and openly whenever he thought she was doing wrong, and especially he often censured her conduct toward her mother, whose cold, systematic ways often provoked the rebellious spirit of the daughter.

When Germaine was alone, she now frequently shed tears; and when her father asked her what grieved her, she replied: "Life gives me so little satisfaction."

He made no reply, for he knew full well that words would not change her present state of mind. However, he had the happiness of his child too much at heart not to try to devise ways and means by which he might give her relief. Solitude and tranquillity were unsuitable for her nature. She had to live in a certain excitement, and, whatever she might do, she had to do it passionately and impetuously; violent conflicts, breathless expectations of the coming minute, did her good. To play a *rôle* in society was the only task for which she was fitted. He took his steps in accordance with this conviction.

One morning he surprised her at an unusually early hour in the *sa'on*, where she stood at the mantel-piece and wrote very rapidly. She was so much absorbed in her occupation that she had not noticed his entrance; and when she saw him now, she hurriedly cast aside her pen, blushing, and in confusion at having been surprised in this manner.

"I should like to see what you are writing," said her father, approaching her. "Will you let me see your manuscript?"

"How can you ask such a question?" she replied, handing the manuscript to him.

He sat down in an arm-chair and turned over the manuscript.

Meanwhile her eyes rested on him expectingly.

The contents began to interest him; at first he read only a few passages here and there, but finally he became absorbed in his daughter's work.

"You have been very industrious," he said, after a while. "Your verses are beautiful, the diction is pure, and your style has improved considerably since you laid your first dramatic production before us."

"Oh, at that time I was still a child!" cried Germaine, somewhat offended.

"Yes, you were a child, but a very promising one," replied Necker, calmly. "And now that we are about to celebrate your birthday, I hope we shall witness the realization of all the expectations to which you have given rise. Is it not so, my daughter?"

"I hope so," replied Germaine, trying to divine the drift of her father's words.

"At that time, you know, I advised you not to continue your literary labors, because I think a woman should lay her works before the public only if her talents justify this step; and as you were still a child, I could not decide positively as to the character of your abilities. Since then I have had repeated

opportunities of admiring your extraordinary talents. Your
reply to the *Compte Rendu* was a masterpiece of eloquence;
your notes on Montesquieu's 'Esprit des Loix' are no less
piquant than able; and what you have written about Rousseau
surprised me in a girl of your age; but, to tell you the truth,
these poetical efforts seem to me unworthy of Necker's daughter."

"Why, father?" asked Germaine, bursting into tears.

"Because they speak only of love and passion, and of the
bitter grief of resignation. I should have expected that you
would have bestowed your attention upon graver subjects.
You are no ordinary girl, Germaine. If you were, I should
willingly forgive you these idle reveries. If you could lend to
your life no higher interest than to hear the confession of love
from the lips of a man, I should not blame you for practicing
the little arts leading to that object. But, gifted as you are
far beyond most women, you must set a wider horizon to your
feelings; humanity, and not a single man, must fill your
heart."

Germaine had buried her face in her hands and made no
reply. Her father's words touched her like live coals. He had
touched the right string; her ambition was sorely wounded.
Necker continued, after a pause:

"Since you are brooding over your feelings, your intellectual development has made no progress. *Sophie, ou les sentiments secrets*. I ask you what new views you will gain by writing on such a subject. Then comes *Jane Grey*. Despite the historical back-ground, you treat the subject in the same limited
manner. The verses are good, and the style is very attractive,
but I do not consider that sufficient. Of my daughter, I expect *ideas*. You have a masculine mind; that is to say, you
possess judgment, and, therefore, stand above the relations of

life, while the so-called feminine natures are pent up and dominated by them. How often did you fill both myself and the friends of our house with sincere admiration, by your profound criticisms and correct appreciation of authors and their works, and now you would allow your mind to walk in the leading-strings of your emotions."

"No, I will not do so, father!" vehemently cried Germaine, jumping up from her seat. "As sure as I live, I will not do so. But pardon me for saying: I long so intensely to love and be loved, that my yearning for this happiness overshadows every other desire of my heart. Is it my fault that my heart throbs impetuously, and that in my bosom burns a fire that longs to be quenched? Is it my fault that in my veins stirs a current of life, intent on asserting itself? I do not know whither to direct the strength which I possess; it seems to me I am like a volcano, in whose depths the elements are struggling with one another, while the cold and dry surface covers the molten lava. I walk my path like other human beings; but what makes them happy, kills me. I find no satisfaction in the petty pleasures and joys of life; there must be a happiness affording us a more exalted bliss, and it is for this bliss that I long."

"You will not find it in the path which you have entered," said Necker, taking her hand, and drawing her to him. "All gifted natures feel as you do. Life seems to them not to afford what they long for; and to satisfy this longing for more exalted bliss, religion points out to them the road to another world. A man has his ambition and glory to quench this flame; a woman has nothing but her love, which pens her up in a narrow circle of duties. Look at your mother. What a simple, unpretending life she has led by my side, humbly and faithfully striving to be a helpmate to me. It is the tighest aim which a woman is able to reach, to become the consort of a man whom she loves and respects, and to whom she willingly subordinates herself, because she acknowledges his superior judgment. You must renounce this kind of happiness, my child; inasmuch as your superior intellect prevents you from pursuing such a modest and humble course. The man to whom you might look up, would have to be born first."

"I revere you, father, as, next to God, I can never revere any mortal; and I do believe that you are on earth the only man worthy of such reverence!"

"You are my child," said Necker, affectionately, and that determines our relationship. In a certain sense I am you, and you are me. We are mutually proud of one another; and that which concerns you, touches me even more sensibly than if it concerned myself. But it is not thus with man and wife. They must first assimilate, and learn how to treat one another. For this purpose the wife has need of self-abnegation. But you are unable to restrain; your nature is too impetuous and independent, and must rule until time will teach you moderation. You are, moreover, too gifted to be able to confine your talents to the narrow circle of domestic duties; you must yield to grand ideas, and warm your heart for the happiness of millions. It is in this extensive horizon that lies the happiness for which you long. Silence your feelings, and let them give place to fame."

Germaine trembled. She pressed her hand to her heart, and became so dizzy that she was fearful she might faint away.

"And you believe that I possess ability enough to obtain fame?" She asked, anxiously.

"I believe it not only, my daughter, but feel convinced of it No woman in France ever possessed such extensive knowledge and refined culture as you do. Lay aside these childish efforts, bestow your attention upon something serious, continue your letters on Ro. sseau, publish them as soon as they are completed, and your success will teach you something about your worth and capacity. All France will pronounce the name of the authoress with ardent admiration, and Parisian society will lavish encomiums on you."

"Oh, if I could obtain fame in this wise!" she exclaimed, with radiant eyes. "Oh, if I should be admired and revered like you! Ah, I feel how tempting the idea is!"

"Rely on my judgment. It is, besides, my intention to procure you now a sphere of your own in Paris. Loath as I am to part with you, I must pursue the same course as other fathers, and secure you a name of your own, and a position in society. Now, inasmuch as you are my only child, I may be pardoned for the desire of keeping you near me, and this is the only difficulty standing in the way of a match suitable and desirable in every other respect."

"With whom?" exclaimed Germaine, crimsoning.

"With the Swedish Embassador, Baron de Stael. He is a Protestant; hence, there is no religious objections to the union. His official position will procure you access to the most aristocratic society, and even the Court must receive you, whether your father be in disgrace or not. M. de Stael, although no longer a young man, is good-looking, and will not impose any restraint on you; only as regards representation, you must submit to the stringent rules of court etiquette. He is not wealthy, and so he desired this union; and inasmuch as I was fearful lest his King should recall him, and bury my child in the woods of Scandinavia, I imposed the condition that he must procure a written pledge that he should remain at the head of the Parisian embassy during his lifetime. He has now applied to Marie Antoinette; and the

Queen, who is as passionate a match-maker as most women, has written an autograph letter to the King of Sweden. As soon as his answer arrives, I shall present Baron de Stael to you, and you may then decide for yourself whether you will accept his hand or not."

So saying, Necker left his daughter, musing on all that she had heard.

CHAPTER V.

The Prince de Beauveau gave a brilliant festival to the members of the Academy, and invited Necker to it. Necker visited now but rarely the soirées to which he was invited, inasmuch as the feeble health of his wife rendered it impossible for her to accompany him; but on this occasion she determined to make an exception, and urged him to accept the invitation for herself and Germaine.

Germaine was overjoyed at her mother's resolution, inasmuch as she hoped to find the most brilliant conversation in the circle of the most distinguished men of France. So she looked forward to the appointed day with considerable interest and pleasure.

Since the interview with her father, which we have related in the preceding chapter, she had zealously devoted her morning hours to her literary labors. However difficult it was for her to renounce the dearest wishes of her heart, she felt the necessity of following her father's advice; for who could tell if she was not mistaken in regard to Montmorency's apparent attachment, as she had been as to that of M. de Narbonne's? Who could tell her that he was able to dispose of his heart and hand in consonance with his own wishes?

Her interviews with him caused her to heave many a heavy sigh. She was not allowed to tell him how much she felt attracted towards him, nor suffer him to read in her eyes how much she liked him. This embarrassed and confused her in his presence.

His changeable conduct added to her perplexity. Now he treated her with the tenderness of a brother, and now he took pains to be cold toward her, as if it was his intention to efface the impression which he had made on her before. This uncertainty in their mutual relations was perfectly intolerable, and she was desirous of bringing about a decision at any cost.

Her beautiful and profound essays on Rousseau's character and writings were on the eve of completion, and she anxiously looked forward to the moment when she would lay them before the public.

She would oftentimes absorb herself so thoroughly in this occupation, that she took no notice of the lapse of time; and to-day, too, when the festival at the Academy was to take place, this had happened to her. Madame Necker entered her room in full dress before she had even thought of her toilet. She jumped up in dismay when she saw her mother's clouded brow, and hastened out of her room.

Madame Necker, shaking her head, followed her with a slow step.

Upon entering her daughter's room, she found Germaine's maid already busily occupied in helping to dress her young mistress. She fastened red rosettes to her dark hair, and put on a green dress fringed with gold; this costume rendered her corpulent form and swarthy complexion so conspicuous, that Germaine's mother started back in dismay as she now beheld her own image beside that of her daughter in the large toilet-mirror.

"You cannot wear this costume, Germaine," she said. "This dress does not become you."

"Never mind," replied Germaine, carelessly. "I never shall be beautiful, and I should not like to keep father waiting."

"He will do so rather than expose his daughter to the sneers of society, which always finds fault with what the Necker family is doing," replied her mother, in a tone of vexation. "You must now the more zealously avoid exposing yourself to ridicule, as you may at no distant time fill a place in society where such things might injure you."

"Of course, if I am to be judged by such trifles, such as the color of a rosette or a bonnet, I shall frequently incur the censure of society; for my nature is averse to paying much attention to such things," said Germaine, angrily.

Madame Necker made no reply, in order not to continue this conversation in the presence of the servant-girl. When they entered the carriage, she said:

"I owe you yet a reply, Germaine. Accept this lesson from your mother now, that it may still be useful to you. Never treat anything as so trifling that it might not influence the happiness or unhappiness of your life. It is a noteworthy fact, too, that we seldom gain the affections of men by brilliant qualities, but rather by the little things by which we enchant their eyes. This truth may seem distasteful to you, but put it to the test, and you will be unable to deny it."

Germaine made no reply, as she used to do when her mother spoke of love; her remarks on that subject always made a disagreeable impression on her, and a painful feeling of envy and jealousy tormented her heart.

When they arrived at the Academy, all the guests were already assembled. The singular contrast between mother and daughter was noticed by everybody to-day. Madame Necker looked even paler than usual. She wore a crimson dress—her favorite color—and her fair hair was dressed in antique style,

with a toupet called *à la Minerve*, which she had introduced because she disliked the tall hair-dress then in vogue. Her delicate and slender figure and white and almost transparent
complexion still imparted to her a very youthful appearance,
although she was already upward of forty years old.

Germaine, on the other hand, looked much older than she
was. Although her white dress, and the plain green wreath
with which her mother had caused her to adorn her dark hair,
were a toilet suitable to her complexion, and distinguished her
from the older ladies, she did not make a pleasing impression, and, above all things, there was wanting to her that graceful composure and tranquillity peculiar to the bearing of a distinguished lady.

She would have certainly herself felt this want most sensibly,
had she been aware of it; but no one is able to draw an im-
partial picture of his own appearance, and never correctly
appreciates the impression which it produces.

Despite her superior mind, which inwardly raised her far
above most men, she always seemed to be deficient in that dignity which self-consciousness generally imparts to us. This
arose, perhaps, from the fact that it was not easy for her to begin a conversation, and usually was exceedingly laconic in
speaking with insignificant persons; and it was not until an
idea excited her interest that she burst forth into a stream of
the most fervent eloquence, which silenced all others.

Necker, therefore, would say, " *Ma fille a besoin d'un premier
mot.*"

There were among the guests several ladies of the court, to
whom Madame Necker hurriedly introduced her daughter;
and then all went to the table.

Germaine was fortunate enough to sit between two gentlemen who were exceedingly agreeable to her—M. de Narbonne

and M. de Condorcet. She missed, however, the Vicomte de Montmorency; and yet, whenever the question rose to her lips, she did not venture to inquire why he was not present.

The general conversation soon referred to the usual topics: the finances, the short supply of grain, Minister Calonne and his golden promises, the purchase of St. Cloud for Queen Marie Antoinette, and the growing unpopularity of her Majesty.

"Let us not talk politics to-day, Mademoiselle Necker," exclaimed Narbonne; "I am in too good spirits to give you any sensible answers."

"And I am too grave to talk anything but sense," replied Germaine. "So we had better keep silence."

"I shall not object, if Condorcet will tell us some pretty stories which would make us laugh."

"I should rather make you shudder, by repeating all sorts of ghost stories about Cagliostro and the Rosicrucians. But you must first promise me to listen without skepticism."

"I shall promise no such thing," exclaimed Germaine. "I must, above all things, preserve my liberty."

"That is my creed too," said Condorcet. "Mademoiselle Necker and I are worthy of being placed by the side of the great Washington."

"By the way," said Narbonne, "where is our young enthusiast of liberty? Why is our friend Montmorency not here?"

"He was suddenly summoned to his old grandmother in the country. The venerable lady had heard all sorts of rumors about him, which rendered her fearful he might prove recreant to the principles of a Montmorency. A family council was summoned; and he is, perhaps, being tried at this very moment."

"Well, we cannot swim against the stream in this world,"

replied Narbonne, carelessly. "They have long ago chosen a wife for him, but could never prevail on him even to look at the girl. For the rest, that may not be so very necessary, provided he consents to marry her."

"His grandmother will be certain to obtain his consent," said Condorcet, laughing. "No one but he who has experienced it himself, knows the power of a grandmother's tears over the heart of a tender young man."

"I think tears are even more effective when the eyes which weep them are not too old," said Narbonne, jocularly.

"I am sure you cannot weep," said Condorcet to Germaine, who had sat absorbed in her thoughts; "the fire of your eyes will immediately dry the tears gushing from your lids."

"You are mistaken, M. de Condorcet. Grief always affects me so powerfully that I shed at once streams of tears, and could fill for you a vial with tear-drops if you wish it."

"In that case I should have to wish to plunge you into grief, which would cause those tears, and God forbid that I should do that," exclaimed Condorcet, deprecatingly.

"Pray look at Cazotte," interposed Narbonne, pointing to a pale young man who sat close by. "He is turning paler and paler, and rolls his eyes as if he had visions."

"I wonder why they invited him," said Condorcet, shaking his head.

"Perhaps he came without an invitation. You know what sort of a man he is."

"Do you know him?" asked Germaine.

"To be sure I do," replied Narbonne. "He is a popular journalist; but he has latterly lost his head, owing to the writings of Saint Martin and the teachings of the Illuminati. He is said to have occasional fits of insanity, when he foretells the events of the future."

"Why do you call the gift of prophecy insanity?" asked Germaine.

"Because I do not believe that it is given to us to foresee future events," replied Narbonne.

"I should like to hear him prophesy," exclaimed Germaine, excitedly.

"In that case I will try to see if the spirit moves him to reveal the future to us," said Condorcet, rising to speak with the strange guest.

"You are so grave, M. Cazotte," he began. "You do not participate in the conversation. May I fill your glass and at the same time drink your health?"

"I thank you," mournfully replied Cazotte, shaking his head.

"What? You are so dejected that nothing will induce you to participate in the general mirth?" Condorcet went on to ask.

A shudder ran through Cazotte's frame, and averting his head, he whispered, "Poor Condorcet! It tastes bitter, does it not?"

"Are you speaking of me?" exclaimed Condorcet. "I do not understand what you mean. What is bitter? Pray tell me what you refer to?"

"The poison tastes bitter," whispered Cazotte.

"What poison?"

"That which you will take in order not to fall under the executioner's ax."

Condorcet turned pale. He smiled, but with bloodless lips. Germaine, who had listened to them attentively, seized Narbonne's arm and clung to it convulsively.

"You let me suffer the death of Socrates," he then said, with forced composure, "but do not tell me the reason why. I cannot, like him, overthrow the false gods, nor proclaim that there is but one God."

"Truth is God; lies are false gods," cried Cazotte, as if absently.

"Ah, well then, let us drink to the victory of truth, gentlemen!"

"You laugh," said Cazotte, shaking his head disapprovingly. "Poor Condorcet. You will soon cease laughing in this manner!"

"Your words are very grave," replied Condorcet, with forced hilarity. "But do you want to let me die all alone for the triumph of truth? That would be almost too cruel."

"Unfortunately, fellow-sufferers will not be wanting to you," said Cazotte, with a deep sigh. "Your neighbor at this table, M. Chamfort, is averse to sharing the bitter cup with you; but he does not want to fall either under the executioner's ax; so he will open his veins and slowly bleed to death. As for you, M. Bailly, and you, Malesherbes, and Roucher, you will hope to the last that they will acquit you; even at the moment when they lead you to the scaffold, you will refuse to believe that your death is at hand."

All the guests now commenced listening to him attentively. Germaine trembled with horror and agitation.

"What will be my fate?" she asked, in a very low voice.

Strange to say, Cazotte seemed to have heard her words, for he immediately fixed his eyes on her, and the longer he looked at her, the more joyous became the expression of his face.

"You are saved!" he said at last, heaving a deep sigh of relief. "You save the life of two friends, and your own is preserved in return."

"And the names of those whom I save?" she cried, in feverish agitation.

"M. de Narbonne and M. de Montmorency, neither of whom

deserve that you should risk your life in saving them from the executioner's ax."

"He does not speak very highly of me, that is certain," exclaimed Narbonne, laughing. It was to be seen, however, that his mirth did not come from his heart. "Henceforth I shall more than ever take pains to keep on friendly terms with you, Mademoiselle Necker, since I know that you might suffer me to expiate the slightest delinquency with my head."

"Not with your heart, too?" she asked.

"Oh, you have long since crushed that."

"But all of us must die. Could he not be prevailed upon to tell us, how, when, and where?"

"The 'how,' at bottom, is indifferent," replied Narbonne; "the 'when' might prevent us from enjoying the present time; but the 'where' cannot lessen our happiness. So let us inquire about the 'where.'"

Cazotte, whose eyes were still turned in the same direction, looked at both of them a while in silence; he then murmured in a very low voice:

"Not on French soil. Narbonne dies at Torgau, and M'lle Necker at Geneva."

The two looked at each other in surprise. "Torgau!" said Germaine. "I should like to know where that is. For God's sake, why should you go to such a place?"

"Yes, if I knew that," replied Narbonne, shrugging his shoulders, "perhaps I should not do so." Both of them laughed.

Meanwhile all the guests had risen in order to hear what was going on. The Duchess de Grammont stepped close up to Cazotte and said:

"Pray, M. Cazotte, prophesy to me, too, as noble a deed as you predicted to M'lle Necker. It would be exceedingly

9

agreeable to me to hear that one of these gentlemen should be indebted to me for his life."

Cazotte looked at the beautiful lady for a moment. He then said :

" I can only inform you, Duchess, that you will be taken, with many other ladies, in a cart, your hands tied behind your back, to the place of execution."

"And M'lle Necker will not accompany me?" she asked, laughing.

" She will not accompany you," he replied, his expression growing still more mournful, and his blue eyes filling with tears. "She will be far away. Her heart will suffer; she will seek assuagement; and that which will afford it to her will plunge her into an early grave."

" You treat me too cruelly, M. Cazotte," said the Duchess. " The prospect of that ride on the cart is decidedly unpleasant. I wish at least I had agreeable companions on the way to the place of execution."

" They will assuredly allow you a confessor, Madame," exclaimed Condorcet, jocularly; " and inasmuch as you will have a long time to prepare for the ride, you should betimes select a very amiable abbé for that purpose. If Cardinal Rohan should be acquitted by that time, you might count upon him; he is fond not only of love affairs, but of all sorts of adventures, and both of them united would crown his wishes. The same may be said of the amiable Talleyrand, who would certainly not shrink from the short journey from Autun to Paris in order to render you this important service. How soon shall we have to send for him, M. Cazotte?" he said, turning inquiringly to the latter.

" It is unnecessary," replied Cazotte. " The last person who will be accompanied to the scaffold by a priest,"—he hesitated for a moment, as if his lips refused to utter the words—"is Louis Capet, King of France!"

No sooner had those terrible words been spoken, than all the guests started up at the same time, and looked in dismay at the prophet, who, trembling at his own prediction, intended to escape from the room. But the Duchess de Grammont, seizing his arm, said, sneeringly:

"As you have predicted such a charming lot to me, sir, I should like to hear what you are going to do about yourself. Is it your intention to share my fate? Do you prefer taking poison like M. de Condorcet, or will the hand of some beautiful lady untie your fetters, as you prophesied in regard to M. de Narbonne and M. de Montmorency? Pray inform me of your fate, too, that I may know how, when, and where we may perhaps meet again?"

Cazotte eyed the beautiful lady gloomily, from head to foot, and then bowed his head, saying to himself in a monotonous voice:

"During the seige of Jerusalem a man walked on the walls of Jerusalem for seven days, and shouted in a terrible voice: 'Woe unto me!' A large stone hurled from the enemy's *ballista* then hit him and tore him to pieces."

Having addressed these words to the Duchess, he bowed to her and left the room.

No one detained him. A shudder ran through the whole company, and all hastened to leave the house without taking any further notice of their acquaintances.

CHAPTER VI.

THE YOUNG EMBASSADRESS.

THE Swedish Embassador, Baron de Stael, held to-day his first reception at his newly-furnished palace.

Thousands of wax-lights illuminated the spacious apartments; the most beautiful exotics transformed the ante-rooms into gardens, and impregnated the atmosphere with the sweet perfumes of the tropics. Servants in gorgeous liveries hastened in all directions, and stationed themselves at the foot of the large staircase in order to receive the guests and announce their names.

In one of the rooms a great many instruments were to be seen, and all preparations had been made for a concert. M'lle Huberti, the first cantatrice of the Grand Opera, had consented to entertain the guests with some airs from the opera *Dido*, which she sang with great skill and taste. The lady of the house herself had selected the airs; for the fate of the unhappy Queen of Carthage always excited her heartfelt compassion. To love a renowned hero seemed to her such a great happiness, that she regarded as quite explicable the Queen's determination not to survive such a loss.

Now all preparations for the festival were completed, and the Embassador walked through the still empty apartments with a slow step and gloomy air.

"Is my wife already fully dressed?" he said to the footman, who entered the room.

"I shall go and ask, sir," replied the footman, turning to leave the room.

"Request the Baroness, in my name, to come hither as soon as her toilet is finished," said the Baron. "I am looking momentarily for the arrival of the guests."

Shortly after, a young lady hastened toward him through the long suite of gorgeous apartments. She was dressed in light-blue velvet, and wore a kind of crimson turban on her raven hair, which fell in heavy ringlets on her shoulders. A set of precious pearls adorned her neck and beautiful arms.* Despite this very tasteful and expensive costume, and notwithstanding the charm which youth imparts, the appearance of the young Embassadress was by no means prepossessing. Her heavy frame, her broad lips, and coarse features imparted to her appearance an air of grossness which did not disappear till one caught a sunbeam from her magnificent eyes, and heard the words of her eloquent lips.

A man's gait corresponds to his character; for it is an expression of his being.

She hastened, as we said before, with somewhat too long steps through the long suite of apartments toward her husband, who awaited her approach, his hands folded at his back. When she was already quite close to him, she suddenly stood still, as if calling something to mind, assumed a stiffer attitude, and then, approaching him more ceremoniously, and bowing slightly, said to him:

"You see I am ready, sir."

Her husband's air had not changed at her approach; it remained as cold as before; only a tinge of irritation was added to it.

"Your gloves?" he said, eyeing her.

---

* "Portrait Inédit de Madame de Stael; par un Homme de Lettres."

She looked at her hands in surprise.

"Ah, *mon Dieu*, I have forgotten them," but in a tone betraying the vexation caused by his censure.

"And your fan?"

"I forgot it, too, in my hurry to join you here. I shall go and fetch the gloves and fan immediately."

So saying, she turned, and was about to leave the room.

"Never mind," exclaimed the Embassador. "It would be my duty to render you this service, if it were not absolutely necessary for me to stay here. So permit me to send my *valet-de-chambre* for the gloves and fan. Etienne, hasten to the dressing-room of the Baroness, ask her gloves and fan of the lady's maid, and tell her I hoped she would henceforth attend more carefully to her duties."

The valet hastened to carry the order into execution. Meanwhile Baron de Stael turned again to his young wife.

"I hope you will bear in mind the rules of etiquette, Madame, which I have taken pains to inculcate upon you, and you will carefully observe the ceremonial in accordance with the rank of the persons whom we shall receive to-night?" he asked, coldly.

"I believe I remember all your instructions on this subject, Baron," she replied, gently.

"You will oblige me by trying to avoid violating those rules in any respect, Madame," he continued, in the same measured tone. "It would be very disagreeable to me if all Paris should laugh at us to-morrow."

"You attach considerable importance to the opinion of the world concerning very trifling matters, sir," she said, taking the gloves and fan which the valet presented to her.

"The rules which etiquette imposes on aristocratic society are by no means trifling matters to persons of noble birth," he replied, sarcastically. "They are the tomb-stone of a good education."

"Fortunately more liberal views begin to prevail in this respect," she said, quietly. "The young noblemen of France have proved in the American war that they hanker after another kind of glory than that of being perfect courtiers."

"The young noblemen will soon recover from their silly enthusiasm, Madame, and then be ashamed of the spurs which they won in struggling for a bad principle. You may depend upon it."

"Pardon me, sir, if I prefer not to give any credence to your prediction; for it would grieve me to doubt the ultimate triumph of a cause for which all my pulses are throbbing."

"Then I advise you to drink a great deal of lemonade in order to get rid of those unfeminine sentiments."

"You use the words feminine and unfeminine so often, sir, that I should like to have you explain to me what qualities you wish to designate by these adjectives? At times, I must confess, the strange idea has occurred to me that you call feminine only natures about which little or nothing can be said."

"Your supposition is quite correct, Madame. We ask of a woman only that she be handsome and try to please us."

"In that case, nature has imposed upon us a task no less agreeable than easy," she said.

"Agreeable, yes; but if it is easy, is somewhat doubtful, inasmuch as it requires charms which many a woman does not possess," he said, significantly.

"Count d'Artois!" shouted a footman at this moment.

"Monsieur and Madame Necker!" shouted another; and while the Embassador went to meet the royal prince, his wife hastened to her parents, and embraced her father with streaming eyes.

Necker turned pale on seeing this outburst of grief on the part of his beloved child. He glanced anxiously about the room, which was rapidly filling with guests, in order to see if anybody had noticed the occurrence.

"My child! my own daughter!" he whispered to her, in deep emotion. "For your father's sake, compose yourself!"

She raised her head.

Her glance met the ray of an eye which, radiant like the eternal sun, gazed with infinite tenderness into hers, and spoke to her the mute language of sympathy, which caused her heart to tremble with unspeakable joy. "Birth and beauty are not the highest boons," cried a voice in her breast, exultingly, and her tears ceased flowing. She gazed into her father's face and smiled.

The Vicomte de Montmorency now stepped up and whispered to her:

"Make haste; the Duchess de Polignac has just been announced. You must receive her at the door."

She dried her eyes and followed the hint.

"I thank you," said Necker, heaving a sigh.

M. de Montmorency remained close to her during the whole evening, and whenever she seemed to be abstracted or inclined to leave her post in order to chat with her intimate friends, he encouraged her, by a word or glance, to persevere in the performance of her duties; and these little marks of sympathy on his part, reconciled her to the conventional phrases which seemed to her so frivolous and insipid.

At parting, Necker whispered to her that her conduct had gratified him exceedingly. She looked at him with a mournful smile and sighed.

He understood this mute reply.

"It will, perhaps, be best for her if we now allow her to publish her writings," he said to his wife, as they were driving home.

"I have always been in favor of it," replied Madame Necker.

"I was in hopes that the splendor of her new position would dazzle her, and calm her passionate heart; but such is not the case. That in which her heart takes no interest leaves her cold. Poor Germaine! She has too much understanding for a woman."

"And too much heart for a man," said Madame Necker, smiling.

Her husband laughed.

"But still they say that she bears a strong resemblance to me."

"That may be. What is called a virtue in you, becomes a vice in us."

"Because you are destined to represent weakness."

"A task which I now perform very satisfactorily," she replied, smilingly, alluding to her feeble health.

9*

CHAPTER VII.

THE CELEBRATED LADY.

NUMEROUS book-stalls, where all the new papers and pamphlets were kept for sale, were to be found on the ground-floor of the Palais Royal. The passers-by stopped there, looked at the titles of the new works, and bought copies of the periodical which contained articles particularly interesting to them. The public took the liveliest interest in everything that was printed, and these alleys had already become a library of passions.

Count Louis de Narbonne one morning left one of these stalls. He held a folded paper in his hand, and went with it to the palace of the Swedish Embassador.

It was quite early yet, but as a friend of the house he was admitted without being announced. Since Necker's daughter had married Baron de Stael, she had a writing-table of her own. She needed no longer to work standing and in a hurry, inasmuch as her father visited her only at certain hours, when she was not at liberty to occupy herself with her pen.

When Narbonne entered her room, she was writing busily; and as she was turning her back to the door, she did not notice his arrival. So he stepped close up to her without attracting her attention, and, looking over her shoulder, he read in a loud voice, in the manuscript which she had before her: "Montmorency: a tragedy in five acts.—Cardinal Richelieu."

She closed the manuscript hastily, pushed it aside, and turned.

"How impertinent you are! I knew it was you; no other man would have done that," she exclaimed, rising from her chair. "Such little traits of yours prove to me again and again, Narbonne, that you are unfit to become a republican. You want to wage war against inveterate prejudices; but you do not want to obey. You are averse to recognizing and honoring a man in every individual, and it is distasteful to you to be only a leaf on the tree. Ah, Narbonne, I wish I could inspire you with the passion that must fill our whole heart when it too ardently espouses a good cause! It is true, your language expresses precisely what I feel; but still it always seems to me as if your heart is not in what you utter."

"And you overwhelm me with this flood of reproaches so early in the morning, so unexpectedly, and so undeservedly, merely—if you will permit me to say so—because I rashly read a name which, it seems to me, is distasteful to you," he said, smilingly fixing his fine eyes on her.

She blushed. To conceal her confusion, she seated herself, and beckoned to him to take a chair beside her. He complied with her hint slowly, and, meanwhile, drew the paper from his pocket and unfolded it. She noticed it, and seeing that he was looking for a certain passage in the paper, she asked:

"What is it? What do you bring to us?"

"Notwithstanding my numerous faults, and the inexcusable coldness of my heart, I take some interest in the welfare of my friends; and to prove this to my esteemed Embassadress, I have hastened to her at the break of day in order to present to her an article criticizing the letters on the character and writings of Jean Jacques Rousseau."

"My God! what does it say?" she exclaimed, almost fainting with agitation, and changing her color every second.

"What should it say, but that you are the most gifted lady

of the century; that the profound understanding with which you appreciate Rousseau, despite your youth, is something truly marvelous; that your style is excellent; that you depict the character of the great and eccentric man with no less warmth than discrimination; in short, that you are such as your friends have always known you to be; and there is only one thing with which you are reproached on this occasion—" He hesitated to continue.

"For God's sake," she cried, trembling, "name it; tell me with what I am charged."

"That you refuse to do justice to Count Louis de Narbonne, and to grant him in your heart the place which he believes to deserve."

"Is that it?" she said, drawing a deep breath, as if a heavy weight had been lifted from her breast; while she held out to him her beautiful hand, which he pressed to his lips.

"You seem to make light of this charge?" he said, reproachfully, fixing his fine eyes on her, archly.

"I reject it as unjust," she replied, merrily, "inasmuch as my friendship has conceived such lofty plans for you that your wings must grow before you reach the summit on which I desire to place you."

"That I might fare like Icarus? No, no! The sun of your wonderful eyes has already heated me so much, that I shall take good care not to approach still other sunbeams; otherwise nothing might be ere long left of me but a small heap of ashes."

"The Parisian ladies would never forgive that to the sun."

"Had they not to forgive it to you?"

"Because the sunbeams of my eyes did not consume anything about you. You have remained the same irresistible Narbonne as before."

"You are sarcastic," he said, looking at her languishingly.

"But while we have been wasting our precious time in chatting in this manner, you might have read the article to me," she exclaimed, suddenly returning to the former subject. "Is my name mentioned in it? Does it speak of me personally? Or does it refer to me only in general terms as the authoress of those letters?"

Narbonne shook his head disapprovingly. "Oh, how unfortunate I am to languish at the feet of a celebrated lady!" he exclaimed, with ludicrous pathos. "She robs us of the most beautiful moments by occupying herself with the object of her ambition, to which she refuses to raise any of us men."

"You try my patience very severely, Narbonne," indignantly exclaimed Madame de Stael, jumping up in order to snatch the paper from his hand. "So you believe, then, that it is a matter of no consequence to be exposed to publicity? To have to expose your defenseless breast every minute to the thousands of arrows which malice may aim at it with impunity? Did not my father's experience show me the high price at which such fame has to be purchased? And he is a man. It is easy to injure a woman; she cannot protect herself; she cannot hide behind deeds which slander is unable to deny. Nothing defends us but our very weakness. That which renders us assailable, makes us strong, and enlists the forbearance of your sex. But when you wish to mortify us, you are not magnanimous. You seize then every weapon you can find, and do not see the wound which your cruelty enlarges a thousand times. Already I feel the pain I shall suffer when everybody aims at this poor heart, and even my life-blood cannot save it any longer."

So saying, she leaned back in her easy-chair, and closed her eyes, from which large tears rolled down her cheeks.

" Is it possible ! " cried Narbonne, dismayed at the sight of these tears, which, like so many men, he could not bear, " that you with your clear understanding should see ghosts in broad day-light? There is not a word of censure in the whole article. It lavishes the most flattering praise on you. When Necker's daughter appears in the capacity of an authoress; when she writes in so lofty a spirit as these letters breathe, she will not only create a sensation, but excite admiration; and not only France, but the whole world will pay homage to her. Your distinguished father has reason to be proud, not only of his own fame, but also of the fact that his daughter is the most gifted woman on earth. That will crown his wishes."

She had raised herself up while he was speaking, and a smile kindled her features.

" Ah, Narbonne," she exclaimed, " you are mistaken about my father. He was averse to my obtaining any fame as an authoress; and if he encouraged me to publish my work, I believe he wished that literary fame should indemnify me for the disappointments of my wedded life. The woman who marries a man whom she does not love, is entitled to constant commiseration. I should compel my daughter to choose the husband whom she loves.* The wife's place is only by the side of her beloved husband; she must see the world only through the eyes of her hero; her vocation, her duty, is to go only arm in arm with him, and to act for him. She cannot live for a principle, she cannot devote herself to a great cause, except through the husband whom she has chosen. My father was unable to bestow this happiness upon his daughter; so he tempted her to go in search of fame."

Narbonne paced the room in great agitation. Suddenly he stood still in front of her.

* " Madame Necker de Saussure."

"If we had got acquainted with one another but one year before we did, our lot would have been a different one. What would you not have made of me!"

She looked at him laughingly for a minute.

"So it is only for that reason that you wished to have known me at an earlier day?" she exclaimed, smilingly. "In that case you will not lose anything, Narbonne; for what your friend can do for you, shall not be wanting to you. But, for my part, I should like to know a man who could make something of *me*."

"Of you?" he asked, wonderingly.

"Of me," she repeated. "I want to be lifted up, and not to lift up."

At this moment the folding-doors were thrown wide open, and the footman announced, "Baron de Stael!"

The Swedish Embassador entered the room with a stiff, dignified step, bowed coldly to Narbonne, and then turned to his wife.

"I have been congratulated on the fame which my wife has gained as an authoress; am I at liberty to accept these congratulations, Madame?"

"You are, sir," replied his wife, in the same ceremonious tone.

"At any rate I hope that you will be liberally rewarded for your labors," he continued, with frigid sarcasm. "After once entering the ranks of the laboring classes, you are certainly entitled to your wages."

"The booksellers of France will pay me as liberal a salary as your King gives to you, sir. The only difference is that you have to serve him here, while they serve me here."

"You draw a very singular parallel. But then, we learn to overlook a great many things you utter."

He bowed as frigidly as before, and left the room.

"Ah, Narbonne, what a prejudiced world this is!" exclaimed Madame de Stael, as soon as they were alone. "Like Jean Jacques Rousseau, I am no longer able to find any place on this earth. I do not know where I belong. And since authorship weighs me down, I am more at a loss than ever before. The women scold me for being what all of them would be, if God had endowed them with talents. What they are unable to perform, they censure in others, simply because the grapes are sour. And as regards the men, they are ready and willing to praise the insignificant talents of a woman ; only she must not venture upon fields where they rule supreme. If we are bold enough to place ourselves beside them, they instantly withdraw their favor from us. Alas, it is a sad fate to be a woman! I pity my own sex profoundly. Naturally destined as we are to make our happiness dependent upon the other sex, we find it to consist of tyrants, and, what is still more unbearable, our love enables them to rob us of honor and fame. I perceive every day more and more clearly how difficult our position is toward you ; especially, too, because we women refuse to stand up for one another, and because every one is ready to throw a stone at her sister. But a truce to complaints. I will go to my father and rest on his bosom, draw from his love fresh courage to live, and steel myself thereby, so as not to feel the thorns hidden under the roses of female fame. Will you accompany me to him, Narbonne?"

They found Necker a prey to unusual agitation. M. de Calonne, the then Minister of France, had lulled both the court and the whole country, by dint of golden promises, into sweet dreams, from which they were now cruelly aroused.

The Notables had been convoked, and the Minister declared in his opening speech that he had found France hopelessly lost, and had therefore not hesitated to loosen the last plank from under the feet of the Government, because the emergency would lead to reforms, which a large part of the nation would certainly resist under different circumstances.

Hitherto, he said, every Minister, including Necker, had deceived both the King and the people; his *Compte Rendu*, which had excited so much admiration, was calculated only to mislead the reader by its round sums.

This charge had made the most painful impression on Necker. He could not bear to have his character attacked in this manner, and he hastened to justify himself in a reply to Calonne. His daughter warned him against imprudent precipitation on this occasion, inasmuch as he might be called upon to take Calonne's portfolio. But he turned a deaf ear to her remonstrances.

She said nothing about her own affairs, not only because the above-mentioned event overshadowed them, but also because she forgot herself whenever she saw her dearly-beloved father a prey to pain and mortification. His affairs were soon to grieve her still more intensely.

Necker presented to the King a memorial in which he proved the correctness of the *Compte Rendu*, and at the same time caused this document to be printed and circulated all over Paris. This step displeased Louis the Sixteenth so much that he ordered him to remove to a place at a distance of at least forty leagues from the capital.

When the news of this measure reached his daughter, she was perfectly beside herself. Her lamentations filled the whole palace; her servants were at a loss to know how to render her assistance; they were unable to comprehend the misfortune which caused this boundless grief. Banishment was at that time something so unheard-of that Madame de Stael could not

bear the thought of seeing her beloved father endure the punishment of a criminal.

As soon as she had composed herself, she ordered her carriage and repaired to the house of her parents.

"I shall accompany you, father!" she said to him, as soon as
she caught sight of him. "Your daughter will share your exile.'

Necker looked at her in profound emotion. He knew how
dearly she loved Paris, how much need she had of society, how
difficult it would be for her to leave the friends, the daily intercourse with whom was almost indispensable to her. His urgent
remonstrances against her making this sacrifice to him were
wasted: his objection that her husband would miss her, only
brought a mournful smile to her lips.

"M. de Stael is content if he retains the palace which we
inhabit," she replied, with a slight sneer. "He will not miss
me if I leave him the comforts of his home. But my friends
will now be able to prove to me if they really esteem me, by
visiting me in our exile."

Necker had finally to yield to her wishes, and she then hastened to prepare for her departure.

In the evening, a small circle of acquaintances assembled in
her room. They conversed cheerfully, and it was not until
the moment of parting was at hand that her heart grew heavy
at the thought that she might not meet them again for a long
time. She mournfully shook hands with all of them, and
nodded a parting greeting to them; for her heart could not
find any words at this sad moment. Now all of them had left
her, except Montmorency. He stood irresolutely at the door,
and tried to find suitable words with which he might take leave
of her. Madame de Stael stood before him, pale and silent.

"Germaine!" he said, in a low voice; "may I accompany
you?"

"If my father will give you a seat in his carriage," she replied, in a voice tremulous with agitation, and dropping her eyes in order to conceal the tears which filled them.

"So we shall not part yet. *Au revoir*, then."

She gave him her hand, which he pressed respectfully to his lips.

When the door closed after him, she stepped to the window and listened to the rolling of his carriage. "He has stood the test," exclaimed a comforting voice in her breast, and she gratefully lifted her clouded eyes to the stars. She then walked a long time yet through the silent rooms, and caused the memories of the pleasant hours which she had spent there to pass once more through her mind, before she turned her back on surroundings to which she had accustomed herself, and which were therefore dear to her.

CHAPTER VIII.

In a large, well-lighted room, whose windows opened upon a garden, there were several persons assembled around a tall, slender, and still youthful-looking lady, whose ghastly paleness indicated that she was in very feeble health. A nervous twitching of her features, and especially of her mouth, betrayed her sufferings when she did not speak. But, although death had already laid his heavy finger on her forehead, she might have still been called beautiful.

M. Necker had returned to Paris in order to try a second time to save the State, and his wife received this evening the congratulations of her acquaintances, who hastened to express their satisfaction at this event. Paris, nay, the whole of France, exulted with them to-day, in the hope that a new era would dawn upon the suffering country.

Madame Necker smiled kindly at her husband; for she read in his eyes how greatly he rejoiced to find that his mission was not yet at an end. He who has once tasted the power which a vast field of action gives to the man who is able to conceive and execute great plans, will hardly ever return very readily and willingly to the petty cares of his own hearth.

All had seated themselves round a large round table, covered with a large, gold-fringed, velvet cloth. A silver chandelier with twelve branches shed its light on them. The young Swedish Embassadress had chosen her favorite seat, beside her father. Her radiant eyes were fixed on him while he spoke, as if she wished to read his opinion in his features rather than learn it from his words.

Necker was now a man of forty-five, and, therefore, at the height of his intellectual strength. He seemed to be taller than he really was, owing to his heavy-set form and the erect manner in which he always turned his head to heaven. His high, angular forehead beamed with intelligence, not a wrinkle was to be seen near his eyes, and his whole appearance was that of a man whom time has not yet touched. The glance of his eyes, especially when they fell on his daughter, was so gentle and tender, that too great mildness might have been ascribed to his character. Lavater consequently said that there was something feminine about him, aside from his great power of combination, with which the fair sex is endowed but very rarely.

Madame Necker alone had not seated herself; for some time past her feeble health had not permitted her to remain quietly at the same spot. So she wandered from one of her guests to the other, and sought to enliven the conversation by pleasant sallies and striking remarks, and to give direction in keeping with the spirit and inclination of the visitors.

Madame de Stael had not yet acquired this art. Endowed with the warmest of hearts, she always remained too much a child of the moment to choose her words cautiously before they escaped her lips; and, without intending to offend others, she did so in a thousand little ways, before she herself was aware of it. Such was the case to-day, too.

She had just begun to relate the story of the portrait of Charles the First, which Count d'Artois had secretly put into the King's room on the day when Necker had advised the King to convoke the States-General. She entirely overlooked for the moment the fact that this anecdote could not be very agreeable to her father's ears. Carried away by the subject, as was always the case with her, she related the occurrence with the utmost animation, which was even enhanced when she depicted the blindness of the members of the royal family, who regarded as fatal a measure which was proposed only for their salvation, and would have certainly led to it, if they, instead of submitting to the stern voice of necessity, had taken the step of their own accord.

"My father alone showed them the road to salvation," added the young Embassadress, in a loud voice. "And what do you believe Count d'Artois did when he found that his hint was disregarded? He caused the picture to be removed from the King's room, and had placed in its stead a copper-plate, representing the execution of Charles the First."

"What did the King say to it?" inquired Marmontel.

"Nothing. He disregarded the second hint, too. But is it not strange that ignorance, nay, stupidity, should be coupled with so much audacity?"

Here she was interrupted by the entrance of a new guest. The footman announced the Marquise de Sillery, and the Countess de Genlis entered the room.

There was a general pause.

Madame Necker went to meet her, took her by the hand, and conducted her to a seat, where she conversed with her in the most polite and amiable manner. Madame de Stael did not follow her example. She rose and joined a group of gentlemen. Since she had visited the celebrated lady at Belle Chasse, her opinion about Madame de Genlis had undergone a marked change. At that time her mother had taken her to the chateau in order to present her to the authoress of "Adele and Theodore," a book which had just filled her with the liveliest enthusiasm, and made her desirous of paying to the authoress the tribute of her heartfelt admiration. With how much enthusiasm had Germaine bowed to the celebrated lady, and kissed the hand to which she was indebted for so many delightful hours. The years which had gone by since that time had cooled this ardor.

Madame de Genlis had publicly spoken with much bitterness of the Necker family, and had frequently censured its members. Her remarks were communicated to those at whom they were aimed, and Madame de Stael had not forgotten them. She easily forgave personal insults; she knew neither hatred nor revenge when she herself was concerned; but such was not the case when her parents were attacked and insulted. An injustice done them, wounded her too deeply to ever be forgotten again. She, therefore, now took her father's arm, and caused him to participate in the conversation into which she had entered. Without being beautiful, she seemed to be so to-day. She wore a plain black-velvet dress, which set off her beautiful arms and hands to great advantage; her eyes beamed with filial love and ardent enthusiasm for all that is good and beautiful; and youth with its hopefulness and happiness shed over everything that inimitable charm which later years never are able to assume. She was to-day the archetype of Corinne.

The conversation between Madame de Genlis and Madame Necker had meanwhile become quite animated, and Voltaire's name fell on Germaine's ears. Dominated, as usual, by the impulses of the moment, Madame de Stael was anxious to know what the two ladies were speaking of, and she immediately approached them in order to listen to their conversation.

Madame de Genlis seemed to be greatly excited, her beautiful eyes were radiant, and her quivering features showed that the subject of the conversation was by no means indifferent to

her. Madame Necker, in her plain white dress without any
ornaments, gentle and well-poised in tone and bearing, presented in every respect a marked contrast to the distinguished
lady who was standing before her, and dissented from an
opinion which Madame Necker had uttered in regard to the
illustrious author of the *Henriade.*

"You say that Voltaire was simple-minded," said Madame
de Genlis; "that assertion is at variance with what I saw
about him at Ferney, especially with that abominable picture
in which he sits enthroned in the clouds, while his feet rest on
a number of persons who incurred his displeasure. He hung
this abominable daub in his study, and banished a magnificent
Correggio to the ante-room, where no sunbeam could fall on it.
Ott, the German painter, was with me at Ferney. He saw
that abomination, too. Do you call that simple-minded?"

"You have misunderstood me, Madame," replied Madame
Necker. "When I said simple-minded, I meant that he was
natural and unaffected. To prove this assertion, permit me
to read to you a letter which he wrote to me in regard to his
statue."

She hastened into the adjoining room and returned presently with a letter, which she read aloud. It was as follows:

"I am sixty years old, Madame, and have scarcely recovered from a dangerous malady. M. Pigalle, I have been told,
is to take a cast of my face; but, Madame, is it not, first of all,
necessary for that purpose that I should have a face? You
would now scarcely find the place where it formerly was; my
eyes lie three inches deep in their sockets; my cheeks resemble old parchment thrown loosely over my bones; and my few
teeth are loose in my mouth. What I tell you here is not an
expression of my vanity, but simply the truth. Never has a
man in my condition sat to a sculptor; M. Pigalle would

think that we intended to mock him, and I must confess that my self-respect does not permit me to expose myself in this condition to his view," etc.

"Now," asked Madame Necker, after reading these lines, "the man who wrote these lines, I should think, must have been entirely exempt from vanity."

"I am sorry to say," replied Madame de Genlis, smiling, "that you have not converted me yet. I regret to differ with you, because I esteem you too highly not to derive the utmost satisfaction from a concurrence of our views; but this time I am unable to change my opinion."

She said this in such an amiable and polite manner that Madame Necker, who felt quite flattered, offered her hand to Madame de Genlis, as if to bring about a reconciliation, and begged her to forget their little quarrel.

"Considering my admiration of every great talent, you must forgive me for warmly espousing the cause of absent persons, and still more that of the dead," she said, kindly. *Les absents ont toujours tort.* Death strengthens every friendship, inasmuch as it immortalizes the virtues of the person who is dear to us; it immortalizes them at least in our hearts." *

"We may be content if we leave such friends behind," politely replied Madame de Genlis, approaching the door, in accordance with the custom prevailing at that period, as quietly as possible, in order to leave the room without disturbing the company.

As soon as the door had closed after her, several persons, especially Madame de Stael, began to censure her in unmeasured terms. They laughed at Madame de Genlis' visit to Ferney, and at the reception with which she had met at the hands of the Patriarch. All the world was familiar with the particulars

---

* "Mélanges de Madame Necker."

of this curious scene, and everybody took pains to deride the lady by commenting on it sarcastically.

"How could Voltaire receive so illustrious a lady without shedding tears of profound emotion?" said one.

"Did she not wear ostrich plumes?" asked another.

"Which fell from her head as she had to go on foot up the long alley," said a third.

"But, if I am not mistaken, he kissed her."

"Yes, but rather coldly; what good did his kiss do her then?"

"How could he remain unmoved when she was accompanied by Ott, the German, who is said to be a celebrated painter," interposed Madame de Stael.

Madame Necker said nothing, but glanced reproachfully at her daughter. She disapproved this tone, and could not bear to see society revenge itself in this manner on an absent person. "If death should overtake a person in this occupation," she would say, "with what face would he appear in eternity?"

M. Necker knew his wife too well not to perceive that this conversation was distasteful to her, and, always anxious to shield her from painful impressions, he adroitly managed to break off this conversation.

"Madame de Genlis is perfectly justified in complaining of Voltaire," he said. "What did Raynal say in his sermon? The truths of christianity are so self-evident that Jupiter himself would have been converted if he had heard them."

"Excellent!" exclaimed Madame de Stael. "Excellent! Our dear Raynal would have robbed us by his eloquence of the whole Olympus, if the gods had been his contemporaries. *Le Silence du Peuple est la Leçon des Rois!* How astonished his audience must have been at such striking arguments. The hurler of thunderbolts a penitent of the Abbe Raynal!"

"The ruler of Olympus would have burdened his discreet ears with a rather long list of sins," said Necker, smiling.

"But we must not forget that Jupiter had delayed his con fession a long time," remarked his wife, who was very glad of the turn which the conversation had taken. "This reminds me of the old lady who came to Fontenelle and addressed him as follows, 'Well monsieur, we still live !' 'Hush,' said Fontenelle, laying his finger on his lips, 'let us say no more about it, Madame; they have forgotten us.'"

"That would not be so bad," exclaimed Marmontel, laughing. "It would not be so disagreeable to me to play at hide-and-seek with death. I do not say, like Maupertuis, that I am as pale as death, and as sad as life. I still like this world, despite its imperfections."

"Your appearance shows that very plainly," replied Necker, casting a jocular glance on his corpulent figure. "But this reminds me of a still better anecdote. A Capuchin preached one day on the marvels of nature. 'My brethren,' he said, 'you wonder at many things, while others that are by far more important seem not to affect you at all. Thus, for instance, you admire the sun, and appreciate the moon but very little; and yet the latter sheds her rays over you when the darkness of night would frighten you; while the sun shines only in broad daylight.' His hearers thenceforth treated the moon more justly than before."

"The Capuchin was a *savant*," exclaimed Madame de Stael. "We ought to have made him acquainted with Buffon."

"Great errors always go hand in hand," interposed Madame Necker. "Do you not know the story of the drunkard who invited a guest, and, wondering why he did not touch the bottle, asked him why he did not drink? 'Because I am not thirsty,' replied his guest. 'In what way do you differ, then, from the animals which drink only when thirst torments them?' Of course he was unable to answer that question."

"I think so, too," said Necker. "The man was right, although he was wrong. He reminds me of Buffon, who knows the universe, but not the world. Now, the more extensive our knowledge, the more easily do we reach those limits where we are unable to make replies."

"Or shall not get any either," interrupted his daughter. "When God gave reason to man, he called upon him to battle with truth and for truth. Providence, therefore, has laid into our hearts all necessary incentives to research and investigation. It wants us to be inquisitive and active. It may be imposed on us for the welfare of all to risk our thoughts, our most precious capital, in a great cause; but it is difficult to find and rivet in the labyrinth of our mind the point which marks the truth; hence, we say, to err is human."

Her eyes were radiant; she raised them in her enthusiasm to the ceiling, and seemed to have entirely forgotten her surroundings. Her father drew her gently to him, and gazed at her with a tender expression.

"As with truth, so it is with our happiness," she continued. "All of us seek it, and who would confess that he has found it? There are on earth still many flowers which we are destined to gather; but the most beautiful flower is withheld from us; its color is red, deep red, and its name is love."

She had uttered these words as if absently. Suddenly a deep blush mantled her cheeks; she turned her eyes in great confusion toward M. de Narbonne, whose glance she caught, and, as if ashamed of herself, concealed her face on her father's breast.

Madame Necker knit her beautiful brows slightly.

"You have not yet redeemed your promise, M. Marmontel," she said, turning to the poet, " to recite to us the beautiful ode which you have written on the death of Leopold, Duke of Brunswick, who perished in the waters of the Oder."

"Pray excuse me," replied the poet. "I assure you I have forgotten the lines."

"Oh, Marmontel, how could you permit your memory this perfidy in regard to so beautiful a subject?" interposed Madame de Staël. "The deed of that Prince is so great and noble, that a crown would have henceforth been an inadequate ornament to his brow. What a great heart of his it was that impelled him to plunge into the waters of the raging river in order to rescue two victims! And this great heart had grown up in the shade of peace! When Cæsar entered a boat and braved the howling storm, he was on his way to Rome, the mistress of the world. He risked his life on the waves on which he might win a throne. But Leopold of Brunswick! What was beckoning to him when he plunged into the Oder? Only two poor wretches who stretched out their arms toward him. He heard their cries, and the noble young man braved the perilous storm without asking if he should have to do so alone. And he did so alone. His hands were full of gold; he offered it to the bystanders. Oh Marmontel, Marmontel, pray recite your verses!"

All had listened to her with growing agitation. The profound emotion depicted on her features, the tears gushing from her radiant eyes, had added to the excitement of the guests; and when she now paused, she trembled with inward emotion, and none of her hearers were able to make immediately a suitable reply. Madame de Staël had risen while she was speaking; now she seated herself again beside her father, leaned her head thoughtfully on his shoulder, and was absorbed in the remembrance of the event which had taken place but a few weeks ago. When she looked up, she met her mother's eye, whose

disapproving expression made a painful impression on her
She dropped her eyes and left her seat. M. de Montmorency
followed her, and pressed her hands to his lips with an expression of ardent admiration. She sighed.

"You know what it is to sacrifice one's self to a great idea,"
she said. "Men find satisfaction and happiness in them. But
I have need of love, fervent love, and all around me is so cold,"
she added, in a low voice.

Her mother's manner and peculiarities weighed her down all
the time; they impeded her at every word, at every step in
her life-path; and, although her position had now seemingly
become an independent one, her heart constantly yearned for
her father, who alone loved and understood her, as she wished
to be loved and understood, but who, like herself, in his conduct toward his wife, had to submit to certain restraints which
were the more painful to him as he felt that they grieved his
child.

Three of the most excellent persons who highly esteemed
and tenderly loved one another were unable to find in their
domestic circle that happiness which beckoned to none of
them without. It is not circumstances that render us happy
and contented; it is not wealth or poverty that gnaw at the
peace of our heart; but the source from which our happiness
springs lies hidden in the inmost recesses of that heart. We
may change our relations to men, but we cannot change ourselves.

Supper was now announced. How often had this message
already made peace between the contending parties, especially
when they talked politics, which was now but too often the
case. Madame Necker was decidedly averse to these excited
discussions in her *salon;* she would not allow the ladies to participate in that which should have engrossed the thoughts of

the men alone. Madame de Stael, however, took the liveliest interest in them; a worthy pupil of Rousseau, she was an en thusiastic advocate of the liberty and happiness of the people; her great heart would not acquiesce in the idea that power and right were inseparable, and that only those had to obey the laws who were unable to defy them. Justice for all, was her motto.

Champagne sparkled in the glasses; witticisms were uttered here and there; the guests chatted merrily about theaters, litera- ture, and art; they called Shakespeare a barbarian, and pro- nounced his dramatic works coarse and in bad taste; while "Attila" was praised as a master-piece of poetical genius; and in the meantime the pale and beautiful lady of the house moved around the table like a fragrant shade, dropping a word now here, and now there, and always taking pains to keep the conversation within the bounds of etiquette and propriety.

Madame Necker recited the description of a character, and the guests had to guess who it was that was thus portrayed—an exceedingly popular pastime at that period. Usually a mem- ber of the company was selected for this purpose, and adorned in the most flattering manner with many virtues. Several per- sons then improvised and offered toasts. Marmontel displayed his brilliant talents on such occasions to great advantage; the word *champagne* being proposed to him, he immediately im- provised the following lines:

> " Champagne, ami de la folie,
>   Fais qu'un moment Necker J'onblie,
>   Comme en buvant faisait Caton ;
>   Ce sera le jour de la gloire :
>   Tu n'as jamais enr la raison
>   Gagné de plus belle victoire."

All praised him, laughed at the clever allusion, and drank to Necker's return to the Cabinet.

CHAPTER IX.

THE WINTER OF 1788.

THE winter of the year 1788 was at hand. An exceedingly dry summer was followed by short crops and hard times. The Government offered liberal prizes for the importation of grain, and stimulated it by all means at its command. The Seine froze over already on the 26th of November, and Reaumur's thermometer was at $18\frac{3}{4}$ degrees below zero.

The oldest inhabitant could not call to mind a winter of equal severity and duration.

The high price of bread caused more and more discontent; several riots took place, and the police had to interfere very often, and to protect the bakers from violence. Such was the general dissatisfaction that everybody was intent on exposing abuses, and nobody showed the necessary patience to wait for the introduction of reforms.

Necker had not returned to the cabinet in a joyous and hopeful spirit. He now came to his daughter with a clouded brow. She discovered his depression at a glance. He sank exhausted into an arm-chair, and rubbed his hands before the blazing fire in the fire-place.

His daughter seated herself beside him.

" This abominable distrust ! " he now burst forth. " The King has appointed me Minister against his will, which he lets me feel now at every step, and Marie Antoinette even insists on being present at the sittings of the Cabinet. If France is to obtain relief in this manner, her prospects are extremely gloomy."

"I told you already that the Queen received me more frigidly than ever before," replied Madame de Stael; "and, to add to my mortification, she even prefers M. de Brienne's daughter to me in the most offensive manner. It is evident that she detests us."

"It is very unfortunate for her that she does. If she had confidence in me, how much useful advice I might have given her! At all events, I should have told her the truth. The people now loudly call her Madame Deficit, and unjustly charge her with having brought about the enormous indebtedness of the country. That unfortunate necklace affair had made her already exceedingly unpopular; but the people now dislike her more than ever before. Last Sunday the boys shouted under her windows: 'We are going to St. Cloud, in order to see the fountains and *l'Autrichienne.*' The King is in a perfect tempest of perplexity. In his rage he has already broken several chairs, but no bright idea has occurred to him yet. He is unable to adapt himself to the spirit of the times. He sees the people shake the royal prerogatives, and perceives also that the nimbus which formerly surrounded the nobility of birth has vanished; and the prospect frightens him."

"Because he has been blind so long," exclaimed Madame de Stael. "Did he not himself, both in Holland and America, arm subjects against their sovereigns? And now he is surprised to see that the people of his own country at length awake to consciousness, and that those who hitherto were slaves, rise to the dignity of freemen. I cannot tell you how glad I am that the States-General are to meet next May."

"You are aware that I do not share your opinion in this respect," said Necker. "In order not to forfeit the confidence

of the people, I could not oppose a measure which my prede-
cessor had proposed. But I am afraid of the consequences.
The people of France are not, like that of England, capable of
self-government. As a nation it is too young; it is still in the
leading-strings. Every form of government, moreover, has its
advantages, provided it performs what it promises. With
honest men at the helm, the Ship of State will always remain
in the right channel."

"But what if the honest men are wanting? In that event
we must be protected by a constitution, and I hope we are
now in a fair way of securing the welfare of France by legisla-
tive means."

"You are hopeful because you see the difficulties only at a
distance. A Minister's daughter shares only the advantages
of his position.* She basks in the sunshine of his power; but
that power at this juncture imposes a terrible responsibility on
his head. I do not see how I can be useful to France under
the present circumstances; I think that honesty is the best
policy, and I detest crooked ways; and yet, in a struggle with political faction, it is advisable not to disdain the means by which
we might secure the assistance of their leaders. My aversion
to such a policy cannot but lead to my downfall. Ah, why
did they not give me the fifteen months of the Archbishop of
Sens! † Now it is too late."

"It cannot be too late," exclaimed Madame de Stael,
warmly. "I have confidence as long as you are at the helm
of government. Only you yourself must not lose heart."

"When I resigned my portfolio the first time, I censured myself severely for the step, inasmuch as I knew that no one was
able to replace me. Now, many persons might act more vig-

---

* "Madame de Stael: Considération sur la Révolution."
† Necker's own words.

orously in my place. I lack confidence, and hence, also, the strength to carry my views into execution. Last night I reflected a great deal as to what satisfied men; and I found that, at bottom, only stupid persons are happy. When I have again leisure to live for myself, I shall complete my essay on the happiness of blockheads.* Stupid persons really still wear the garb in which God clad Adam and Eve in Paradise; the cloak under which they hid their nakedness were the pleasant illusions, the sweet confidence and self-opinion which we censure now because we do not appreciate their value. A stupid man is never guided by experience; even though he should reach an age of two hundred years, he would still see the world in the same rose-colored light. He draws no inferences, follows up neither cause nor effect, does not look beyond his nose, and looks forward to the future with the *naïveté* of a child.

"Stupid persons never doubt their own strength and sagacity. They are inaccessible to the ideas of others, stick obstinately to their views, and pass opinions on everything with the utmost promptness, because it seems to them that everything has but one side.

"Hence, stupidity is a source of great happiness, and a considerable advantage. But when the slightest idea about the true sources of his happiness occurs to the stupid man, his happiness is at an end, his self-love is disturbed, and he will never again repose any confidence in himself. He is then a very wretched creature."

Madame de Stael burst into loud laughter at this serio-comic definition.

"In truth, I almost wish I could get rid of what little understanding I possess," she exclaimed, merrily; "because it de-

* "Le Bonheur des Sots." Necker's sprightly essay.

prives me of so many joys; but, above all things, I should like
to make the very embodiment of stupidity Prime-Minister of
France, in order that a man of true self-reliance might be at
the head of government. But I am afraid the capitalists
would not throw their money into his lap, nor would stocks
rise thirty per cent. twenty-four hours after his appointment.
Such an event occurs but once in history, and fortunately I
was the daughter of the man in whom this extraordinary confidence was reposed."

Necker, greatly pleased with this clever little flattery, smiled,
and held out his hand to his daughter, who pressed it warmly
to her lips.

"Now I have to communicate yet a singular event to you,"
he said. " You are aware people said that the gifted Bishop
of Autun had assisted Minister Calonne in his labors; and
others said that he was the author of an excellent pamphlet
defending my *Compte Rendu*. What surprised me in regard to
the latter, was the fact that the pamphlet in question was sent
to me anonymously, while the Bishop of Autun at the same
time caused me to be asked if I would permit him to make
my acquaintance. I must confess that I was anxious to see
the versatile man. Well, then, this morning, accompanied by
Condorcet, he called at my office."

"And what impression did he make on you? Did you like
him?" asked his daughter, eagerly.

"I am glad I was a man," replied Necker, with a sarcastic
smile; "for his reputation is by no means undeserved. Prepossessing and gifted as M. de Narbonne is, Talleyrand eclipses
him in every respect. I have invited him to dinner. So you
will be able to get acquainted with him."

"I must confess that I am anxious to do so," replied Madame de Stael. "A young Bishop who, to all appearance, is

engaged only in stealing the hearts of the ladies, suddenly meddles with financial affairs. That is very singular indeed."

"And that is not all. He spoke very gravely about our political affairs, and dwelt on the necessity of curtailing the prerogatives of the clergy and nobility. Inasmuch as he combines both classes in his person, and cannot but lose heavily if we curtail their privileges, his disinterestedness astonished me beyond measure."

"Nor do I repose any confidence in such disinterestedness," exclaimed Madame de Stael.

"And yet Lafayette has shown that one may honestly prefer the welfare of the people to one's own interest."

"The exception here only proves the rule. I am sure Montmorency is animated by the same spirit. He wants merit alone to mark the various grades of society."

"I think St. Jerome was right in saying that wealth alone was the origin of nobility; and it is certainly a hazardous undertaking to dig new beds to the rivers," said Necker, gravely. "But the everlasting discussion of this question will lead to nothing. We are unable to create new social relations by laws and revolutions; they must spring up from the ground; and if the soil is healthy, the fruit will be in keeping with it. First let us regulate the disordered state of our finances and give bread to our people, and then we shall see about further reforms."

He rose. His daughter accompanied him to the ante-room, and, at parting, promised to dine with him.

M. de Stael did not accompany her to the house of her parents. He dined with M'lle Clairon, for whom he had purchased a very fine villa, which he had not yet paid for. His wife being very wealthy, he spent her money very freely, until Necker finally put an end to his extravagance. Ger-

maine did not find an affectionate protector in her much older
husband; she had to pursue her path alone through the bustle
and commotion of Parisian life, where at this juncture no head
was any longer in its right place, and all minds had fallen a
prey to a fermentation which mixed up all ideas prevalent up
to that time in a motley chaos.

The young Bishop of Autun was introduced to the Swedish
Embassadress.   A certain apathy which characterized his
whole being was to be noticed, too, in the somewhat languid
expression of his blue eyes, as he fixed them searchingly on
the face of Madame de Stael, of whose talents he had heard
the most enthusiastic accounts.   In fact, after the appearance
of her work on Rousseau, no one ventured any longer to question her ability, and many persons now visited Necker's house
only for the purpose of getting acquainted with his daughter.
It was suspected that the young bishop had caused himself to
be introduced to the Minister for the same reason; the expression of his face, however, did not betray this desire.   With
that reserve of manner which imparts an indisputable superiority to men who are able to assume it, he addressed a few
polite words to the young Embassadress, and, when they were
about to go to the dinner-table, he courteously, but rather
coldly, offered her his arm.

"You dislike my class, and I venture to seat myself beside
you," he said, with his half sarcastic, half malicious smile, which
added to the prepossessing expression of his face, while his
delicate white hands coquettishly unfolded his napkin.

"You are mistaken," she replied, fixing her radiant dark
eyes on him, as if she wished to penetrate the inmost recesses
of his heart.   "Every class has legitimate claims to recognition; only it must not attempt to over-step the bounds set
to it."

" Well, did *I* do so ? " he asked, fixing his fine eyes on her.

" My remark was not a personal one," she replied, evasively because she deemed an allusion to his love affairs unbecoming. " I spoke as the daughter of a statesman. The people is very severe in its criticisms of priests and soldiers.* It demands that both of them should scrupulously perform their duties. Soldiers are expected to be brave, and clergymen are required to be pious; these classes derive from these qualities the respect that was paid to them; and they forfeited it by no longer being brave and pious. Hence, both the nobility and the church have lost most of their former authority."

" That is the reason why I have joined the third estate," replied the Bishop, with a significant smile.

" But, it seems to me, without renouncing the other two."

" *La moitié vaut mieux que le tout*, is my motto."

" And mine is to devote myself entirely to every truth."

" What a tempting prospect for the man on whom you will bestow your affections."

" It is true, I am warmly attached to my friends, and am constant in my devotion to them, inasmuch as I know why I love them. Our mutual affections are not blind."

" One might expect that of your understanding, but should, at the same time, be afraid of your penetration."

" I am not very rigorous toward others. Only he who wishes to hold intercourse with me, must not be entirely destitute of mind. In that case, I can get acquainted with him in a day, as well as in ten years."

" Your words fill me both with hopes and fears. At all events, it is best for us to be executed immediately, when the sword hangs once over our heads."

" What do you want me to reply to this remark ? "

---

* " Considerations sur la Révolution Française."

"Whether you will receive me, or close your door to me."

"The latter would be something new to the admired Bishop of Autun," she said, laughing; "and, even though I should not injure myself by taking such a step, I should like to do so in the interest of my whole sex. But where our self-love is concerned, justice is not always triumphant."

"The flattering result of your decision fills me with just pride," he replied, gratified at what he had just heard. "I shall humbly lay my thanks at your feet."

"So you intend to stay here in Paris, M. de Talleyrand?"

"At least for the present."

"I can imagine that you have always longed to go to the capital," she exclaimed. "It is only here that men live, while the rest of the world seems to vegetate. I pity every talented man who is not permitted to participate in solving the great problems which the times propose to us. By the way, have you read my father's new work, '*Sur l'Importance des Opinions Religieuses?*' It is a wonderful book. The seven years of his exile were not fruitless; he has turned them to account like a sage, and devoted himself to the welfare of humanity like a youth. Had it been possible for me to admire and love him still more, his self-abnegation could not but have enhanced these feelings of my heart. To belong to the best and noblest of men is such an exalted happiness, that I should be an ingrate if I should quarrel about other things with fate, which, in this respect, has blessed me too richly not to grudge me other blessings from its cornucopia."

"But I am unable to see that any blessings are wanting to you," said her neighbor; "you seem to be a favorite of fortune in every respect."

Madame de Stael sighed.

"I am a woman," she said, sadly. "Our sex does not exist

for its own sake; it is our task to win the love of men who never bestow their whole heart upon us. Now, we are happy only if we are loved as dearly as we love. All other ends of life are, to us, mere palliatives, by which we assuage our grief, soothe our heart, and silence our rebellious desires."

"You can never be justified in practicing this kind of resignation," replied the fine-looking prelate, with a significant glance.

"But I am compelled to do so," she cried, mournfully "Nor could it be otherwise. I did not choose my creed, I did not select the relations by which my life-path was to be regulated, and the cold word *duty* written over the gate leading to my happiness. Providence indemnified me by giving me my father. May it not frown on me for longing to have received other boons, too, at its hands!"

"It indemnifies us for everything," said the young Bishop, significantly.

"It gives us no compensation for a clear conscience, such as Calvin's teachings require of us," she replied, gravely; and M. de Talleyrand dropped his eyes before the stern glance of hers.

CHAPTER X.

THE PROCESSION.

On the 4th of May, 1789, the sun rose radiantly over the city of Louis the Fourteenth. All France was in Paris, and Paris was in Versailles. The States-General were to be opened next day, and it had been determined that a religious solemnity of imposing character and common prayer should prepare the minds of all for this momentous event. The day was very fine, and the splendor that was displayed on this occasion had never been equaled before. But what constituted the grandeur of the spectacle, were not the crowded and sunny streets, not the glittering lines of bayonets, not the beautiful ladies assembled at the windows, not the rich draperies floating from the balconies, not the grave voices of the priests, not the peals of the bells ascending to heaven amidst the flourish of the trumpet, the roll of the drums, and the loud shouts of the officers—no, the most impressive and novel feature of the ceremony was the language that was used throughout the city, the drift of the remarks which passers-by exchanged everywhere, the animation of all faces, the proud expression of all glances, the unwonted self-consciousness of everybody's bearing, the feverish excitement of the minds, and the manly and impressive agitation and solicitude of a nation visited by liberty.*

At the appointed hour the Three Estates left Notre Dame in order to repair in solemn procession to the Church of St.

---

* Louis Blanc.

Louis, and the multitude hastened up from all quarters to witness the imposing spectacle.

Madame de Stael stood at a window beside Madame de Montmorin, the wife of the Minister of Foreign Affairs, and gave the reins to her joy at the fact that the representatives of the French people had at length been convoked.

Madame de Montmorin listened to her a long time in silence, and finally replied to her gravely.

"It is very wrong in you to rejoice to-day; this day will bring terrible calamities upon France and upon us." *

Madame de Stael, deeply moved by these words, made no reply for several moments. She looked inquiringly at the Minister's wife; but it was not written on her features that she would ascend the scaffold with one of her sons, that the other would drown himself, and that her husband would be slain during the September massacre.

The procession meanwhile moved past. It was headed by the Franciscans and the clergy of Versailles, in whose midst marched the band of the royal chapel. Then followed the deputies of the commons. They were dressed in plain black cloaks; but the firmness of their step, and their calm, dignified bearing, showed sufficiently that they represented the bones and sinews of the nation.

Next came the deputies of the nobility, resplendent with their rich embroideries, white plumes, and costly laces; and then, separated from the bishops in surplice and camail, the plebeians of the Church—the curates.

The King and Queen accompanied the Host which the Archbishop of Paris carried under a magnificent baldachin, the strings of which were held by the Counts of Provence and Artois, and the Dukes of Angoulême and Berry.

---

* "Madame de Stael: Sur la Révolution."

Marie Antoinette looked very pale; and when no popular acclamations greeted her, but only shouts of "Orleans for ever!" were heard, an expression of disdain quivered round her beautiful lips, and, in order not to sink to the ground, she had to seize the arm of the Princess de Lamballes.

"Poor woman!" exclaimed Madame de Stael, repeatedly, on seeing this, and a tear rolled down her cheeks. "How she must suffer! How dreadful this walk must be to her!"

"What? You pity her who dislikes you so much?" asked her neighbor, in surprise.

"The fact that she is prejudiced against me cannot make me insensible to the sufferings of a person who, moreover, belongs to my own sex;" she replied, gently.

On the following morning, the National Assembly was opened amidst imposing ceremonies. A hall hitherto used for the amusements of the court had been arranged for this purpose, and a dense throng of spectators soon filled it to suffocation. On an estrade in the back-ground, under a baldachin, was to be seen the throne, decorated with golden fringes; beside it stood an easy-chair for the Queen, and chairs for the Princesses of the royal family. At the foot of the estrade stood a bench for the Secretaries of State, and, in front of them, a table covered with violet velvet.

Louis the Sixteenth had himself directed the arrangement and decoration of the hall. On the eve of events of such magnitude, the decoration of the hall engrossed his thoughts; and the rest of the time he spent in learning his speech by heart, and trying to improve his delivery of the most pointed sentences.*

A number of amphitheatral rows had been reserved for the select audience and the ladies, dressed in the most gorgeous and fashionable style. Here sat Madame Necker beside her

---

* Madame Campan.

daughter. The latter gazed upon the scene with eyes radiant with joy, and it was not until the King seated himself on the throne that a vague apprehension stole upon her.

She noticed how agitated and pale the Queen was when she entered the hall some time after the appointed hour. She watched her with anxious eyes during the whole of the ceremony.

Beside the Ministers of the Robe and the Ministers of the Sword stood M. Necker in a plain civilian's dress—the only Minister who had disdained to appear in a courtier's costume. Enthusiastic applause greeted him. His daughter, whose heart trembled with joyous pride, would have liked to join in the acclamations which were repeated again and again.

Now Mirabeau made his appearance, and a murmur ran through the Assembly. He knew its meaning, and went to his place with a proud step, and an air plainly indicating that he would make them rue this reception.

Louis the Sixteenth wore the large royal mantle, and a plumed hat, whose ribbon sparkled with brilliants, and whose agraffe was the Pitt diamond. When he entered, the whole Assembly rose; but Mirabeau whispered to his neighbor, " There is the victim ! " *

The King delivered his speech, and then the Chancellor of State and M. Necker addressed the Assembly. All three of them expatiated on the improvement of the financial condition of the country, while the Assembly was looking for the draft of a constitution. Madame de Stael noticed with the liveliest regret that the deputies were exceedingly disappointed at her father's speech, the gist of which was the phrase " *Ne soyez pas envieux du temps.*" She trembled on reading an unmistakable expression of disappointment on all faces, and she

---

* " Memoirs of Weber."

could hardly refrain from jumping up and calling out to them, "Have patience! Do you not hear the words, '*Ne soyez pas envieux du temps?*' My father is the King's Minister; he must act in accordance with His Majesty's wishes, and is not at liberty to propose what the latter disapproves. As an honest man, he cannot do otherwise; for to prove recreant to the confidence reposed in him, would be impossible to him."

She left the hall in an agony of impatience, and hastened back to her house in order to converse with her friends about the great event of the day. She found that Madame d'Aiguillon had preceded her thither. The latter came to meet her in the utmost agitation, and complained of the disappointment of her hopes.

"*Ne soyez pas envieux, du temps,*" replied Madame de Stael, partly to soothe her, and partly to defend her father in his own words.

"How can you expect us to be patient," replied Madame d'Aiguillon, "when the moment has come at length that calls upon the nation to govern itself? What we do not now demand, what we do not now wrest from the Government, we shall never obtain. We must have a constitution; we must insist on this safeguard being granted to the nation. A constitution alone can save France."

"You are aware that I fully concur in that opinion," replied Madame de Stael; "but I cannot allow you to charge my father with causing your disappointment. He acted in accordance with his character. He had to subordinate his individual wishes to his sense of duty. He is unable to compel the King to be and do what the times demand of him. He does not stand firm, but is swayed by a thousand influences; and what is obtained from him in one minute, may be lost again in the next one. My father is unable to manage him, and you can hardly expect that he should have such a decisive influence over him. We should concentrate all our efforts on prevailing upon the deputies to demand a constitution. You have friends among them, friends whom you are able to influence, and so have I. Madame de Coigny, Madame de Castellane, and Madame de Luynes are likewise surrounded by a small circle of men who share our views; and if we join hands, we shall certainly be able to exercise considerable influence upon the course of events. We should even make the daily press subservient to us if it should be able to promote our ends."

Madame d'Aiguillon concurred in these views, and hastened home in order to receive her friends. As soon as she had left, Madame de Stael went to her boudoir and took up a pamphlet which she had received that very day. The author, M. de la Luzerne, Bishop of Langres, one of the most gifted men of France, proposed in it that the three chambers should be transformed into two, and that the high clergy and the nobility should form the first chamber, and the low clergy and the representatives of the people the second;—so deeply impressed was everybody with the necessity of bringing about measures that would exclude all needless debates, and immediately solve the great problem with which they had to deal.

She was still reading the pamphlet when Mathieu de Montmorency was announced.

"Is it so late already?" she said, when he entered the room; "I have not yet dressed for receiving the guests who are to dine with us."

"I have preceded the others in order to converse confidentially with you. What do you think of the King's speech?"

"Ah, let us not speak about it," she exclaimed, mournfully; "I know it has not satisfied anybody. Passion does not count the obstacles, and hunger does not wait. I may be frank

toward you, Montmorency, and confess to you that I look forward to the future with great anxiety. Two dreadful evils
menace us: bankruptcy and famine. How are they to be met
but by thorough-going measures ; and how are they to be taken
as long as three chambers can veto every bill ? To improve
our financial condition, the clergy and nobility must be taxed
as heavily as the people, and their inherent selfishness will
never permit these two classes to consent to such necessary
measures. Their vote will neutralize that of the third estate;
we have not made a single step forward ; nay, what is worse,
we hopelessly stand on the brink of a precipice."

"How can you believe that the nobility would reject so just
and equitable a measure," exclaimed M. de Montmorency,
proudly throwing back his fine head. "One should be ashamed
of being a nobleman, if that class possessed so little nobility of
the heart. What! A nobleman should not be willing to con-
tribute his mite toward sustaining the crown, when the lowest
classes of the nation readily perform this duty toward their
country ? A nobleman should cling to his *sous* like a Jew, and
refuse to make any sacrifices in such an emergency ? That is
impossible, utterly impossible; and if I should be mistaken,
I should no longer be proud of my name. I swear to you, as
sure as my name is Montmorency, should my class ever sin so
heinously against my class, I myself, the heir of this ancient
name, shall move to divest a nobility that displays so little
nobility of all its prerogatives, and I shall then be first to join
the third estate."

He had drawn himself up to his full height as he uttered
these words ; his eyes shot fire ; his cheeks glowed ; and he resembled an enthusiastic Antinous. Madame de Stael gazed at
him with admiration and profound emotion, and her dark eyes
filled with tears, as, holding out her hand to him, she said:

"To be animated with such generous feelings, my friend, is a great blessing, and I should like to offer a libation to the gods for this sublime minute. Nothing is so grand as a glance into a human soul truly ennobled by nature."

"You attach too much importance to sentiments, which, at bottom, are quite natural," replied the young man, modestly; "and I hope you will discover yet a great many noblemen who share my opinions."

"I am afraid there are very few of them," said Madame de Stael. "I am quite familiar with the spirit of the nobility at court; it will submit, if it cannot help it; for it is accustomed to obey the sovereign; why, then, should it not also yield to necessity? But it will not do anything from conviction. Now, the provincial nobility is still worse; it clings to its privileges as if it had received them at the creation of the world, and speaks of its titles as if the whole world paid homage to them; when, in reality, no one but their neighbors has ever heard their illustrious names. All the arguments of these provincial noblemen may be reduced to the three words, ' *C'était ainsi jadis.*' If you reply to them that the times are changed, that the world does not stand still, that nations cannot go backward, but must go forward, they smile incredulously, and their expression indicates that nothing would convince them. There is nothing they despise so much as knowledge and intelligence."

"Your criticisms are very severe," mournfully replied the young man, laying his hand on his forehead; "but I cannot but admit that they are true in many respects. But how are we to bring about a change for the better? What are we to do in order to save what can be saved?"

"The National Assembly must demand a constitution," exclaimed Madame de Stael, emphatically. "We must have a

11

government similar to that of Great Britain. When the younger son of a lord becomes a commoner, the aristocracy can no longer treat the third estate with haughty disdain, and encroach upon its rights, which, in a measure, are its own. The clergy, however, must not represent itself; in that case, we should have to strengthen the influence of the third estate again, and that would also be dangerous. As I said before, the English constitution seems to me well-nigh perfect; and the closer we imitate it, the greater will be the happiness of France."

At this moment the Bishop of Autun was announced.

" I came a little earlier to congratulate you on M. Necker's masterly speech," he said, on entering the room, and bowing to her in his black robe, which sat so well on him. " He did not promise anything, and thus kept the whole game in his hands. I admired his tactics sincerely."

" They were those of an honest man; of a responsible Minister," exclaimed Madame de Stael, warmly. " But, above all things, tell me now if we may count upon you. Will you bring your influence to bear on your class, in order to cause it to pursue a course of moderation and conciliation? Will you act honestly for us and with us?"

He smiled significantly.

" What would one not do in the name of the most gifted woman on earth," he said, gently. " But you refer to my class. Unfortunately," he added with a sigh, "I combine three classes in my person, so that I am at a loss to know to which you alluded."

" You are at a loss to know it, M. de Talleyrand? You do not know it, because you do not want to know it. You are a deputy of the third estate, and at the same time you wear the dress of a high prelate. You are a nobleman, and, as such,

occupy a place close to the throne. You are courted and consulted by all parties; every one believes to have won you as
long as you listen to him; but as soon as you leave him, the
conviction dawns on him that your smile was no pledge. Put
an end to this game."

The handsome Bishop smiled all the time.

"And what do you want me to do, my adorable friend?" he
asked, in a gentle voice.

"I only want you to break with the Court, turn your back
on the Duke of Orleans, and vote in the Chamber for a union
of the estates and a constitution."

"Now, I must remind you of the momentous words of your
illustrious father, '*Ne soyez pas envieux du temps.*' In breaking
with the Court and the Duke of Orleans I should not gain
anything but the impossibility to inform myself any further of
their plans and intentions. Had the Count d'Artois followed
my advice at an earlier day, when I was ready to join the
Court party on condition that the Duke of Orleans and Mirabeau should be sacrificed, the fall of these two heads would
have rid us of two powerful leaders of the enemy, and
smoothed our path. But as it is, and at a time when no one,
not even M. Necker, acts in keeping with Beaumarchais'
words, '*Oser tout dire, oser tout faire,*' I do not deem it incumbent on me to obstruct my path needlessly. Where
there is power, there is in the long run right, too; let us
wait and see. '*Ne soyez pas envieux du temps,*' says Necker.
Will his daughter be angry with me for walking in his footsteps?"

"Ah, M. de Talleyrand, if you would, if you could do so!"
she exclaimed, mournfully. "But I am afraid you are by far
too gifted, too objective to pursue the path of justice inflexibly
and inexorably. You continue visiting the Palais Royal. You

hold intercourse with Mirabeau. You feel at ease among men who profess the most objectionable principles."

"I am a little of an epicure, I admit," he replied, jocularly. "To enjoy myself the better here, I frequent those circles. The lower I descend there, the higher I ascend here."

"You cannot ascend very high, for never yet have I been able to fill you with ardor enough to declare that you would like to sacrifice yourself for an idea—to die for an idea."

"It is true, I should prefer living for an idea, if it is a beautiful one; nor am I entirely destitute of passion, as you seem to believe. So pray do not give me up yet!"

"You cannot do anything with him," she said, turning to M. de Montmorency, and shaking her head. "He always escapes by a back door. And yet, we cannot now accomplish anything by half-words and half-measures, by which inconsistent humanity always likes to defend its cause. We cannot reiterate too often, that individuals, as well as law-givers, have but moments of luck and power; they must resolutely seize them, for the same opportunity never returns, and he who allows it to pass by without turning it to account, will thenceforth meet with nothing but failure and losses."

At this moment, Barnave, a young lawyer from Dauphiné, highly gifted and destined to become an eminent parliamentary speaker, entered the room. Madame de Stael built great hopes on him, and welcomed him now in the most flattering manner. She then withdrew, in order to change her dress, and the footman announced soon after that dinner was ready.

M. de Stael received his guest with the air of a diplomatist, and performed the duties of hospitality with the frigid politeness peculiar to courtiers. The exalted position and great popularity of his father-in-law silenced his aristocratic pride; and the circle of guests whom his wife of twenty-three assembled around her, was such as not to justify the slightest objection on his part. Her extreme kind-heartedness had, moreover induced her to fulfill some of his most unreasonable wishes : so that, mindful as he was of her generosity, he did not want to prevent her from yielding to the great current of the times and wishing with all her heart to see her country happy and free As for himself, such a cause did not arouse his enthusiasm ; his life lay behind him. The brief span of life which was still left to him, he wished to pass in enjoying himself as much as possible—a task which grows the more difficult, the more the senses are blunted. Opposite to this man now sat his gifted young wife, and indulged, with her sympathizing friends, in golden dreams for the welfare of France.

CHAPTER XI.

THE FAMINE.

INTENSE excitement reigned in Paris and throughout France. The assembly of the States-General riveted the attention of the whole nation. All eyes were fixed on their proceedings, politics engrossed all thoughts, and even the most fashionable ladies had become ardent advocates of constitutional reforms.

The moment had come when talented men were able to distinguish themselves. Many a young lawyer who, under different circumstances, would have continued leading an obscure life in his provincial town, had now been called to Paris, where he displayed his brilliant abilities. At the same time, there were found in the ranks of the aristocracy many gifted young men who were deficient neither in knowledge nor zeal to serve their country, and who joyously joined those who advocated the rights of the people.

Madame de Stael was now surrounded by a brilliant circle. As the daughter of an almost all-powerful Minister and wife of an Embassador, her house was frequented by the most eminent men. Despite her diplomatic relations with the court, she was allowed to receive many representatives of the third estate, and consult with them as to the best means by which the royal prerogatives might be curtailed, and equality before the law established. She demanded a new constitution with the head of a man and the heart of a woman. She did not want to see the humblest persons excluded from their share in the fruits borne by civilization.

Necker's political demands did not go so far; still he did not disturb his daughter in the aspirations and plans which she advocated with heartfelt enthusiasm. She was at liberty to declare in favor of measures which his position as a Minister prevented him from supporting.

Dinner-parties, suppers, social parties, nay, the theaters, seemed to exist only for the purpose of giving the upper classes fresh opportunities for engaging in heated political discussions. On all sides were to be heard words referring to the strife of the various parties. Literature had lost its charms; the members of the Academy no longer cared to deliver addresses on such subjects.

Hopes of better times filled all hearts with joy and gaiety, and caused them to forget the perils and calamities of the moment. Madame de Stael went almost every day to the sittings of the Assembly. A great many other ladies from the highest circles of society were also frequently present; but none of them obtained as much influence as Necker's daughter.

Meanwhile a terrible foe put his pale face into the hall of the Assembly, and threatened to hinder their deliberations as to the future by the grave exigencies of the present; it was—hunger!

When the brilliant equipage of the Swedish Embassadress rolled through the streets of Paris, she could not but notice the thousands of wretches, who, covered with rags, stared at her with hollow cheeks and sunken eyes, and lifted their hands to her imploringly. What could she offer them to relieve such terrible distress?

She averted her face in dismay. Had matters come to such a pass before the Government had consented to grant the safeguard of salutary laws to the poor country?

Of these new laws she now hoped everything. Meanwhile the condition of the poor became more and more deplorable. The bad and scanty food engendered malignant fevers and other wide-spread diseases; on the market places and public squares encamped the shelterless multitude, like vast bands of gypsies. During the dark nights death crept softly through their ranks, and released those who were weary of their sufferings.

Whenever a wagon filled with provisions made its appearance, a riot took place; the multitude quarreled fiercely as to who was to obtain the food, and the military had to be called out to prevent violence and bloodshed.

When the sufferings of a people have reached this degree, an untoward accident or the machinations of an ambitious man may lead to the sudden overthrow of a throne.

Notwithstanding her political hopes, Madame de Stael was deeply impressed by the deplorable condition of the lower classes, and she would have willingly divided the courses of her sumptuous table with all the poor sufferers. Above all, those men who wished to honestly earn their livelihood in the sweat of their faces, seemed to her deserving of sincere compassion; for the morsel which charity gives to such men tastes bitter, very bitter.

She came to her father with streaming eyes, depicted to him what she had seen, and asked him what was to be done.

Necker had left no stone unturned to check the growing famine, but all his efforts were wasted. Deeply depressed, knitting his brows, and folding his hands on his back, he stood before his daughter, and was unable to give her the answer which she called for.

"My God! My God!" she sighed. "How fearfully this terrible sin against the people will have to be atoned for."

Necker replied bitterly:

"Ah, if this were the only sin! but if you could see the prisons; if you could cast a glance into those dungeons where so many are languishing without knowing what crimes they may have committed; if you could just once walk through the cells of Bicêtre, you would find out what a mockery human justice is. I am unable to help. When a house is everywhere on fire, a fire-engine can do but little good."

"She buried her face in her hands, and remained a long time standing before him in silence.

"Spring is at hand, and in the course of a few months there will be another crop; must, then, so many thousands starve to death before that time?" she asked, despondingly.

"God knows, my child," said Necker, drawing her to him and imprinting a kiss on her forehead. "I cannot but believe that such is the will of Providence, inasmuch as I see the evil here without being able to fathom its source."

On her way home her carriage was stopped repeatedly. The populace had gathered in front of the bakers' shops, and demanded imperiously to be admitted to them. Some bakers had sold them bread mixed with earth, which had caused dreadful sufferings to those who had eaten of it. The court still used the finest white flour; nobody suffered there from the famine which had stamped its fatal imprint on the livid faces of the poor wretches who were assembled here.

Madame de Stael was perfectly beside herself when she reached her house.

"Great God, how is all this going to end!" she lamented; and she then implored her friends to devise means by which an end might be put to the heart-rending sufferings of the people; but they responded to her only by shrugging their shoulders and shaking their heads.

Finally, she took all her money, and walked out on foot. She intended to bring relief to sick and suffering women, and forgot that money had lost its value, since bread could no longer be bought with it.

She wandered from street to street, as if she could not satiate herself with the sight of all this misery; her eyes followed this ever-varying scene, which hunger and extreme wretchedness had created.

She had unwittingly wended her way to the garden of the Palais Royal, when she suddenly heard the shout, "To the Abbaye! To the Abbaye!" The voice belonged to a young man, who, standing on a chair, was haranguing the multitude. Loud cheers burst forth as he now signed to the crowd to follow him. A vast concourse of people started with him, and Madame de Stael was carried away by the throng.

She glanced anxiously around in order to find an outlet. She had never before been in such a crowd, and ignorant as she was of its irresistible force, she vainly tried to escape from it.

Fortunately for her, the Bishop of Autun stepped at this moment from the Café Foy, and perceived to his utmost surprise the wife of the Swedish Embassador in the midst of the tumultuous crowd. He suspected at once that she did not follow it of her own accord; so he hastened to offer his arm to her, and take with her a position where the crowd might sweep past them. He succeeded in so doing.

As soon as they were alone, he said, "You have been beforehand with me, Madame. You have practically joined the third estate, while I was still reflecting whether or not it would be theoretically worth while for me to do so."

"You are always jesting, M. de Talleyrand, even when grim earnest is staring at you from faces distorted with hunger. But pray tell me, whither is this crowd hurrying?"

"Did the people not shout, 'To the Abbaye?' They want to deliver the eleven guardsmen who are imprisoned there; and who, it is rumored, are to be taken to Bicêtre to-night. The soldiers begin to mutiny; they refuse to submit any longer to the regulation disqualifying them to hold commissions in the army because of their plebeian birth. Old Ségur should not have revived this old law."

"It was an unaccountable blindness on his part to do so," exclaimed Madame de Stael. "When are these men going to perceive that talent, and not birth, should alone be regarded in filling those positions? But let us say no more about it to-day. Help me to devise means to deliver Paris from the horrors of this famine. I cannot tell you what I am suffering at the present time. If my tears would give bread to the poor, they would flow perennially over their dreadful fate."

"I can unfortunately serve you only with the proposition of confiscating the estates of the high clergy, and I am ready to be the first to surrender mine," he said, with the same graceful calmness, as if he were conversing on the most indifferent subject.

"My God, you would really do so?" exclaimed Madame de Stael. "Do you know, Talleyrand, that you have just uttered a great and noble word."

"You are able to obtain anything from me," he replied, with a sidelong glance from his fine blue eyes at the young Embassadress, who was gazing at him with an air of heartfelt enthusiasm.

"Ah, Talleyrand, I have often doubted your sincerity; but, if you will take this step, I shall beg you with all my heart to forgive me for distrusting the sincerity of your sympathies for France."

He smiled strangely. "I shall afford you a great deal more

joy than I have hitherto led you to believe," he said, signifi
cantly. "I shall prove to you that you have mistaken my
character."

"I will do you full justice," she exclaimed, in deep emotion ;
"only help me to save these poor, poor people from death by
starvation. Just look at the group yonder! How they are
staring at me, those women with their pale faces! Is there,
then, no baker's shop where we might buy bread? Ah, I wish
only to obtain the satisfaction to know that I saved those whom
I was able to save!"

"What you give to some, you have to take from others," replied Talleyrand, in the same tone as before, averting his face
with a slight shudder from the dismal group. "I am afraid
still worse scenes are in store for us. Free institutions cannot
be obtained without bloodshed."

"God grant that we may not have civil war!" cried Madame
de Stael, in dismay. "Concessions obtained by force may be
easily taken from us by the same means."

At this moment a carriage rolled past.

"That was Mirabeau," said Talleyrand. "He is sick. It
would be very fortunate for France if he were to die. It was
a deplorable oversight on the part of M. Necker not to try to
win Mirabeau over to his party."

"My father is no diplomatist. He always pursues the
straight road."

"And suddenly stands on the brink of a precipice."

When they reached her palace, they found Necker's equipage
at the door, and, in the *salon*, Madame Necker, awaiting her
daughter's return.

"I have just been at the hospital," she said. "There are so
many patients there, that all the beds are occupied, and typhus
is spreading very rapidly. I wished to request you to drive to

Bailly, and ask him to give us some public building where more patients might be placed."

While they were still conversing on this subject, Condorcet entered the room.

"I bring you here the latest literary production," he said, with his habitual sarcastic smile, presenting a paper to Madame de Stael. She unfolded it. It represented John Bull mounted on the British Constitution, and driven by an old gentleman, exclaiming: '*Laissez-les faire, à force de la faire galopper ils la crèveront.*'" *

"Always jest and earnest side by side!" exclaimed Madame de Stael, shaking her head. "At a moment when rebellion and famine knock at all doors and call upon all hearts for sympathy and mercy, there are men still capable of deriding the poor constitution which has made England great and happy."

"We must try to forget what we cannot help," interposed M. de Talleyrand. "So I propose that we say no more about bread and constitution to-day, but go to the opera. Gluck's 'Iphigenia' will be performed to-night."

The proposition was approved. Madame Necker, too, longed to repose, after witnessing so many heart-rending scenes. Notwithstanding the general distress and anxiety, the theaters still were crowded. Frequently, however, there arose quarrels among the spectators, which often came to blows. The exasperation of the lower classes was constantly on the increase; and inasmuch as they thought the boxes were occupied by the aristocracy, they disturbed the performance by throwing apples at some ladies with painted cheeks.

It is true, Necker's family were safe from such insults; but the sight of this brutality greatly depressed the mother and daughter, and they went home in gloomy spirits.

---

* "Mémoires de Condorcet."

M. de Stael had been at court. Contrary to his habit, he inquired if his wife was at home, and, upon receiving a reply in the affirmative, he entered her *salon*. She supposed that some unusual event had led him to her, and looked at him in eager expectation as he entered the room. He seated himself and talked about indifferent matters. This added greatly to her curiosity. She listened to him absently, and finally interrupted him by saying:

" Did the King say anything about my father to-day, or did he not mention his name ? "

" That would have been impossible," replied M. de Stael. " A man whose name is in the mouth of all France cannot be passed over in any conversation."

" So he praised him ? "

" By no means. The courtiers put on mysterious airs, and whenever Necker's name was mentioned, they cast singular glances at one another. Struck with their strange demeanor, I took M. d'Esprémenil aside, and asked him what it all meant. ''That he will be hung in less than three weeks' time,' he replied, with a confident smile."

"How can they do so?" cried Madame de Stael, turning pale. " All Paris would rise in rebellion if they should dare to touch a hair of my father's head."

" They will take good care not to do so publicly," replied M. de Stael, gravely. " They will arrest and cause him to disappear. The grave does not give up its dead."

Madame de Stael uttered a piercing cry on hearing these words. Breathless with terror, she rang the bell and ordered her carriage.

It was late already when she reached Necker's house ; but her father's solicitude for France kept him awake; and he stood musingly at the window and gazed into the dark night which shrouded so many scenes of heart-rending misery. Suddenly an arm was wound round his neck, and the radiant eyes of his daughter gazed up to him with tender anxiety.

"You here?" he asked, in surprise. "What brought you hither at this late hour? What has happened?"

"Let us flee!" she cried, breathlessly. "They are intent on killing you. Save yourself while it is time."

Necker turned pale, but he composed himself in a moment and replied:

"God is with me, and so is my conscience. So never fear, Germaine. When your father is protected by them, no one will harm him."

She gazed up to him with reverential admiration. "But what if they use force?"

"In that event I shall die as I must die, my child. Would you not rather have your father fall at his post, than desert it in a cowardly manner?"

She made no reply. Leaning her head on his breast, she wept a long time in silence; she then raised herself up, kissed him, and, without uttering a word, left the room.

Necker gazed after her a long time in deep emotion. "My child loves and understands me better than all the world," he said to himself, and he raised his eyes thankfully to heaven.

CHAPTER XII.

NECKER'S TRIUMPHANT ENTRY INTO PARIS.

THE oppressive sultriness preceding a violent thunderstorm rested heavily on the capital of France, and added to the discouragement reigning everywhere. Suddenly, in the evening of the 12th of July, the *Courier de Versailles* brought, in its eighth edition the news that the King had dismissed Necker.

It needed only such a spark to kindle the existing combustibles into a terrific blaze.

As soon as the newspaper in question appeared on the tables of the coffee-houses, and was taken up by the first readers, they rushed out into the street, and rent the air with lamentations, shouting that the country was in danger, and Paris was lost, inasmuch as Necker had left the capital.*

The performances at the theaters were interrupted; frantic despair seized the people, who rushed everywhere into the streets, and surged in dense masses toward the Palais Royal. Here the leaves were torn from the trees, and fastened as cockades to the hats; the crowd then brought the busts of Necker and the Duke of Orleans from a store, and carried both of them in triumph through the streets.

Night set in during these tumultuous scenes, but it was a tepid summer night, lit up every now and then by flashes of lightning, and which rendered it unnecessary for the Parisians to seek the shelter of their homes.

---
* Marmontel.

Thus the climate and season play an important part in the great epochs in the history of the world;—a shower, a snow-storm, and a widely different morning would have dawned on Paris.

Madame de Stael had entertained a few guests at her house, and, absorbed in an animated conversation, she had not noticed the commotion reigning in the streets, nor the anxious and in-quiring expressions with which her servants watched her. Now she was alone, and stepped to the window in order to breathe a little fresh air before retiring for the night. At this moment there fell on her ears the startling notes of the tumult raging through the streets. Turning very pale, she started back, and was about to leave the room, when M. de Montmor-ency rushed in breathlessly.

"Great God, what has happened?" anxiously cried Mad-ame de Stael, lifting her hands as if imploringly.

"You do not know it yet?" asked M. de Montmorency, in surprise. "You do not know why Paris is ringing the tocsin, and threatens us all with destruction and death?"

"I do not," she cried, beside herself.

"Because Necker has left Paris."

"Left Paris!" exclaimed Madame de Stael, trembling so violently that she had to lean against the wall in order not to fall to the ground. "He has left Paris without saying a word to me? That is impossible, utterly impossible!"

"And yet it is true. He departed in obedience to the King's order, without a word to anybody. He was at the dinner-table when the King's letter was handed to him. He read it without losing his self-possession, laid it aside, and finished his dinner. He then ordered his carriage, as he said, to take an airing, and entered it with your mother in the white dress which she wore at the time. We saw him drive away, and did not learn until an hour afterward that he would not return."

"Oh! I warned him!" cried Madame de Stael, mournfully. "Thank God, my worst apprehensions have not been realized. I was fearful they might arrest him, in order to protect themselves against an insurrection."

"They did not venture to do so, for there is no dungeon from which the French people would not have rescued him. The only way to prevent an outbreak, was to banish him. But, even now, the interference of the military is necessary to restore order and tranquillity. I should not wonder if the people should force the King to recall M. Necker."

"My poor father! Such is the gratitude of kings!" cried Madame de Stael, mournfully. "Yesterday, still all-powerful on the soil of France; he is hastening to-day to the frontier, a powerless exile! I shall follow him. He has more need of me in these gloomy hours than ever before. Nothing but love of his child can indemnify him for the bitter ingratitude of the world."

"Wait until he informs you where he has taken up his residence. I have been told that he has taken a circuitous route, in order not to be overtaken by the people."

"How generous! How magnanimous!" she exclaimed, enthusiastically, bursting into tears. "Even now he acts so considerately toward a king who never appreciated his worth, and, if he did, never was courageous enough to stand up for him. He sits in his palace, and must hear now that hundreds of thousands are mourning over the loss of a man who was a father to all of them. The voice of the people is the voice of God. Ah, Montmorency, how difficult it is for kings to rise to that true humanity which recognizes the rights of man!"

She paced up and down her spacious apartments a long

time, while the tumult outside was constantly on the increase. She heard shouts for arms, and the terrible notes of the tocsin, and pressed her trembling hand to her impetuously throbbing heart.

"My father is far away, and my husband, I do not know where.   How deserted I am, in spite of my brilliant position !" she sighed to herself, painfully impressed with the difference between ardent admirers of her genius and faithful friends in times of need.

Early next morning there arrived a courier with a letter from Necker, who informed his daughter of the route which he had taken, and requested her and M. de Stael to leave Paris as quietly as he had done himself.

She entered her traveling-coach with a heavy heart.   She had not taken leave of any of her friends, and did not know when she would return to the capital.   She caused her coachman to drive her through the most deserted streets, leaning in a corner, and shutting her eyes to the frightful scenes which were enacted in Paris.   When the capital lay behind them, and the green summer landscapes extended before them so quietly and smilingly, as if peace reigned everywhere on earth, she drew a deep breath of relief.   She left the horrors of civil war behind her in the city which she loved so dearly, and wept with all her heart over the fate which was in store for the Parisians.

Upon reaching Basel, she met her parents, who had arrived shortly before.   Necker was deeply dejected.   It was with extreme dissatisfaction that he looked back to his second term of office, which had terminated in so disastrous a manner.   He sat most of the time grave, and absorbed in his thoughts, and even the presence of his daughter was unable to divert him

However, he was not long to remain the only French exile. To his astonishment he learned, early on the following day, that the Duchess de Polignac had arrived; and a few hours afterward she requested him to visit her.

Necker smiled bitterly as he crumpled her note in his hand.

Like most of the ladies of the Queen, the beautiful Duchess had treated the parvenu with undisguised disdain, and often given him to understand that she did not consider him her equal. Necker, on his part, had severely censured her extravagance, and never forgiven her for accepting so many costly presents at the hands of the Queen.

Adversity was now to bring them together, which prosperity had never been able to do.

Necker learned from her that his removal had caused a terrible rising, in consequence of which many aristocrats had fled, and that the Queen had dismissed her in order to conciliate the people. "Without taking leave of me!" she added, bursting into tears.

When he returned from this visit to his family, not without inward satisfaction, Madame de Stael came to meet him with a triumphant air. "A letter from the King!" she exclaimed, exultingly. "He requests you to return to Paris."

Necker took the letter, but then he shook his head gravely and said, "I shall not go. I will not risk my reputation in a lost cause."

"A lost cause!" exclaimed Madame de Stael, in dismay. "You give up France when your hand is still able to guide her at pleasure, when your word is all-powerful there, and your name alone is sufficient to fill her treasury? You can do everything there; you can make everything of France, and she is lost only when Necker deserts her."

He contemplated his daughter mournfully. "It is your heart

that looks at the matter in this light," he replied, shaking his head. "Your head would cause you to think otherwise, if I were not your father."

"Believe me just once," she said, coaxingly; and she knelt down before him and pressed his hands to her lips.* "Yield for once to the prayers of your daughter, who lays the destinies of France into your hand. Look forward to the future with courage and confidence, and surmount with bold energy the objects obstructing your path, and you will be certain to achieve the most brilliant success. Just try again, my dear father, and you will attain your object. Place yourself, like Washington, at the head of the State. If need be, seize the helm with the strong hand of a Cromwell; secure respect for the laws by compelling everybody without distinction of rank to obey them; cause the King to grant constitutional liberties to the nation; and your name will be mentioned in history side by side with those of the greatest benefactors of mankind. The French nation loves and idolizes you; it longs for your return; do not desert it in this hour of need! Listen to its supplications, and do not avert your face from those who raise their eyes imploringly to you!"

Madame Necker joined them now, and likewise tried to persuade her husband to return to Paris. She felt how difficult it would be for him to renounce the exciting life of the capital, where his popularity made him the hero of the day, and admiration followed every step he made. Much as she herself had need of the quietude of Coppet, and greatly as she longed to live in that solitude with her husband, whom she still loved with all her heart, she was fearful lest the lonely life which he would lead there should cause him to regret not having embraced the opportunity which was now offered to return to Paris.

* Madame de Crequis.

The Minister now yielded to their joint prayers,* and his daughter ordered the carriage exultingly, that they might immediately set out for the French capital.

His return was hailed with universal applause and enthusiasm. In all the villages through which he passed on his way to Paris, the church-bells were rung; the field-laborers left their work in order to see him; the people unharnessed his horses in order to draw his carriage; women and children knelt by the wayside and implored heaven to preserve their protector.

This flattering reception did not leave him unmoved. He loved his fellow-men, and so he believed in their love. Madame de Stael sat opposite to him with radiant eyes, and was overjoyed at the enthusiasm with which her beloved father was greeted.

At a village-inn he fell in with Baron Bezenval, whom the people had arrested. He interceded immediately in behalf of that worthy nobleman, and begged the people to release him, and never to listen to the voice of revenge. To forgive and forget should be their motto, and regenerated France should obey only the dictates of justice and humanity.

Madame de Stael had performed the same route with widely different feelings two weeks ago. At that time she left behind her scenes of murder and arson, and looked forward to an uncertain future; now she brought peace and harmony back to Paris, which was agitated by all kinds of impetuous passions.

Necker stopped at Versailles in order to wait on the King. He appeared in deep emotion before Louis the Sixteenth. He had served him faithfully, and had been rewarded with exile. The thought of his ungrateful treatment prevented him from finding immediately the right kind of words in his address to the King.

---

* Madame de Crequis.

Marie Antoinette received with frigid politeness the Minister who had been forced upon her husband. Necker, in his
agitation, did not notice the Queen's reserve; and seized,
deeply moved, her hand, and pressed it to his lips. At this
moment, an expression of pain quivered round the lips of the
beautiful lady. The violation of etiquette mortified her, even
at this grave juncture, so much that it rendered her insensible
to the pulsations of a warm heart filled with sympathy for her.
So difficult is it for queens to feel like human beings.

Amidst the jubilant acclamations of the people, Necker
continued his triumphal journey to Paris. The whole population of the capital filled the streets; even the roofs were covered with spectators, and enthusiastic shouts of "Long live M.
Necker!" rent the air.*

When he arrived at the Hotel de Ville, the cheers grew even
more deafening than before. Necker alighted here, and ascended to the hall, in order to communicate to the municipal
authorities the steps he had taken for Bezenval's release.
Madame de Stael paused here for a moment, and gazed upon
the vast concourse of people who had assembled here in order
to pay homage to a man whom she called father.

It was the happiest moment of her life. If her soul had
panted for fame, her longings had been more than fulfilled
to-day. She felt that popular admiration and enthusiasm
could not be raised to a higher pitch.

Meanwhile Necker urged the authorities to grant a general
amnesty, and all hearts joined in this appeal for mercy; † the
whole people desired to participate in this act of general
clemency ; they embraced and kissed each other, and swore to
be friends for evermore. The great words *liberté, égalité, frater-
nité*, were uttered for the first time.

---

* "Madame de Stael: Sur la Révolution."   † Bertrand de Moleville.

Necker now stepped out in deep emotion upon the balcony opening upon the Place de Grève, and, accompanied by his wife and daughter, showed himself to the vast multitude in order to repeat in a loud voice the heart-stirring words of peace which he had spoken in the hall.

Thousands upon thousands of voices cheered him to the echo; not an eye remained tearless; even Madame Necker was profoundly moved; and while she fondly clung to her husband, and pressed his hands to her lips,* her daughter, overcome by her agitation, sank senseless to the ground.†

When Madame de Stael an hour afterwards awoke to consciousness in her house, she asked herself if she had not dreamed. She slowly called to mind all the scenes through which she had just passed, and built on them anticipations of a golden future, forgetful of the fact that the path leading to the longed-for goal was already marked by bloody traces, and that the terrible specter of anarchy would not be long in attaching itself to the still pleasant-sounding word *Revolution*, which had been uttered for the first time after the demolition of the Bastile.

Her eyes still red with the tears which she had shed for joy over the happy scenes of that eventful day, she sat in the evening opposite to her father, and spoke of the glorious time when the people would no longer suffer from hunger, and law and order would be re-established in Paris.

At this moment somebody handed to Necker a paper containing the news that the decree granting a general amnesty had been rescinded. Necker turned pale.

The Government repented already of what they had granted only four hours ago. This would be a sad blow to his own authority; his power would be merely illusory; and his return

---

* Bertrand de Moleville.   † "Madame de Stael: Sur la Révolution."

was evidently a *faux pas*. Henceforth he did not believe any longer in his mission.

Madame de Stael read in his face that something had deeply mortified him. But he kept silence. She was so happy, that he would not make her heart heavy at this joyous hour. Reminiscences of her childhood, of Voltaire and his laurel-wreath, arose in her mind. Then, as now, she had seen the people of Paris ascend to their roofs, and longed to achieve a similar triumph one day.

This thought caused her to sigh. Since politics overshadowed all other interests, she, too, thought only of laws and reforms, and no longer found time for literary employment. Her life was so eventful, it engrossed all her thoughts, and she could no longer think of writing books.

When she rode next morning through the streets, she noticed on all hats and caps the revolutionary cockade—that first symbol of popular rights. At the same time she learned that many aristocratic families, headed by the Count d'Artois, had left Paris. When she visited the spot where the Bastile—that ancient bulwark of the French monarchy—had stood, she vividly felt how deeply its demolition had shaken the foundations of France. She lingered a long time on the place, which now presented a desolate appearance, and a foreboding told her that a constitution could not be easily built on such a ground.

CHAPTER XIII.

THE DREAMS OF THE EIGHTEENTH CENTURY.

EVERY century is the bearer of certain ideas, which, after being followed up to their extreme limits, are suddenly deserted and exposed to the derision of coming generations. When we call to mind on what grounds France built her hopes at that time, we feel tempted to call them childish dreams; for we have long since advanced beyond the stand-points occupied by the politicians of that period.

Parisian society had never perhaps been so interesting and versatile as at that juncture, and despite the black clouds rising in the political horizon, the higher classes still gayly indulged in the wonted pleasures of social life. Every one now formed political views of his own; men and women joined certain parties; and, in trying to win adherents, all became eloquent, and hankered after popularity. They tried to convince those who differed with them not only by oral, but also by written arguments; and thus the number of pamphlets and journals was constantly on the increase, and every club and every party had soon an organ of its own.

Only Necker, as before, stood alone and confined to his own strength. His third term of office began with a defeat, followed by several others, all of which were entirely unexpected. In the day-time he was tormented with petitions, many of which wrung tears from his eyes; and in the night-time he would often start up from his bed in order to escape the terrible apparitions staring at him with hollow eyes, and crying for bread. His heart suffered so much that he fell a prey to a disease which afterward killed him.*

Whenever Madame de Stael went to her father, she met in the streets crowds of persons in quest of bread; in front of the bakers' shops they formed in long lines, and were admitted one after another. But she was still full of hope—hope in the ideal of her life; hope in the salutary effects of a liberal constitution.

Man lives on illusions. As soon as they are realized, he drops them and takes up new play-things.

Necker and his wife had taken up their residence at Versailles in order to be close to the King. His daughter was unable to accompany him; she had given birth to her first child, and Necker pressed his grandson, Augustus, with tears of joy to his heart. The more eagerly she read every word referring to her father. Every morning, as soon as she awoke, the newspapers were brought to her, and as poor Necker was now held responsible for a great many things of which he was entirely guiltless, her indignation at such unjust criticisms frequently knew no bounds, and her agitation in consequence often was so great that she fainted. The free press availed itself of its rights; it refused to acknowledge that it was admissible only in a nation whose moral sense was highly developed; for they looked upon France as the world; popularity, the idol to which all were now paying homage, had not yet lost its halo either, despite what experience had taught her in regard to her father.

The summer had passed by; of its verdure but little more had been seen than the leaves from the garden of the Palais Royal, which had been used as cockades. Who cared whether

---

* Bertrand de Moleville.

or not the roses had bloomed? Nobody devoted his precious time to the beautiful, and the arts were neglected; everybody wanted to know only if·the crops would be good, so that the people would have bread again, and that the deficit might be paid.

Autumn came, and the leaves fell from the trees; but the hopes of the people remained as green as ever. Madame de Stael received now only friends of the constitution, and took pains to influence them so that the constitution might embrace such features as she deemed peculiarly desirable. As a woman she could participate but indirectly in the great task of the regeneration of France, which she often felt very bitterly. It was very difficult for her to amuse and direct the enthusiasm of men sympathizing with her, and yet to prevent them from entering the wrong path. It is so difficult for men to understand that the ardent sympathies of a woman may be bestowed on a grave cause, and their vanity always is prone to transfer to themselves the interest which she manifests.

Every gifted woman meets with this difficulty; how, then, could Madame de Stael expect not to encounter it? She had loved Mathieu de Montmorency as she would never be able to love again. Such early love-affairs leave in the heart traces which never fade from it. She felt for him a certain tender attachment, which manifested itself in the delicate solicitude with which she always treated him; and his excellent character permitted her to convert this attachment into relations of friendship, which were to terminate only with her death.

The gifted and prepossessing Narbonne had endeared himself to her in a different manner. She had recognized his susceptibility for all that was great and beautiful, and it afforded her the most exquisite pleasure to play on the strings of his lofty and cultivated mind. To dominate such a char-

acter, gladdened her heart; to guide such a man, gratified both
her vanity and pride. As he, on his part, longed to attach
himself to a person who took pains to convince him of the
truth of· his views, the intercourse with Madame de Stael became daily more indispensable to him.

Beside these two friends, she now saw the Bishop of Autun
very frequently ; she could not boast, however, of exercising
any influence over him. When she had seemingly won a
victory over him, she found that he adroitly slipped from her
hands. Inasmuch as he never warmed in any cause, the advantage always remained on his side ; the more so, as Madame
de Stael always got excited in her argument, and allowed herself to be carried away by the subject which engrossed her
thoughts, so that she made a long speech on it before she
permitted her opponent to reply. This way of repelling contradiction often misled her as to the real views of her opponent, and prevented her from fully mastering her subject, in
consequence of just objections made to her argument.

One morning in October, when she was still reading the
news of the preceding day, her *valet de chambre* told her that
half the population of Paris had set out for Versailles in order
to ask bread of the King. Madame de Stael turned pale on
hearing this. If they intended to apply to the King, they
would not forbear to ask the same thing of Necker. She ordered the carriage and started immediately for Versailles.

She could not go thither by the high road, which was occupied by the riotous populace of Paris, but took a circuitous
route, by which she arrived at Versailles before the Parisians
had reached it. Her father was already with the King, and
her mother had followed him as far as the royal ante-room, in
order to share his fate, no matter what might befall him.

She hastened likewise to the royal palace.

Madame Necker sat on a tabouret in a window-niche in the
room of Louis the Sixteenth, while a number of courtiers
were assembled in various parts of the room, and conversed
with an air of intense anxiety.

Madame de Stael walked through their ranks and seated
herself beside her mother. The uneasiness of the courtiers
was constantly on the increase, until Lafayette made his appearance and promised them protection. "There is our
Cromwell," whispered a cavalier, as he entered the room.
"Cromwell would not come *alone*," calmly replied Lafayette,
and entered the King's room, where he found Necker, his face
buried in his hands, and his heart full of grief at the new cries
of distress uttered by the famished people.

It was not until midnight that the Minister and his family
retired. By a covered passage they repaired from the King's
apartments to Necker's residence, some of Lafayette's guardsmen having previously been stationed at both outlets of the
passage. They passed a dreadful night.

Necker shudderingly looked forward to the coming day, and
his wife and daughter likewise were a prey to the most intense
anxiety. He trembled for France, and they were fearful of the
dangers to which *he* was exposed.

At break of day Madame de Stael was aroused by a noise in
her room. She started up and saw a lady with whom she was
not acquainted. "Pardon me for begging an asylum of you!"
she said. "I am the Countess Choiseul-Gouffier. Assassins
have penetrated to the Queen's room; she has fled to the King.
There is no longer any safety for us in the palace."

"And my father?" cried Madame de Stael, jumping up and
ringing the bell.

M. Necker had already repaired to the King. Mme. de Stael
hastened to follow him thither. On the way to the palace

reports of muskets fell on her ears, and in the gallery her feet touched bloody traces. She averted her face, shudderingly.

In the ante-room she found the Garde du Corps exchanging cockades with the National Guard, and shouting, "*Vive Lafayette!*"

The young Embassadress passed courageously through the ranks of the soldiers, and entered the second room, where she found Madame Necker and many ladies and gentlemen of the court. The Queen entered the room at the same moment. Her hair was disheveled, her cheeks were livid; but her bearing was dignified. Her appearance made a deep impression. In obedience to the shouts of the multitude, she had stepped out on the balcony with her children, her features expressing disdain; but better counsels prevailed among her enemies, and she was greeted with cheers. When she withdrew from the balcony, she said, sobbing, to Madame Necker:

"They want to compel the King and me to go to Paris, and they are going to carry the heads of our Garde du Corps on pikes before us."

Madame Necker deplored this purpose of the populace with all her heart.

When the royal family finally left Versailles, Necker and his wife and daughter likewise returned to Paris by a circuitous and deserted route. They conversed but little on the road. The sun shone brightly in the cloudless sky, and nature was clad in her richest attire, but men did not feast their eyes on it. At the Bois de Boulogne, tepid zephyrs played with the first-falling leaves, and kissed caressingly the cheeks of the passers-by. Necker gazed thoughtfully upon the quiet landscape, while his ears listened already for the voices of the hundreds of thousands who were returning to Paris. His heart was overwhelmed with grief. What will be the end of all this? he asked himself.

Madame de Stael, noticing his depression, pressed his hand to her lips, and looked at him tenderly. "Courage, my dear father!" she said. "As soon as the constitution has been adopted, the people will cool down."

Necker shook his head, despondingly. The constitution would not furnish bread to the people.

When the King reached Paris, he repaired to the Hotel de Ville. Necker and his family followed him thither. The Mayor of Paris received him there.

"I return with pleasure to my dear Paris," said Louis the Sixteenth.

"And with confidence," added the Queen.

On the following morning, Marie Antoinette held a levee at the Tuileries. The whole diplomatic corps, and M. de Stael and his wife, too, were present, in order to render their respects to the royal couple. For a whole century the ancient palace had been deserted by the kings of France, and the eyes of the beholders fell everywhere on the traces of a past, which strangely seemed to mock the present. The Queen had found that no preparations had been made for her reception; in the hurry, a room had been arranged for her and her children. Field-beds had been placed in this room for them. It was amidst such surroundings that the proud daughter of Maria Theresa had to present the spectacle of her fallen greatness to the eyes of the Embassadors of all courts.

" *Vous sauriez que je ne m'attendais pas à venir ici,*" she said, as if apologetically. to the assembled ladies, who could not but look at her compassionately. The parvenu's daughter, whom she had formerly looked down on so haughtily, would not have liked to be in her place now.

Necker remained in Paris, whither the Assemblée Constitu-ante had likewise to transfer its seat. The more convenient it was for Madame de Stael to follow its debates. But she was not long in perceiving that no one was any longer at liberty to act in consonance with his convictions, but had to swim with the tide of popular opinion, unless he was ready to re-nounce all influence over the course of events.

"It cannot be reiterated too often," she said to Narbonne, "that both nations and individuals have only moments of luck and power, which, if allowed to pass by without being turned to account, will never return. So you should profit by the favorable moment." '

In this manner she sought to stimulate his ambition, and incite him to vigorous action. But as her father was unable to lend his character to the King, so she could not infuse her energy and enthusiasm into Narbonne.

With the approach of winter came the wonted series of amusements. Despite the deficit and famine, the embassadors received their friends regularly, and Necker gave quite a num-ber of soirées. Dinner-parties and concerts added to the gayety of social life in the circles of the aristocracy, while the people grumbled loudly at the extravagance reigning in the palace. Many noblemen, however, deemed it prudent to leave the country, and every day were heard the names of new fami-lies who sought abroad protection from the storm which was about to burst forth, and whose outbreak they accelerated by their precipitate flight from France.

Meanwhile a new page had been added to the geography of France; she had been united into one state, with the same coins and laws, and the whole people looked with intense de-light upon the extensive boundaries of the new united country. A brilliant festival was to be celebrated on the Champs de Mars

in honor of this important event; and the King, as if derisively,
had appointed M. de Talleyrand to consecrate the oriflamme
on this occasion upon the altar of the country. Madame de
Stael was present at this ceremony, whose symbolic meaning
made a deep impression on her. With tearful eyes, she gazed
upon the vast concourse of people, who greeted each other exultingly, as sons of a common country. "They are now
awaking to a sense of their dignity as men," she said to herself;
"they learn to appreciate the meaning of the great words,
liberty and *equality*." Overjoyed, like the rest of the spectators
she returned from the festival to her house.

Necker, meanwhile, became more and more desponding in
looking forward to the future; his popularity decreased very
rapidly, and his health was sensibly affected. The situation of
the King was not less deplorable. Despite her longing for a
constitution, Madame de Stael could not see him without profound compassion in this dependent position; and, always ready
as her warm heart was to help and relieve sufferers, she reflected
on the best means by which the King might be extricated from
this piteous predicament. She conceived a plan for his
escape, and caused it to be laid before him. But Louis the
Sixteenth had no confidence in the plan of such an enthusiastic lady, whose ardent and sanguine temperament had always
been distasteful to him. So, shaking his head, he pushed her
letter aside.

She was very sorry at this rejection of her suggestions. Like
all women who always act with their hearts rather than their
heads, she would have staked everything on everything, while
men never lose sight of their own interests in promoting those
of others.

The unsuccessful flight of the royal family proved this
abundantly.

On the 8th of September, 1790, Necker, with his wife and grandson, quietly left Paris, never to return to it. Fifteen months had elapsed since he had made his triumphal entry into the capital, and since the people had fastened to his door a plate, bearing the inscription, " *Necker, le Ministre, adoré.*" And now no one took any notice of his departure.

Deeply grieved and despondent, he bade a long and mournful farewell to his daughter. In doing so, he took leave of life, of his political life, of his wishes and hopes, and, above all, of his fame, whose shadow now pursued him.

Madame de Stael remained in Paris. She could not now leave the scene of her hopes; what her father had been unable to accomplish for France, she might help her friends to achieve. Necker himself was desirous that she should stay in Paris; for he knew his daughter too well not to foresee that her feverish agitation would prove fatal to her in the solitudes of Coppet.

The King's sisters, accompanied by Narbonne, had set out for Rome. When he returned, Madame de Stael's sagacious counsels enabled him to obtain the office of Minister of War.[*] She was delighted with this success, which she enjoyed as if she herself had obtained that important position. Mirabeau had died; a powerful party-leader disappeared with him from the scene, and she hoped to replace him by Narbonne, and inspired him with that self-reliance which a man needs, who wants to exercise influence over the people, and render it obedient to his wishes.

---

[*] Bertrand de Moleville.

CHAPTER XIV.

THE TOCSIN OF PARIS.

GREAT characters are products of their times. A struggle for ideas developes ideas. Never before, therefore, had so many gifted men appeared in the public arena, as at the beginning of the French Revolution.

Madame de Stael admired nothing so much as a gifted mind. She was unable to appreciate the beauties of nature, whose low and sweet notes did not charm her ears, and the vast realm of art was as yet closed to her. Intercourse with talented men was the only pleasure which she was able to enjoy. Wherever she discovered an able man, she paid homage to him, even though he belonged to the party of her adversaries.

Hitherto, she had lived in and with her father, and had looked upon his fame as her own. Since his star had set, since his popularity had vanished, and he had finally turned his back upon France, she was surprised to find how dependent she was on others. Her sex prevented her from taking an active part in political life, and she had to remain invisible, in bringing about measures which she deemed indispensable to the welfare of the nation. She thirsted for political fame and popularity, and could not obtain either, except through others. She had to infuse her sagacity and energy into a man, and let him turn her talents to account. It cost her a struggle to do so; but she could not gratify her ambition in any other way.

She was now twenty-five years old. Taking a very bold view of political affairs, she desired to shape the course of events in accordance with her convictions. For this purpose, she gathered representatives of the various parties about her, and even attempted to bring about a compromise between them. But these efforts were wasted. She was unable to stem the tide of events.

From under the long lashes of her lustrous black eyes there beamed no less pride than tenderness.* The flames which burned in them kindled enthusiasm, not only for the cause to which she sought to win adherents with the eloquence of a Mirabeau, but also for the lady who advocated it with so much ardor. She was generally admired, and the applause bestowed on her gladdened her heart. The days which she passed amidst these political troubles were the happiest of her life.

The Constitution, for which she had longed so ardently, had, meanwhile, been completed and submitted to the King, who, since his flight, had been imprisoned at the Tuileries.

Madame de Stael dissented from this mode of proceeding. She felt the disgrace heaped on royalty, and sympathized, from the bottom of her heart, with the King and Queen, at every humiliation which was inflicted on them. In her person were mixed the three elements of the Revolution; according to her rank, she was an aristocrat; by birth she belonged to the popular classes, and her talents placed her in the ranks of the representatives of science and literature. Thus one principle was always in conflict with another in her breast, and she would not allow any of them to achieve a complete triumph over the others.

Her wish to procure M. de Narbonne a seat in the Cabinet

---

* Lamartine.

after her father's resignation had been fulfilled; through him she now had a vote in the Cabinet, and she left no stone unturned in order to realize her plans.

But she found again on this occasion, that, as she had often said, we are unable to infuse our character into other persons; for M. de Narbonne proved unequal to his position. Guided by an able woman, he pursued the path which she marked out for him; but his heart was not enthusiastically in the cause. Like Madame de Stael, he wished to see equality before the law established in France, but not at the expense of the existing relations and institutions; and such moderate views were repudiated everywhere.

M. de Montmorency had proposed to abolish the titles of the nobility. Madame de Stael differed with him on this point. Reminiscences cannot be effaced, and the merits of his ancestors are sacred to every cultivated man. She warned him against the inefficiency of this step, but he refused to listen to her. The Bishop of Autun moved to confiscate the estates of the clergy; he it was, too, who made them secular priests, and set them the example of repudiating the celibate. Madame de Stael did not approve this either. She wished for a constitution such as England possessed, and she declared that these means were not in keeping with the object. But the universal thirst for popularity shut all ears to sensible advice; everybody paid homage to the clamor of an excited multitude which did not understand its own interests, and, instead of leading, should have been led. They yielded, from cowardice and selfishness, to the most senseless demands, in order to rule by the favor of the people.

M. de Stael took no part in these events. Satiated with life and in feeble health, he allowed his young wife to do as she pleased. The death of his King finally aroused him from his apathy, and compelled him to make a trip to Sweden. His wife did not accompany him. Madame de Stael would not have left France at this juncture under any circumstances, inasmuch as she still hoped to exercise a salutary influence over the destinies of the country. She was fearful lest Narbonne, without her assistance, should be unequal to his task; but he was unable to maintain himself even with her aid. Talleyrand was in England, where he was to try to enlist the Cabinet of St. James in the cause of the French Revolution; when he returned to Paris, he heard that his friend Narbonne had been dismissed.

"He was unable to maintain himself, because he makes a most injudicious use of his tongue," said the handsome Bishop to Madame de Stael. "He always wants to express his thoughts with it, while language was given to us for the purpose of concealing them."

This did not console her. She had lost the organ by which she gave utterance to her ambition, and she was now at a loss to know how she might influence public opinion.

Narbonne had set out for the army of the North as soon as he had been removed. Accustomed as she had been for a long time to see and consult with him daily as to the course to be pursued by him, she missed him painfully, even in her domestic circle. She longed for his return, and accused herself of not having taught him that prudence and caution which she possessed least of all.

The clubs and meetings did not now interest her near as much, since no voice spoke for her there any longer. She walked sadly through her apartments, which seemed so lonely to her. Although the stirring events of the day still attracted her attention and sympathies as much as ever, they no longer gladdened her heart, since she could no longer play a part in them.

She tried to enter into more intimate relations with M. de Talleyrand. Vain endeavor! No matter how amiable, interesting, and agreeable he was at her soirées and in her *téte-à-téte's* with him, she never was able to draw from him a word in regard to his true intentions. "He is like a sensitive plant," she said one day; "he closes at the slightest touch." *

Meanwhile the summer of 1792 came, and now there ensued convulsions which rendered a sojourn in Paris exceedingly dangerous. Péthion and Marat began to rule supreme. All those who were able to leave the soil of France went abroad, but Madame de Stael remained in Paris. Distasteful as the progress of the Revolution was to her, she was unable to leave the capital, where she was a prey to incessant excitement and suspense.

Social life lost its charms since a coarse and brutal tone began to prevail. The newspapers breathed a spirit highly distasteful to a lady brought up in the school of Rousseau and Voltaire. She disliked the practice of using such bad and vulgar style. Human language, in her opinion, had never been abused in this manner, and she said only the howls of wild beasts could be rendered in such words.

The anniversary of the 14th of July was to be celebrated. Madame de Stael, as the wife of a foreign embassador, occupied a seat close to the Queen, and perceived distinctly the painful impression which the celebration produced on the unfortunate princess. Marie Antoinette sat bathed in tears, and looked on, as her husband, in his powdered wig, the only one among so many black heads, and in his gold-embroidered coat, ascended the altar of the country, and took another oath to obey a constitution which was to bring him to the scaffold. The people saw him to-day for the last time.

---

* Monsieur de Talleyrand. Vol. II.

Madame de Stael returned from the celebration in profound grief, to her house, and for a long time was unable to banish from her mind the painful impression which the poor royal family had made upon her.

"Matters cannot go on in this manner!" she cried, wringing her hands. "This cannot be tolerated any longer. It is cruel. It is cowardly murder."

But all her friends turned a deaf ear to her; none of them were willing to risk anything in behalf of a lost cause.

"You are like those," said Talleyrand to her, smilingly, "who first set fire to a house, and then want to save the inmates." *

"The remark is charming," replied Madame de Stael, "but unfortunately it does not improve the prospects of the cause."

Her words met with no response amidst the uproar. The evening of the 9th of August came. The forty-eight bells of Paris rang their gloomy and monotonous alarm. Madame de Stael, who stood with her friends at the open window, listened to this death-knell of an ancient monarchy, and anxiously looked forward to the events of the morrow. The whole night passed in breathless suspense. At 7 in the morning, finally, the booming of artillery drowned the dull sounds of the tocsin. The people hurried through the streets. Madame de Stael received every quarter of an hour reports of the progress of the insurrection. The Tuileries had been surrounded, the sentinels had been attacked and slain.

Upon receiving this news, Madame de Stael immediately ordered her carriage. She had many friends among the officers at the Tuileries, among whom was M. de Narbonne, too. She wanted to ascertain whether or not they were safe. When she arrived at the bridge, her coachman was stopped, and informed

---

* Allouville, Mémoirs.

that he and his mistress would doubtless be murdered on the other side of the bridge. Madame de Stael, however, insisted on advancing. Two hours elapsed in vain efforts to do so. At length word was brought to her that her friends were safe; but they had been compelled to conceal themselves.

After nightfall she hastened on foot through the streets, and visited her friends in their places of concealment. Everywhere were to be seen drunken men, who, sword in hand, had fallen asleep on the threshold or door-steps of the houses. She performed her self-imposed task courageously, frequently shutting her eyes to the horrors which obstructed her path.

Henceforth no one was safe in Paris; even the most ardent advocates of the constitution could save themselves only by precipitate flight, and hastened to the army of the north. The troops of Austria and Prussia had already crossed the frontier; as soon as they should come close up to Paris, a wholesale massacre might be looked for at the capital.

M. de Narbonne and M. de Montmorency were no longer safe in their hiding-places; so Madame de Stael took them in the dead of night to her house, locked them up in one of the back rooms, and watched herself over their safety. Narbonne, being an ex-minister, would have been immediately killed if his whereabouts should be discovered, and she listened tremblingly to all footsteps, fearful lest some traitor should conduct the police to her house and cause her friend to be arrested.

This terrible state of suspense could not last for any length of time; the danger was so threatening that something had to be risked. At this juncture Dr. Bollmann, an honest Hanoverian, the same who afterwards rescued General Lafayette from an Austrain dungeon, visited Madame de Stael, and, deeply moved by the anguish of the young Embassadress, offered to convey M. de Narbonne in disguise, and under an assumed name, to England.

She heaved a deep sigh of relief when she had been freed from this anxiety, and still more so when she learned that both of them had safely reached the frontier.

She felt now, that she herself must no longer try to brave the storm. So she applied for a passport to Switzerland; but, even after she had received it, she could not yet make up her mind to fix the day when she was to bid farewell to so many friends whom she was loth to leave amidst so many dangers.

Victims fell daily now, and daily grew the list of the names of those over whom the sword was suspended. The prisons were crowded with sufferers, and Madame de Stael sought to save whomsoever she could. No hour was too early for her, no walk too long, to serve those who had need of her aid. She had just succeeded in saving the life of a worthy man, M. de Jancourt, by interceding with Manuel in his behalf, and this noble deed was to close her career in Paris. On the following morning she intended to leave the capital, and the Abbe Montesquieu, disguised as a servant, was to escape with her to Switzerland; they were to meet at a certain point in the suburbs.

At this juncture the Parisians heard that Longwy and Verdun had been taken, and there was rung again that tocsin whose sounds again struck terror into her heart, and all Paris was again in commotion. Madame de Stael persisted, nevertheless, in her intention to set out for Switzerland. Although she could as yet be safer at her house than on the road, the Abbe's life would be endangered in case she should not meet him at the appointed place, and this consideration induced her to start. In order to show distinctly that she was the wife of a foreign embassador, she ordered a berlin drawn by six horses, and told her servants to don their gala liveries. This proved to be a serious blunder. In driving in this ostentatious manner through the streets, she attracted the attention of the multitude, and a number of furious women were not long in shouting that the carriage which they said contained the treasures of the nation should be stopped. Excited men surrounded the carriage, dragged the postillions from the box, and ordered Madame de Stael to repair to the office of the district authorities.

She patiently obeyed their order.

She was charged with helping persons sentenced to death to escape from the country; and her passport, too, it was said, was not in good order. It is true, one of her servants who was mentioned in it was absent; she had secretly dispatched him to inform the Abbe of what had occurred. In consequence of this irregularity, she was to be sent to the Hotel de Ville, and subjected there to a formal examination.

To reach the Hotel de Ville she had to cross one-half of the capital; nothing could be more dreadful to the poor lady, whom it took three hours of mortal anguish to perform that distance. She implored the gensd'armes who surrounded her, to have mercy on her, and bear in mind that she was pregnant, and that the upsetting of the carriage might be fatal to her. She met with no response, but threats and disdain.

The danger became more imminent by the time she reached the Place de Grève. Surrounded by men bearing pikes, she walked to the Hotel de Ville. When she reached the hall of sessions, she felt comparatively safe. She had escaped from the furious multitude, and stood now before a Robespierre. The hall was crowded; men, women, and children shouted, " *Vive la nation !* "

Madame de Stael did not admire these voices any longer

A chair was offered to her. She took it and tried to compose herself. At this moment her eyes fell on the Embassador of Parma, who had been arrested like her; and, finding that she had recognized him, he rose and declared that he did not know "that woman," and that he took no interest in her fate. Indignant at his miserable cowardice, she rose to defend herself. Fortunately, Manuel arrived at this moment. Surprised to see her in this condition, he stepped forward and became her bondsman; he then took her and her maid to his private office, where he locked them up.

He left them there for six long hours. Meanwhile they looked down on the Place de Grève, where the bare-armed and blood-stained assassins rent the air with horrible shouts.

It was not until after nightfall that Manuel dared to take her back to her house. The street-lamps not having been lighted, no one was able to recognize her. A new passport was given her, and, escorted by a gensd'armes, she left next morning Paris and France.

BOOK III.

CHAPTER I.

MADAME DE STAEL AT COPPET.

MADAME NECKER, leaning on the arm of her husband, was slowly walking up and down under the tall elms which lined both sides of the road leading to Coppet.

The setting sun shed its last rays on the earth, and bathed the snow-clad summits of the Alps in a flood of purple light; while the lower landscape, already half enshrouded in the evening mist, vanished more and more from their view.

A low sigh escaped the lips of the ex-Minister. His thoughts had wandered far away, while his eyes gazed dreamily upon the magnificent scenery. He thought of his child. Here reigned peace; in this happy solitude, everything breathed the most profound tranquillity; but where she lived, the tocsin incited the multitude, perhaps at this very moment, to arson and murder.

For several days past he had received no letters from her. The cause of this silence was perhaps the fact that she had already left Paris, or that fresh disorders had detained the mails and carriers. He would have gladly believed the former supposition to be true. To have her with him, and under his protection, would have greatly reassured him; still, he did

not wish to persuade her to leave a city to which she was so
much attached, while the quiet life in the country could not
but be exceedingly injurious to her vivacious and ardent spirit.
The growing danger, however, had convinced Madame de
Stael herself that it was time for her to leave the scene of so
many horrors. Her husband was absent; she was looking forward to her speedy confinement—reasons enough for her to
long for a safer place of abode.

Hitherto, no women had yet fallen victims to the Revolution; but no one could tell how long the fair sex would be
spared; and the imprudence which characterized every step of
Necker's, could not but expose her to incessant danger.

While such and similar thoughts arose in the mind of the
ex-Minister, his eyes descried, at the distant end of the alley,
a traveling-coach, approaching in the direction of the villa.
His eyes became radiant with joy, as he stood still, and called
his wife's attention to what he had seen.

Madame Necker trembled at this discovery. She faintly
leaned her pale head on her husband's shoulder, while she
pressed her right hand to her heart.

Her growing weakness rendered her sensible to the slightest emotion of her heart; and with the thought that she would
presently embrace her daughter, there mingled now the foreboding that her end was drawing nigh. Although Germaine
had never occupied the first place in her heart, she was her
mother; and at the moment when she thought of a final separation, all jealousies gave way, and the heart alone warmly
spoke the language of the purest affection that exists on earth
—the love between parents and children.

The post-horn now sounded a merry tune, a head emerged
from the traveling-coach, a loud "Halt!" was heard, and,
a minute afterward, Madame de Stael, sobbing, was folded to

her father's heart. As her grief, so her happiness always manifested itself in the most vivid manner.

In front of the door of the villa, there played her little boy, who had almost forgotten his mother, as children of his age are apt to do. But her loving words were not long in reviving in his memory the sound of a voice than which none can appeal more powerfully to a child's heart.

The joy of meeting her family again made an almost overwhelming impression on a woman whose emotions were so vivid, and whose affections were so ardent. The expression of happiness which she read in her father's face, added greatly to her joy; she kissed his eyes, his hands, and caused him to feel that ambition, fame, and the passions of this world, were as nothing compared with the love which she felt for him.

Madame Necker had withdrawn, and did not return until she had rested for several hours; she then remained for a few moments with her husband and daughter, whose vivacity she was unable to bear.

Madame de Stael had, meanwhile, related to her father the events which had taken place in Paris, and depicted to him the scenes of the September days, in words as graphic and impressive as a painter's pencil. Necker shook his head mournfully as she unrolled those horrors before him.

He was beyond measure astonished to hear that Narbonne and Montmorency had been saved, and he asked himself whether they had escaped in consequence of Cazotte's prophecy, or if that gloomy visionary had really been able to penetrate the veil of the future. Although he had kept up a regular correspondence with his daughter, there still remained for her so much to add, and for him so much to ask, so many lives had suddenly taken such a strange turn, that the first days passed

12

mostly on his part in questions, which his daughter took pains to answer as explicitly as possible.

, Madame de Stael had left Paris in the utmost agitation, and the news which she received thence since her departure, the melancholy and precarious condition of her best friends, kept her constantly in a state of painful uneasiness.

A protracted indisposition, and the birth of her child shortly after, contributed greatly toward soothing the tempest in her heart, and conjured up in her breast a certain resignation which, following as it did in the wake of her prolonged feverish agitation, at times almost frightened her.

Time wore on. Winter had come, and snow covered the flanks of the mountains. She gazed sadly on the cold landscape that fell on her heart with icy coldness, and filled her mind with that *ennui* which caused her wings to droop.

Her hopes in regard to France were blasted; tears streamed from her eyes whenever she called to mind what she had expected, and what she had lost. That constitution for which she had longed so ardently, what had become of it? Her friends whose fame she had shared, were reduced to want and misery; Paris, the pearl and ideal of all cities, was bleeding under Robespierre. The cause of liberty had become a cause of terror.

" What remains to me now? what am I to do with my life?" she secretly asked herself; and she felt deeply and painfully how lonely her life was, after all, inasmuch as the sound foundation of domestic happiness was wanting to it. Profound melancholy seized her.

Necker urged her to form a social circle; but all acquaintances which she formed here added to her despondency. In Geneva lived Madame Rillet, *nee* Huber, who had formerly been her companion at St. Ouen; since that time circumstances

.had separated them still further, and everybody knows how painful it is to meet old acquaintances with whom we have no longer any sympathies in common. She had been estranged from female life in its usual relations; she never sympathized very ardently with the interests to which it is devoted. Accustomed as she was to pay homage to the mind, and to follow with ardent enthusiasm whatsoever it creates, she contemplated with a sad air the petty cares and troubles which engrossed the attention of other women as wives and mothers.

Moreover, the hypocrisy to which her sex stooped, the insincerity with which women concealed their thoughts and feelings, were exceedingly distasteful to her. She was at a loss to understand how any one could be ashamed of his feelings. She appreciated only such words as were the immediate expression of the heart; she treated men in social intercourse as if they were women, and charmed them by her candor and honest straightforwardness. The women, on their part, took umbrage at her unusual conduct, which they censured as wanting in good breeding.

Madame de Stael saw that she was not appreciated, and this discovery saddened her heart, for she wished to be loved, and she was well aware that she was unable to bring about a change for the better. "*C'est ma nature ainsi*," she said, and it was beyond her power to transform it. She remained truthful to indiscretion, and concealed neither what moved herself nor what grieved or gladdened others.

During the last six years she had not written anything, the political events having completely overshadowed all literary interests; and whenever she was able to use the living word for communicating her thoughts, she abstained from writing. Now, in her solitude, she took up her pen again.

An active and animated correspondence with her friends in

demnified her, in the first place, for her separation from them.
Narbonne remained in London, and took pains to defend the
interests of France at the British capital.   Though he was poor
and proscribed, the most aristocratic and influential circles
opened to him; Fox and Grey, Erskine and Granville invited
him often to dinner; and Madame de Stael tried now from afar,
as she formerly had done in Paris, to exercise her influence
over him and guide his steps.

The condemnation of the unfortunate King of France
caused her the most profound grief, and she consulted incessantly with her friends as to the means by which he might be
saved.   Narbonne had offered to go under a safeguard to Paris
and defend the King; when his offer was rejected, he nevertheless wrote a justification of Louis the Sixteenth, and had it
published.

Madame de Stael, animated by the same spirit, wrote a defense of Queen Marie Antoinette, and issued it anonymously.
Everybody divined the name of the authoress, although it was
not on the title-page, and admired the heart from which such
words emanated to justify a princess who had treated her so
unjustly and offensively.   It is difficult to overcome our
wounded vanity.   But Madame de Stael was in this respect,
too, the most kind-hearted creature on earth; she never re-
sented an insult; she never revenged herself upon a person
in adversity for having mortified her in the days of his prosperity.   The sufferings of the unfortunate appealed irresistibly to
her heart, and silenced any other feelings in her breast.

As Narbonne's justification was unable to save the King, so
Madame de Stael did not succeed by her pamphlet in bringing
about the acquittal of Marie Antoinette, and both of them had
to bleed on the scaffold. When the news of their execution
reached Coppet, the Necker family mourned for them as deeply

and sincerely, as if the most beloved relatives had been taken from them.

As soon as Madame de Stael's health permitted her to travel again, she made in the spring of 1793 a trip to England, and tried to bring her influence to bear on Pitt and Fox; but her self-imposed mission was unsuccessful.

Her maternal duties called her back to Coppet. By this time a great many exiles had arrived in Switzerland, and their frequent visits rendered her life less monotonous and lonely than heretofore. Still the tone of these visitors was anything but cheering. The days of hopefulness and joy were gone; all looked forward to the future with the gloomiest forebodings; and even the thought of the ultimate triumph of liberty had lost its charm, since the road to it had been drenched in blood.

There was no gayety even in the circles of the most intimate friends, and no one was courageous enough to begin a sprightly and witty conversation. The Phrygian cap, and the cockade, had driven away the *esprit* of the French.

M. de Narbonne had to leave England again, and seek an asylum in Switzerland. Want and privations dogged his steps, and he wandered about in deep despondency. The favorite of fortune could not accustom himself so easily to the whims of fate, and it was not until he met the young Duke of Chartres, and saw at Lucerne how bravely the Prince entered upon his position as schoolmaster, that he took heart and, like him, resolved to look adversity courageously in the face.

Mathieu de Montmorency, too, arrived at Coppet, and remained with Madame de Stael until he received from Paris the intelligence that his only brother had been sentenced to death. He hastened thither in order to save him, but he came too late.

Inasmuch as everybody trembled for his own life, or for that

of his friends, nobody was able to console others, and, least of
all, could this be expected of Madame de Stael, whom grief
prostrated so easily, and who had tears only to weep over an
inflexible fate, but was unable to brave it.

Necker vainly tried to comfort her, and encourage her by
his example to submit patiently to what could not be helped.
Life was dead and void for her when she had no desires and
hopes to connect with her future. Even fame had lost its
charms, if it was not to adorn her forehead in France. She
was like an actor who is to play before an array of empty
benches; the right kind of spur was wanting to her, and even
her eloquent words died away on her lips because she had no
listeners with whom she cared to converse.

She received Narbonne with a mournful smile at Coppet.
He had been to her a brilliant star, whose rise she had watched
with enraptured eyes, and whose setting now filled her soul
with quiet grief. She had not faith enough to exclaim at
every failure, "What has happened was inevitable," and so
there mingled with her grief the self-reproach that many a step
would have been more successful if she had guided her friend
with more judicious advice.

Her defense of the Queen had appeared anonymously; in the
same manner she now published a number of papers on the
peace question, on which even Fox, to whom Narbonne sent
them publicly, bestowed the most flattering encomiums.*

These works occupied her, but they did not engross her
heart. She had long since perceived that her life in a certain
respect was a failure, owing to her thirst for fame and distinction, which did not indemnify her for the lack of that quiet
happiness which a woman is to find in the bosom of her family.
Whenever she glanced at her mother, she heaved a sigh, for

---

* Villemain.

she could never hope to love and be loved as Madame Necker loved her husband, and was loved by him. Even her children did not afford her the joy felt by a mother who seeks in these precious pledges a resemblance to her beloved husband, and presses them with redoubled tenderness to her heart because they belong to him. She could never feel, never hope for, the proud satisfaction of enjoying this sweet and quiet happiness.

Madame Necker's disease, meanwhile, grew more and more alarming, and the physicians finally declared that there was little or no hope of her recovery. Sustained as she was by her firm religious faith, she courageously looked forward to her death, and closed her eyes with a serene air.

This quiet sick-bed, this gentle death, affected Madame de Stael most injuriously, unable as she was to lock any of her emotions in her breast, and to fight out any heart-struggles within herself. Grief to which she was not allowed to give vent, made her sick.

Necker was deeply afflicted at the loss of a wife whom he had esteemed so highly and loved so dearly; and he mourned for her long and profoundly. Madame de Stael wished sincerely to indemnify him for this loss, and to cling to him with redoubled tenderness; but at the same time she saw that it was impossible for her to pursue the same course as her mother, and it was not until now that she recognized her high worth. Her eyes were fixed on Paris; her thoughts were at the French capital while she was walking at her father's side, and she looked forward to every coming day in the anxious hope that something—she did not know herself exactly what she longed for—might turn up.

M. de Stael had been appointed again Embassador to Paris. He arrived there two months after the death of Louis the Sixteenth; he was the only foreign embassador that set foot on French soil during the Reign of Terror.

In order to add to his personal safety, he distributed on the day of his arrival the sum of three thousand francs among the poor of the district; nevertheless, he considered his life endangered; and much as he desired to prolong his sojourn in Paris and call Madame de Stael to his side, after a few weeks time he hastily turned his back on France. It was not until after Robespierre's overthrow that he ventured to return to his post.

CHAPTER II.

BENJAMIN CONSTANT DE REBECQUE.

THERE was no place in Switzerland where the French exiles met with a less friendly reception than in the small town of Lausanne. The young men of Lausanne were such ardent adherents of republican liberty that they not only rejected all moderate ideas, but furnished the representatives of such views with public marks of disrespect.

In the autumn of the year 1794, Benjamin Constant de Rebecque returned to Lausanne, his birth-place, in order to visit his relatives. His father, a general in the Dutch service, had died at Dole. Young Rebecque had been educated abroad, heard lectures at the University of Edinburgh, studied then at Göttingen and Erlangen, imbibed the principles of Kant's philosophy, and acquired a vast store of knowledge. His family had escaped from France after the promulgation of the Edict of Nantes; he had grown up as a Calvinist, and, although a native of Switzerland, remained at heart a Frenchman. He returned now from the petty court of Brunswick, where the Duchess, whose special favorite he was, had appointed him chamberlain a year ago.

Although he was only twenty-seven years old, he had in many respects arrived at his full maturity. His tall, slender form, the enthusiastic glance of his large blue eyes, which were constantly turned to heaven, made his appearance no less striking than prepossessing. His blonde hair, which he wore
13*

very long, after the fashion of the German students, imparted to him at the same time the naïve air of a youth who has just entered into life, and thinks that some fresh pleasure is in store for him behind every mountain.

Easily carried away by his impressions, he had already at an early age put upon his heart fetters which he was not courageous enough to break. At a later time, when he formed the acquaintance of the Hardenberg family at the court of Brunswick, the niece of the prince charmed his impressive heart; and as his love was returned, he built the boldest plans on the future, and secretly promised to marry the beautiful young lady, who had been brought up in the most brilliant circumstances. He took this imprudent step without considering how difficult it would be for him to redeem his promise.

She did not suspect what chains he bore already, and hoped in his and her good star.

No sooner had Constant de Rebecque set foot on his native soil, than he heard from all lips the names of the illustrious Necker and of his no less celebrated daughter; and the ambitious young man naturally desired to get acquainted with these distinguished personages. The kindness of Madame Necker de Saussure, Madame de Stael's cousin, enabled him soon after to attain his object. On a beautiful September morning he put his letter of introduction into his pocket and set out for Coppet.

Necker happened to be in his study, where he read and wrote all day long, and refused to be disturbed. When the visitor was announced to Madame de Stael, she was standing sadly at the window and gazing into vacancy. It was the longing of her heart that caused her eyes to wander far away.

Narbonne had just left her. He had been the bearer of bad tidings, which his own discouragement had rendered still gloomier. At the same time she had perceived how little he valued her friendship since wealth and position were wanting to him. "Oh, these men!" she said, shaking her head, after he was gone. "Instead of being props to us women, it is we that must support them. They accept our services as though it were our principal destination to promote their interests; and they forget that, with all our seeming disinterestedness, we feel at the bottom of our hearts the longing to be rewarded for our services with a little love and tenderness. Poor sex! The vulnerable side turns up everywhere."

Her large, lustrous eyes, half veiled under her long lashes, and an expression of profound melancholy stamped on her features, she went to meet the young stranger, and bade him welcome.

He stood before her in surprise. He had thought that the appearance of the author of the letters on Rousseau was widely different from what he found her to be.

"You come from Germany," she said to him in her deep, sonorous voice. "You have drawn your intellectual food from the fountain of German philosophy, but at the same time learned to pay homage to monarchial principles. They know there but very little of the writings of our Rousseau, and the chapter of the 'Rights of Man' is still a closed book for those dreamers. So my grief will be inexplicable to you. I have no hopes of happiness but such as are connected with the liberty of France, with a representative constitution, and the recognition of the *droits de l'homme*. The tocsin of Paris has tolled the death-knell of all my wishes."

So saying, she paced the room in great agitation.

Constant followed her, meanwhile, with his clear eyes, and sought to penetrate the singular being of the gifted lady.

"We were by no means indifferent lookers-on, while such

stirring events occurred in France," he said, at last.   "I myself take the liveliest interest in all that is going on there; for
I look upon France as my own country, and am at heart a
Frenchman. And I say, even to-day, 'Thank God, I am a
Frenchman.' The petty German States could not win my
sympathies, inasmuch as I found everything there too insignificant and narrow-minded.   To entertain great ideas and
noble feelings, one must belong to a great nation, and play a
part in the arena of humanity."

"And that you can do only in France," she said, standing
still before him, and looking him full in the face with her radiant eyes. He dropped his eyes before the wondrous luster of
these stars. "In France as it was, but not as it is. I wish
you had known it in its glory, in its greatness; I wish you
had witnessed the majestic rising of a people determined to
throw off its yoke, and to break with the traditions of the
past, in order to rise to a new and nobler greatness. Ah, that
time will never come back. I wish you had seen the suspense
pervading all classes of society, and how every one wished to
co-operate in the great work, and thought he existed only for
the welfare of the whole nation.   And now, and now! to what
extremes has too much resistance driven this poor people!"

"It is a transition," replied Constant de Rebecque, rising
likewise. "History never advances in a straight line; we
overstep the right measure, now on one side, and now on the
other; and we learn only by our excesses when we should
have pursued a course of moderation."

"You speak like a philosopher," replied Madame de Stael,
eyeing him with growing interest. "The right measure is
reason; and what you call excesses, passion. I have grown
up in a school which granted to the latter a power, the fruits
of which were reaped under Robespierre. You have been

brought up in a country where the "Critique of Pure Reason" founded its systems. So both of us have started from opposite points; and yet I wager, M. de Rebecque, that, no matter what theory may have taught us, we shall practically meet in the same path. Forbidden fruits are always so sweet!"

"And yet they leave such a bitter pang behind. It is so beautiful to love virtue and hate vice; it is so beautiful to ardently admire all that is great and noble, and it is still more beautiful to believe in a demi-god. You do not know how magnificently we are *dreaming* in Germany. There is in Germany an ideal world for which we gladly risk the very ground under our feet. To think is there the first duty of man. Oh, you must get acquainted with Germany. The very contrast between that country and France will make it interesting to you."

She sighed deeply.

"How I envy you for being able to feel so warmly," she said, mournfully. "Although I am still young, I have suffered a great deal, and met with many disappointments. There is but one thing that remains to me: an everlasting unsatisfied longing for some unspeakable happiness. Whenever I thought it within my reach and stretched out my hand for it, it escaped from me. Now I do not hope for it any more; there is a deep gloom in my breast; my illusions have vanished; my life seems aimless, and my heart is so poor, oh, so poor!" Her eyes filled with tears as she said so.

Constant rose in deep emotion and seized her hand; she gave it to him willingly, and allowed it to rest in his.

"Your tears show how rich your heart still is," he said, feelingly. "How deep and pure its feelings must be, when it is able to weep such pearls after past and lost happiness."

A sunbeam from her eyes was her response. He wanted to withdraw his hand in confusion, but she held it and said naively:

"To get acquainted with one another, we might need an hour or ten years.* I believe I understand you, and it is my habit to say frankly and openly whether people please or displease me. I feel that you can be a great deal to me, inasmuch as you possess all that is wanting to me—hope, faith, and enthusiasm. Kindle with them once more the dead spark in my soul. Become my friend. Let us try and see what we can be to one another."

Confused, surprised, and flattered, M. de Rebecque pressed to his lips the beautiful hand still resting in his own, and meanwhile tried to find words for a reply. What was he to answer? He was a prey to strange feelings. The most gifted lady of the century offered her friendship to him, an obscure young stranger; that was a triumph most gratifying to his vanity; and yet something told him that, in accepting her offer, he added another chain to the fetters which he already bore, and which would thereby be rendered still more intolerable and oppressive.

At the dinner-table he was introduced to Necker. The conversation was exceedingly animated, and gave him an opportunity to admire the genius of his new friend. They talked about the usual topics, the latest events in France, the war between the allied powers, the condition of the French exiles, and the probable *denouement* of all these complications.

Necker inquired, also, about the German universities, the policy of Prussia and Austria, and the spirit and sympathies of the youth in whose hands rested the future of the States. M. de Rebecque gave him satisfactory information about everything, and interspersed his remarks with many witty sallies, which delighted Madame de Stael, and caused Necker to smile approvingly.

---

* Her own words.

Brilliant rather than profound, sustained by a sanguine temperament, accessible to all impressions, and destitute of that firmness of the soul which teaches us to avoid noxious influences, he was a man of the moment, catching with his sprightly. heart fortune on the wing, and never taking umbrage at its fickleness.

Frank and communicative as he was, he willingly disclosed the events of his brief career. He told them all about his youth, his studies, his life at the English and German universities.; He only passed over his sojourn at Brunswick as less important, and adroitly evaded all questions propounded to him in regard to it.

When Necker's eyes happened to fall on the small golden ring on his left hand, he became embarrassed, and soon after the treacherous ornament disappeared from his finger.

Necker liked Benjamin Constant from the very first, on account of his birth-place and religion ; and the pleasure which the amiability of the young man afforded him, added greatly to the partiality which the ex-minister felt for him, so that Necker was not long in treating him like an old acquaintance. So he was not surprised to hear Madame de Stael say to Constant at parting, she wished him to consider Coppet his home during his sojourn in Switzerland. She would cause a room to be fitted up for him.

It is true, this kind of hospitality was by no means unusual at that time, and it had always been practiced with especial liberality at Necker's house.

Young Rebecque replied to these kind words only, that, under these circumstances, he should be loth to leave Switzerland again.

"So much the better," replied Madame de Stael, casting at him a glance which contained the assurance that she would gladly consider him her property.

The stars had risen already when the young man reached Lausanne.

He threw himself moodily on his couch, but could not fall asleep. Whenever he shut his eyes, the gifted lady stood before him, fixed her radiant eyes on him, and said, "Let us try and see what we can be to one another."

The idea of her friendship made him dizzy.

He thought of his first love—how timidly he had approached the very young girl, and indicated his love for her by glances rather than words. He recalled the sweet happiness of those days; but alas! it seemed to him like a childish dream. And then appeared before him the beautiful and elegant lady whose acquaintance he had formed at Hardenberg's house; before her the humble picture of his first love had sunk into the dust; and his passion, enhanced by his ambition, had stimulated him to win a heart for which he had to betray another.

And now he was to add to these relations, from which he had not yet freed himself, a friendship which began too warmly and affectionately not to lead to more tender relations.

But what was he to do?

The courage of truth he did not possess. He despised his own cowardice, his head reproached him with his discreditable conduct, but his heart sinned none the less. His lips refused to utter the word that would mortify a woman dear to him, and so he sinned still more grievously against her.

He returned to Coppet on the third day. Madame de Stael thought that he tarried too long for a friend who valued her friendship as highly as she wanted to be esteemed. She received him with a clouded brow.

"*Jamais je n'ai été aimé comme j'aime*," she said to him, reproachfully.

Henceforth he had always to tell her beforehand the day

and hour when he would return, which was to him both new and disagreeable. He sighed, but did not venture to disobey her wishes.   She manifested so much gratification at his visits, her interviews with him were so agreeable to her, that he could not tell her that he would feel happier if she were less exacting toward him.

Letters from Brunswick called upon him to return to that city. He responded to them by lame excuses, subterfuges, and promises, which, on the following day, he was not courageous enough to fulfill. How could he inform Madame de Stael that he intended to leave her, when she assured him every day that his presence lent a new charm to her life!

He began to write his work on religion,* to which his conversations with Necker and his daughter constantly stimulated him afresh, especially as the ex-minister himself devoted considerable attention to this subject. At the same time he looked anxiously forward to the immediate future. He could not possibly continue this mode of life for any length of time. To repose in this manner at his age was a crime against himself. He had to obtain a position and secure his future. But, whenever he alluded to this subject, Madame de Stael fell into an agitation which rendered it impossible for him to come to an understanding with her ; and finally carried him away to the most passionate assurances that all his other interests should always be secondary to the desire of living as near to her as possible.

As soon as he left her, this falsehood weighed down his soul like an incubus. Vexed and out of humor, he determined to tell her the truth at his next interview with her, but these resolutions always terminated in the same discomfiture. And thus the winter of 1795 drew nigh.

---

* Biographie Universelle.

CHAPTER III.

It was in March, 1795, that M. de Stael returned again as Embassador to Paris, the only representative of a foreign power authorized to recognize the new government.

The Directory, highly flattered and gratified at his appearance, received him with the utmost distinction. He was conducted to a chair opposite to the President of the Assembly, who received him at his entrance with the fraternal kiss, and addressed him with the republican " thou."

The affectionate treatment which he received at the hands of these men, most of whom belonged to the lower classes of society, seemed intolerable to him. With an air of confusion he suffered the embrace which was by no means to his taste, and fortunately did not perceive the ridiculous figure which he cut among them.

He had gone to Paris with the firm determination to submit to the exigencies of the times, in order to be able to live at the French capital. The sojourn at Stockholm was no less distasteful to him than the limited income which was at his disposal in that city. He was a spendthrift, and addicted to luxury. Inasmuch as he had no fortune of his own, he was unable to gratify his expensive tastes as long as he was separated from his wife, and so he longed intensely to return to his post.

" As soon as he had reached Paris, he wrote to Madame de

Stael, and informed her that she would now be perfectly safe at their Parisian residence. She hastened in great agitation with this letter to her father.

"You cannot accompany me, and I shall not leave you here alone," she said.

"You will do so, nevertheless," replied Necker, with gentle earnestness, folding her to his heart. "Your mind has need of a larger sphere of development than Coppet is able to offer you. You are destined for the great world, and cannot adapt yourself to limited fields of action and narrow horizons. So follow your destiny, my child.' I have arrived at an age when solitude is a blessing, and I shall enjoy with you from afar all the triumphs which you are certain to achieve."

She was, however, unable to make up her mind immediately. She paced her room in great agitation until Benjamin Constant arrived.

Without a word of preparation she handed him her husband's letter, and fixed her eyes steadfastly on him while he read it.

"So you will return to Paris," he said; and the thought that he would now regain his liberty, removed a heavy burden from his heart.

"Is that all you have to say to me in regard to that letter?" she asked, panting for breath.

He dropped his eyes in confusion.

As she still continued fixing her eyes on him inquiringly, he composed himself at last, and replied:

"That I shall be grieved to part with you, I need not tell you; you know how much I shall miss you; still, it is no use complaining of what is inevitable."

"Inevitable!" she exclaimed, curling her lips angrily, while her increasing agitation swelled her nostrils. "Inevitable is only what fate imposes on us, and not what we choose to do of our own accord. Both of us are free and enlightened enough to rise above prejudices and surmount obstacles. Where there is a will there is a way. To the bold belongs the world. He who is able to overcome circumstances knows no other law than his own inclinations. I am only a woman; but my courage, I believe, surpasses that of many men."

M. de Rebecque made an evasive reply. He tried to allay her anger by assuring her of his fervent attachment, and told her that his affairs had long since rendered it necessary for him to go to Brunswick, but that his aversion to a separation from her had caused him to postpone the journey again and again; now, however, he said, he was glad that her determination to return to Paris put an end to his hesitation.

This reply did not satisfy her. A violent scene ensued. She insisted on learning what induced him to go to Brunswick. He could and would not tell her. He had always shrouded his relations with that place in a veil of mystery, and refused now to lift it.

Madame de Stael asked him to accompany her to Paris.

"Why defy public opinion? Why give M. de Stael cause to complain of me?" he said.

"At all events, *your* reputation would not suffer in consequence," she replied, bitterly.

He represented to her that, as her companion, he would be placed in a state of dependence on her, which was repugnant to his self-respect. A man, he said, must be something by himself, and not allow himself to be supported by a woman. He would repair to Prince Hardenberg, who was at this juncture at Basel for the purpose of concluding peace between France and Prussia, and try to obtain some position through his influence.

"A position that would separate you from me? No, Constant, you must not, *shall* not, apply for such an one. Your knowledge and talents will open you an honorable career everywhere. Do you want to be rich? I will give you my whole fortune, and shall be glad to receive a mite from it at your hands. A woman will not degrade herself by such a state of dependence."

Constant divined the reply which she expected, and dropped his eyes in confusion. He was a prey to the most painful emotions. When he raised his eyes again, he met hers, which were fixed on him with an expression of the most profound grief. He threw himself at her feet in the deepest contrition, pressed her hands with the most affectionate exclamation to his lips, and then suddenly rushed out of the room.

Madame de Stael looked after him in surprise.

An hour went by, and he did not return; but a messenger brought her a letter written at the neighboring village. Constant informed her in it that he was ashamed of being unable to devote his whole life to such a friend; he implored her not to banish him in consequence from her heart, but to permit him to enter upon his political career under her guidance in Paris. He would set out for Germany this very day, in order to meet her the earlier at the French capital.

She buried her face in her hands after reading the letter. A violent pain gnawed in her breast; a flood of tears finally gave her relief.

After composing herself, she sent a messenger after him; but he was unable to overtake Constant, who had already returned to Lausanne. She wrote to him that she must see him once more previous to his departure. He replied that he had already engaged a traveling-coach and packed his trunk.

She ordered her carriage and drove to Lausanne. When

she halted in front of his house, the shutters of his windows
were closed, which told her that he had left. She nevertheless
went up to his room, which was in a somewhat disorderly state.
Everything was still lying about as he had left it. Everything
here spoke of him, and reminded her of the days which she
had passed with him. She closed the door, seated herself, and
mused on the events of the past.

Torn letters and scraps of paper littered the floor. She
picked them up and tried to recognize the handwriting. The
characters were German, and she was unable to decipher them.
Only the hand of a young lady could have penned these neat
yet firm letters. The signature, in French characters, was
"Hardenberg." She concealed these scraps tremblingly in her
bosom, and hastened from the room. Hardenberg! He had
often mentioned that name to her, but in a different connection.

Fortunately the preparations for her departure engrossed all
her thoughts for the next few days.

When the moment was finally at hand when she was to take
leave of her father, her heart failed her. Necker had lately
grown obese, and everything indicated that he would not
reach an advanced age. The loss of his wife had, moreover,
inflicted on him a wound which had scarred over, but would
not heal. Her remains had been buried in a bosquet of his
garden. He daily wended his way thither, and conversed with
her in thought.

Madame be Stael led her father to this hallowed spot in
order to bid him here a last farewell. Her children were not
to accompany her. She urgently recommended them to her
father at her mother's grave, and begged him to educate them
in her spirit. Then bursting into loud sobs, she hastened into
her carriage, buried her face in her hands, and saw no more.

She rolled quietly toward her destination.

When we reach after a prolonged absence the place where our cradle has stood, we find that the picture thereof which lives in our memory has lost its colors, and no longer fits the frame which we bring along for it.

We are at a loss to know if we contemplate the picture with different eyes, or if the objects we see have assumed another shape; certain it is that we are no longer at home in these surroundings.

When Madame de Stael descried the spires of Paris, tears of joy filled her eyes. She would have liked to greet every passer-by, and fold every stranger to her heart.

The houses and streets were the same; only they bore different names. The coats of arms had disappeared; the word *citoyen* expressed everything. Luxury had become a vice, and simplicity was a proof of patriotic sentiments.

M. de Stael came to meet his wife without the insignia of his rank, and clad in a simple black dress-coat. She hardly recognized him in his burgher-like costume.

On the following day she drove with him to Grosbois. and visited Barras, who held a reception. Here she saw only *toilettes* of the Grecian fashion, and so low-necked that they made her blush. The hair was worn without powder, and either closely cropped *à la victime*, or in ringlets *à la Titus.*

Her dress created such a sensation that she perceived she would have to change it.

When the footman announced her and her husband, he said, " *Le citoyen Embassadeur Stael et son épouse.*" These words were highly distasteful to her ears. Her admiration of the *Droit de l'homme* had never extended far enough to solicit for herself the appellation, " *La citoyenne Stael,*" or " *Citoyenne Embassa-*

drice." With these words was coupled a certain tone of familiarity which never prevails in good society, and to which she was not accustomed.

Refined manners had disappeared from society ; people used bad language in conversation, and wrote even worse. Nevertheless, she had to take pains to conceal the disgust with which all this filled her. Barras was now a powerful man, and she had to ingratiate herself with him in order to enable her friends to return to France. She conversed with him on this subject, and interceded with her habitual warmth in behalf of the suffering exiles.

Barras himself was of noble extraction, but he carefully concealed his descent, which could not but be injurious to him. Nevertheless, his early education had imparted to him the refined manners of good society, which he still preserved.

He listened smilingly to the enthusiastic encomiums which the celebrated lady bestowed upon her exiled friends.

" You first set fire to a house and then want to protect the inmates against the flames," he said, laughing.

" Help me, and it will be all the same to me whether you accuse me of inconsistency, or not," she said, imploringly.

However, she did not attain her object so easily. The Directory was already accustomed to flattery. The old nobility tickled with it the ears of the parvenus, either to save their estates, or to introduce relatives ; and thus the aristocrats used toward the *bourgeoisie* a language which had never been heard at court, and which would have been less offensive there, inasmuch as it would have been an expression of submissiveness, than here. where sneaking self-interest used it for the purpose of attaining its petty ends.

There being no court and no embassadors, M. de Stael did not hold many receptions. He gambled a great deal, and spent his evenings with M'lle Contat. His wife saw him very rarely. Already accustomed to being left to herself, she devoted her attention, as formerly, to politics, and to the welfare of her friends. She opened her *salon* and gave the first soirée— a faint shadow of what social life had been before the Revolution. At the same time, however, she took pains to attract many of the leading men, partly in order to gain political influence, and partly to enable her proscribed friends to return to France. These efforts were injurious to her character as a woman, and she was called an intriguer; but she never spared herself whenever she tried to obtain an object upon which she had set her heart.

Talleyrand had been compelled to leave England, and lived now in America. By interceding with Barras in his behalf, she obtained permission for him to return to France. Trembling for joy, she seated herself at her writing-table in order to communicate the glad tidings to him.

In regard to Narbonne she was unsuccessful. He lived in obscurity in the Canton of Glarus, where he underwent a great many privations; nevertheless, he refused to return to France as long as it was in the hands of a government which he hated and despised. Vainly did Madame de Stael attempt to change his mind in this respect; vainly did she represent to him that he might use his influence in bringing about a better state of affairs; he persisted in his refusal to erect a structure on such a foundation, inasmuch as it would be certain to break down over his own head.

Mesdames Beauharnais and Tallien likewise opened their *salons;* the theaters were more liberally patronized; and, as formerly, Madame de Stael had many opportunities to display her surpassing talents, and to assert her superiority. Nevertheless she did not feel happy.

14

From week to week since her arrival she had looked forward
to Benjamin Constant's return, and her impatience knew no
bounds. When he asked again and again for delays, without
being able to give her any plausible reasons for these requests,
she was often perfectly beside herself, and almost determined
to follow him. But how can we attach to us by dint of
prayers and reproaches, a friendship which refuses to grant
any rights to the other side.

Her head told her that this was impossible, but her heart
always silenced its voice. She knew by experience how many
relations in life a man will prize more highly than his friendship for a woman, and how easily he can do without her when
his ambition, self-interest, or another passion of the same
description guides his steps. She had had to submit sighingly
to the refusal of her friends to break other fetters for her sake,
and to the readiness with which they allowed her to enter a
union which was a mere *marriage de convenance*, rather than
grant her a position to which she believed herself to be perfectly equal. She had suffered and forgotten all this, and had
constantly remained a faithful friend of these men. But was
she to prove again and again how gladly she sacrificed herself
in order to promote the interests of others?

She wrote daily to M. de Rebecque, and reminded him of his
promise. She depicted to him in glowing colors how deeply
she felt his faithlessness, and how sorry she was to be unable
to hasten to him in order to impress him orally still more vividly with the wound which he had inflicted on her happiness.

Such letters filled Constant with the most painful emotions.
Enchained as he was by a genuine affection, it was difficult for
him to leave the lady of his heart. And yet Madame de Stael
exercised over his imagination an influence which attracted
him to her almost against his will.

CHAPTER IV.

THE NEW PARIS.

ON a warm August morning, Benjamin Constant de Rebecque, after making a trip through the Rhenish provinces and Holland, reached at length the capital of the French Republic. Upon arriving at the *Barrierè*, he left the stage-coach and walked slowly along the road which had been pointed out to him, in order to receive undisturbedly the first impressions which the great city would produce upon him. To see Paris was then an important event for a young man. He looked curiously at the houses and people. Suddenly his eyes fell on a cart filled with twenty gensd'armes, who were being taken to the place of execution. He averted his head shudderingly from the dreadful sight. These gensd'armes were the old retainers of Fouquier Tinville, who had joined the insurgents of the first of Prairial. Good-looking young men, armed with sabers and pikes, hastened through the streets, and drove before them the working-men who had taken part in the attack upon the Convention. Batteries were planted in the streets, and Paris resembled a battle-field after a battle.

Benjamin Constant reached Madame de Stael's house in the highest agitation.

The servant had misunderstood his name; she did not know that it was her friend whom he had announced, and she greeted him with a loud cry of surprise, terror, and joy. She repeated to him the invitation to take up his abode at her house. Constant begged her to permit him not to avail himself of this offer. As M. de Stael was unacquainted with him, it could not be agreeable to him to see a young stranger treated as a member of his family. She pouted at his refusal, and eyed him distrustfully. The name "Hardenberg" was on her lips; but she still hesitated to utter it. She was afraid of its sound.

On the same evening she gave a soirée, at which he formed the acquaintance of Suard, Morellet, Lacretelle, Laharpe, the brilliant Lauraguais, Castellane, Choiseul, and many other eminent men. When he went to bed that night, his head swam, from all that he had heard and seen.

On the following morning, Madame de Stael drove with him to Barras, and recommended her protégé to that all-powerful man; she then introduced him to the ladies of her acquaintance.

M. de Stael was at Passy. When he returned from thence after a few days, he met his guest for the first time. He greeted him coldly, and evidently took no interest in the young man whom his wife so visibly distinguished.

Benjamin Constant was ill at ease in his presence. When he was alone again with Madame de Stael, he begged her to bestow less attention on him in the presence of others. She gazed at him for several minutes in speechless astonishment.

"You wish to teach me that falseness and deceit which you like so well in my sex," she then said, half mournfully, half bitterly; "but it is a vain endeavor! I am my father's daughter, and, above all, want to remain truthful. I shall never deny my friendship for you."

Constant kept silence, as always when he saw her sad or vexed. He was not courageous enough to make her unhappy, and re-assured her, in his cowardly way, by words and assurances in which he did not believe himself.

She took him out to Saint-Brice, and introduced him to Marmontel, who had lost his fortune and his salary during the Revolution, and now looked anxiously upon his young family, whom he was scarcely able to protect against want. It afforded Madame de Stael a great deal of pleasure to show her young friend the place where she had passed her youth, and to speak of by-gone times which were so rich in hope and fame.

Marmontel was exceedingly glad to see her again, and vividly depicted to her the years of anxiety and care which he had passed here, so close to the scene of terror. So many of their common friends had perished so piteously, she shuddered as he related to her the details of the mournful fate which had befallen them. He alluded also to Condorcet, and told her how that able and brilliant man, who had just completed his noble work on the progress of the human mind, persecuted as he was by Robespierre, had taken poison.

" The fictions of us poets are so dull when we compare them with the wonderful complications of human destinies, which real life offers," said Marmontel, thoughtfully.

They parted most cordially.

On the following day, M. de Stael was even more morose and taciturn than usual. Constant, gathering all his courage, spoke to him, and tried to enter into a conversation with him. Vain endeavor! When he asked the Embassador if there was any political news, M. de Stael replied that the *Ami du Citoyen* contained only the news that Citoyen Benjamin Constant was the *Déjeûner à la fourchette* of Madame de Stael. So saying, he left the room. Constant looked after him in confusion.

He and Madame de Stael sat opposite to each other in silence. Neither of them dared to utter the first word. Finally

Constant jumped up, intending to seize his hat and hasten from the room; but Madame de Stael laid her hand on his arm and detained him. As usual, so he yielded to-day, too, to her prayers.

A new life had dawned upon Madame de Stael. She wanted to open to her young friend the road to that fame to which she herself was not at liberty to aspire; she wished to plunge him into the political career, and then enjoy the successes which her ambition would enable him to achieve.

She presented him to Madame Tallien and Madame Beau-harnais, the aunt of the future Empress, both of whom received at their *salons* a large number of the most eminent men. The German, or at all events German-looking, young man, with his long, golden hair, and his open, radiant eyes, was well liked; and before long many felt inclined to take him under their protection, in order to gain political influence by his talents.

Madame de Stael, however, was by no means disposed to give him up so easily. She believed to have found in him at length the friend to whom she might devote herself entirely, and sacrifice everything; and who, in return, would bestow on her the affections of a true and constant heart. His German ideas, his philosophical systems, his enthusiasm, and his *naïve* and simple bearing enchanted her! Why had she not met him at an earlier day? Neither his religion nor the objections of his family would have prevented a union between her and him; and by his side she would have enjoyed that happiness which she considered the greatest and most enviable: a union with a beloved husband. "I shall compel my daughter to marry the man whom she loves," she would often say, with a sigh, when thinking of her own disappointments.

But then, was her case really hopeless?

' M. de Stael would not have objected to a divorce, provided
he received a suitable pecuniary compensation for the loss of ·
his wife. He was, moreover, old and infirm, and by no means
disposed to husband his strength ; so his life could not be of
long duration.

. But could Madame de Stael broach the possibility of such a
solution of her union with her husband ?

Benjamin Constant evaded every conversation whose drift
was in that direction, and so she contented herself with the
expectation that his growing attachment to her would lead to
that declaration for which she longed so intently.

Meanwhile she guided his steps in the path which his ambition and hankering after popularity had caused him to enter,
and rejoiced at his success.

In autumn Talleyrand returned likewise, and hastened to
thank her for her intercession in his behalf. He had been at
Hamburg, where Madame de Genlis lived in exile, and brought
Madame de Stael news in regard to the life which her present
rival and former idol was leading in that city. The love
affairs, however, in which he had engaged in Hamburg, he
took good care not to mention.

Madame de Stael was occupied with her toilet when Talleyrand sent in his name ; and, in consonance with the custom of
that period, she received him in her dressing-room. M'lle
Olive dressed her while she herself rolled a small green twig
between her fingers. Like all vivacious persons, she had to
keep her hands busy in this manner in order to divert her natural restlessness. Standing before her large mirror, she conversed with him in the most animated manner, when suddenly
the beautiful Madame Recamier, dressed in white, entered the
room and seated herself on a light-blue sofa, bordered with '
gold. Talleyrand had risen at her entrance in order to bow to

her, and he now remained standing before her with an air of
ardent admiration.   The beautiful lady gayly chatted with
Madame de Stael for a few minutes about the manner in
which they could pass the day.   She then disappeared as
noiselessly as she had come.

"How beautiful and charming she is!" exclaimed Talleyrand.

"She is an angel!" warmly replied Madame de Stael.   "I
did not get acquainted with her until recently, at the sale of
my father's house, which she purchased.   She was very bashful
on that occasion; she was afraid of my intellectual superiority,
and I had considerable difficulty in winning her.   But now she
is mine.   We are tenderly attached to one another.   She lives
at Chateau Clichy, and is but rarely in Paris, inasmuch as she
is afraid of the great world.   At her Chateau she sees a great
many interesting persons, among whom is also Lucien Bonaparte, whose affections she has completely won.   But what
heart could remain indifferent to such a charming personage?"

"Mine, I hope," replied Talleyrand, jocularly.   "Women
cause us so much more pain than joy, that it really seems to me
they must have been created in order to punish us rather than
to gladden our hearts, unless they possess such a gifted mind
as yours."

Madame de Stael took no notice of this compliment, and
recommended her new protégé to the kind favor of the experienced politician.

"You ask me to be so disinterested as to promote the interests of a young man who is evidently dear to your heart?"
he said, smilingly.

"I am sure you do not expect me to solicit your influence
in behalf of my enemies?" she asked, laughing.

"Very well. But in what way can I serve him?"

"By teaching him to turn circumstances adroitly to account.".

"You are a dangerous woman," he replied; "for you see through my policy as you once saw through my heart."

"Until you locked the door of it," she interrupted him, laughingly; "for you felt that I might discover too much in it."

"Ah, those were glorious times," said Talleyrand, covering his smooth forehead with his white hand. "Now I am growing old, and no one cares any more for me."

"You cannot be in earnest. You really do not look like a man determined to renounce the pleasures of life. But tell me now, how do you like our republican Paris? How did, it strike you?"

"Citoyenne Stael, I find the tone somewhat vulgar, and the language rather coarse and blunt. One believes at times to have descended into the kitchen of one's hotel."

- "The Parisians speak, at all events, a very plain and expressive language; they use no smooth words, no unnecessary phrases. Buffon would laugh at his florid style, if he should compare it with his plain and sober language."

Thus the aristocratic classes laughed and joked about republican France, and a society of young cavaliers who called themselves *Incroyables* even marched about publicly, and derided the manners and costume of the new democracy.

Madame de Stael disliked the new tone of society, and the social changes brought about by the Revolution; but she acquiesced in everything, inasmuch as the *droit de l'homme*, to which she still adhered as ardently as ever, could not be secured in any other way.

Benjamin Constant was now her inseparable companion; she clung to him with all her wishes and hopes, and built on

14*

him both the happiness of her future and that of the present moment.

She appropriated, as it were, his talents, and turned them to account. He often painfully felt the fetters which she thus imposed on him. Whenever he made an attempt to free himself from her influence, she flew into a towering passion, and overwhelmed him with a flood of reproaches and tears. He longed to escape from her, and yet he could not do without her.

"*Jamais je n'ai été aimé comme j'aimé*," she said to him, mournfully, one day; and, more profoundly moved by the reproachful expression of her eyes than by the vehement words of her passion, he came near betraying his secret to her. Kneeling down before her, and pressing her beautiful hands to his lips, he said: "Would to God I had been at liberty to offer you my whole heart."

"At liberty!" she exclaimed, in the utmost agitation. "What do you mean, Constant? Pray do not goad me to madness by such terrible allusions!"

Instead of disclosing anything to her, he reassured her again, on seeing the state of mind into which his words had thrown her.

Thus passed the summer. Benjamin Constant was at work upon his book, *Les Effets de la Terreur*, and issued his *Réactions Politiques*.

He was now carried away more and more by the political current, and allowed himself to be guided by this gifted lady, who used him as a tool of her ambition. The solemn festival of the promulgation of the Constitution was celebrated; it was the Constitution of the year III, that was offered to France; and the excitement ran very high in Paris, when this palladium of national liberty was publicly read.

Benjamin Constant could certainly not remain a passive looker-on at a moment when he saw a whole nation in a blaze of excitement; and Madame de Staël had no difficulty in persuading him to enter the public arena at this juncture, and render his name famous. So he published in the newspapers three letters in opposition to the decree by which two-thirds of the members of the Convention were to enter the new National Assembly. These letters created the greatest sensation. Everybody wanted to get acquainted with the author. He was overwhelmed with the most flattering invitations, and the most beautiful ladies tried to ingratiate themselves with him, and offered him their protection.

These singular demonstrations opened his eyes. He perceived that he had defended a cause to which he was hostile at heart; and this first misstep in his political career taught him henceforth to be more prudent. He had found out how difficult it is for a man to take back what he has once said, and, at the same time, how humiliating it is to be praised for a grievous blunder.

The young stranger had now made his name famous. He could no longer act the humble protégé of Madame de Staël. She was proud of his successes, and yet it was painful for her to feel every now and then that he had now less need of her than heretofore. She followed him in thought at every step he made. Whenever he left her, she asked him when he would return to her; and when he tarried too long, he found her in an agony of impatience, and her beautiful eyes bathed in tears.

This state of dependence often tried his patience severely; still, he was unable to free himself from it.

She wished to visit her father and her children before the beginning of winter, and to take the latter to Paris in case Necker should not miss their presence.

" Will you accompany me to Coppet ? " she said to Benjamin Constant.

He looked at her in surprise.

" I ? " he asked at last. " What would the world, what would M. de Stael say to that, and how should I be able to meet your father and your children, after undermining the reputation of their mother ? "

" This answer is dictated by your head, but not by your heart," she said, angrily, and stepped to the window. His reply had mortified her deeply. She was at a loss to understand his course. He was attached to her ; she had no doubt that he longed to be with her, and yet he seemed to shrink from the idea of uniting his destiny with hers. She sighed profoundly. It was always the same story ; she met again and again with men who, weak and vacillating, could not make up their minds either to belong to her, or to break with her.

Phèdre was performed for the benefit of M'lle Contat, the price of admission having been raised to three times the usual rate. Constant sat at the opera behind Madame de Stael, while her husband passed the evening behind the scenes, and presenting to the actress costly gifts, for which his wife had to pay. The luxury that was now displayed in Paris was greater than ever, and the number of brilliant festivities and equipages was constantly on the increase. The ladies had recovered their power. On the 4th of October Madame de Stael heard for the first time the name Napoleon, which was to become so fatal to her ; and Napoleon soon wrote to his brother Joseph, " Every woman should pass six months in Paris in order to learn how powerful she is, and what is due to her."

It was difficult for Madame de Stael to leave Paris at this juncture ; yet she yielded to her father's wishes, and set out for Coppet.

CHAPTER V.

GUILT AND EXPIATION.

WHEN Madame de Stael, on the morning after her return from Coppet, sat in deshabille at the breakfast-table, Mathieu de Montmorency entered her room. She greeted with loud joy the friend who was so dear to her heart. He had been the hero of the most beautiful dreams of her youth; and no woman ever forgets such reminiscences.

She was overjoyed to see him once more in his native country, in his wonted surroundings, and in the same city with her. "You were wanting to me, Montmorency!" she said, holding out to him her beautiful hand, and tenderly fixing her large eyes on him. "Even though France may not have become what we wished to make of her, she has at all events gained a great deal. Grievous abuses have been abolished, the rights of man are acknowledged, and all men are equal before the law. These are steps forward in the path of humanity, which we must not lose sight of when the imperfection of our constitution makes a disagreeable impression on us."

"Let us say no more about it," said Montmorency, with a deprecating gesture, while a shudder ran through his frame. "I saw my only brother die on the scaffold, and no one can ever forget such a scene. The remembrance of it follows me at every step. The streets of Paris are in my eyes drenched in blood; a constitution written with a guillotine is abhorrent; and so are the rights of man, asserted as it were by wholesale assassination. My past life was an error which I shall repent of all my lifetime."

She vainly endeavored to excite his interest in the political events of the day. His eyes would not kindle when she spoke of her hopes in regard ·to them, and her most impassioned appeals met with no response from him. He said he would devote his strength only to deeds of charity, and to expiation.

She looked at him mournfully. He was no longer the youthful hero who spoke so ardently of the happiness of mankind, and sacrificed so readily his name, his fortune, his whole self to the welfare of France. How quickly this enchanting dream had vanished! In the prime of life, handsome and strong, he displayed the resignation of an old man. A life destitute of hopes and wishes, is the mere prelude to death.

She paced her room repeatedly in great agitation, while these thoughts passed through her mind. Her breast heaved profound sighs. It always costs a struggle to part with the companions of a period of our life which has taken root in our soul in this manner. She asked herself if she had not likewise grown poorer in hopes, and had ceased to wish. But she did not wait for the reply which frightened her. She clung fearfully to the blade which her hand still was able to grasp, lest her life should become utterly aimless and blank.

She had nothing to regret, nothing to lament, inasmuch as only the prompter's part had fallen to her share.

They parted in deep emotion. Both of them felt that henceforth they could no longer love in each other what they prized highest, and that they had to share each other's sensibilities, and that they had to use the past as the base of the friendly feeling of the present.

She glanced at the clock after he had left her. The hour had come when she looked for Benjamin Constant, but he did not make his appearance. She counted the minutes in an agony of impatience. To-day she had more need of him than ever before. The impression which Montmorency had left on her mind was so crushing, that she longed to derive strength and comfort from his fresh and hopeful being. With him, she could dream of a brilliant future.

He tarried long beyond the appointed time. When he made his appearance at last, she feigned to be absorbed in a book, and took no notice of him. This irritated him, and he said, "You have no need of me to-day; so I will leave you immediately. I am sorry for the precious time which I have lost in coming to you."

A violent scene ensued. Constant complained of the restraints which she imposed on him, and of her distrust, which called him to account at every step he made. She burst into tears, and as usual he was vanquished. But he could not take back the harsh words which he had uttered, nor could she forget them.. The worst consequence arising from such scenes is that the reproaches uttered on those occasions are certain to be repeated sooner or later.

Imprudent as she always was, she had not locked her door. M. de Stael suddenly entered the room in the midst of this scene. He looked in surprise at the tearful eyes of his wife, and cast a contemptuous glance at the young man who stood before him in confusion, and did not know what excuse he should offer to him.

"Inasmuch as your conversation seems to afford but little pleasure to Madame de Stael, I believe it would be best for you not to visit our house any longer," he said, with frigid politeness.

Constant drew himself up to his full height, took his hat, and left the room.

Madame de Stael sent an imploring glance after him, but he

took no notice of it. In despair at the insulting manner in which her friend had been driven from her house, she now vented her anger on her husband.

"I do not know, sir, what right you have to meddle with my private affairs in this manner," she said, in a proud tone. "I think it should be left to myself to get rid of acquaintances whom I dislike, and you should refrain from anticipating me in this respect. You have grievously insulted M. de Rebecque, and I now ask you to beg his pardon."

"I do not deem it incumbent on me to use very prudent language toward a young adventurer who forces himself as a parasite into my house," replied M. de Stael, coldly. "As to you, Madame, I ask you not to sully a name which your children are going to bear. If you are unable to perform your duty as a wife, you will, as a mother, certainly take pains to submit to the rules of decorum and propriety."

"Your reproaches are utterly groundless," she said, coldly.

"All I have to say on this point is, that the wife of the Swedish Embassador receives a young stranger at the most unseasonable hours of the day, and enacts with him noisy scenes, to which all the servants may listen at the doors. That seems to me sufficient. You have always regarded imprudent steps, which scandalized the world, as eminently praiseworthy; and I overlooked many of them, engrossed as my attention was by political affairs; but now I have leisure to watch over your honor, which is mine, too, as long as you bear my name."

"An honor for which my father has paid half my fortune; I should think that that made us even, sir."

"Not quite," he replied, coldly.

"What else do you want?"

"I want you to discontinue your acquaintance with Con stant."

"In that case I suppose I am at liberty to ask you to pursue the same course toward your fair friends?" she asked, sarcastically.

"No," he said, with icy calmness. "A man's position in the world is different from that of a woman. I may defy public opinion, but you must bow to it."

"But what if I refuse to do so?"

"You must, then, stand the consequences. I am the master of this house, and the servants have hands to eject intruders."

So saying, he rose and left the room.

Madame de Stael sank to the floor in an agony of grief and despair. It took her a long time to regain composure enough to ring for her maid and dress herself. When she had finished her toilet, she left, on foot, her house, to which she did not intend to return.

When Benjamin Constant, at a late hour in the evening, returned to his house, he was informed that a lady, who insisted on seeing him, was waiting for him.

He hastened up-stairs in dismay, and entered his room.

At his entrance Madame de Stael rose and came to meet him with a timid air.

"For God's sake," he exclaimed, in an undertone, locking the door anxiously, lest inquisitive persons should disturb them, "for God's sake, what brought you here?"

She told him what had happened.

"And what are you going to do?" he asked, anxiously.

"I count upon you," she said, timidly.

"Upon me!" cried Constant, as if in despair, burying his face in his hands. "Upon me! Have mercy on me, and take back these words! It is time yet; your house is still open to you. Do not lose a moment. Every minute is precious. Remember your children. Remember your old father, and the

honorable name which you bear." He implored her by all
that was sacred to her, not to venture so desperate a step which
could never be retrieved. She listened to him with a mournful air.

"If you turn me out, very well; I shall go to a hotel," she
said, with an expression which made him tremble. No matter
what he said to her, she turned a deaf ear to his appeals.

"You are the last hope of my life," she repeated to him. "I
am forbidden to receive you at my house. Well, then, I shall
see you elsewhere. M. de Stael can do without me; but I cannot do without you."

"But you cannot intend to take up your residence in these
humble rooms," he objected; "they do not offer you any comfort
whatever."

She now cast the first glance at her surroundings. A smile
lit up her features as she did so. "Yes, I see your rooms do
not allow you to receive your friends here," she then said.

"Well, then, you can and will not stay here; so you will
now return to your house. I shall get you a carriage. As yet
you can go back without exciting any suspicion. To-morrow
you will try to find a house suitable to your circumstances; as
soon as you are there, send for me, and I shall hasten to you."

He threw himself at her feet and implored her to comply
with his wishes. She looked at him compassionately.

"I shall go," she said, "but alone."

So saying, she rose and left the room.

Constant remained in a state of indescribable anxiety. He
did not touch his bed, but paced his room all night long, and
shudderingly looked forward to the coming day. He was determined not to go to the house of the Swedish Embassador
to inquire whether or not Madame de Stael was there. He
would not cross the threshold of that house again.

He was still in hopes that she would rue a resolution which he clearly foresaw would be fatal to her reputation. He passed the day in a constant tempest of perplexity, hope, and fear. Already he had tried to persuade himself that her continued silence was owing to her return to her husband, and her probable determination to stay with him, when he received from her a note in which she requested him to come to her. She begged him not to object to her invitation on account of its being written at her husband's house; she would remain there, but he would henceforth reach her rooms by another door, inasmuch as she had taken possession of the house which belonged to her, and had granted to M. de Stael a suite of rooms, where he would now live entirely by himself and be his own master.

Constant, agitated by conflicting emotions, hastened to comply with her request. He could not upbraid her for what she had done. He felt that she was making sacrifices for which he was unable to indemnify her; and he perceived this in moments of calmness, the more as, at bottom, she had good cause to be dissatisfied with him. What other woman would have borne to see him accept the sacrifices which she made to him, without offering her his hand and the protection of his name? He felt, to his shame, that his conduct could not but give rise to the most unpleasant misconstructions.

Although her separation from her husband was by no means strange, rumor was not long in inventing a thousand ridiculous stories in regard to the cause which led to it. Her name was soon on all lips, and she could not prevent people from circulating the most unpleasant rumors about her. This was most painful to her ambition and pride. She had made an immense sacrifice, and was not even allowed to complain of the consequences, against which Constant had cautioned her so cloquently. So she kept silence and devoted herself to politics and to the interests of her friend even more zealously and energetically than before.

Marmontel was now elected to the Council of Ancients, and therefore returned to Paris.

She met her old friend in visible confusion. "You must not be angry with me," she said to him, bursting into tears. "I have need of some one who shares my life, and whose interests are my own. *C'est ma nature ainsi.* I cannot walk my path alone. Would to God I could! But I cannot. I am not like other women. If I see that happiness is within my reach, and I am not to enjoy it because the so-called rules of decorum forbid me to do so, I cannot obey them. God has given me a heart which throbs impetuously. It has carried me away to many a good deed which I had to perform with great self-abnegation; and if it now for once urges me to do something gratifying to myself, I must yield to it likewise."

Marmontel folded her to his heart with paternal tenderness. "I pity you," he said, "but I do not censure you. Those whose emotions are powerful, will every now and then slightly overstep the rules of decorum. Let them be called to account for it by Him who gave them such a nature."

No less unexpectedly than Marmontel had been called into the Council of Ancients, he saw that body dissolved, and himself sent back to St. Brice, where he died soon after.

Moreau commanded the army of the Rhine at this juncture; Bonaparte was at the head of the French troops in Italy; and Madame de Stael watched attentively the glorious career of the two young heroes. The free press took pains to lay all the news from the seat of war before the public, and there was so much stirring intelligence to relate and read that the days were not long enough for doing so.

Constant had become a member of the Salm Club, which opposed the Directory. He was soon after elected Secretary of this Club, in which, by the aid of Madame de Stael, he was all-powerful. She was now desirous of procuring Talleyrand, too, a position suitable to his talents, and by their joint efforts he obtained the appointment of Minister of Foreign Affairs. In return, he wished to recommend Constant to Bonaparte. But Bonaparte was already prejudiced against him, owing to his speeches in the Salm Club, where he had inveighed with brilliant eloquence against all hereditary privileges, and generally assumed a tone which seemed objectionable to the future of France, and caused him to decline his services.

CHAPTER VI.

MADAME DE MONTESSON.

MADAME DE MONTESSON, who had been secretly married to the Duke of Orleans, received at her house in the Rue Mont Blanc, on the corner of the Rue de Provence, a circle of the most eminent Parisians, among whom was also M. de Talleyrand. Here he formed the acquaintance of Josephine Beauharnais, and conceived the plan of bringing about a union between her and the General-in-Chief of the army of Italy.

Madame de Stael had long since ardently admired the young hero, and longed to get acquainted with him. At Madame de Montesson's house she had at last an opportunity to do so.

Talleyrand had informed her that she would meet him there on a certain evening, and she did not fail to be present on that occasion. Easily excited by every new acquaintance she made, especially when, as on this occasion, she was swayed by her imagination, which depicted the young hero in the most glowing colors to her, she looked in breathless suspense forward to the moment of his arrival.

She had chosen a very simple toilet, because she had been told that the General disliked too gorgeously dressed women. She wore a white satin dress, beautifully trimmed with lace; her arms and neck bare, and red-velvet ribbon studded with pearls wound round her short and curly hair.

"How beautifully you are dressed!" said Talleyrand, gazing at her admiringly. "Would I could think you had done so for me!"

"Oh, you do not wish it, Talleyrand. Such an attention would only embarrass you. Your heart is by far too large to be a suitable present for one lady."

"You know that there are so many amiable ladies that I cannot bestow my exclusive admiration upon one of them," he replied, with a polite smile toward the other ladies.

"Suppose we were at sea, and should be shipwrecked; to which lady would you offer your hand at the moment of danger, in order to save her?"

"Not to you, *car vous nayez si bien, Madame.*"

An answer of this description enchanted Madame de Stael. She admired this skill of getting so advantageously out of a difficulty, the more as she was deficient in it. Persons who speak much and well, and like to hear themselves, never are noted for skill at repartee.

"You are irresistible whenever you wish to be so," she said, taking his arm in order to pace the not very large room till Bonaparte's arrival. It was long after midnight when he entered the room. Madame de Stael watched him attentively while he paid his respects to Madame de Montesson. Her imagination had drawn a widely different portrait of the young hero, and she had now to recover from her surprise before she was able to meet him with composure. She had fancied that he was much taller. His somewhat awkward and embarrassed bearing made an unfavorable impression in a *salon.* He listened to the polite welcome of Madame de Montesson with an air of superiority which displeased her. He was at home only on the battle-field.

Many persons thronged around him already. Talleyrand, disengaging himself from Madame de Stael's arm, approached

Bonaparte and whispered to him that Necker's daughter wished to get acquainted with him.

" *Je n'aime pas les femmes qui se mêlent de politique*," he said, briefly.

" Well, in a country where their heads are cut off, they like to know the reason why it is done," replied Talleyrand, smiling.

Bonaparte then allowed him to conduct him to her.

Madame de Stael had overheard his words. Instead of meeting with admiration at his hand, she found that he was prejudiced against her. This vexed her.

He said to her that he was very sorry not to have formed her father's acquaintance during his journey, although he had gone to Coppet in order to pay him a visit. M. Necker had not been at home.

She replied to him without much presence of mind. All that she had intended to say to him had vanished from her memory as soon as she discovered that he would never admire, never love her. This discovery plunged her soul into the deepest gloom. She could not appear otherwise than she was ; and if he refused to pay homage to her gifted mind, she felt full well that their meeting could not but make a painful impression upon each of them.

Thus she foresaw their mutual relations from the very first, and henceforth she opposed, with Constant, his progress toward a position which was to destroy the whole structure of her ardent hopes.

She soon after saw the day when the word *Citoyen*, which she still regarded as an expression of the acknowledged rights of man, was changed into the humiliating term *Subjects;* she saw that, despite all the thundering speeches of her protégé, the rights of birth were reinstated in their former importance;

she had to follow the nation step by step to the old regime, and the only reward which she received for her sacrifices and efforts to oppose this reactionary movement, was persecution, and finally exile from a city which was vital to her existence. At a distance from Paris she merely vegetated, and her tears flowed constantly during the slow and tedious days.

Madame de Stael now met Bonaparte frequently in society, while he was preparing for his expedition to Egypt; but she no longer sought to approach him. She was already afraid of him. The laconic questions which he always propounded to those with whom he conversed, were distasteful to her. She called this peculiarity of his a " *vocation naturelle pour l'etat de prince*," and deemed it contrary to good breeding to ask of others information about their affairs, which they did not offer of their own accord. "Are you married?" "How many children have you?" "When did you arrive?" "When are you going to leave?" Who had a right to address a citizen of the republic in this manner?

She censured Talleyrand for not calling his attention to the fact that his conduct was impertinent; but he escaped her, as usual, by a witty phrase.

The world had ceased noticing the fact that M. de Stael did not appear any longer in the apartments of his wife, and Benjamin Constant met no more with reproaches and allusions which were indescribably painful to him.

Switzerland being threatened with invasion, Madame de Stael left Paris in January, 1798, and hastened to Coppet. Her father's name was still on the list of French exiles, and in case one of these exiles was apprehended in a country occupied by French troops, his life was forfeited.

She tried to persuade Necker to leave Coppet, but he refused to do so.

"At my age," he said, "one must not wander about the world."

He would not leave his wife's tomb. As she had never left him during her lifetime, so he wished to remain near her in death.

It was a fine morning in midwinter when they were informed that the French were approaching. Madame de Stael and her father stepped out upon the balcony of the château, where they surveyed the long alley, and awaited the arrival of the troops. The air was so pure, the sky so blue, the water of the lake so transparent, that the lofty summits of the Alps were reflected in it. The sound of the drums fell on their ears from afar, and filled Madame de Stael with anxiety for her father's life.

At the moment when the French troops crossed the frontier, she noticed that an officer left the ranks and rode toward the château. She awaited his arrival tremblingly.

The Directory had commissioned him to inform M. Necker that a safeguard had been granted to him. The bearer of this news was Suchet, who afterwards became a Marshal of the Empire, and who performed his mission in the most courteous and pleasant manner.

Madame de Stael was now reassured as to her father's fate; but she watched the course of events in Switzerland with incessant anxiety. The first battle took place soon after. Although Coppet is thirty leagues from Berne, the echoes of the distant mountains wafted the roar of artillery over to them and struck terror into her heart. She scarcely dared to breathe while the struggle continued, and Necker suffered even more than his daughter from this war, which France, his adopted country, waged against his small fatherland. The French were able to drive back the Swiss forces, but they could not conquer Switzerland; for the will of a united people, no matter how small it may be, renders it invincible.

On the famous 18th of Brumaire she returned to Paris. While her horses were changed at the last station, she was told that Barras, escorted by gensd'armes, had just passed by on his way to his villa at Grosbois. All along the road she no longer heard the people speak of the National Assembly, but only of Bonaparte.

Scarcely had she reached the house when Benjamin Constant entered her room.

" Our cause is lost!" he said, sitting down in front of her with a desponding air. " This Corsican is master of the situation."

" At the first moment already you speak to me *de ce petit homme?*" she asked, deeply mortified.

"I know that you love your country better than yourself and me," he said, in confusion.

" Still it would not have offended me if you had forgotten France for my sake for a moment," she replied, reproachfully.

After regaining her composure, she begged him to communicate to her all that had happened, and now almost regretted having stayed so long at Coppet, believing as she did that her presence might have prevented much mischief.

" We shall have to bow to the dictator's power," he said, " or share the fate of Barras."

A shudder ran through Madame de Stael's frame at the mere thought. The phantom of *ennui*, which always pursued her, rose before her more terrible than ever. Nevertheless, she felt that she must not and could not prove faithless to the cause of humanity, and must defend the *Droit de l'homme* to her last breath. In this spirit she now spoke to Constant, and the lofty and noble enthusiasm which she breathed, fascinated him again as irresistibly as ever. His heart belonged to M'lle de Hardenberg; but his head loved and admired Madame de Stael.

While Bonaparte's power became daily more unlimited, and while his heroic deeds captivated the imagination and dazzled the judgment of the people more and more, the opposition redoubled its efforts to conjure up a counter-revolution, and to depict in glowing colors the dangers threatening the cause of liberty.

The mouth-piece of this party was Benjamin Constant; the spirit animating his speeches was that of Madame de Stael.

He published a history of the Revolution of 1660, which gave great umbrage to Bonaparte and his adherents. He prepared, furthermore, a speech, which was to depict the dawn of the new despotism. This subject was in consonance with the views of his gifted friend, and although she was well aware of the dangers which might arise for her from this significant manifestation, she was determined not to deprive her protégé of this brilliant triumph for the sake of her own safety.

For some time past she had been acquainted with Joseph and Lucien Bonaparte. The former was even warmly attached to her; he did not share his brother's prejudice against gifted women; her views about liberty and the rights of man were not at variance with his opinions and schemes; so he gladly yielded to the charm of her conversation, and passed the most agreeable hours at her house.

Meanwhile, the day when Benjamin Constant was to deliver his speech, was drawing nigh. On the eve of this important demonstration, Madame de Stael had gathered around her a circle of friends, most of whom, tired as they were of political convulsions and of persecution, were ready to acquiesce in any measures of the Government, provided it did not disturb

them any more. They were engaged in the most pleasant and
animated conversation, which the lady of the house illuminated
with the incessant coruscations of her genius.

Constant gazed musingly upon the company. He fixed his
eyes thoughtfully on his fair friend, who chatted so gayly and
looked so serene, as he had not seen her for a long time past.

Suddenly he rose, approached her, and whispered in her
ear :

" Look at this circle of eminent men now gracing your *salon ;*
when I have delivered my speech, all of them will desert you ;
do not forget that."

" I cannot be recreant to my convictions," she said, in her
enthusiasm for the good cause, which she thought she was promoting. To an uncertain success she was ready to sacrifice
her own existence, but only because she had miscalculated the
consequences of this step. But no one is able to swim alone
against the tide without becoming a martyr to his cause.

She threw down the gauntlet to Bonaparte, and he took
it up.

Benjamin Constant delivered his speech.

Madame de Stael had invited a few friends to dinner on that
day. When the clock struck five, one of the guests sent her a
note, excusing his inability to be present ; another note of the
same tenor arrived a few minutes after, and finally no one remained to share her dinner but Constant himself.

They sat opposite to one another in silence.

Despite her efforts to conceal her vexation, she was unable
to do so ; but she felt that she would not be justified in vent-
ing her disappointment on her protégé.

Joseph Bonaparte was severely rebuked by his brother for
visiting the house of a woman animated by such sentiments.
Since that time he no longer ventured to appear at her house,

and his example was generally imitated. Even those who had hitherto shared her opinions, now denounced her loudly, and disapproved what they had formerly advocated. She was severely censured for having assisted Talleyrand in obtaining a seat in the cabinet; and yet the same men who blamed her on this account, flocked to Talleyrand's house and praised every step he took.

This inconsistency gave much pain to Madame de Stael. For the first time she now experienced a feeling of bitterness which had never stolen upon her before. It was not fate, but the injustice of men that gave rise to it.

Owing to her natural and almost irresistible communicativeness, she had the utmost difficulty in restraining her impetuous feelings; and the consequence of this was, that her intercourse with Benjamin Constant became exceedingly painful. Both of them were vexed and dejected, and silently charged each other with having caused their misfortune, without venturing to confess it.

Fouché, the Police Minister, sent for Madame de Stael and informed her that the First Consul ascribed Benjamin Constant's speech to her. He had no proofs; general reflections on the liberty and rights of nations, devoid of personal allusions, were no crime.

Such was her reply; and Fouché, admitting the pertinency of her answer, advised her to leave Paris for a time, in order that the matter might be forgotten.

She returned, deeply dejected, to her house. She was exiled, then—exiled from a city which she loved so dearly—exiled, as it were, of her own accord. Deserted by her friends, and excluded from society, nothing remained for her but to flee the place where her feelings were wounded so cruelly.

She paced her apartments mournfully. She needed not

to shut her doors. No one visited her. No one seemed to care for her any longer. No one desired to have a seat at her table.

She thought she had followed her convictions, and yet she did not feel that tranquillity of mind proceeding from the consciousness that we have sacrificed everything to our principles. She did not care to fathom the cause of her present state of mind, inasmuch as a low, low voice, in all probability whispered that she had this time set her heart not so much upon the cause alone as upon its representative, and that her hatred of despotism was enhanced by the fact that Bonaparte was the despot.

Her hours dragged through slowly and wearily. She longed to arrive at some resolution, and yet she was unable to make up her mind. She was waiting for Constant in order to consult with him. She glanced uneasily at the clock. Already the hour had come when she had expected him, and he did not make his appearance yet. What detained him so long to-day? Did he intend to shun her likewise, because the others had deserted her?

At this moment she heard the footstep of a man in the anteroom. She listened. It was not that of Benjamin Constant.

Mathieu de Montmorency entered the room.

"I hear that you are in trouble, owing to Benjamin Constant's speech," he said, "and want to inquire how you are."

"So *you* are not afraid of visiting her whom all the rest of her friends have deserted?" she exclaimed, with streaming eyes; and, already relieved by the sympathy of this faithful friend of hers, she told him what had occurred.

He listened to her calmly, until she was through.

Although he no longer shared her views, nor approved her conduct, he was still able to sympathize with her feelings and pity her. He had not been at liberty to offer her his hand. Had he been able to do so, how different her fate would have been! Conscious as he was of this fact, he never uttered a word of censure against her, and he never proved recreant to the faithful friendship which he had once pledged to her.

He now tried to sooth her and to convince her that the displeasure with which the First Consul looked upon her would be certain to pass away in a short time.

"Accompany me to my estate for a few weeks," he said; "meanwhile the storm will blow over, and you will return to Paris with fresh hopes and courage."

She looked at him in deep emotion. With such a friend life was still beautiful. His very presence would comfort her, and the thought that she was not utterly alone, gave her fresh strength. She accepted his offer.

When he had left her, Constant arrived at last. He was in a high state of irritation. That a woman should be held responsible for his actions, vexed him greatly; that she was considered dangerous, while no notice was taken of him, as if he had nothing to do with the whole affair, wounded his vanity. He expressed his mortification in bitter terms, without considering that in so doing he poured poison into an open wound.

Madame de Stael, deadly pale and panting for breath, strode up and down the room while he uttered his long and bitter tirade. Finally she paused, and stood still in front of him. Her eyes shot fire as she fixed them on him. She then represented to him in a torrent of words the cruelty of his conduct in wounding by harsh words a woman unhappy enough without his reproaches, and to treat with such base ingratitude her who was devoting her whole life to him, and making to him every sacrifice conducive to his happiness. In her rage she upbraided him, for the first time, with the unmanliness of his conduct; she portrayed him in his indecision, his weakness; and told him that for his sake she had broken with her husband and tarnished her reputation, when he had been able to keep her honor unsullied.

He was unable to deny the truth of these charges, and, like all wrong-doers, he defended himself by preferring against her counter-charges, which she indignantly repelled because they were groundless. Both of them grew more and more excited, and they used constantly more scathing and bitter language in giving vent to their hatred; this time a speedy reconciliation was out of the question. Hour after hour passed in this useless quarrel; and Benjamin Constant, tired of the endless altercation, hastened from the room, and rushed wildly into the street. Madame de Stael fainted as he closed the door after him.

No sooner had he reached his room, and was alone with himself, then he regretted what he had done. He was at a loss to comprehend his own conduct. He tried to find reasons for justifying himself in his own eyes. The hours of the night slowly dragged through as he was doing so. He was up betimes in the morning, and immediately went to her house, the doors of which were still locked. A walk through the streets, he thought, would refresh him, and give him courage to appear before her. After an hour's lonely promenade, he was again at the street-door of her house.

The porter looked at him with surprise. "Madame de Stael has left Paris," he said, wondering at Constant's ignorance of her departure.

"Left Paris!" echoed Constant, pressing his hand to his forehead, as if he had to compose himself in order to understand these words.

15*

CHAPTER VII.

THE civilized world greeted the new century with eager expectations. At its beginning, mankind had reached a turning-point of history, and strove for aims never known before. The intellectual development of the nations of Europe had made immense progress in the last fifty years. German philosophy imbued all minds with the idea of the perfectibility of the human race, and thereby gave a new stimulus to the faculties of the soul. The word "perfectibility," which had hitherto not been used, was now added to the language to denote this idea.

France had dreamed all its political dreams. The ardent love of liberty had disappeared, tranquillity and moderation took its place, and the soil which had been drenched in blood pushed out new shoots. A longing for enjoyment rose in all minds. Art and science awoke from their slumbers, and literature began to shoot out new buds and blossoms.

Goethe had written his *Werther*. All Paris papers bestowed the most enthusiastic encomiums on this singular production of a great genius, and the public commenced taking the liveliest interest in German affairs. The sorrows of young Werther filled young France with deep emotion and ardent enthusiasm, and tempted many an unhappy youth to go in search of similar misfortunes, and make real or imaginary sorrows the destiny of his life.

Schiller's *Robbers* had been performed at all theaters, and it became fashionable to carry both virtues and vices to extreme length. This enthusiasm of the public never thought of the consequences; it feasted its soul on fine words. *Wallenstein* was already being rehearsed at the Berlin theater.

Frederick von Gentz issued his Report on the finances of Great Britain, and the *Journal de Paris* never tired of commenting on this curious and interesting work.

Madame de Stael had watched this revival of literature with the liveliest interest in the solitude of Coppet. It was, at bottom, the most essential element of her life. She had grown up under its influence, her childhood had drawn most of its nourishment from its blossoms; so she could no longer exist without that to which she had been accustomed so long, and she deemed life dull and vapid without this intellectual fragrance.

Bitter disappointments had bowed her courage and weighed down her heart, and in her present state of mind she derived consolation and exhileration only from literary employment. She wrote and read a great deal. At the beginning of the new year she intended to publish her production, and was now polishing and revising her book for the last time before sending it to the printer—the authors of the eighteenth century having taught her that the style of a writer will alone impart a true and lasting value to his works.

She had chosen a grave subject. She treated of the progress of mankind in the realm of the mind, as manifested in the productions of literature; and she inferred from these manifestations of progress that the Creator intended that the human mind should become perfect, and that it was incumbent on all men to strive to attain that object; in a word, she discussed the question of perfectibility. She had entered upon her

task with ardent courage, in order to strengthen her mind
and cure herself of her gloomy despondency.   Since Parisian
society had deserted her so cruelly, she was animated by a bitterness painful to herself; for, according to her nature, she
could entertain only feelings of kindness and generosity toward her fellow-creatures, and try to win their love; but this
love, she now asked herself—what was it?   What had it
proved to be in her case?   How they had applauded and flattered her; how they had praised her talents; and yet, at a
beck from the First Consul, they had deserted her and passed
her as if they had never known her !

So friendship and love were mere words; for men could
hardly sacrifice so readily what they really esteemed and admired.   How they could boldly exhibit the weakness of such
perfidy, was an enigma to her.

She had not profited by her father's experience in regard to
the fickleness of public opinion and popular favor; for every
one believes only in what he has experienced himself.

In these days of severe trials, Mathieu de Montmorency tried
to soothe her by the influence of religion.   She was to recognize the finger of God in everything, and bow to him in de-
vout humility; she was to perceive how immaterial it was to
be appreciated by men, when one was sure of his love.   She
listened to his words; she smiled at him gratefully when he took
pains to point out to her the path in which his own mind had
found peace; but she did not act upon his suggestions.   Life
still knocked so impetuously at her doors, that she was unable
to appreciate the blessing of resignation.   She could not bring
herself to submit to suffering as a salutary trial; she desired
to be happy in accordance with her innate qualities, and said
it was the Creator's intention that man should be happy.

Her sojourn at Coppet, her intercourse with her father, and

the joy which her children afforded her, did not tranquilize her mind. The thought of the humiliation which she had suffered, drew from her every morning new murmurs and complaints, and moistened her eyes with new tears which her wounded heart caused her to shed. She could not reconcile herself to the idea that she had been deserted and treated so ignomin-iously. She asked herself again and again if it was true, or if some dismal dream had not deluded her; and, whenever her mind replied in the affirmative, she would wring her hands despairingly.

This thought was upon her all the time. No matter where she was, it did not leave her; and an imperative voice in her breast commanded her to reconquer her position in society. Necker grieved profoundly at his daughter's despondency, and vainly tried to cheer her up. What was to be done about it? How could he help her?

Benjamin Constant had not been able to bear the separation from her a long time. With his usual weakness, he had fol-lowed her. She received him coldly. His words of repentance, his protestations, to which his conscience gave the lie, misled her, and she forgave him; for what the heart wishes, it is al-ways ready and willing to believe.

Besides, she felt so lonely; she needed so much to have with her a man whom she could influence; who became, as it were, the instrument of her dreams in regard to the future, and with whom she could dream, hope, and wish. So she was glad that he had returned to her.

His position as Secretary of the Constitutional Club, however, did not permit him to stay away from Paris a long time; he had entered upon his political career there, had become a pop-ular orator, and could not now, by a prolonged absence from the capital, risk all he had gained thus far. So he proposed to her to return with him to Paris. She could easily recover her position in society; all she would have to do for this purpose would be to bring about a reconciliation with M. de Stael, and the wife of the Swedish Embassador would stand again in the midst of the best society.

It was generally known in Paris that M. de Stael was pressed by his creditors, and frequently very hard run for money. Formerly, he had been at liberty to refer his creditors to his wealthy father-in-law, and got rid of the importunate duns by telling them that M. Necker would pay them; but since he had separated from his wife, he was no longer allowed to do so. No one would trust him any more, and the consequence was that he saw the splendor and comfort of his household pass away, and had to do without his wonted luxuries. Nothing could be more disagreeable to him, and it was more than probable that he would gladly grasp the hand offered him for reconciliation. Why, then, should Madame de Stael not offer it to him, when such a reconciliation would be so advantageous to her, and enable her to return to Paris, where she longed to live? Why should she not pay the insignificant price of a first word for so great an advantage? Why not recover so cheaply the prominent position which she had formerly occupied in Parisian society?

Benjamin Constant was justified under the circumstances in supposing that conciliatory steps on the part of Madame de Stael, how insignificant soever they might be, would be most joyously met by her husband. If Madame de Stael returned to Paris in order to resume her place as Embassadress of Sweden, the First Consul was obliged to receive her and treat her politely; and no one would thenceforth have any reason to shun her house; no one would dare to offend the Embassador of a foreign power by slighting her.

He wrote her a long letter after his return to Paris, and laid all these arguments before her. His letter closed as follows: "The laws of society are stronger than the human will. The pride of independence bows in the long run to stern necessity and to circumstances. It is for us to determine to follow only what our hearts long for; sooner or later we must, nevertheless, comply with the requirements of our reason. I can no longer allow you to occupy toward the world a position which mortifies me in your soul, and which is, moreover, a silent reproach against me. You owe it to me, you owe it to yourself to put an end to this struggle."

After reading these lines, she threw them angrily on the floor. She thought it was evident that he did not wish to share the humiliations of her position.

"I shall put an end to this struggle, but in my own way," she said. "Never shall I submit to the humiliation of begging of M. de Stael a position which I once threw unhesitatingly at his feet. Never shall I do so! Never! I must by my own efforts recover the place of which a word from the First Consul deprived me. Paris once admired me; it bowed before the sound of my name. It shall be subjected again to the same charm. I am too old to bow my head; I am too old to adorn myself with borrowed tinsel. I feel my worth too much to beg for what I have a right to demand! They shall admire my genius; they shall pay homage to me again! I will achieve this triumph or none! If I do not succeed in doing so, I possess less genius than I believe I do, and I deserve to disappear in the multitude. I deserve to be overlooked."

After this soliloquy, she hastened to her writing-table and worked with redoubled energy at the book by which she intended to obtain this triumph. The winter drew to a close before her work was completed.

Early in the spring of 1800, she suddenly returned to **Paris,** it was said in order to superintend the publication of her book. She made no calls after her arrival. She remained at home all the time, and anxiously looked forward to the day when her work would be issued, and the public criticize it.

To Benjamin Constant she said not a word about her expectations; for he, too, was to be surprised by her success, like the rest of her former friends. Whenever he upbraided her for disregarding his advice, she smiled and shook her head mournfully.

"Oh! how little do you know me, Constant!" she said to him. "How little are you able to appreciate the difference between the conventional respect granted us for the sake of our official position, and the distinction for which we are indebted to our personal merit, our own fame and talents. I am sorry to find that you believe the former would satisfy me."

A few days afterward, Talleyrand called on her. She asked him, wonderingly, what had led him to the house of a lady that had incurred the displeasure of his master to such a degree as to drive away all her friends? Those swimming with the tide should not show themselves at her house; so she could not but admire his courage."

"Extend your admiration also to the power which I serve, and we shall live again on the most amicable footing," he said, with a smile.

She looked at him in surprise. Had he perhaps come to her only in order to suggest this prudent course to her? Had Napoleon sent him to her? She told him she would not bow to that power, and he seemed dissatisfied.

On the following day, Joseph Bonaparte visited her. He held in his hand a letter from his brother, which he handed to her with an air of embarrassment, and begged her to read in his presence. It was as follows.

"March 19, 1800.

"M. de Stael, I have been told, lives in abject poverty, while his wife enjoys all the comforts of affluence. If you should continue to visit her while she lives in Paris, beg her to grant that poor man a monthly allowance of one thousand or twelve hundred francs. What a pass we have come to! I am ready to treat Madame de Stael as a man; but in that case she should bear in mind that a man possessed of a large fortune and a celebrated name is not at liberty to let his wife be in want, and that the world will condemn him for so doing."*

A deep flush of anger crimsoned her cheeks as she glanced over these lines.

"Your distinguished brother is very kind to take so much interest in my private affairs," she said, returning the letter to him with a sarcastic smile. "Pray inform him that the King of Sweden pays to his Embassador, or, if he does not, should pay to him, a sufficient sum for living decently, provided he knows how to keep his expenses within reasonable bounds; and I am sure it is not my duty to pay out of my own means for festivals in which I do not take part, and for love affairs which are a disgrace to his advanced age. For the rest, I am obliged to him for intending to treat me as a man; as no one can deny that, as a general thing, men surpass us in intellectual endowments, it certainly flatters me to be placed on a footing of equality with them. That I have remained a woman at heart shows my sensibility to malevolence and persecution, and to every act of hostility which tells me how much need my sex has of support and protection. But if my talents are equal to those of a man, it must not be inferred that M. de Stael's relations to me are those of a woman—of a wife—and

* Memoirs of Joseph Bonaparte.

that he is dependent on me for his daily bread. Natural relations cannot be inverted in this manner, even though the all-powerful First Consul of France tries to shake them."

"I regret my brother's irritation toward you," replied Joseph, "the more so as it often deprives me of the pleasure of seeing you. You know how highly I esteem you, and prize my acquaintance with you. In order not to incur his displeasure, I have often to abstain from visiting you, lest he should forbid me to call on you at all. You ought to be kind and friendly enough to spare me this pain. You ought to think of your friends, and bear in mind how much they suffer in consequence of obstinacy."

"What can I do," she exclaimed, vehemently. "It is my nature to be truthful."

"Pursue a more conciliatory course. Be cautious in speaking of him. Make about him some flattering remark which will be reported to him, and which will neutralize the effect of your former unfavorable criticisms."

"Then I should have to do violence to my convictions, and I cannot do that; I should be untruthful."

"At all events keep silence."

"That will not satisfy him, inasmuch as he wants me to admire him, and I cannot do so. All honor to his military skill, but as a law-giver and ruler of France he is distasteful to me."

"You do not know him. Get better acquainted with him."

"How can I do so when he shuns me, and purposely avoids me wherever he can?"

"We shall manage to bring you in contact with him. For the sake of your friends, embrace the opportunity to bring about a reconciliation. You do not promote the interests of France by expressing your dislike of my brother, and you injure yourself no less than you grieve your friends."

" Such a friend I cannot refuse anything," said Madame de Stael, deeply moved, and gave him her hand. "I shall henceforth love you more than ever, since your heart has manifested so much sympathy for me."

A few other acquaintances gave her similar advice. They told her she would have no difficulty in ingratiating herself with the First Consul, and the advantages arising from his favor were so great, that, in acting as she did, she must be perfectly blind to her own interests. She could not deny that these arguments were excellent, and she would gladly have pursued a prudent course, but she could not bring herself to do so.

" I am no longer at an age when we form new views on such subjects," she replied. " I have reached my four-and-thirtieth year, and my experience adds as many years to my age. I am, moreover, my father's daughter, *c'est ma nature ainsi*, to be candid. I owe it to his fame, and to the honor of his name, not to sacrifice my political opinions to my personal advantage. No matter what I may do, I must remain true to my convictions. To such sincerity of character even an enemy will pay respect. They fear me only because they are unable to win me."

Benjamin Constant had listened silently to this conversation. When he was at last alone with her, he said, in a tone of vexation :

" It is unfortunate for women to meddle with politics. How tranquil and agreeable a life you might lead ; how pleasantly and merrily your days might pass in the bosom of your family, but for this passion of yours for playing a political *rôle!* "

She made no reply, but sat motionless, opposite to him, wildly gazing into vacancy. Constant hastened to her in dismay and seized her hands. They were cold as ice. She seemed to be

senseless. When he touched her, she awoke to consciousness as if from a dream. She pushed him back and said in a
hollow voice:

"What do you want of me, M. de Rebecque? You have
said to me all that can be said. We have henceforth no longer anything to do with each other. Go! What do you want
here?"

She rose, for the purpose of leaving the room, but her feet
refused to carry her. She tottered. He hastened to her in
order to support her; but before he reached her, she sank
senseless at his feet.

Almost beside himself, he bent over her and called her by
the fondest names. She did not hear him. At last he rang
the bell, and when the footman came in, he ordered him to call
Madame de Stael's maid, and tell her to undress her mistress
and lay her on her bed. He tried once more to appeal with
his voice to her heart. A deprecating gesture silenced him,
and the large tears which now gushed from her long dark
lashes, showed him how unsuitable the moment was to an ex-
planation and reconciliation. He left her, in an agony of conflicting emotions, and hastened home, where he locked himself
in his room.

Madame de Stael kept her room for several days after this
scene. She did not eat, she did not speak, and was not at home
for anybody. Even Benjamin Constant was not admitted to
her. He wrote to her. His letters remained unanswered.
Goaded almost to madness by her silence, he finally determined
to force an entrance into her room. He succeeded in gaining
access to her, and, throwing himself at her feet, covered her
hands with glowing kisses of repentance. She looked at him
sadly and reproachfully, and had not the heart to repel him.
When he commenced excusing himself, she closed his mouth,

and told him to be silent. " Say not a word reminding me of the past," she said, gravely. " Since we are on such terms as we are now, we had better speak of indifferent matters."

She handed him the *Mercure de France*, then edited by Fontanes. It contained an open letter addressed by Chateaubriand to Madame de Stael, and in which he tried to refute her opinions.

"The young man will make himself famous by this essay, and by thus attacking my views," she said. " All Paris will speak of him to-day. The religious tone which he assumes is new to us ; the spirit of the times is tending in that direction. He will be much applauded and find plenty of adherents. His religious enthusiasm, moreover, springs from genuine conviction, and the truth never fails to interest us, even though it does not harmonize with our own views. Pray call on him and tell him that I wish to get acquainted with him. I am much interested in him."

In this manner the interview, so painful to both of them, passed without a real reconciliation.

A few days afterward, the booksellers advertised Madame de Stael's new work on Literature. This book treated neither of Napoleon, nor of his policy, but expatiated on the civilization of the human mind, and pronounced *belles-lettres* its most beautiful flower. This book, therefore, created an extraordinary sensation.* The times had as yet brought forth few productive talents ; it was the first truly great book since the Revolution, and the author of this book was a woman. All the newspapers commented on it, all authors hastened to criticize it ; in all circles nothing was spoken of but Madame de Stael and her work, and the Parisians bestowed more encomiums and admiration on the gifted lady than ever before. Carriage after

* Journal de Paris.

carriage drove up to her door ; and all those who had been the first to desert and deny her, were now again the first to return to her. She witnessed this sudden zeal with a bitter smile. She did not receive anybody. Her servants had been instructed to inform all visitors that she would be at home for those who wished to call on her next Monday evening. She was anxious to find out how large the number of her friends would be by that day. She wanted to celebrate her triumph with this satisfaction, which was so painful to her heart.

Beautiful Madame .Récamier alone was not included in this order. She alone had been courageous enough to visit Madame de Stael at a time when all her other friends had deserted her; and for this noble trait of kindheartedness Madame de Stael rewarded her by the most ardent attachment and friendship. She loved Madame Récamier, not because she was beautiful, but because she was good.

Napoleon had meanwhile removed from the Luxembourg to the Tuileries. His power became daily more absolute, and he gradually matured his vast and daring plans. The world was henceforth to occupy itself with him alone, and now the press devoted its principal attention to a book on literature and perfectibility of the human race, and to excite the minds of the public by dwelling on a subject so foreign to his glory, and, moreover, treated by a woman whom he wished to see ignored and shunned by everybody. The growing popularity of his gifted enemy irritated him more and more. He was unable to counteract it. His power and authority were insufficient for that purpose. He could not prohibit her book ; nor could he compel her to leave Paris on that account. So he had to allow the mad enthusiasm of the Parisians to go on without let or hindrance.

Monday evening, when Madame de Stael had promised to receive her friends, had meanwhile come. The apartments of her house were brightly illuminated; the servants were in readiness at the doors. Madame de Stael herself, attired in a light-green satin dress with a long train, her short curly hair adorned with a bandeau and plumes, her beautiful arms covered with long gloves reaching up beyond the elbows, was sitting at the door leading to the ante-room, and was listening for the rolling of the first carriage.

Benjamin Constant stood before her.

"If we grow richer in experience only to have our confidence in men diminished, the shortest life, at bottom, would be the most desirable," he remarked.

"I am not of your opinion," said Madame de Stael; "we learn to be satisfied with what life offers us; in other words, we grow wise by experience. Having been so long deprived of social life such as I like best, I am overjoyed to see my old friends around me to-night, and ask neither why they come, nor why they leave me. We never learn to appreciate the full value of anything until we are deprived of it. A conversation in a Parisian *salon* is the highest enjoyment I know of. The springs of my life are the winters which I have passed in Paris. *Je compte mes printemps par mes hivers.* I feel to-night as if I were awaking to new happiness."

Her room was soon crowded with visitors, among whom the most eminent names of the capital were represented, and all of whom paid homage to her genius. So she had attained her object and recovered her celebrity and popularity. She smiled triumphantly.

All *salons* of the capital were now open to her; she was invited to all soirées; wherever she made her appearance, all eyes followed her, and everybody paid homage to her. She fairly reveled in this triumph which she had taken so much trouble to achieve; a heavy burden had been removed from her breast.

Time wore on. Summer was close at hand, and Parisian society dispersed in order to enjoy rural life. Madame de Stael, therefore, had likewise to leave this scene of her happiness. She returned in the best of spirits to her father's villa at Coppet, where she arrived at the very time when the French army crossed the Alps, and detachments of soldiers disturbed the peaceful valleys of Switzerland.

When she now, on fine summer evenings, stood on the balcony of the villa, while the quiet landscape was reflected in the transparent lake, the snow-clad summit of the mountains looked down on her so grandly and gravely, and her children played so merrily in the park, she was almost ashamed of the fact that she sought her happiness in things which she knew to be nugatory, and which, moreover, never afforded it to her. But she vainly attempted to get rid of her inward restlessness She was constantly haunted by a vague, nameless longing, an incessant dissatisfaction which clung to her through life, and allowed her to find repose only in death.

Saints and martyrs have pursued the same path in the hope of finding in heaven full compensation for the imperfections of their earthly existence.

She watched Bonaparte's victorious career with the liveliest interest, hoping all the time that it would terminate in defeats which would lead to his downfall, and restore liberty to her beloved France. Vain hopes and wishes!

Those fine summer days, meanwhile, passed away very rapidly; and in November, 1800, when social life in Paris began to revive, Madame de Stael, too, returned to the capital of France. Peace had not yet been concluded, but Moreau's victories had prepared the way for it. No one, however, saw as yet through the ambitious schemes of the First Consul, and his adherents still entertained the most patriotic hopes for the welfare of their country.

One evening, while engaged in an animated conversation with a few friends, Madame de Stael heard a deafening report, which no one was able to account for. It was the explosion of the infernal machine.

It was not until the following day that she heard of the plot and its failure, and unfortunately she was imprudent enough to express her regret at it. Her remarks were reported to the First Consul, who never forgot them.

As her position in society now depended upon her literary successes, Madame de Stael continued most zealously, turning her genius to account. She was now working at her *Delphine*. But her social relations engrossed her attention so much, that her work progressed rather slowly, and she counted, therefore, upon the coming summer, and the leisure which she would have at Coppet.

She passed the winter this time in the most agreeable manner. It is true, the First Consul never visited her, nor did Talleyrand show himself at her house; but all distinguished strangers who visited Paris, were presented to her, and especially the diplomatists of the foreign powers visited her very frequently. She spent much of her time at Joseph Bonaparte's beautiful villa, Morfontaine, and Lucien always invited her to his brilliant festivals.

Napoleon alone treated her constantly with the same coldness, despite the partiality of his brothers for the gifted lady.

One day she met him at the house of General Berthier. She had been prepared for it, for her friends hoped that Madame de Stael and the First Consul might be reconciled, and they had therefore taken pains to bring about this meeting.

16

Vain endeavor! Madame de Stael refused to appear in deep humility before him ; she wished to meet with admiration and flattery at his hands, and he did not admire anybody. His remark that he did not appreciate the genius of a woman, but only the number of children whom she had given to the country, wounded her to the quick. Henceforth friendly relations between her and such a man were out of the question.

CHAPTER VIII.

IN EXILE.

MADAME DE STAEL was well aware that the sword was hang‧ing over her head, and was held only by the silken thread with which public opinion still reined the ruler of France. Nevertheless, she disdained to avert the threatening danger by pursuing a more prudent course than before.

She knew that Napoleon was informed of all that took place at her house; that, with Fouché's ears, he listened to every conversation held in her room; that, by the aid of his police-minister, he read all her letters; * that all she did, said, and wrote was reported to him; and yet she continued giving the reins to her tongue. She was a woman, and availed herself of the privilege of woman to speak her mind with impunity.

But Napoleon would not grant this privilege to the fair sex. The great man was little enough to show to the world that he was afraid of a woman.

In France, the *salons*, and the gifted ladies shining in them, have always exercised considerable influence upon public affairs. Napoleon was not ignorant of this fact. Madame de Stael held intercourse with the most eminent statesmen of France; she gathered around her all men of mind and genius; and Napoleon noticed that those who visited her house, always left it with a less favorable opinion of him. He was unable to prove in what way she exercised this unfavorable influence

* Mémoires de Constant, valet de chambre de l'Empereur Napoléon.

over her visitors; otherwise he would have had no hesitation in punishing her for it; he only knew that such was the case, and it was but natural for him to try to remove or destroy a power só injurious to him.

A woman had thrown down the gauntlet to him, and he took it up.

Owing to the peculiar political situation in France, it was utterly impossible for Madame de Stael to take any part in the management of public affairs; for where the voice of one man decides everything, none but those who are on intimate terms with that man can have influence. So she had to play the part of a mere looker-on; and all she could venture to attempt, was to obtain permission for her exiled friends to return to France.

Fouché deemed it prudent to avoid needless rigor, and, although he surrounded Madame de Stael with spies, and secretly opened her letters, he treated her with marked favor, perhaps only to lull her suspicions. Many a poor exile, therefore, now, through her intercession, obtained leave to return to his native country; and she was overjoyed to be able to place Narbonne, too, on the list of these privileged persons, and to welcome him in Paris after so prolonged a separation.

It is true, she did not suspect at that time that he would one day enter the service of her enemy, and assist him in his victorious career to the best of his power.

In the autumn of 1801, she returned, as usual, to Paris, and opened now, in the zenith of her celebrity as an authoress and gifted woman, her *salon* once more to the brilliant world of the capital. All eminent men gathered around her immediately; all distinguished foreigners were presented to her; but, above all, her house was frequented by those who were secretly hostile to the First Consul, and envied him his marvelous suc-

cesses, by which he had here and there crossed their ambitious
purposes. Among those who rallied around her for this reason was also Bernadotte, the future King of Sweden, who
would have preferred the imperial throne of France. With
him she was, therefore, soon on terms of the most intimate
friendship; for both of them were animated by secret dislike
of Napoleon.

M. de Chateaubriand had published his " Genius of Christianity," and acquired great celebrity by it. Madame de Stael
rejoiced at his success. She was free from that contemptible
envy of those who are intent only on adding to their own
fame, and, for that reason, tolerate no other talents by their
side, but disparage them wherever they can. Many flowers
bloom in the garden of the Lord; the rose need not be afraid
of the pink, for both are flowers of peculiar beauty, and can
not be compared with one another. Thus she looked also
upon other persons endowed with poetical talents.

. Although Chateaubriand's principles were widely different
from her own, she highly appreciated his works, and often told
him how warmly she admired them. " Mere echoes weary
me," she would reply to those who told her that a new book
was not written in her spirit. She liked and praised all works
which showed that their authors were gifted men. She possessed the enviable faculty of appreciating the peculiarities of
all talented authors, and it never occurred to her to mark out
for it a path which was repugnant to it.

She had to do without Benjamin Constant this winter. As
her friend, he spoke and wrote in consonance with her views,
and thereby incurred Napoleon's displeasure; the consequence
was that he lost his place as Secretary of the Constitutional
Club.

Unjust as he always was, he hastened in the first ebullition of his anger to Madame de Stael, whom he charged with having caused his misfortune, and informed her that he would immediately set out for Germany and try to enter a more prosperous career.

"Should I have, perhaps, persuaded you to conceal your sentiments, because self-interest commanded you to pursue that cowardly course?" she said to him, gravely.

This answer caused him to blush. But Paris had become distasteful to him for the time being, and so he departed.

Madame de Stael did not detain him. She was already accustomed to his running away in his fits of anger, and expected that, as usual, he would return immediately.

She did not believe that he would stay away from her a long time, for she knew full well how little he could do without her. His vacillating character had to be guided by as strong a mind as hers, in order to avoid those weaknesses by which characters so constituted so often forfeit the confidence and esteem of their fellow-men.

Madame de Stael wrote often to him. Amidst the brilliant social life of the capital, she did not forget her absent friend. It is true she was ignorant of the bonds which detained him in Germany, and he did not deserve the pity which she felt for him.

Early in the spring she intended to hasten to her father and gladden his heart by telling him how successful and happy she had been. Suddenly, however, her physician informed her that M. de Stael had had a stroke of apoplexy, and was at his house, deserted by everybody, and without a woman to nurse him in his helplessness.

"Oh, my God! my God!" she exclaimed, compassionately, and hastened to him.

He was suffering; that was enough for her to forgive what

had separated them. He was sick and helpless; how could she then still bear in mind how he had wronged her?

She found him in a pitiful condition. A partial paralysis of his limbs rendered him helpless and entirely dependent on his attendants, while a repetition of the fit threatened to put a speedy end to his life.

She consulted with the doctor as to the course that should be pursued in regard to him; she said that no sacrifice would be too great, no trouble too arduous for her, provided she could give him relief.

The baths of Aix, in Savoy, were to be tried; the hot springs might perhaps cure him of the palsy.

She immediately caused a comfortable traveling coach to be fitted up for the patient, furnished it with every possible convenience, so that he could be most as in a bed, and bid farewell to her dear Paris in order to journey, by short stages, at the side of the palsied sufferer, toward their mournful destination.

M. de Stael was deeply moved by her kindness and magnanimity, and expressed his gratitude by glances and words as far as his condition permitted him to do so. He felt inwardly with profound remorse that he had not deserved such generous treatment at her hands, inasmuch as he had never taken pains to win her affections, and to be to her a tender and loving friend. So his heart smote him, although she, in her kindness, never thought of making him ashamed of his conduct toward her.

They traveled very slowly, for long stages exhausted the patient's strength. When they reached the small frontier town of Poligny, he had another fit, and died.

Madame de Stael stood in profound emotion at the coffin of the unfortunate man whom she had called husband. She had been unable to save him, unable to preserve his life.

She now went to Coppet, and arrived quite unexpectedly at her father's house, with the remains of his son-in-law, who was buried there. Madame de Stael could not mourn for her husband; and yet his death made her very grave for a time. While she had scarcely aroused herself to a full sense of her new liberty, Benjamin Constant suddenly entered her room. He stood still before her in surprise on seeing that she was in mourning.

"I am a widow," she said in response to his inquiring glance, and was herself astonished at the sound of this word as applied to her, for her relations with M. de Stael had been such as almost not to justify her in calling herself his widow.

Benjamin looked at her with an embarrassed air and blushed. The last barrier had now fallen between them. He dropped his eyes, lest she should read in his soul what he took good care to conceal from her. She noticed his confusion. Her eyes rested on him mournfully for a moment; she then began to talk of indifferent matters. She still took as much interest in political affairs as ever before. In a letter to Joseph Bonaparte, she wrote on this subject as follows:

"COPPET, October 9, 1802.

"The peace with England is the joy of the world; I am glad that it was you who concluded it, and that you have every year fresh opportunities to win the love and esteem of the whole nation. You have conducted the most important negotiations in the annals of France. Universal applause and gratitude await you; the terms will be excellent; if they were less satisfactory, this peace would exercise such a salutary influence upon the domestic prosperity of France that you would have a thousand opportunities to display your tact and sagacity, inasmuch as so many commercial interests are connected with this peace, that your achievement will create a much greater sensation than the conclusion of the peace of Luneville.

"Pardon me for occupying myself on so important an occasion with your personal welfare; I gradually accustom myself to measuring the most momentous events only with reference to you, and it is agreeable to concentrate my mind in my love for you. I think, already, with pleasure of all that we shall talk about you next winter.

"The First Consul must be very happy; you serve him most efficiently, and your great kindness enlists all hearts in your successes.

"Adieu! Go forward to the greatest and most brilliant event of your life. Enjoy the friendship of her whose wishes may indemnify you ——(illegible)——I hope you will earn glory enough, and always remain my friend; if you have glory, and I your friendship, the advantage is still on my side.

"STAEL."

"P. S.—Be kind enough to convey my respects to Madame Julie. I wish her joy, and I am glad that she bears the name of the Peace-maker, as everybody calls you."

She now resumed her literary labors, and occupied herself particularly with the last revision of her *Delphine*, which was to be published in the course of the winter. She did not venture to return to Paris in autumn and superintend the publication of the work; for she had been informed that the First Consul had said it would be good for her not to return to the capital, and such a remark from his lips was sufficiently indicative of the course he intended to pursue toward her. She stood mournfully on the balcony of the château, and gazed over toward France, where there reigned now such an active and stirring life, in which she longed to participate. Should she risk it? should she go to Paris despite the hint which she had received, and expose herself to banishment? Should she pass the long,

16*

long winter all alone at Coppet, where she enjoyed herself so little?

The Prefect of Geneva had not yet been ordered to refuse her a passport, so the road to the capital was open to her; only she lacked the courage to set foot on it. Finally she resolved to remain at Coppet until her *Delphine* had been published. The reception of this book was to show her the feelings of the Parisians toward her before she ventured to make her appearance at the capital.

Her days dragged through in anxious suspense. Necker himself suffered greatly in consequence of her constant agitation. He loved his daughter so dearly that he grieved deeply to see her deprived of something which gladdened her, and he laid all sorts of plans in order to induce Napoleon to desist from his rigorous measures toward his child. Aged as he was, and arduous as a journey would have been for him, he was ready to go to Paris and intercede personally with the First Consul in her behalf.

Autumn was drawing to a close, and the day came when *Delphine* was published. As soon as the book had appeared, it created a great sensation; all *salons* conversed about it alone, all coffee-houses resounded with criticisms on it, all newspapers published long articles on it. With trembling haste Madame de Stael opened the first Paris paper which was sent to her. It was the *Mercure de France*, edited by Laharpe, which fell into her hands. But alas! instead of criticizing the book, the editor had written about the personal appearance of the authoress. She glanced in dismay over the lines. He said that she was utterly destitute of enthusiasm, and the article closed as follows: " *Regardez la! Elle est grosse, grasse et forte; sa figure est enluminée de trop de santé.*" What had her figure to do with her book? How could they allude to her appearance?

"Oh, how mean! how despicable!" cried Madame de Stael, beside herself with indignation; and her loud lamentations drew the other inmates of the château into her room. Vainly did Necker try to comfort her, vainly did Benjamin Constant assure her that such malicious criticisms of a book would not make a lasting impression on anybody, nor detract from the value of the work in the eyes of any sensible person. No consolations were able to soothe the poor lady. These very remarks on her personal appearance, her character, and even her private affairs, mortified her deeper, perhaps, than if the book had simply been pronounced bad and unreadable. They wounded her in her heart of hearts, and she felt as if the very stones could not but look at her, pity her, and defend her.

A great many critics, however, censured the book, too. They charged her with having reviled religion in her book, recommended dueling, and advocated divorce, and they condemned the work as immoral. Only a few voices were raised in her defense, and they were drowned by the large majority of unfavorable criticisms. Lalande fearlessly called *Delphine* " *Le beau roman de Madame de Stael;*" and Sueur devoted to it an article in which he bestowed the most flattering encomiums on it. But the book was prohibited even at Leipzig, and the Elector of Saxony threatened those who were in possession of a single copy of it with a fine of one hundred dollars. That was too much. She had not expected that her book would meet with such a reception.

Necker had read his daughter's work before she had published it, and he had approved of it. The more painful were these attacks to him now. So he was inclined to ascribe the cause of this renewed hostility of the First Consul to himself, and not to his daughter's novel. He had sung his last strains, as Madame de Stael called his book, which he had entitled

Dernières vues de politique et de finances. Napoleon was exceedingly displeased with the spirit of this work, and said that
Madame de Stael had misrepresented the present condition of
France to her father. In a paroxysm of rage he dictated to
Consul Lebrun a letter to Necker, in which he informed him
in unmeasured terms of his indignation, and which wound up
with the announcement that Madame de Stael would no longer
be permitted to reside in Paris. So she had been prepared for
her exile even previous to the appearance of her *Delphine.*
Nevertheless, the certainty of what she had feared now made
the most painful impressions on her. Not to live in Paris was
in her case equivalent to renouncing all enjoyments of existence ; people lived there, and merely vegetated elsewhere.

So she resolved to pass the winter at Geneva. But what
could Geneva offer to her ? She caused her guests to perform
parlor theatricals and represent charades ; she gathered around
her the foreign residents, among whom were a great many
Englishmen ; she recited and read to them, and created a great
sensation ; but she herself derived from this social intercourse
no other enjoyment than that of gratified vanity. A conversation, such as she liked, could be held only at the capital of
France, and this conversation was the highest and only enjoyment of her life.

In the following autumn she was lead to believe that Napoleon had forgotten her. Her friends wrote her from Paris
that the contemplated expedition to England engrossed all his
thoughts, and that he hardly thought of her any more. So she
resolved to profit by this opportunity to approach the capital.

She took up her residence at Maffliers, a villa situated within
ten leagues of Paris. Here she intended to pass the winter, receive her friends, and visit every now and then a theater or
art-gallery at the capital.

She had spent two months undisturbedly at this villa, and began to look about with less timidity, and rejoice at the success of her plan, when the First Consul was informed that the road to Maffliers was covered with carriages and men hastening to Madame de Stael. This information, no doubt, came from Madame de Genlis, who was indebted for her return to Paris and a pension to a correspondence with Napoleon, which informed him of a great many things which he would not have learned otherwise. To tolerate a rival whose literary celebrity far eclipsed her own, could not be expected of a vain woman, and so she availed herself of this opportunity to remove the envied Madame de Stael from the capital.

Madame de Stael was informed by one of her friends that a gensd'arme would bring her the order to leave France. At first she refused to believe in the truth of this communication, inasmuch as it seemed to her incredible that a lady should be subjected to such arbitrary treatment. She believed that Napoleon would hardly have the courage to pursue such a course toward a lady of her rank, nay, that he would be unwilling to confess how much he was afraid of her.

However, she was not long in finding out that she was mistaken.

She ordered her carriage and fled to Madame de la Tour, to whom Regnault de Saint Jean d'Angely had recommended her. She was hardly acquainted with this lady. She found her at her villa, surrounded by a number of persons who were almost entire strangers to her, and to whom she would not betray the fear gnawing at her heart. At every unwonted noise she would give a start; her color changed from minute to minute; she scarcely listened to what was said, and her answers indicated that she had not followed the course of the conversation. What if the gensd'arme, with whose arrival she had been threatened, should follow her thither? What if he should arrest her in the presence of all these guests?

Glad to escape this almost intolerable constraint, she retired to her room. But here she did not find any rest either. She opened the window and listened if the sound of a horse should be audible in the stillness of the night; and she looked from minute to minute for the arrival of the tyrant's messenger. She wrote to Joseph Bonaparte and depicted to him the whole extent of her humiliating situation. She told him that she had only sought an asylum at a place ten leagues from Paris, and that she had not been desirous of returning to the capital. She implored him to intercede for her, and, above all, to prevent the dread word "exile" from being pronounced against her; for those who had once been exiled always had the utmost difficulty in obtaining permission to return to Paris.

Her days dragged through in anxious suspense. Madame Récamier, who had returned from a trip to England, invited her to come to her house at Saint Brice. She accepted her invitation gratefully, without anticipating how grievously she would injure her beautiful friend by so doing. The most agreeable company was assembled there, and she yielded once more to the charm of the enchanting conversation, of which she was so very fond. She met Talma there. He read to her a scene from *Othello*. Madame de Stael told him that all he had to do, to be the Moor of Venice, was to pass his hand through his hair and knit his brow. Madame Récamier sung with her enchanting voice, and Madame de Stael recited scenes from *Romeo and Juliet*, or represented Hagar in the desert, with Madame Récamier, who performed the part of the angel on such occasions. The effect which she produced by such tableaux-vivants was indescribable. She represented the expression of grief with such striking vividness that all the spectators were irresistibly carried away by her performance. Her long black hair hung disheveled upon her shoulders and back. Her dark eyes beamed with heavenly radiance as they assumed the expression of despairing maternal love. All eyes rested, spell-bound, upon her face, and attentively followed her slightest movements. Although she was not good-looking, she seemed surpassingly beautiful at such moments, and no one had any difficulty in understanding how, destitute as she was of personal charms, she had been able to inspire men with the most passionate love.

She passed several days in this manner, as if in a sweet dream, so suddenly and unexpectedly had those longed-for enjoyments and charming intercourse with her friends been restored to her. As no one alluded to her exile, she, too, commenced forgetting the dread word, and tried to persuade herself that Napoleon no longer intended to punish her.

Almost perfectly reassured, and satisfied that he had only threatened her in order to frighten her, she finally returned to her villa.

Several friends visited her there, and she merrily sat down to dinner with them. The garden-hall opened upon the highway, and allowed her to see the entrance gate. It was a bright September day; heaven and earth were radiant under the rays of the autumnal sun, and Madame de Stael's face likewise beamed with satisfaction at her safety from arbitrary treatment. She merrily surveyed the small circle of her friends, and enjoyed their pleasant conversation.

At this moment the clock struck four.

A man dressed in a suit of gray clothes appeared at the gate and demanded admittance. He was on horseback.

No sooner had Madame de Stael cast a glance upon him, than she knew her fate. She started up in dismay.

He demanded an interview with her. She left her guests and went to him in the garden. The flowers were so fragrant, the sun shone so brightly, she stood still and yielded for a moment to a meditation on the difference between the effects produced on the mind by nature, and those which society makes upon us. The man in gray now approached her, and said he was the captain of the gensd'armes of Versailles; in order not to frighten her, he had not put on his uniform. He then showed her a letter, signed by Bonaparte, ordering him to remove her forty leagues from Paris; he was to start with her in the course of twenty-four hours, but to treat her with the utmost respect.

Madame de Stael trembled, and was scarcely able to compose herself.

"Such an order is issued against criminals, but not against a lady of my rank, not against a lady who has to give up housekeeping and to take her children along with her. Accompany me for three days to Paris, sir, that I may make my preparations." He bowed and said that he was willing to comply with her request.

She now returned to her guests, apologized for her departure, ordered her carriage, and entered it with the officer and with her children. Her friends looked after her regretfully. When would they meet her again?

She caused her carriage to stop at Madame Récamier's villa, and alighted in order to see her friend. She met here General Junot, who promised her to bring his whole influence to bear in her behalf upon the First Consul. Vain promise!

Madame de Stael had rented a new house in Paris in the hope of passing the winter there; she now entered it for the first time, accompanied by the gend'arme. She hastened sadly through the apartments in which she had hoped to spend many merry hours with her friends. Every morning the gend'arme made his appearance here, and told her that she must set out; and every day she met him with the urgent request to allow her to remain another day at her house. She wished to see her friends once more; she wished to be merry with them once again in these apartments, before bidding farewell to Paris and to happiness.

Joseph Bonaparte tried to persuade his brother once more on the day previous to her departure to desist from a measure which seemed unworthy of his greatness, directed as it was against a woman; but his efforts proved unsuccessful. His amiable young wife hastened to Madame de Stael, and requested her to spend a few days with them at Morfontaine, an invitation which she accepted with heartfelt gratitude under the existing circumstances. Her oldest son, Augustus, accompanied her thither. But however gratefully she acknowledged the kindness of Joseph Bonaparte, she could not enjoy herself in a family where she had to conceal the bitter feelings gnawing at her heart; so she left, three days afterward, this hospitable house, where she had formerly passed so many pleasant hours.

But whither was she now to wend her way? Was she to return to Geneva, where the monotony of social life seemed intolerable to her, and where everybody would tacitly say to her, "You have been sent back to us?" Her pride revolted at this humiliation. She had always said to the Swiss, that France was her native country, and that she was utterly averse to being considered a daughter of Switzerland. France had now disowned her; what if Switzerland should do likewise?

Hence she resolved to go to Germany. In Germany her name was well known; in Germany her father was loved and esteemed, and the ancient dynasties would be certain to receive her in a flattering manner. She requested Joseph to inquire if she might go to Prussia. He hastened to St. Cloud, while she awaited his answer at a small tavern two hours from Paris. The answer was in the affirmative. Joseph sent her letters of introduction to distinguished persons in Berlin, and wished her, in the most courteous manner, a happy journey to Germany.

This was the last word. She was obliged to go.

Benjamin Constant accompanied her on her journey. She sadly leaned back her head in a corner of the carriage, and inwardly regretted every step of the horses which removed her from Paris. Never, perhaps, did a traveler set out on a journey in gloomier spirits. It was not until they reached Châlons, that Constant—*par son étonnante conversation* *—succeeded in arousing her from her apathy. At Metz she was slightly exhilarated by the presence of a M. Villers. Nevertheless, she was unable to forget Paris, and to accustom herself to the idea that she should not live there any more.

---

* Her own words.

CHAPTER IX.

FRANKFORT, Dec. 3, 1803.

" *Madame de Stael to M. de Chateaubriand*—

"Oh, *mon Dieu*, my dear Francis, how your letter saddened my heart! Already yesterday the newspapers had conveyed the dreadful tidings to me, and your heart-rending account then stamped it in bloody letters upon my memory. Can you speak to me of different opinions about religion and the priests? Are there two opinions when there is but one feeling? I have read your letter with scalding tears. My dear Francis, call to mind the time when your friendship for me had reached its height; do not forget the moments when my whole heart belonged to you, and tell yourself then that the same feelings still reign at the bottom of my heart, only more so than ever before. I loved, I admired the character of Madame de Beaumont; I never knew a more magnanimous, grateful, and affectionate one. Ever since I entered the world, I have been on intimate terms with her; and even amidst many disagreeable circumstances, my attachment to her has never been shaken. *Mon cher* Francis, grant me a place in your life. I admire and love you; I loved her for whom you are mourning. I am a faithful friend. I shall be a sister to you. I shall honor your sentiments more than ever. Mathieu, who shares them, is as kind to me as an angel, whenever a calamity befalls me. Give me again opportunities to spare you; let me be useful to you or afford you pleasure. Have you heard that I have been exiled to a place forty leagues from Paris? I shall profit by this decree to make a trip to Germany; but next spring, if I can obtain permission, I shall return to Paris, or at all events take up my abode in its vicinity, or go to Geneva. Let us then meet somewhere. Do you not feel that my mind and soul comprehend and appreciate yours? Do you not feel that we are similar to each other, despite our dissimilarities? M. von Humboldt wrote to me a few days since, and alluded to your works in terms of admiration, which, coming as they did from a man of his merit and views, could not but be flattering to you. But am I at liberty to speak to you, at this moment, of your successes? She, you know, loved these successes, and attached the utmost importance to them. Continue adding to the celebrity of him who was so dear to her. Adieu, my dear Francis. I shall write to you from Weimar, in Saxony Address your replies to me thither, care of M. Desport, Banker. What heart-rending words do I find in your letter! And your determination to keep poor St. Germain! You will one day take him to my house.

"Once more, an affectionate, a mournful farewell.

"N. DE STAEL."

Contrary to expectation, Madame de Stael was detained for some time at Frankfort by the sickness of her youngest child, a little girl of five.

The *Journal de Paris* stated that she had left Paris in order to issue in Berlin a new edition of her *Delphine*, with a preface justifying the purpose and contents of the book. Benjamin Constant was mentioned as her companion, and as author of several pamphlets and of a translation of Kant; "*dont la doctrine*," said the editor, "*est au dessus de la portée de l'esprit humain.*"

At this very juncture, Frederick Schlegel lectured every Sunday morning in Paris, and sought to familiarize the French public with the spirit of German science; to judge from the above-mentioned article, there remained to him a vast field for his lectures on German literature and philosophy.

Madame de Stael, however, received also from Paris other newspapers alluding to her journey in less delicate terms, and closing with calumnies which caused her heart to tremble. She had to drink both honey and wormwood from the cup of life; of both of them a measure full to overflowing was presented to her lips.

In Germany, the name of Madame de Stael had long been very favorably known, and her writings had been read with great admiration. Already, in the year 1795, Sophie la Roche had written to Wieland:

"Tell me, would you like to read *Les Réflexions 'sur la Paix*, which Madame de Stael, Necker's daughter, wrote in her leisure hours, and dedicated to Pitt, and to the French nation? And shall I send you *Zulma*, the fragment of a very interesting work by this same gifted woman? Intent as she was on writing on the influence of the passions over our happiness, she of course tried first to depict that of loves, and *Zulma* appeared. I confess I am glad to own the works of father, mother, and daughter, and to be personally acquainted with all three of them."

The inhabitants of Weimar had already been prepared for her arrival, and awaited her impatiently, while so sad a cause detained her at Frankfort. It was the first German city where she stayed for some time, and the grave apprehensions with which the sickness of her little daughter, Albertine, filled her, did not render more agreeable the impression which the stillness of the place, the sound of the foreign language, and her longing for Paris and for her friends, made upon her. Few physicians spoke French at that time, and owing to this fact she had considerable difficulty in conversing with her doctor, which was extremely painful to her maternal heart.

She received daily letters from Coppet, with advice and consolation, and medical instructions from her doctor in Geneva. Necker always accompanied his daughter in thought, and shared both her joys and sorrows.

She wrote to him from Frankfort:

" But for prayer, what would become of a mother who knows that her child's life is endangered ? This condition would lead to the discovery of religion, even though it had been unknown up to that time."

She did not breathe more freely until the physician declared that her little daughter was out of danger.

The days had, meanwhile, grown shorter—a cold shroud of snow covered the earth, and all the terrors of winter set in. She had considerable difficulty in continuing her journey, and was glad if every day brought her a few miles nearer to her destination.

Benjamin Constant was no stranger to this soil. He had formerly already passed through these regions, although with a lighter heart, and a destination holding out to him the most brilliant prospects and hopes. Now he gazed with a gloomy air upon these desolate fields, and seemed to be a prey to constant despondency. There was something unsteady in his gaze; and a certain anxiety, which Madame de Stael perceived full well, had seized him since they had reached Germany.

She fixed her radiant eyes on him inquiringly. He noticed it, and tried to avert her thoughts from him by entering into a conversation with her. Familiar as he was with what was most interesting to her, he nearly always succeeded in drawing her into a conversation when he wished to do so; and then she would speak so beautifully and charmingly that he had likewise to banish his thoughts from his mind, and hang upon her lips.

Madame de Stael wished to be acquainted with the poets of Germany, and therefore she wended her way to Weimar. The muses had at that time fled to the banks of the Ilm, and shed over the small duchy a lustre which was to illuminate the whole world. Pilgrims flocked thither from all quarters of the globe, in order to worship at its shrine.

On a dark evening she reached the small town, whose streets were not lit up by any lantern save that of her own traveling-coach, and alighted at the not very comfortable hotel. Already, an hour after her arrival, the news that the celebrated lady had arrived at length, spread from house to house; and early in the morning all asked each other how and where they would meet her.

Madame de Stael had been urgently recommended to the court of Weimar, and no sooner had she arrived than she was invited to the ducal table, and received in the most flattering and honorable manner. After dinner was over, the Duke introduced Schiller to her. The celebrated lady fixed her eyes searchingly on the face of the German poet, whom she met with proud self-consciousness. Her heavy, corpulent form contrasted strangely with that of the pale, slender poet, with the angular features, upon which the lofty aspirations of his mind were stamped, while the singular figure now standing before him evidently belonged to earth.

When his clear blue eyes met her ardent gaze, he dropped them almost in terror before those dazzling rays.

She now addressed him in her fine deep voice in a language which he did not speak fluently, and which he understood only through her excellent pronunciation, and the vivid expression of her face. He listened to her attentively, while his high, thoughtful forehead looked even more thoughtful than usual.

"Sit by me," she said, beckoning to him to seat himself at her side; "I have known you for a long time past; we are old acquaintances, and *c'est ma nature ainsi*, to treat all gifted men as my friends. I have come to Germany in order to familiarize myself with your philosophy. I should like to get acquainted with your Kant and Fichte. Pray tell me all about them. Which of them do you prefer? Which of them do you consider most profound?"

Schiller had some difficulty in replying to her numerous questions. Nevertheless, he was soon engaged in an animated conversation, and absorbed in philosophical discussions such as these rooms had perhaps never heard before. The court listened from afar in the utmost surprise to the singular conversation of the two illustrious personages. Both of them grew more and more excited; Madame de Stael raised her fine voice louder and louder, and caused its sonorous tones to fall charmingly on the ears of the listeners. Suddenly, however, as if actuated by a quick impulse, she jumped up from her seat and walked with her bold, firm step toward the Duke; all looked at her in astonishment, and awaited eagerly what she was about to do.

"I have just learned that M. Goethe is at Jena," she said, vividly; "and when I requested M. Schiller to present him to me, he replied he could not do so, inasmuch as he would not return to Weimar, but would expect me to visit him there. Is this really in accordance with German etiquette, sire? Is it customary for ladies at your court to pay homage to gentlemen in this manner? If such is really the case, I must submit to this strange custom."

The Duke glanced in confusion at Schiller, in whose eyes he read the confirmation of this charge, and replied after a moment's reflection, " Your wishes, Madame, will be respected by all the members of my court; it will be flattering to Goethe that you desire to be acquainted with him, and I myself shall inform him to-morrow of the happiness which awaits him."

Reassured by this reply, Madame de Stael allowed the conversation to turn to other topics, and thus closed a day so memorable in the annals of Weimar.

On the following morning, Schiller caused himself to be announced to her in order to introduce to her Wieland, who made a very agreeable impression on her. In the meantime, the Duke sent a messenger to Goethe in order to induce him to return to Weimar; but what Goethe had before said to Schiller, he repeated now in his reply to the Duke, only in more respectful terms. " In order to enjoy the celebrated lady, he must have a *tête-à-tête* with her, and would have, therefore, rooms fitted up for her in Loder's house." *

The Duke did not venture to communicate this answer to her, and preferred informing her that Goethe was sick, whereupon Madame de Stael resolved to prolong her sojourn at Weimar.

Although Weimar was not Paris, it offered many attractions to her mind; and there remained so many questions for her to propound that she did not lack material for the most animated discussions.

Schiller wrote to Körner: " She is a most gifted and accomplished woman; and if she were not so very interesting, I should not pay so much attention to her. But you may imagine the striking contrast of this gifted creature, standing on the summit of French culture, and thrown into our midst from

* *Vide* Schiller's Letters to Körner.

17

an entirely different world, with our German peculiarities, and, above all, with my own being. She diverts me almost entirely from poesy, and I wonder that I am still able to write anything. I see her very often, and, as I do not speak French very fluently, I really have a hard time of it. But her wonderful mind, her liberality, and her great susceptibility, entitle her to our warmest esteem."

While Madame de Stael achieved these triumphs, Benjamin Constant received a letter which embarrassed him beyond measure. M'lle de Hardenberg proposed to him in it to visit him at Weimar, in order to get acquainted with his generous protectress. He had not told her that this protectress was and had to remain ignorant of her existence, and hence he was at a loss what to do in order to prevent her from coming to Weimar. Now that he was in Germany, it was but natural for him to join the lady of his heart; but, on the other hand, he could not find it in his heart to leave Madame de Stael at a moment when, owing to her ignorance of the German language, she had more need of him than ever before. He sighed deeply. His predicament was painfully embarrassing.

A thousand bonds attached him to the gifted lady; she treated him so kindly and generously, she shared with him her position in society, and the honors which were bestowed upon her; and, in return, he was always to deceive and cheat her! This *rôle* oftentimes was exceedingly repugnant to his self-love.

After passing several days in the most painful agitation, he wrote to M'lle de Hardenberg that he could no longer restrain his impatience to see her again, and that he was about to hasten to her. In this manner he prevented her from visiting him; but he was now to verify his words, and that was a somewhat difficult undertaking. Under what pretexts should he enter upon this journey? He mused a long time on this problem.

As he had resumed his work on the religions of the nations with redoubled zeal since politics was silent, he thought he might use this as a pretext. "I must go for a few days to Göttingen," he said to Madame de Stael, "in order to examine several works at the University Library."

She looked at him wonderingly.

"Could you not defer that until we reach Berlin?" she asked, with an inquiring glance.

"If I could defer it, would I wish to leave you at this moment?" he replied, in a tone of irritation. "Do I deserve this distrust with which you watch all my steps? Do I deserve this suspicion with which you always look upon my attachment to you? Have so many years of an intimate acquaintance not yet sufficed to convince you of the lasting character of my affection, which, no matter what may have happened, always leads me back to you, and causes me to forget all wrongs and injuries as soon as I see you again?"

"I find that you bring on this scene without any cause whatever," replied Madame de Stael, proudly and gravely. "Confidence deserves confidence. I allow you a full insight into my heart; you know the motives of all my actions. Can you wonder, Benjamin, if my friendship for you tries to give me the right to penetrate likewise into the inmost recesses of your soul?"

"Certainly not," he replied, touched by the gentle tone of her voice; "certainly not, Germaine. But to desire confidence and entertain suspicion are two widely different things. It does not become a man to be called to account for every step he makes, even by the woman whom he esteems highest. It mortifies and insults him if she insists on it."

"Well, then, go, Constant; I shall not ask you why you leave me at this juncture."

He kissed her hand gratefully, and left her, greatly relieved, in order to engage a seat in the stage-coach.

He felt that he was wronging her. During the whole of the evening his eyes rested on her mournfully. She had scarcely been two weeks at Weimar, she was still a perfect stranger to the place, and he who was so much indebted to her, was capable of leaving her! It seemed to him impossible to part with her. Schiller and Wieland had arrived, the conversation had become exceedingly animated, and the brilliant eloquence of his friend enchanted his ears. What if he should never hear that voice again?

Folding his arms on his breast, he leaned against the door, and gazed sadly upon the group before him. The servant informed him now that it was time for him to go to the post-house. He drew his watch from his pocket, and found that the appointed hour was at hand. He threw it angrily on the floor and trampled it under foot.*

"What is the matter?" asked Wieland of him, in surprise.

"The watch is my enemy; otherwise, it would not have shown me the minute calling me away from here." He embraced Madame de Stael as if in despair, and rushed from the room.

"The air in Germany does not agree with him," said Madame de Stael, while her eyes followed him wonderingly. "He is too old for a period of storm and stress, and, it seems to me, is playing a comedy with himself. As he is going to spend his Christmas with some old manuscripts, he is very likely to feel at parting how much he leaves here behind; nevertheless, he so willed it, and he has now to keep his aim in view."

---

* Letters of M'me de Stein to her Son.

This little scene was soon generally known in Weimar, and gave rise to a great many rumors. Goethe heard of it, too, and became daily more anxious to see the wonderful woman, who, Schiller had written to him, was made of one piece, and entirely free from strange, false, and incongruous traits.

He determined at length, toward the close of December, to go for one day to Weimar. Madame de Stael was prepared for his visit, and received him with more coldness than she used to display; for, despite his indisposition, she knew full well that he might have visited her at a much earlier day. His tardiness in coming to Weimar had offended her.

Goethe spoke French very fluently, and met her without the slightest embarrassment. The reports of his friends having familiarized him beforehand with her appearance, he was not surprised to find that she was not prepossessing. They were soon engaged in an animated conversation, while she was rolling a small green twig between her beautiful white fingers, a habit from which she was no longer able to wean herself. She could get along much better with him than with Schiller, whose idealism—which in her opinion could not but lead to mysticism and superstition—almost frightened her. She wanted to penetrate everything with her mind—to explain, perceive, measure everything; she would not admit anything mysterious and inaccessible, and that which she could not illuminate with her torch, did not exist for her.*

Goethe was more favorably impressed with her from minute to minute; and, at parting, he promised to return speedily to Weimar, and to remain there until her departure, if she would now accept his invitation and come for a few days to Jena, where he wished to make her acquainted with a guest who would surpass all she had hitherto seen in Germany, and give

---

* Goethe's Letters to Schiller.

her a deeper insight into the mysterious realm of the human mind than the philosophy of Kant and Fichte could do.

"But who is it?" she asked, in great surprise. "Whom do you refer to? You have no Cagliostro or St. Germain, for aught I know!"

"No, but something better—a real ghost; something without a body—a genuine German apparition you shall see there with your wondrously beautiful eyes."

"But where shall I find this nameless being? where does it stay? where does it walk? In this land of legends and fairy-stories, I should like to see the places where your ghosts take up their abode."

"For this reason, I have fitted up for you rooms in a house where a little ·man, such as our poets have portrayed to you, walks about every night, and will have the honor to appear before you personally. Will you not be afraid of this guest?"

"Not at all. I shall be exceedingly glad to form his acquaintance, and shall now be certain to come."

"So you are willing to grant to a ghost what you refused to me?" he said, leaving her smilingly.

But whether Madame de Stael enjoyed too healthy a sleep, or whether the ghost was afraid of the celebrated lady, with whose language he was perhaps not familiar, he did not make his appearance during her sojourn at Jena; and upon her return, she said that only German eyes could see German ghosts, for belief in them would do wonders.

Schiller always disliked such remarks. He did not know how to take a jest, and raillery was distasteful to him; he scented in everything of the kind personal allusions, and felt offended when he should have laughed. But he did not know how to laugh. So he was now very angry with Madame de Stael for boasting that the German ghosts had run away before her, and said, "He was not at all surprised at that, inasmuch as Satan's assistant himself would have refused to have anything to do with her." *

Goethe was on better terms with her. He confessed that he had never met with so much mind in a woman, and that he would never have deemed it possible to find so gifted a woman. Her ardor, her glowing enthusiasm, made an agreeable impression on him; he liked to draw strength and inspiration from such a flame, and, as Madame de Stein acknowledged, became in consequence again accessible to other noble ladies.

However, nearly a month went by before Goethe took up his abode in Weimar again, and received the distinguished stranger at his house. Her great vivacity, her constant questioning, denying, and arguing against the opinions of others, at times tired him, too; for he felt only too well how vain were their endeavors to convince one another, when they started from such opposite points.

Constant had meanwhile suddenly returned to Weimar, and both his departure and arrival gave rise to more rumors in the small town, as he took pains to enshroud his journey in a mysterious veil. Madame de Stael, who always missed him during his absence, received him in the most cordial manner.

Constant sat before her in confusion, for falsehood was again on his lips.

"I know you have missed me, *mon cher* Benjamin," she said to him. "No matter where you may be, you do not find anybody to replace me. Is it not so?"

He could answer this question at least in the affirmative. The mysticism of M'lle de Hardenberg had tried him, and in the long run filled him with a genuine longing for his gifted friend. He loved the former because he could rest at her heart;

---

* Reminiscences of Henrietta Herz.

he was attracted toward the latter because she was certain to impart fresh elasticity to his mind.

"I wish to appoint an evening for reading to my friends," said Madame de Stael; "and I rejoice the more to have you here, as your opinion concerning the play which I shall read will be decisive.   What shall I select?"

"Read *Macbeth* to them, or perform *Juliet*, a *rôle* in which you are inimitable," he replied.

"Yes, if there were no women in Weimar! But they look upon me now already with visible ill-will. Because they themselves are so insignificant, they grudge me my mind. Ah, Benjamin, if there were more women as gifted and cultivated as I am, how different men would be! Female society has created in Paris that spirit of conversation, which is so inimitable, so seductive, so enchanting. The influence which we exercise over your sex is incalculable. But here the women do not comprehend their position; they do not even try to rule by their mind, tact, and amiability. Here they choose husbands only to become mothers, and forget that with their minds they shall educate citizens to their fatherland."

"Their ill-will must not disturb you," replied Constant. "The grapes are sour, says the fox, when he cannot reach them."

"You have learned that word from me, Constant," said Madame de Stael, smiling.

"Will you censure me for knowing how to pick up pearls?' She looked at him tenderly.

Madame de Stael postponed her departure from week to week, and a visit of a few days was prolonged to one of several months.   The Court treated her in the most flattering manner, and the people of Weimar became more and more accustomed to the presence of the stranger who, in the consciousness of her superiority, disdained the nimbus imparted by hypocrisy and artificial means. What distinguished her most strikingly from other women, was the frankness and straight-forwardness of her being; and what her own sex feared more than anything else, were the words of naked truth on her lips.

Johannes von Müller arrived at Weimar. She wished to form his acquaintance, too, and postponed her departure again. Schiller almost grew impatient at it. For a short time, he had suffered this stranger to disturb him in his peculiarities; but in the long run he rebelled against being taken back, in so spirited and ingenious a manner, from the world of his dreams into the realm of reality, so that his words, "The earth does not exist for me," died away before it. Like all idealists, he could not bear contradiction, and the refusal to acknowledge his stand-point always irritated him. And Madame de Stael would not and could not do that.

"*Je marche avec des sabots sur la terre quand on veut me forcer à vivre dans les nuages,*" she said, smilingly, when he had left her in great agitation, after wrangling with her a long time.

After her departure, Madame de Stein wrote to her son:

"I believe Madame de Stael has caused Goethe to long again for intercourse with somewhat more cultivated women than those who have surrounded him of late."

17*

CHAPTER X.

THE HYPERBOREAN ASS.

THE mists of winter still enshrouded the capital of Prussia, when Madame de Stael reached Berlin. Joseph Bonaparte had furnished her with the best of recommendations to distinguished men in that city, and especially had he written to the Embassador, M. Laforest, and requested him to render her sojourn at Berlin as agreeable as possible ; for the ill-will of the First Consul was unable to lessen his personal friendship for her.

Upon her arrival, Madame de Stael was presented to the Court, and received with great distinction. The beautiful Queen Louisa met her in all her gracefulness, and said to her in her amiable manner :

" *J'espère, Madame, que vous me croyez trop bon goût pour n'être pas flattée de votre arrivée à Berlin. Il y a longtemps que je vous ai admirée et j'ai été impatiente de faire votre connaissance.*"

The King, too, took pains to be courteous toward her in his laconic manner. Despite her enthusiasm for constitutional government, Madame de Stael was so much pleased with the Prussian Court that she said, " *Berlin était un des pays les plus heureux de là terre et les plus éclairés.*"

She made the acquaintance of Prince Augustus; but, above all, she was most favorably impressed with the noble and chivalrous bearing of Prince Louis Ferdinand—his ardor and enthusiasm. Like herself, he sought *les émotions qui peuvent agiter la vie ;* like herself, he hated Bonaparte, not only as a usurper

but also because of the moral assassination which he perpetrated by slandering those whom he hated, and whom his arm
was unable to reach. *"Je lui permets de tuer, mais assassiner
moralement, c'est là ce qui me révolte,"* he said.

The learned world, then so numerously represented at Berlin, was not long in thronging around her, and the busy and
stirring life of a great capital soon engrossed all her thoughts.
The rumor that the celebrated lady was in Berlin spread like
wildfire, and all now wished to get acquainted with her and to
be introduced to her.

The cultivated society at Berlin possessed at that time already
its *côteries*, its tea-parties, and literary ladies whose principal
task it was to gather about them a small circle of gifted and
interesting men. The Court, however, lived entirely apart from
this sphere, and only the princes tried to gain access to these
parties.

A great many of them were held at the houses of Sander,
the bookseller, and of the beautiful and gifted Henrietta Herz;
besides, Nicolai and Kotzebue received all distinguished foreigners at their *salons*. Madame de Stael was introduced to
this circle, and thus met with an opportunity to come in
contact with the most cultivated personages of the Prussian
capital.

Kotzebue had reached the zenith of his fame. He had recently returned from Siberia, and written his travels, which had
made him the hero of the day. His plays also were performed
amidst rapturous applause; he was the Scribe of his time, and
his talents entitled him to the popularity which he obtained.

He lived on the second floor of a house on Täger Street, in
good style, which a present from the Emperor Paul, consisting
of three hundred serfs,* enabled him to do. His rooms were

---

* *Vide* Recollections of Frederick Laun.

the rendezvous of all strangers, who were received there in the most hospitable manner.

Madame de Stael was not long in directing her steps hither. She was very fond of the stage, and liked to perform dramatic *rôles*. She had assiduously studied German at Weimar, and was now able to follow a dramatic performance. The witticisms which she did not understand, had to be explained to her, and she laughed very heartily as soon as she comprehended them. One of her most ardent wishes, upon her arrival at Berlin, was to get acquainted with the author of so many comic scenes, and to see his comedies performed by Iffland. She, therefore, sent Benjamin Constant immediately with a note to him, and looked now impatiently for the arrival of the famous dramatist.

Already on the following morning, his handsome equipage halted in front of her house, and M. de Kotzebue was announced to her. When he entered the room, Madame de Stael started back with an involuntary "Ah!" of surprise. Her imagination had traced to her a widely different portrait of the famous dramatist; and now she stood before a man, who, aside from a certain expression of shrewdness, had a very common and by no means intellectual face.

She begged him to be seated, and hoped that the wit and humor of his conversation would indemnify her for this disappointment. She was mistaken, however. Kotzebue was one of those men whose pens alone overflow with wit and humor, but who in their intercourse with the world are grave, taciturn and laconic. *Les frais de la conversation* were left to her alone.

However, he had to reply to her direct questions, and she had no hesitation in asking him for information concerning the most various subjects. " Can I be useful to you in any way, Madame? " asked Kotzebue, in the course of the conversation.

"Yes, you can, Monsieur," she replied, politely; "by affording me the pleasure of your company as often as possible."

"You are very kind. But can I not be useful to you in some other way, too, without deriving any personal advantage therefrom? Pray command me."

"I should like to get acquainted with Tieck, who is said to read so exceedingly well. I hear he is every now and then in Berlin. And Augustus William Schlegel, who, I have been told, is reading somewhere, Calderon's *Devotion at the Cross.*"

"Unfortunately, I am unable to introduce these two gentlemen to you, for both of them belong to the new poetical school, which I try to overthrow in the journal which I have established here," he replied, regretfully.

"So there is war between you—open war!" exclaimed Madame de Stael. "I like that. There is life and activity in it. You attack your adversaries, you defend yourself, and thereby arrive at new results. But may I inquire what is the cause of this literary war?"

"They reproach us with standing on the ground of reality, while they want to have poetry transferred to the realm of enchanting dreams. They intend to found a romantic school."

"Ah, if that is the case, I shall side with you, Monsieur," exclaimed Madame de Stael, warmly. "I shall never relish those airy 'phantoms inhabiting the mists of Ossian,' and coming to us from a world which our eye has not seen. Where and how can I meet those gentlemen? For I should like to form their acquaintance for all that."

"The house of Madame Bernardi, where Augustus William Schlegel lives, is the rendezvous of their clique; just signify your wish to be introduced there, Madame, and you will be invited immediately."

"But Iffland I shall find at your house, Monsieur, shall I not?"

"Certainly, if you will afford me the pleasure of spending an evening at my house, you will meet him and Rhigini, the composer."

"Now, you must tell me also all about Fichte. I am very anxious to get acquainted with him in order to penetrate the spirit of his philosophy. You must communicate to me your views about him."

"Well, I am less familiar with that subject than with theatrical matters," replied Kotzebue, smiling. "Authors writing as much as I do, do not find much leisure for reading all the new productions of literature. Permit me, however, to recommend you to read my *Hyperborean Ass*. It will show you the standpoint which I occupy, and what I oppose in literature."

"The *Hyperborean Ass!* That is a dreadful title. What does it mean?"

"The Hyperboreans offered to Apollo, asses whose pranks amused him. In the same manner, the world is amused by the senseless phrases of our opponents, whose turgid twaddle they call poetry. Frederick Schlegel has reduced this nonsense to a definite form in his *Lucinde*, and erected to literature a monument which cannot but cause it to blush. My *Hyperborean Ass* is to punish him for it. We must exercise poetical justice, Madame."

"You are a stern judge," said Madame de Stael, wonderingly. "It is here, then, *tout comme chez nous*. Everybody thinks he has found the truth and hates those who deny it. Philosophy, I hope, will be wiser. I hope the philosophers are brethren, and will together strive for light."

"But one must be the first to find it, and what will then become of the rest?"

When he had left her, Madame de Stael sent for Benjamin Constant and requested him to get her a copy of the *Hyperborean Ass*, and to invite Augustus William Schlegel to visit her.

The dreaded animal appeared in the shape of a small volume of fifty-eight pages, and contained in dramatic form an attack upon *Lucinde*, Frederick Schlegel's notorious novel, which preached the emancipation of the flesh. She had to read this novel before being able to understand Kotzebue's book, and for this purpose she had need of a teacher. While she was looking at these books and musing as to whom she should ask to interpret them to her, Augustus William Schlegel was announced to her.

He entered the room with the studied bearing and manners of a dandy, and bowed deeply to the celebrated lady. Madame de Stael had risen and come to meet him, in order to thank him for complying with her request.

"You have made me the happiest of mortals," he said, laying his hand on his breast. "To gaze into these eyes which promise a heaven to us, is a bliss which is not purchased too dearly at the price of half a lifetime. I have read your *Delphine*, and learned to adore its authoress. May I respectfully press to my lips to-day the hand that wrote such beautiful words?"

Madame de Stael granted his request, somewhat surprised at the stiffness with which the German *savant* practiced French gallantry. She asked him to take a seat, and then inquired of him about Fichte and his philosophy. He would have preferred speaking of himself and his works; but inasmuch as such were the wishes of the lady, he took pains to portray Fichte's teachings and influence to her with all the eloquence at his command. She listened to him attentively, interrupted him with many questions, and finally seemed much pleased with him.

"You possess a very fine talent to clothe your thoughts in words, M. Schlegel," she said; "I have not conversed in Germany with anybody whose conversation afforded me so much pleasure; and, if you will take the trouble, you can give me information on a great many subjects. I understand you very well, and am much pleased with your method of explaining intricate questions. Suppose you accompany me during my journey? I want a tutor for my eldest son. If you should be willing to take this situation, I should be the gainer, the more as I should derive so much profit and pleasure from my constant intercourse with you."

"Your offer is a very flattering one indeed," said Schlegel, in surprise; "and nothing could be more agreeable to me than to live all the time in such close proximity to you; but I have to devote too much time to my literary labors, to be able to be useful to your son. I am engaged in translating Shakespeare, and I hope my production will be creditable to me. I should not like to relinquish it now."

"You will have plenty of spare time for that purpose, Monsieur. Two or three hours a day would be all the time I should expect you to devote to my children. You would, moreover, be treated with all the consideration which an honored guest of my house may expect. The only thing which I demand of my son's tutor is *qu'il ait fait l'amour et ne le fasse plus.* * I believe, however, you will be able to fulfill this condition. You know the world and life, and are done with them."

Schlegel grew visibly confused, and hesitated to reply.

"You may think so, Madame, in regard to my marriage; and yet a man of my age, and who is perfectly free and inde-

* Allonville, p. 312.

pendent—I should not like to promise you anything in this respect."

"Very well," said Madame de Stael, smiling, "let us say no more about it now, and you will think of it. If you will in the meantime be kind enough to read with me for an hour every morning, you will put me under great obligations, and as you will thus get better acquainted with me, you will find out whether or not your constant intercourse with me would indemnify you for what you would leave behind in Berlin."

"It would; you need not doubt it," exclaimed Schlegel, vividly. "I hesitate from a widely different motive. I am first an author, and then only a man. For the time being, it will afford me the greatest pleasure to make you acquainted with what our Germany is able to offer you, and I request you to appoint an hour when I am to wait upon you."

"At 10 to-morrow morning, if you please; I desire to read the *Hyperborean Ass* with you; owing to the allusions which it contains, I am unable to understand it."

"What, the *Hyperborean Ass?*" exclaimed Schlegel, in surprise. "My antagonist's book? Why do you wish to read it?"

"The author recommended it to me, and I am anxious to see what your literary quarrels are about, and why you wage war with each other."

"It is envy on his part—nothing but envy," warmly exclaimed Schlegel. "But we have managed to avenge ourselves. These frivolous comedies, destitute as they are of any genuine value, and by no means in keeping with our civilization, excite the enthusiasm of the multitude, and make their author more popular than any other literary man. We cannot tolerate this; we shall annihilate him; we *must* annihilate him."

"I should be very sorry if you did; for he entertains me very pleasantly, and I like to laugh," said Madame de Stael.

" If such be the case—if these trivial comedies entertain you, I shall keep silent," replied Schlegel, angrily, and left the room.

" Strange, very strange," said Madame de Stael, shaking her head, after the door had closed after him. Although she could not approve the spirit from which these enmities arose, they amused her, and, to inform herself about this literary war, she asked, wherever she went, if the old or new poetical school was represented there. But at her own receptions, representatives of both parties were present, and the most relentless enemies met there quite unexpectedly. After one of these soirées she wrote to Wieland:

" BERLIN, March 31, 1804.

" Yes, my dear Wieland, I am here in Berlin, amidst a rather noisy social life; but at heart I long for the pleasant intercourse which I held with all of you in Weimar. I was received here with the utmost politeness; but people in Berlin have no time to see enough of one another, so that their acquaintance always remains a superficial one; and the complete separation of the two societies, that of the court and that of the literary world, imparts to the former often a most tiresome frivolity. They speak French here, and make French *calembours ;* and yet, ignorant as I am of the German language, I long for the quaint humor with which you speak French, inasmuch as I am convinced that Germany will not be the gainer in imitating our French sprightliness.

" I have seen the learned men here. Fichte, Ancillon, and Spalding interest me most among them. I caused Kotzebue and Schlegel to meet in the same room, as might have been expected of a stranger to whom their private feuds were unknown; and I told Schlegel that he injured not you, but himself, by attac':ing the foremost literary celebrities of Europe.

How I regret that the time is past when there was still a noble emulation between the *savants* and authors of Germany! I repeat it; only Frenchmen are able to insult each other gracefully."

"I cannot do anything here but read German books with Schlegel, who has kindly consented to be my teacher. Translations and studies are incompatible with four invitations *par jour*. But I have been told that social life would be much duller in the month of June.

"Tell me that you still love me, and that you still protect my life by your wishes and friendship. I have written to your seductive Duchess, as you call her, and addressed three letters to M'lle de Goechhausen, with the request to remember me to you. Did she do so?

"I have not yet written to Goethe. You call him my favorite, without bearing in mind that I must be more attached to you, because you are more susceptible of love. Adieu, adieu; give me your poetical blessing; I prefer it to that of Capuchins and Idealists. Adieu!

"N. DE STAEL."

CHAPTER XI.

AN EVENING WITH HENRIETTA HERZ.

MADAME DE STAEL had rented the ground-floor of a house on the banks of the Spree, which reminded her of those of the Seine, and, therefore, filled her every now and then with the illusion that she was in her dear Paris.

One morning, when she was yet fast asleep, her maid woke her up, and informed her that Prince Louis Ferdinand was halting on horseback under her window, and wished to see her. It was not yet eight o'clock. Much surprised at the unseasonable time of his visit, she rose in haste and stepped to the window in order to speak with him.

The Prince presented a very handsome appearance. The fresh morning air, as well as a certain agitation, added to the charms of his prepossessing face to-day. Madame de Stael's eyes rested with pleasure and admiration on his fine, chivalrous form as he saluted her.

"I wish to inform you," he began, "that the Duke of Enghien has been arrested on the soil of Baden and carried to Vincennes, where a military commission has sentenced him to be shot. This outrage has filled me with the most intense indignation."

"What a story!" replied Madame De Stael. "Do you not see, Prince, that the enemies of France have invented and circulated it?"

"If you do not believe what I say," said the Prince, "I shall send you the *Moniteur* containing the sentence."

So saying, he spurred his horse and galloped off, with an air expressive of vengeance or death.

Madame de Stael withdrew thoughtfully from the window.

A quarter of an hour afterward, a footman brought her the number of the *Moniteur* containing the account of the execution of the Duke of Enghien, and a letter from the Prince, which read as follows:

"Louis of Prussia sends to Madame de Stael the paper to which he referred, and it affords him pleasure that he will meet her to-day at the house of the Duchess of Courland." *

He wrote thus because he was perfectly beside himself at the disgrace inflicted upon the royal blood of the Duke of Enghien.

Madame de Stael now convinced herself of the truth of the intelligence which he had communicated to her. She paced the room in great agitation, and soliloquized aloud in order to give vent to her indignation. With her heart still overflowing with bitter feelings, she finally dressed herself in order to drive to the Duchess of Courland, who had invited her to dinner.

The Duchess had but few guests to-day.† Madame de Stael met at her house, beside Prince Louis Ferdinand, Johannes von Müller and Henrietta Herz, whose beauty and grace made the most agreeable impression upon her. The conversation referred exclusively to the mournful fate of the unfortunate Duke of Enghien; and it was not until after dinner—when Prince Augustus and several other gentlemen made their appearance—that it became more cheerful.

Madame de Stael requested every guest to tell her something about Fichte's philosophy, which she wished to understand. These requests were frequently somewhat out of place and em-

---

* "Dix Années d'Exil, par Madame de Stael."
† "Reminiscences of Henrietta Herz."

barrassing, inasmuch as it was difficult to say much about so grave a subject in a company of merry guests. So, when Prince Augustus greeted her to-day, he asked her, jocosely, if she had already succeeded in mastering the whole of Fichte's philosophy. " *Oh! j'y parviendrai,*" she replied, most decidedly, but withal with a sharpness of tone showing very plainly that she had understood the hidden meaning of the question.

As she knew that Henrietta Herz was intimately acquainted with Augustus William Schlegel, she embraced the opportunity to inform her that she was anxious to engage him as a tutor for her children, and that she could not imagine what prevented him from accepting her offers, inasmuch as she was ready to fulfill all conditions which he might impose upon her.

" *Vous avez quelque ascendant sur lui,*" she said to her in the course of the conversation. "All I want him to do is to give German lessons to my son and daughter; the rest of his time shall belong to him. His pretext is that translation of Shakespeare at which he is working; but I cannot see," she exclaimed, very warmly, "why he must live in Berlin in order to translate the English poet. Pray persuade him to accept my offers."

The fact was, that Schlegel wished to remain at the Prussian capital, not on account of the English poet, but for the sake of a lady of Berlin. He was the devoted friend of Sophie Bernardi, *née* Tieck, afterwards Madame de Knorring. As soon as Madame de Stael learned this, she requested Henrietta Herz to invite Schlegel and his fair friend to a soirée at her house, that she might get acquainted with the lady. But Sophie Bernardi did not speak a word of French; the two ladies, therefore, would be unable to converse with each other; and Henrietta Herz, foreseeing the painful embarrassment of an interview between them, hesitated to fulfill the wish of her

celebrated friend. Madame de Stael, however, would not permit her to refuse her request, and so she appointed a day when
Necker's daughter was to meet Sophie Bernardi at her house.

" *Je la verrai parler !* " exclaimed Madame de Stael, with her
irresistible vivacity, and impatiently looked forward to the
hour when she was to form the acquaintance of the lady whom
Schlegel admired so intensely.

Henrietta Herz had invited a large number of guests, in
order to mask Madame de Stael's intention as much as possible; it would have been marvelous, however, if Sophie Bernardi had not divined it, nevertheless. For no sooner did she
address a word to Schlegel, than Madame de Stael would say to
him with her habitual vivacity, " *Qu'est ce qu'elle dit ?* " and as
he stood behind her chair, he could not but translate to her the
remarks which Sophie had made. He rendered them, however, by no means faithfully. When Sophie had said anything
at which Madame de Stael might take umbrage, he changed
the meaning of her words. This caused the other guests to
smile, and Henrietta Herz finally was fearful lest Madame de
Stael should notice it and take umbrage at it. So, in order to
prevent an unpleasant scene, she suddenly put a stop to the
deceitful conduct of the distinguished translator. Sophie Bernardi asserted that the French language was not musical at all,
and, hence, unfit for singing; when Madame de Stael asked
Schlegel, " *Qu'est ce qu'elle dit ?* " he translated a remark bestowing a flattering encomium on the melodious element of the
French language. Henrietta Herz then corrected the translator;
and Madame de Stael, instead of propounding any further
questions to him, contented herself, as she had promised, with
hearing Sophie Bernardi speak.

Madame de Stael gave, during her sojourn in Berlin, every
Friday, a soirée, to which she never invited more than three

ladies. Henrietta Herz was frequently among them, and she was invited also to the last party which Madame de Stael gave in the Prussian capital. Her other female guests were the Duchess of Courland and Madame de Berg, and the conversation was exceedingly animated, sprightly, and interesting. Especially amiable was Prince Louis Ferdinand, who was even kind enough to offer Madame de Stael to have his piano brought to her house, and play to her guests on Friday next.

But—man proposes, and God disposes. On Friday next, Madame de Stael was not to be any longer in Berlin. A sudden end was put to her sojourn in that city, by the intelligence that her father had been taken sick. She had been but six weeks at the Prussian capital when this mournful news reached her, and suddenly thwarted all her plans. The philosophy of the German professors was immediately forgotten, the *Hyperborean Ass* was flung aside, the many new relations were broken off, her trunks were hurriedly packed, and she set out for Coppet. She did not know yet the terrible calamity that had befallen her; she was still full of hope and confidence and refused to yield to serious apprehensions.

It was not until she reached Weimar that another letter informed her of what had occurred. Her grief knew no bounds; her words, her tears, were those of despair; she had fits and convulsions; she screamed and raved; and was, in the full sense of the word, on the verge of madness.

Madame de Stein to her Son.

"WEIMAR, April 29, 1804.

"Madame de Stael returned from Berlin before Goethe was able to answer her letter, because her father had died in the meantime. She sets no bounds to her grief, has convulsions, and screams and wails all the time amidst her streaming tears.

How sad it is that Nature did not add a little wisdom to all the extraordinary talents which it bestowed upon her. But that is wanting to her. William Schlegel accompanies her as tutor of her son, Augustus. She will set out to-morrow for Coppet.

"She was unable to compose herself. Her grief had so over-powered her that her physical indisposition prevented her soul from recovering its tranquillity.

"William Schlegel and Constant sat opposite to her in the traveling-coach, and took the utmost pains to console her; but all their efforts were in vain. She felt that no one would ever love her as her father had loved her; that no one would hence-forth accompany her in her life-path with so much solicitude, confidence, and tenderness, as he had done; and the most ter-rible loneliness, that of the heart, fell like a pall on her soul.

"'One day—one more day,' she exclaimed, imploringly, that she might see him once more, hear his dear voice again, and read in his eyes that he perceived and pitied the grief of his child; but this one day—who did not implore it in the course of his life, and who did not hear the terrible, 'No?'

"For the first time, the dread silence of the grave struck terror into her heart; for the first time, this weird stillness and lone-liness caused her restless and active soul to tremble. Her eyes gazed upon the landscape around her, in order to discover in it a picture analogous to her grief; she contemplated the trees of the forest in their beautiful foliage, in the lovely verdure of May, and envied them for their constantly renewing vitality, which enables them to outlive centuries; and to man, whose mind embraces time and eternity, was granted but such a brief span, scarcely sufficient to perceive the good, but not to reach it!"

Bettina von Arnim to Goethe's Mother.

"This time I am angry with you, Madame; why did you not

18

send me Goethe's letter? Since August 13th, I have not received a line from him, and now September is already drawing
to a close. Madame de Stael may have helped him to while
his time away, so that he did not think of me. I dined with
her yesterday in Mayence; as the other ladies refused to sit by
her, I took the seat next to her. It was uncomfortable enough,
as the gentlemen crowded around the table in order to speak
with her and look her in the face. They even bent over me;
and when I said, '*Vos odorateurs me suffoquent,*' she laughed.
She told me that Goethe had alluded to me in his conversations with her; I sat still in order to learn what he had said
about me; and yet I was displeased, for I do not want him to
talk of me with anybody; and, after all, I do not believe that
she told me the truth; finally, the crowd of men bending over
me, in order to converse with her, became so large that I could
not stand it any longer; so I said to her, '*Vos lauriers me
pèsent trop fort sur les épaules.*' I rose and elbowed my way
through the throng of her admirers. Then Sismondi, her
companion, came to me, kissed my hand, told me I was very
talented, and said so to others, too; and they repeated it at least
twenty times, as if I were a prince; for everybody admires all
that princes say and do, no matter how insignificant it may be.
Afterwards I listened to what she said about Goethe; she told
us she had expected to find another Werther, but she had been
mistaken, neither his bearing nor his figure being in keeping
with that character, which had greatly disappointed her.
Madame Goethe, I waxed wroth at these remarks. Turning
to Schlegel, I said to him in German, 'Madame de Stael was
mistaken both in her expectation and opinion of Goethe; we
Germans expect that Goethe will have no difficulty in producing twenty heroes that would make the same deep impression on the French; and we believe and know that

he himself is a widely different and much superior hero. Schlegel has acted foolishly in not imparting to her better information on this subject. She threw a laurel-leaf, with which she had been playing, on the floor; I put my foot on it, pushed it aside, and walked away. That is all I can tell you about the celebrated lady. . . . ."

When the travelers approached the mountains of Switzerland, Constant pointed out to her a cloud, bearing the shape of a gigantic man, and which, after covering a summit for some time, disappeared at setting-in of night. Madame de Stael looked upon it as a sign sent her from Heaven ; she considered it a symbol of the life of her father, whose existence was now likewise concealed from her view by the gloom of an everlasting night.

Her grief was heart-rending when she reached Coppet and entered the room which he had inhabited, where everything reminded her of him, and everything spoke to her of him. Here she was now to live without him whose love had shed so much sunshine over her path, and who alone had known how to render her abode endurable. To the last moments of his life he had occupied himself with her, with the most affectionate solicitude; during the nine days of his sickness he had only uttered her name and thought of her, only manifested the utmost uneasiness concerning her future, and expressed deep regret at having published his last work, and thereby brought about his daughter's exile, which would be more intolerable to her than ever before, when she would not be welcomed at Coppet by anything but the graves of her parents. With a trembling hand he had written, yet in the heat of his fever, to the First Consul, and assured him that Madame de Stael had had nothing to do with the publication of his last book, and had, on the contrary, requested him not to issue it.

There is a wondrously persuasive power in the words of a dying person. It seemed impossible that the last prayer of a man who had borne so conspicuous a part in the history of France, and who implored the First Consul to permit his child to return to her native country, should be disregarded. With this hope Necker had closed his eyes.

When his daughter heard of this step of her father's, she thanked him tearfully for the tender solicitude with which he tried on his death-bed to enable her yet to return to her dear Paris.

She could not believe that the First Consul would turn a deaf ear to such a supplication. But when she heard that her father's letter had made no impression on him, she smiled bitterly at the folly of her expectation that the death of a man would hush the hatred of a Napoleon.

CHAPTER XII.

THE settlement of her private affairs had afforded Madame de Stael a certain diversion from her grief, and engrossed all her thoughts. Up to her father's death he had attended to all her business, and saved her all the trouble connected therewith. It was, therefore, an entirely unwonted task for her to enter upon the management of the vast fortune which she now inherited of him, beside the two million francs which Necker had lent to the French Government during the Revolution, and which France had never refunded to him.

Little as this kind of business was to her taste, she determined not to intrust it to others, but to watch personally over the fortune which she was resolved to hand down intact to her children.

She devoted herself to this task with praiseworthy circumspection. She did not want anybody to say that, gifted as she was in other respects, she was disqualified to fulfill the practical requirements of life. She had to indemnify her children for the loss of her father, and she was determined to do so.

Her son Augustus, who was on the verge of adolescence, had hitherto been educated by his grandfather alone. It was now incumbent on her to direct his education and to watch over his studies. The lessons which Schlegel gave him were insufficient; and as she was prevented from living in Paris, she went for the time to Geneva, where good schools and teachers of all branches of knowledge were at her command.

These duties and occupations produced a favorable effect upon her state of mind, and added to her tranquillity. As long as she remained as active as she was now, as long as these exigencies of reality knocked at her door, she forgot her grief, and experienced a certain satisfaction at the thought that she was acting in consonance with the wishes of her late lamented father, and that she was certain of his approbation. This consciousness did her good, and imparted fresh strength to her.

At length, however, everything was settled; lawyers and courts no longer claimed her attention, and a profound silence reigned again around her. Her children were poring over their books; Schlegel worked with them or for himself; Benjamin Constant read the papers, cast longing glances up to the clouds, all of which he thought were moving towards Paris, and turned over the works of Schiller and Goethe in order to find something, the translation of which might render him as famous as Schlegel had become by that of Shakespeare; for his vanity craved for applause; he could not bear a life of tranquillity; he was bound to play a *rôle*, and to obtain laurels as an actor on the political stage.

His presence could not comfort and soothe Madame de Stael, but only entertain and excite her. He was exceedingly eloquent, he argued with her, he raised paradoxes and dropped them again, and these intellectual contests diverted both of them for hours.

It was still impossible for her to take up a book. Whenever she was vividly excited, whenever she was a prey to pain or grief, she was unable to turn her thoughts upon anything not connected with it. Such was now the case again. She turned over page after page, and did not know what she was reading.

In her present state of mind, she was only able to write; but she lacked the courage to do so. Her father could no longer

read what she wrote; he could no longer rejoice at the encomiums bestowed upon her; he alone had taken such an affectionate interest in her; without him she felt lonely and deserted.

"Why do you complain of loneliness?" Constant said to her.
"Is friendship, then, nothing to you? Am I not here to share
sunshine and tempest with you? Do I not stand by your side
to rejoice at your successes? Do you care so little for my applause that you do not deem it worth while to write in order
to obtain it? Is your muse silent when she is to play her
cithern before me?"

Madame de Stael shook her head mournfully. "Only a
father can love purely and disinterestedly," she said, sadly;
"he alone rejoiced truly at my successes. But you, Benjamin,
with all your friendship for me, you resemble all men in
granting to your self-love the first place in the catalogue of
your passions."

So saying, she left the room.

Benjamin Constant looked after her in surprise. No doubt,
he felt that she did not misjudge him.

Ever since her father's death, Madame de Stael had been in
feeble health. A doctor was sent for, and declared that only a
change of place, a different climate, other people and other
surroundings, could dispel her grief and cure her of her sleeplessness. He therefore advised her to go to Italy and spend
the winter in Rome, whose art-treasures, he hoped, would
arouse her from the apathy following in the wake of long-con-
tinued grief. She had to follow this advice, but insisted on not
leaving Coppet until she had written a biography of her father,
which was to show to the world what virtues he had possessed,
from what motives he had acted, what he had been as a husband and father, and how dearly he had loved his daughter.

After performing this task, she was ready to undertake a journey upon which she entered without hope or joy, and filled with forebodings of her death.

All night long she walked about like a restless ghost. To put an end to her fast-increasing sleeplessness, the physician prescribed the use of opium, which, since that time, she was unfortunately unable to give up again.

Augustus William Schlegel was not long in accustoming himself to his new position. He treated the gifted lady with so much courtesy and kindness, and bestowed such enthusiastic encomiums on her genius, that Benjamin Constant could not refrain from suspecting that the German professor desired to be even more than a friend and the tutor of her children. The present circumstances, however, were decidedly unfavorable for bringing about closer relations between the two. Her grief was so profound that she took his efforts to please her as expressions of his compassion, and thanked him in this spirit.

The eldest son of Madame de Stael was already a youth, and assisted his mother with the kindness and prudence of a friend; she treated him thus, and asked on all occasions his advice and approval. His boundless love rewarded her for this confidence.

The summer months had slowly elapsed in this manner. Benjamin Constant had profited by them to begin a translation of Schiller's *Wallenstein*. While she was working at the biography of her father, and therefore had no need of him during the morning hours, he could devote himself uninterruptedly to this task.

At noon she made her appearance, with eyes red with weeping, in her family circle. The recollections of past days, the jotting down of so many affectionate remarks which her father had addressed to her during the closing months of his life, filled her eyes again and again with tears.

She wrote these reminiscences in the same cabinet of the château of Coppet where Necker had worked—at the very window where his writing-table had stood. There she had a fine view of the grove where a monument had been erected over his grave, as well as of the long alley where he always, at parting, had waved to her a last farewell.

She called to mind an evening in the preceding autumn, when she had sat by his side at the same spot, and, filled perhaps with a momentary foreboding of the loss that was in store for her, had asked him what was to become of her if she should ever be compelled to live without him.

"My child," he had answered in a broken voice, " *Dieu mésure le vent aux brebis depouillées.*"

"Ah!" she now said to herself, "I am very unhappy; I have neither a country nor a home: the grave of my parents is my only home."

But, profound as her grief was, never did it render her hardhearted; never did she forget her friends, and become indifferent to that which concerned them. Thus she wrote to Madame Récamier, when that beautiful lady lost her fortune:

GENEVA, Nov. 17, 1804.

"Ah, my dear Juliette, how much pain that dreadful intelligence has given me; how I execrate an exile which prevents me from hastening to you and pressing you to my heart! You have lost all that makes life sweet and agreeable; but even though you were better loved and still more interesting than you are, the same calamity would have befallen you. I shall write to M. Récamier and tell him how much I pity and honor him. But tell me, would it be possible for me to see you here

18*

this winter?—if you could make up your mind to pass three
months in a small circle where you would be received in the
most affectionate manner? But then your friends in Paris
are sure to treat you in the same manner. *Enfin*, I shall go at
all events to Lyons, or to the utmost limit of my forty leagues
in order to see you, embrace you, and tell you that I love you
better than any woman in the world. I do not know how to
comfort you, save by saying that the noble traits of your generosity and benevolence will become more conspicuous in adversity than ever before. Your circumstances, no doubt, are
no longer what they were; still, could I envy her whom I
love, I should give everything in order to be you. A beauty
unequaled throughout Europe, a stainless reputation, a proud
and generous character—what sources of happiness even in
this life; *où l'on marche si dépouillé.*

"Dear Juliette! May our friendship grow firmer and firmer;
may it be strengthened, not only by the generous services which
you have rendered me, but by a continued correspondence
and the mutual desire of a constant interchange of feelings
and of a common life. Dear Juliette, you might obtain for me
permission to return to Paris, for you are always an all-powerful personage, and we should then see each other every day;
and as you are younger than I, you would close my eyes, and
my children would be your friends. My daughter has wept
to-day over the tears of both of us. Dear Juliette, the affluence which surrounded you has served to afford us pleasure;
your fortune was ours, and I feel as if I were poor because you
are no longer rich. Believe me, those who are loved so dearly
are still happy.

"Benjamin will write to you; he grieves at your misfortune.
Mathieu de Montmorency wrote me a very touching letter concerning you. Dear friend, may your heart throb calmly amidst

so much grief! Alas! Neither the death nor the indifference of your friends threaten you; they alone are incurable wounds. Adieu, dear angel, adieu! I reverently kiss your sweet face."

At length, on the 25th of October, 1804, Madame de Stael had arranged the posthumous papers of her illustrious father, and sent them to the printer with the sketch which she had written of his character and private life; it was not till then that she set out for Italy.

Hitherto she had not shown a due appreciation of the fine arts. With the exception of music, of which she was passionately fond, she was indifferent to everything which did not engross the mind. It was not until now, under the mild sky of happy Italy, that she was to awake to other views, and learn to enjoy with her eyes. A new world arose before her; a new life dawned upon her.

Accompanied by Schlegel, Benjamin Constant, and her children, she visited Rome and Naples. Although she had entered upon her journey in the gloomiest state of mind, the novelty of the scene made an overwhelming impression on her, and hushed all her mournful recollections. The fine arts brought their powerful influence to bear on her. Paris, politics, the longing of her lonely heart, the memories of the past, all the grief of the present, faded away at the contemplation of the countless monuments which so many ages had accumulated. She breathed a different air, she heard another language, the centuries of the past spoke to her, and unrolled the most remote periods before her view. In Rome she met the fair-haired young Canova, whom she had formerly received at her house in Paris; she met there, furthermore, the two Humboldts, Eliza von der Recke, a number of *savants* and artists from all quarters of the globe, and, finally, Sophie Bernardi, from Berlin, who had come to Rome probably in order to see if the gifted Schlegel had not forgotten her, exposed as he was all the time to the rays of the lustrous eyes of the most interesting lady on earth. If she met with a sore disappointment, and if his fidelity had not stood the test, she confessed only to herself.

Joseph Bonaparte had furnished Madame de Stael also with letters of introduction to eminent men in Rome, in order to make her sojourn there as pleasant as possible; so she met with the most flattering reception. Her house became speedily the rendezvous of the most distinguished personages; and in the midst of this brilliant circle, her genius beamed as a bright star, and animated all who approached her.

Her gift of improvisation, her skill in reciting poetry and performing dramatic *rôles*, awoke here to renewed life; and as if the applause and admiration bestowed upon her, and her new-born enthusiasm for the fine arts, kept her in a constant state of rapturous excitement, she forgot herself, and the real happiness that was wanting to her heart, and her grief was hushed for a while.

Her impressions gave rise to the creation of a new work of art, and *Corinne*—a book with which all my readers are familiar, was the fruit of her sojourn in Rome.

CHAPTER XIII.

NAPOLEON'S HATRED.

MADAME DE STAEL returned from Italy, in the summer of 1805, with a rich store of recollections, and took up her abode again at Coppet. Time had exercised its soothing influence over her. She had learned to do without the ever-watchful solicitude of her father; she had accustomed herself to his eyes no longer following her every step, and to his approval no longer stimulating her energy and ambition. Gentle melancholy filled her heart when she arrived at Coppet, and met him no longer in the rooms where he had welcomed her so often with tender glances and words of affectionate consolation.

In order not to relapse into her former grief, she now began to work very assiduously at her *Corinne.* This occupation, as well as the instruction of her children, which she herself directed in part, kept her busy during the morning hours, while the afternoon and evening belonged to her friends.

Guests were not wanting at her house, where everybody met with the most hospitable reception. The name of Madame de Stael had already obtained a world-wide celebrity. All strangers who came into that part of Switzerland took pains to visit Coppet. Hence, there were plenty of visitors during the summer and autumn; and only in the winter months reigned at Coppet that monotony which is so tedious to inhabitants of a large city. In order to escape from this stillness, she removed to Geneva as soon as the roads were passable again.

The social life of this city did not afford her much pleasure, inasmuch as the austere republican ladies of Geneva treated her with marked disrespect, and their prudery shrank from the frank and straightforward bearing of the gifted lady. Their views of propriety were stiff and narrow-minded, the tone of the Parisian *salons* grated on their ears, and the social customs of the French capital gave umbrage to them.

It was impossible for Madame de Stael to make concessions to the prejudices of others. Her motto was, "*Fais ce que dois, advienne que pourra.*" She set no other bounds to what she would do, and would not do, than such as were in consonance with her inclinations and taste, and she refused to be restrained in this respect by persons who were mentally so greatly inferior to her. This pride and firmness made her unpopular.

Those who do not go with the multitude, will incur its enmity, and it is then a dangerous opponent.

The fair but austere ladies of Geneva visited Madame de Stael's parties, but only to censure her bitterly for reading, reciting poetry, performing dramatic *rôles*—in short, doing all she could to entertain herself and her guests as pleasantly as possible. Because they themselves did not possess these talents, she was not to display them in their presence.

The ever restless and active mind of Madame de Stael stimulated also the friends who lived at her house to measure their own strength by a higher standard. The intellectual atmosphere in which they moved, produced a crushing effect upon weak minds, but it added to the vigor of intellects strong enough to breathe it. Such was the case with Augustus William Schlegel, whose energy and enthusiasm were greatly enhanced since he lived at the house of this remarkable woman, who knew how to awaken slumbering talents, and unearth hidden treasures.

Whenever there were no visitors, each of the three read in the evening what they had written during the day, and listened to the criticisms of the hearers. This interchange stimulated the ambition and efforts of all of them.

Madame de Stael read the chapters of *Corinne*, as they were completed, to this small circle of friends, who listened to the work with admiration and astonishment. They felt that the heroine was the authoress as she wished to be, and, in fact, was, with the exception of Corinne's beauty. Her own heart-struggles, the disappointments with which she had met, her thirst of fame, her bearing toward the world, the weakness of the men, everything was here idealized and presented to the hearers in a form of great artistic beauty; and the authoress and heroine often embarrassed them greatly by asking them what they thought of the work.

Benjamin Constant, especially, recognized himself but too often in Lord Nelvil, although he took good care not to confess it. Very disagreeable feelings would steal upon him on such occasions. He then turned his eyes searchingly upon Schlegel in order to see whether or not he suspected who was meant; Schlegel, however, seemed to notice only the artistic form of the work, without paying any attention to the source whence the subject had been taken. He bestowed the most eloquent encomiums on the authoress, and predicted that she would obtain a celebrity such as no woman had ever enjoyed before.

Schlegel did not suspect the painful interest which Benjamin Constant took in the work, and he therefore often called upon him to join in his praise, but such exhortations were wasted. He persisted in keeping silence, because he felt greatly offended, although he refused to confess it even to himself. The picture of his own weakness arose before him so distinctly, as he heard the delineation of Lord Nelvil's character, that he felt a sort of exasperation against Madame de Stael, which he vainly tried to master. His wounded self-love refused to be soothed.

In order to get rid of these disagreeable impressions, he likewise began to write a novel which he entitled *Adolphe*. He depicted in it his soul-struggles, and represented himself the victim of a passion which he was unable to return ; but, despite his persistent efforts to hold the heroine responsible for the embarrassing position of the hero, we find here again a feeble character, whose will is always overcome by his inclinations. He himself, however, did not perceive the strong resemblance which the hero of his novel bore to his own character, and, while he wrote this book, he enjoyed the silent triumph of what he considered his complete justification. The winter passed amidst many little wranglings between him and Madame de Stael, and in the spring she left Geneva in order to return to her dear France.

She was still exiled from Paris, but was at liberty to take up her abode at a distance of forty leagues from the capital, and she now tried to find a place where she might superintend the publication of her new work.

Her eldest son, Augustus, whom her father had educated, and who bore a strong resemblance to him, both in his appearance and character, had entered the Polytechnic School; he was thus enabled to visit her at least once a week ; and no one, she thought, would prevent her from going every now and then to Paris, the control at the gates of the city being not so rigorous as that she needed to fear lest she should be refused admittance upon her arrival. Fouché, she knew, was decidedly averse to needless rigor. Bonaparte, who was then at the acme of his power, had little to fear from a woman, who was now, moreover, exclusively occupied with literary labors, and he would certainly not carry his personal hatred toward her so far as to resort to extreme measures against her.

Madame de Stael went, in the first place, to Auxerre; after residing there for some time without being molested by the authorities, she moved to Rouen; and as the Government still failed to throw any obstacle in the way of her return to the capital, she ventured to approach Paris again by several stages, and took up her abode at Auberge en Ville, where her friends could visit her more frequently than before.

Here she saw Mathieu de Montmorency at her house; here she was visited by her beautiful friend, Madame Récamier; here she yielded again to the whole charm of Parisian society. Augustus William Schlegel now saw her for the first time in her proper element. All the memories of her past happiness awoke again in her mind; all the dreams of her youth arose again before her eyes. That sweet happiness for which she had vainly longed for so many years, appeared before her soul in the radiance of renewed hope; and the thirst of fame, which had once engrossed her, filled her breast again with irresistible desires. What if the appearance of her *Corinne* should realize her proudest dreams?

She could now hear from her friends in Paris daily, nay, hourly; every minute she was able to hold intercourse with her acquaintances; seated on the balcony of her villa, she gazed upon the road and espied those who intended to surprise her with their visit. She was delighted with this change in her circumstances, and built on that which she had already obtained, the hope of still greater favors. After approaching so close to Paris, she thought she would soon be permitted to return to the capital.

" Ah, Constant," she said one day, when this subject engrossed all her thoughts, " I believe the future will indemnify me, after all, for the sufferings and privations which I have undergone. I think it would be delightful for me to return to Paris at the very time when my *Corinne* appears, and to witness with my own eyes the impression which my book will make on the public."

" There is no capitol in Paris," he said, sneeringly; " the Parisians do not crown female poets; heroes alone obtain honor and glory in that city."

" The applause of my friends will crown me; I shall read my praise in their faces, and be happy; they will love me on account of my talents, and their growing attachment will offer me the most beautiful laurel-wreath."

" I doubt it," he replied.

" You doubt it? " she asked, in surprise.

" Because Corinne, despite her triumphs, died of a broken heart," he replied, harshly.

"*You* can tell me so, Benjamin!" exclaimed Madame de Stael, passionately. "You can reproach *me* with that? Do you not feel, then, how contemptible such language is toward a woman who might have been indebted to you for her greatest happiness, and, inasmuch as she was unable to obtain it, went in search of consolation wherever she could find it? You are cruel."

" You do not know yourself, Germaine," replied Constant, in an unusually grave tone. " You think that your restless spirit, and the yearning of your heart for happiness, is owing to the lack of a certain, indissoluble tie attaching you to a man whom you love; but you are mistaken. Matrimony is a state of tranquillity, and tranquillity is repugnant to you. Wedded life confines all emotions to certain limits, and you love only that which exceeds these limits; wedded life requires mutual forbearance, while you want to see the man of your heart at your feet, and insist on dominating him. Every man is afraid of such a yoke. You have led me, your younger companion, into the path of fame, Germaine; I have admired your genius; your conversation enchanted me; and no matter how often I attempted to break loose from you, I was always irresistibly drawn back toward you, and I could not help returning to her whom I intended to flee. In this struggle my best years have elapsed; will you reproach me with having sacrificed them to you? Believe me, it was better for us that no indissoluble bonds united us, and that we were mutually free. Had we been chained to one another, the compulsory character of our intercourse might have turned our love into hatred; while now, when the years of passion have gone by, the noblest relations of friendship will remain to us for the evening of our life."

"Remain to us, Constant? But who tells me that you will remain to me?" exclaimed Madame de Stael, passionately. "Is not everything in life subject to constant changes? Who warrants me that you will not form new relations and leave me? What then? Attached to you by an intercourse of so many years, I shall remain all alone, with the crushing consciousness of being spurned and deserted by my old friend! I have always looked forward fearfully to this contingency, and tasted its whole bitterness beforehand in portraying it in my *Corinne*. There is no happiness for a woman save in wedded life; she must be sure of one friend; she must know *one* relation in life not subject to a sudden change; she must be able to cast anchor somewhere on this little earth, where nothing is stable. Who warrants me that you will not desert me, Constant?"

"I myself," he replied, in a faltering voice. "I myself, Germaine!"

She gazed at him, thoughtfully, for a moment.

" You yourself ? " she then repeated, incredulously. " Yes, if you *could* be responsible for yourself! For your sake, Benjamin, I have incurred the frowns of the world. I have purchased the happiness of having you at my house with many a tear, for which my children may call me to account one day. My attachment to you has caused many a sad hour to my noble father ; and I shall, perhaps, meet with the grievous disappointment to find that I built everything on sand. I have a foreboding as if bitter hours are in store for me, in consequence of my connection with you."

" Why are you so distrustful of me ? " exclaimed Constant, in confusion. " What is this distrust grounded on ? "

" On your character, Benjamin. In order to stand firm, you have need of a prop, of a support. You are a child of the moment ; every new impression carries you away ; you cannot be responsible for yourself; moreover, I find that your conduct toward me has undergone a marked change since our return from Italy. What ails you ? "

" To tell you the truth, Germaine, you have offended me by the delineation of Lord Nelvil's character. I do not deserve it."

" Why do you recognize yourself in a picture which, you say, bears no resemblance to you ? " she asked, smilingly.

He was at a loss for a reply, and in his mortification reproached her with preferring Augustus William Schlegel to him. She burst into loud laughter.

" In that event, you have found a rival who resorts to artificial means in order to please me," she replied, alluding to Schlegel's careful toilet, which made him look like a fop, and gave rise to many jests on the part of Madame de Stael.

At this moment they were interrupted by a visitor, and a conversation to which it would be difficult for them to recur, was brought to a sudden close. Ochlenschläger, the gifted young Dane, was announced to Madame de Stael, who was greatly surprised to see before her the poet from the distant North, with whom her friend, Frederica Brun, the female poet of Copenhagen, had made her acquainted.

She received him in the most cordial manner, and invited him to visit her at Coppet, during his journey in Switzerland, and to spend some time at her house.

"You must get acquainted with Schlegel," she said, casting a smiling glance on Constant, to punish him a little for his jealousy. "I am sure, M. de Rebecque will be kind enough to call him."

Schlegel made his appearance, and was introduced by Madame de Stael in a manner indicative of her desire to distinguish him; for she felt that his vanity would not permit him to stay at her house merely as tutor of her children, and so she took pains to inform every guest of the distinguished services which he had rendered to literature, and of his talents as an author, before mentioning the duties which he had promised to perform toward herself and her children. Her generosity and kind-heartedness would not suffer the world to look down on Schlegel, on account of the valuable services which he rendered to her and to her house.

Corinne was printed and published. Madame de Stael awaited with breathless impatience the impression which this work would make upon the public, and the fruits which she would reap from it so far as the emperor was concerned. She did not anticipate the grievous disappointment with which she was destined to meet.

She was, therefore, perfectly dumbfounded when she was informed that a new decree of exile was about to be issued against her. On the first anniversary of her father's death, she

received the order to part again with her friends and to leave
her Parisian home. She refused for a long time to believe that
the Government had really issued this order; and when she
could no longer doubt it, she gave way to her despair. Wringing her hands, she paced her rooms, and heart-rending sobs
and groans choked her words. If she was not to be allowed to
reside in Paris—if she was not to enjoy there the applause and
admiration of her friends and contemporaries, life had lost its
charms for her, and she felt that she would pine away in
sorrow and despair.

She was treated unjustly, and she had no arms to defend
herself. Napoleon was now so great and powerful, how could
his glory be dimmed if the Parisians should occupy themselves
awhile with a woman who had written a good book?

But her lamentations did not move him—her tears left him
cold.

She was compelled to leave Paris and return to Coppet.
She submitted to stern necessity with sighs and tears.

Schlegel and Constant accompanied her. Constant did not
conceal his dejection; for he was loth to leave France, which
he likewise considered his native country, and almost indispensable to his happiness.

"Oh, how I long to turn back," said Madame de Stael,
when they reached the frontier of France, and cast a longing
glance toward the country which she was to leave now for
years, and perhaps for ever. "*Il y a comme une jouissance
physique dans la résistance à un pouvoir injuste,*" she added. But
what resistance was she to offer to Napoleon?

"France grieves at the departure of her muse," said Schlegel,
in the florid manner to which he had accustomed himself as a public speaker. "Nothing can be more flattering to you than that
a Napoleon should deem his glory dimmed by your presence."

I shall no longer sing now," said Madame de Stael, mournfully. "The caged nightingale is silent; and exile is to me a prison."

"And so it is to others," said Constant, peevishly. "Had you praised Napoleon, instead of censuring him, we should now be very merry in Paris."

"And I should have sacrificed my convictions to my interests, and lost my self-respect. Did you wish me to do that?"

"All we men expect of women is that they should be amiable, and try to please us," replied Constant, carelessly. "As regards the more serious affairs of life, we shall attend to them alone."

Madame de Stael gazed at Constant; when their glances met, he dropped his eyes. She contemplated him for a minute, while he sat blushing before her; she then averted her face without adding another word, and spoke with Schlegel on another subject.

CHAPTER XIV.

PRINCE AUGUSTUS AT COPPET.

PEACE had been concluded. Europe breathed more freely, and looked forward to its blessings with renewed hopefulness. The soldiers hastened back to their homes, in order to recreate themselves in the bosom of their families, and social life assumed a more brilliant and animated character. Prince Augustus of Prussia profited by this opportunity to make a trip to Switzerland, and visited Coppet in order to greet Madame de Stael, whose acquaintance he had made at Berlin, and whom he had learned to esteem, at her own house.

He arrived quite unexpectedly.

Since her return to Switzerland, Madame de Stael had been at work upon an important book on Germany, which required considerable preparatory studies. The first chapter was completed, and she was about to read it to Schlegel and Constant, when the Prince was announced to her. Uttering an "Ah" of agreeable surprise, she rose, in order to go to meet the august guest.

She received him, not ceremoniously, but with the utmost cordiality. Prince Augustus was still in the prime of life, his uniform sat exceedingly well on him, and there was in his bearing something chivalrous, which made a most agreeable impression, and to which Madame de Stael was by no means insensible. She talked with him about Berlin, about her sojourn in that city, and the numerous common friends of whom the hurry of her departure had prevented her from taking leave, and all of whom yet lived warmly in her remembrance.

They had not yet sat long together and chatted of the past and present, of Berlin and Paris, when the door opened, and a charming lady entered the room with a light swinging step. She stood still and blushed when she perceived the strange guest; already she was about to turn to the door in her timidity, when Madame de Stael, casting a sidelong glance of triumph toward the Prince, seized her hand, and begged leave of her guest to present to him her friend, Madame Récamier.

This name was not unknown to the Prince, for the rare beauty of its bearer had already familiarized all Europe with it. The more was he surprised at her appearance, which bore no resemblance to the picture which his imagination had drawn of her.

This girlish bashfulness of a lady accustomed to the triumphs of her charms, astonished him; and this timidity of a beauty of whom the most decided self-consciousness might have been expected, was inexplicable to him.

He remained standing before her as if spell-bound. He felt strongly tempted to kneel down before this lovely creature and worship her. He had much difficulty in regaining his composure, and concealing what was going on in his mind.

"Fortune smiles on me," he said at last. "Genius and beauty, in their most fascinating form, are going to indemnify me for the hardships of war. How am I to resist such a reunion?"

"Stay with us, sire," exclaimed Madame de Stael. "Let us nurse you, and try to recreate yourself here."

"I should, no doubt, find here the most charming, but withal the most dangerous recreation," replied the Prince, casting a significant glance on Madame Récamier, who was looking at him with sweet *naïveté*.

19

He did stay, not for days or weeks, but for several months, and thought he could never leave this place any more. It was not the social life at Coppet, nor the fascinating conversation of Madame de Stael that detained him here, but the surpassing beauty of her friend. Her charms captivated him more and more, until he was ready to sacrifice everything in order to possess her. But all he was willing to sacrifice, was insufficient for the attainment of his object. Madame Récamier was too pious to consent to obtain a divorce from her husband, and too virtuous to live with the Prince without the sanction of the church and the courts.

She accepted his homage, without detracting for that matter from her dignity or sweetness; she saw him at her feet, and raised him up with angelic grace, without betraying in her face the painful struggle which it cost her to do so, and without showing that her vanity was gratified at having secured the affections of so august a suitor. She was glad to see that he loved her, and rewarded him with a certain humble gratitude for thinking her so amiable. Madame de Stael was delighted with the homage which he paid to Juliette, and was more than ever attached to him since she knew that he admired her fair friend; for her great and noble heart was free from petty jealousies, and neither malice nor hatred ever gained access to it.

Prince Augustus passed three months at Coppet, and during his sojourn there he was indefatigable in his efforts to persuade Madame de Récamier to leave her husband and become his wife; but his impassioned appeals were wasted. Madame de Genlis made this episode the subject of a novel, entitled *Mademoiselle de Clermont*, and the scene of which was laid at Coppet, at the house of a rival whom her envy pursued to the last days of her life.

Madame Récamier left Coppet at last; and no sooner had

she departed, than the Prince likewise bade farewell to Madame de Stael, in order to forget his love in the noise and bustle of the world.

Madame de Stael now went to Vienna to complete her preparations for her work on Germany. She remained there during the winter. Benjamin Constant went with her eldest son, Augustus, to Paris, where he read his translation of *Wallenstein* in several *salons.*

Some critics have asserted that Madame de Stael's knowledge of German literature was very superficial; but such was not the case. It is true, Schlegel's advice was very useful to her in this respect, and she concurred in many of his views; but her opinions, in the main, were perfectly independent, and based on her own studies. She read a volume every morning, and was then perfectly familiar with its contents, as was shown by her conversations on it, which, it is true, often modified her opinions on the subject.

These grave occupations and a pleasant social life produced a salutary effect upon her, and restored the tranquillity of her mind. She had passed the winter without serious heart-struggles; she had been received in the most courteous and flattering manner; she had formed a great many new and agreeable acquaintances, and returned in the best of spirits to Coppet, where she was soon visited by her Parisian friends.

With Madame Récamier she had meanwhile kept up an animated correspondence, which, on her part, was so full of generous and noble sentiments, that it is a nobler monument of her mind and heart than the rest of her works. Now the two friends were united again, and enjoyed together the fine summer days, during which they often called to mind Prince Augustus and his love.

In autumn, friends joined them, and passed the monotonous

winter months with them. Among them was Baron Voigt, from Altona, who read a number of German works, among them Lessing's *Nathan,* to her. Ochlenschläger, too, arrived at Coppet, and Madame de Stael had at once a room fitted up for him at the château.

She received him in the most cordial manner, and invited him to spend several weeks with her. She remarked jocosely that he spoke French far better than he did at the first visit which he paid her at Auberge en Ville, and she repeated to him a few remarks which he had addressed to her at that time, and which seemed to him now so ludicrous that he could not help in joining her laughter at his expense.

Ochlenschläger, however, was not long in discovering that he might use in his conversations with her the German language, which she understood perfectly, but did not like to speak. Her son Augustus spoke German very fluently, and so did her daughter Albertine, who was now a half-grown girl.

The young Dane soon felt perfectly at home at Coppet. The society there could not be better, and the comfortable elegance of the life at the château pleased him exceedingly. Sismonde de Sismondi, the celebrated historian, and Count de Sabrin, joined them soon after; so that the domestic circle became the more interesting and lively, the more the season compelled them to remain in the house. Ochlenschläger generally was quite taciturn. " *C'est un arbre, sur lequel il croît des tragédies,"* said Sismondi, one day, about him to Madame de Stael—a remark with which the young poet was much pleased. Schlegel treated him coldly, perhaps, because he deemed his talents as yet hardly worth noticing. He rode out every day for an hour on a tame horse, in order to take exercise. Once the groom wanted to give him a fiery horse, but he refused to take it. Madame de Stael bantered him. Benjamin Constant then offered to mount the horse, in order to convince Schlegel that it was not dangerous. It was a humiliation which he gladly inflicted on the German professor.

The whole company went down to the gateway to witness the occurrence, in which all took sides one way or the other.

Constant mounted the horse and galloped away. All eyes followed him; but scarcely had he performed a short distance when he was thrown into a wet ditch. The horse ran away and returned to the stable.

Constant rejoined his friends in great confusion, and Schlegel received him with profound compassion, which sounded to him like bitter irony. He went to his room in the worst possible humor; the others followed him amidst laughter and jests.

Young Oehlenschläger was delighted with the genius, wit, and amiability of his hostess. He had never seen a woman like her; and, with the susceptibility of his age, admired her rare gifts. She enjoyed his admiration, as we like a fragrant flower; for ardent admiration of human genius is the finest blossom of a pure mind.

The grave, taciturn Northerner listened attentively whenever she spoke, and was always filled with fresh surprise at the piquant and profound character of her remarks, which made her so agreeable a companion. Wherever she made her appearance, youth and beauty had to retire from the field; so resistlessly did her attractive conversation captivate all men.

She was rich, she was hospitable, and, in his opinion, sat enthroned like a queen or a sort of fairy in her enchanted palace, whither eminent men flocked in order to be dominated by her. Her scepter was the small twig which the footman laid every day beside her napkin, because it was no less necessary to her for keeping her hands in motion, than knife and fork were indispensable to her for taking food.

Zacharias Werner, too, arrived quite unexpectedly one day, late in autumn, with a large snuff-box in his narrow vest pocket, and with a great deal of snuff in his nostrils, and with many bows. Oehlenschläger was glad that Werner spoke French as imperfectly as he did, and laughed at his blunders. At the same time he admired Werner's writings, although not so ardently as Madame de Stael did, and so both of them became warm friends, and made daily excursions in the environs of Coppet.

One day Madame de Stael entered the room when they were engaged in an animated conversation. She asked them what they were speaking of. "I am scolding Werner," said Oehlenschläger. "I communicated the plan of my tragedy to him, and he now wants to conceal the plan of his tragedy from me. Is not that too bad? Is it not unfair?"

"Ah," she replied, gravely and reprovingly, "*c'est une autre chose, vous êtes encore jeune ; vous avez besoin de vous former.*"

Without replying to her, Oehlenschläger quickly turned his back to her and left the room. She vainly waited for his return. When she finally sent a servant to his room, she was informed that he was packing his trunk in order to leave Coppet. Her words had offended him.

She now went herself to him, and tried to pacify him by protestations of her esteem and friendship. His vanity was wounded. She had not yet read any of his writings, and he allowed himself at last to be persuaded to remain till the arrival of his *Aladdin* and *Hakon Jarl*, so that she might acquire a better appreciation and knowledge of his poetical talents. He had sent for the two books, and, when the packages arrived a few days afterward, the warm encomiums which she bestowed upon him, conciliated him entirely, and he no longer thought of his departure.

He intended to pass the winter in Italy. Madame de Stael represented to him that it would be better for him to stay with her and learn Italian, and then to cross the Alps in the spring, when he would be familiar with the language. We easily allow ourselves to be persuaded to do that which we like to do. So he gladly remained with her, and accompanied her and all her guests to Geneva, where he took dancing lessons in order to waltz with the fair ladies of that city.

A constant whirl of dinner and supper-parties, theatrical performances and concerts, entertained them here. Madame de Stael recited poetry and lectured; and the pedantic women of the republic gazed again in surprise at the brilliant comet whose orbit they were unable to follow, and whose passage, therefore, caused them to shake their heads.

Benjamin Constant had now at length completed his translation of *Wallenstein*. He had imitated Racine's style and peculiarities in arranging this tragedy, and was now anxious to learn the reception with which his production would meet; for he was tired of being eclipsed by Schlegel's literary celebrity; and, destitute as he was of productive talents, he had to content himself with translating one of Schiller's plays. He therefore appointed an evening on which he intended to read his translation to his friends at Geneva.

The encomiums which were bestowed on him seemed to him by far too cold. He forgot that what he had written was a mere translation, and that the genius of the author had engrossed the thoughts of his audience as he read the book. So the applause with which the translation was received did not content him, and he gazed with sullenness and dissatisfaction upon the audience.

It is very disagreeable for a talented man to play a secondary *rôle* by the side of a celebrated lady. At the outset of his career, Constant had created too great a sensation; he had then been admired too much as an orator, to be satisfied with a slight measure of incense bestowed upon him in the field of literature, where he was not in his proper element. The longer his friends now talked about the drama, the more distinctly did he perceive that he was not the author, but only the translator; and this added greatly to his disappointment.

For a long time past he had been dissatisfied with his position, and scarcely been able to conceal his mortification. But the reading of his translation of *Wallenstein* caused him to come to a sudden determination.

Madame de Stael had no idea of what was passing in his breast. She was engaged in rehearsing a musical performance which she had arranged, and did not notice his absence immediately. The superb music which Shulz had composed to the lyrical parts of Racine's *Athalie*, was to enchant Oehlenschläger's ears before he left them; for he said that nothing moved him more profoundly than these heart-melodies of the North, as he called them. She did not notice, therefore, that Constant was absent; and when he did not make his appearance in the evening either, she thought it was owing to a whim, such as often made him sullen and morose.

Occupied as she was with Oehlenschläger alone, she did not even think of sending for him. When all the guests had left the house, the Northern poet asked her to write a few lines in his Album. She wrote as follows:

"*J'introduis pour la prèmiere fois le Français dans ce livre; mais bien que Göthe l'ait appelé une langue perfide, j'espère, mon cher Oehlenschläger, que vous croirez à mon amitié pour vous et à ma vive estime pour l'auteur d'Axel et Vallborg.*"

They then parted in the most cordial manner, and did not

see each other for many years afterward, until an accident caused them to meet again for a short time.

When Benjamin Constant did not make his appearance on the following day either, Madame de Stael sent a servant up to him to inquire why he kept his room all the time; and now she was informed that he could not be found anywhere, and that he had not touched his bed at all last night.

This news surprised her greatly. She revolved in her mind all that had happened and had been spoken of for the last few days, but she was unable to find anywhere a key to his sudden disappearance, and to divine whither he might have gone.

Messengers were sent out after him in all directions, but they did not find him. She wrote to Madame Récamier and to M. de Montmorency in order to ask them if he had gone to them; she made inquiries in Paris, but no one was able to give her any information about him.

In the meantime she returned to Coppet, and hoped that he would surprise her here one day; but she waited in vain for his re-appearance. She was deeply afflicted at his prolonged absence. What could have induced him to leave her in this manner—her who had sacrificed everything to him! She was at a loss to comprehend his conduct.

Literary employment was again her only consolation for the disappearance of her old friend. It was only in devoting herself to this occupation with more zeal and energy than ever before, that she found forgetfulness and tranquillity. But her nights, during which her agitation made her sleepless, and when no occupation diverted her thoughts from the subject which she was anxious to forget, were exceedingly painful to her. So she had to resort again and again to the remedy which gave her a few hours of artificial repose, and slowly take the poison that was to hurry her to a premature grave.

Spring had meanwhile drawn to a close, and already she commenced mourning for Constant as if he had died. One day, however, an acquaintance told her that he had met, and conversed with, M. Benjamin Constant de Rebecque, who had been accompanied by a lady, on the road between Lucerne and Interlachen.

Madame de Stael was utterly unprepared for this intelligence. She felt as if something was torn in her breast, and fell senseless to the ground.

When she awoke to consciousness, the outbursts of her grief were so terrible, that her friends began to tremble for her life. He lived while she mourned for him; he lived and deceived her! That was more than she was able to bear. This thought broke her heart.

She ordered her carriage, begged Schlegel to take care of her children, and set out without informing her friends whither she was going, or when she would return. The fact was that she did not know it herself; she had not yet fully made up her mind whither to wend her way. She wanted to go in search of him, no matter where he might be; and she was at a loss to know whither he had gone.

She took the route which the above-mentioned acquaintance had indicated to her, but she did not find a trace of him. At length, several days afterward, she reached Interlachen at setting-in of dusk. The snow-clad summit of the Jungfrau was already shrouded in clouds; in the western horizon some purple streaks were still to be seen; the air was cool, although it was in midsummer; and the place was as deserted as if no strangers ever wended their way to it.

Madame de Stael wrapped herself in a warm shawl, and walked alone through the streets. She was not sure that she would find her faithless friend here, but something in her heart made her restless; her eyes wandered about as if in search of somebody, and as if she would recognize him in every passer-by, and see him step forth from behind every tree.

There was a light in a low-roofed villa which illuminated the street through the open windows. Thither she wended her way; she did not know why; whether it was a foreboding, or fate. In short, an irresistible power drew her thither.

A gentleman and a lady sat opposite to each other at a table in the room. They seemed to be engaged in an animated conversation. Suddenly the lady rose, approached him, leaned on his shoulder, and imprinted a tender kiss on his forehead.

A shrill, piercing cry under the window startled her suddenly, so that she gave a violent start. The gentleman had turned deadly pale at the sound of this voice, and glanced about in terror and confusion. He then took a sudden resolution, and hastened out of the room.

He found Madame de Stael lying in a swoon under his window.

Several persons who had heard the cry, rushed from the house. The strange lady was lifted up; and as Madame de Stael used to recover immediately from such powerful emotions, so she was now again in a few minutes erect and restored to consciousness.

She gazed long and mournfully at Constant. "So you were here, Benjamin," she said in her deep, sonorous voice. "Here, then, I was to go in search of you, and find you in such company? Alas! I had a foreboding that you would desert me so perfidiously one day!"

"Let me escort you to your rooms, Germaine," he replied, in an undertone, deeply moved by her words. "There I will explain everything to you. Pray follow me."

He offered her his arm, and, leaning on it, she walked slowly to her hotel. Not a word passed between them on the way thither. Both made an effort to compose themselves, and call to mind that with which they might upbraid one another. Constant tried to find new subterfuges with which to justify his conduct, but it was not easy for him to do so this time.

They parted company in a very unpleasant state of mind, at an advanced hour of the night.

He felt that he could not convince or rather deceive Madame de Stael. She refused to believe that Count Hardenberg had requested him to accompany his niece on a trip to this watering-place, and that he had concealed it from her, inasmuch as he had felt convinced that her jealousy would prevent her from permitting him to comply with the Count's request.

But the lady whom Constant had left at the villa had likewise been greatly surprised and alarmed at this nocturnal adventure. Upon his return to her, he called upon her to confirm his statements, to avoid Madame de Stael as long as she was at Interlachen, and, even if he should accompany her at her departure, quietly submit to this step, and patiently await his return.

She passed a sleepless night.

In the morning she was dressed long before Constant was about, and on her way to Madame de Stael, without informing him of her intention. She caused herself to be announced to her as Madame de Rebecque, and was admitted; for Madame de Stael was no less anxious to see the strange lady, than the latter was to have an interview with her.

The fair daughter of Germany stood before her, pale and grave. In a voice tremulous with emotion, she begged her to tell her why Constant was afraid of informing her of the rights which she had in regard to him.

"Rights!" cried Madame de Stael, turning red and pale.

"Rights! *Mon Dieu*—" She stopped short. She felt only too painfully that she had no rights to him.

" He wants me to conceal from you that I am his wife," added the other.

"His wife!" exclaimed Madame de Stael. "Impossible! What should I be, then!" She trembled.

"Here is the proof," said the stranger, showing her the wedding ring. " We were married on the 5th of June."

"That is dreadful!" exclaimed Madame de Stael. "Dreadful! How do you come to belong to him, when he has been mine for many years past, and is to remain mine?"

"You will not leave him to me?"

"Never! What claims do you have to him? His love? It has belonged to me for many years! The benediction of the Church? But I—I—oh, dreadful treachery! How could you take him from me?"

"All is clear to me now, suddenly—all, all!" said the other. "His irresolution, his seeming fickleness—all, all. I knew him long before his eyes ever fell on you, and he was engaged to marry me long before you ever heard his voice. Year after year went by, and still he deferred the moment when he was to belong to me. And now he comes at last, redeems his word, and —is about to leave me again! I shall not submit to this disgrace. I shall rather end my life here at your feet; with this intention I came to you; he must either be mine, or I cease standing in your way."

So saying, she quickly seized a glass standing near her, threw something into it, and swallowed the contents before Madame de Stael was able to prevent her from so doing.

"For God's sake, what have you done?" cried the latter in dismay, and hastened to her in order to snatch the glass from her hand; but it was already too late.

" You have got rid of your rival," cried the poor lady, with much resignation, and sank into a chair, where she looked for her speedy dissolution.

At this moment Constant rushed breathlessly into the room. " What has happened here?" he exclaimed, wildly, glancing now at one, now at the other.

" Send for a doctor!" cried Madame de Stael, perfectly beside herself. " She has taken poison! She is dying! For God's sake, quick!"

Upon hearing these words, Constant rushed away like a madman. A physician arrived in a few minutes, and fortunately succeeded in saving her. The unfortunate lady was restored to a life in which she was to enjoy but little happiness. The inconstancy of her husband was an incessant source of trouble to her.

Reassured and cooled down after this terrible catastrophe, all three of them were in a conciliatory mood, and Madame de Stael, kind and generous as usual when her heart spoke and her passion was silent, deeply pitied the poor lady, and assured her of her own accord that she would not encroach upon her rights, and that Constant should belong to her alone. Having comforted her in this manner, and bidden Constant a conciliatory farewell, she returned alone to Coppet.

She arrived there in a sad state of mind, kissed her children, and locked herself in her room.

This journey to Interlachen was an epoch in her life. A mere fickleness she would have gladly forgiven, for she knew the human heart, and was aware that even the strongest will is not always able to regulate its pulsations. This was the reason why she did not count upon any attachment which was not strengthened by the voice of duty.

But treachery—treachery toward her most sacred feelings—

treachery where she looked for fidelity—treachery where she had a right to expect sincere and durable friendship—that was too bitter a disappointment. She was not equal to this trial. It violently shook her faith in human nature.

And yet, despite his unworthy conduct, she could neither hate nor despise the man who had sinned against her in this manner.

She knew his character; she knew that he suffered most in consequence of his treachery; she pitied him sincerely, and lamented his weakness.

With deceit in his heart, he had met her so many years with an open forehead, and she had trusted him! She herself was so candid, how could she suspect that he was false?

She did not want to see him any more. "God! God! Grant me forgetfulness!" she prayed, in order to get rid of her poignant grief.

Suddenly there was a low knocking at her door. She did not hear it. It was repeated again and again. It was at an unseasonable hour of the night. It was past midnight. At last she opened the door with her own hand.

Benjamin Constant, deadly pale and perfectly beside himself, stood before her.

"Is it you, Benjamin?" exclaimed Madame de Stael, in dismay.

He sank at her feet.

"Forgive me, or I shall die here. Be my friend again, or I have lived enough," he cried, passionately.

"For God's sake, do not trouble me any more," exclaimed Madame de Stael, angrily. "I have suffered enough through you. Your sight re-awakens my whole grief. Stay now with her to whom duty attaches you."

"I shall not do so unless you forgive me, Germaine. I shall

not do so without having heard from you a word comforting me, and causing me to appear less hateful to myself. I shall not do so without receiving from you a glance restoring my courage and tranquillity to me. I shall remain on my knees before you, Germaine, until your hand lifts me up; and I shall die here, if you turn from me inexorably!"

"I do not hate you, Constant," said Madame de Stael, weeping gently. "I do not shut my door against you. I only want to forget how deeply you have offended me; and then—then—I shall hold out my hand to you, and be reconciled to you."

She burst into loud sobs, and buried her face in her hands. Constant crept close up to her, pressed the hem of her dress to his lips, and called her by a thousand fond names, shedding tears all the time.

"Go now!" she said, imploringly. "I can say no more. I forgive you," she added in a low voice.

"God be praised!" he cried, as if animated with fresh hope, kissed her feet, and rushed out of the room. She gazed after him. Had it been an apparition, or had she really seen him?

CHAPTER XV.

THE SICK HERO.

A YOUNG man, descended from a noble family, had excited the liveliest interest among the ladies of Geneva, by the fame of his heroic deeds, the contrast of his age with his tottering step, the pale complexion of his prepossessing face, and his feeble health.

Wounds which he had received in the Spanish war threatened him with a premature death. They had confined him to his bed for a long time, and he had not risen from it until quite recently, with a faint hope of ultimate recovery.

Madame de Stael listened sympathetically to the account of his fate and of his present sufferings. She asked herself if he would exchange his physical pain for the trials imposed upon her heart, and a low voice in her breast whispered to her that, compared to her, he was still the happier of the two. Admiration, praise, and sympathies were bestowed upon young Rocca; but no one suspected her sufferings; only the silent midnight hour was the confident of her complaints.

To a woman it is humiliating to be betrayed and deserted; and the compassion to which she is entitled, wounds her heart.

She could forgive Constant's offense, but not forget it; her heart continued bleeding.

One day, when she was walking out alone, she saw the sick young man who attracted so much attention, pacing up and down in the sun. She stood still and looked thoughtfully after him.

"He is very young yet," she murmured to herself, her eyes filling with tears, "and is already to renounce the joys of life."

When he turned now, and was about to pass her again, she laid her hand on his arm, looked at him compassionately with her fine dark eyes, and said gently, in her deep, sonorous voice:

"Hope, hope on, poor sufferer; God is great. Your youth may surmount a great deal; your wounds will heal, and will then be proud ornaments. But when the heart is wounded in its inmost depth, time brings no relief, and all is irretrievably lost. Console yourself with the thought that there are still greater sufferings than those which weigh you down."

So saying, she turned from him and went on her way; but the young patient remained standing, as if riveted to the spot, and gazed after her until she had disappeared from his view.

"It was her," said a voice in his breast; "it could be no one but her; she alone is able to utter such words, and cast such glances on me."

Her words still vibrated on his ear. Waking, dreaming, he heard and saw her alone. She engrossed all his thoughts. All he wished for, was to meet her again; all he hoped for, was to hear her voice once more, and to bask again in the sunshine of her eyes, which had rested on him so sorrowfully and sympathetically.

"But," he was asked, "what could you, a poor invalid, be to her? Of what could you talk with her? She takes no interest in anything but politics and literature; what could you offer to this highly intellectual and cultivated lady?"

"A heart beating warmly for her."

"Who tells you that she cares for that heart?"

"She is unhappy, and has need of the consolation of love. *Je l'aimerai tellement qu'elle finira par m'épouser*," replied Rocca, half angry at the obstacles thrown in his way.

His friends laughed at his presumption, and informed Madame de Stael of what the young invalid had said in regard to her.

She listened to them mournfully. If it should comfort his oppressed soul, why should this consolation not be granted to him? She herself was so unhappy, so weary of suffering—her life was so lonely, so monotonous, and she felt how a person in such moments of loneliness might grasp at a straw.

"We have something in common—both of us are sufferers," she replied, and sent word to him that she would be glad to see him.

The young officer made his appearance, trembling with happiness. Fresh life coursed through his veins since he saw her; his pulse beat more impetuously, and he felt that he *must* recover.

Madame de Stael perceived this impression with heartfelt joy. "Happiness is such a rare flower," she said; "may it bloom to him through me!"

She now continued her work on Germany with fresh courage. Since a new flame warmed her heart, she was able to work again, and she looked forward to the completion of her book toward the close of the winter.

In order to superintend the publication of the work, she wished again to move closer to Paris, and pass beyond the bounds of the forty leagues which had been set to her. A dangerous step!

So she repaired to France in the spring of 1810, and took up her abode in the ancient château of Chaumont-sur-Loire, which

Cardinal d'Amboise, Diana de Poitiers, Catherine de Medici, and Nostradamus had inhabited before her. The present owner of this romantic building was in America, and upon his return she removed to the neighboring estate of Fossé, which offered to her plenty of room, but very little comfort beside.

Madame Récamier visited her here, and cheered her solitude by her warm friendship. As soon as Madame de Stael set foot on French soil, her state of mind underwent a marked change. The very air seemed to produce a salutary effect on her; or was it only the thought that she was again in her native country, and no longer in exile, which cheered her so visibly?

The environs of Fossé were monotonous, and it was so far from Paris that her Parisian friends could visit her but very rarely. So she was confined to her domestic circle; she and her companions amused themselves by music and singing; Madame Récamier played on the harp, an Italian music-teacher on the guitar, and Madame de Stael and her daughter sung, often in the presence of the whole population of the village.

Every now and then she made secret trips to Paris, her negotiations with her publisher rendering personal interviews with him almost indispensable.

One day, at the very moment when her carriage drove up to his door, she was suddenly met by Benjamin Constant. Joy and surprise animated his glance, while he tried to read in her face what reception he would meet with at her hands.

Madame de Stael held out to him her hand with her amiable frankness. "I hope you are happy," she said; "that is more important than anything else."

"Without you? Never!" he exclaimed, passionately. "As the flower has need of the sun, so I have need of the light of your eyes, and of the flashes of your genius, to enjoy my life, and arouse my soul to energetic action. I can no longer live without you."

"And your wife?"

"She is here, and knows that I am in search of you."

He followed her into the house. He told her in a desperate tone that he would throw himself under the wheels of her carriage if she refused him permission to accompany her. So she yielded at last.

"You are foolish," she said; "but how am I to prevent you from following me?—*Comment se fâcher contre d'autres que ceux qu'on aime?*"

"That is a harsh remark!" exclaimed Benjamin Constant, looking at her in surprise.

"But, I hope, it is true; at all events, if it is not, it deserves to be true," she replied.

After attending to her business, she wished to pay a visit to Henrietta Mendelssohn, who was an intimate friend of Schlegel; and in whom she, therefore, took the liveliest interest. Henrietta Mendelssohn lived in a villa on the Richter, where she educated a number of little girls belonging to the most aristocratic families. Accompanied by Constant, she now repaired to this quiet, shady villa, to pass a few hours with the talented and interesting teacher.

This secluded life, the resignation with which she performed her task, her gentleness and modesty, made a singular impression on a lady whose whole nature had always longed for intercourse with the outer world, and who, despite all her longing for happiness, had never been able to reach it. She was not very talkative to-day. She sat absorbed in grave and gloomy thoughts about her immediate future.

Constant did all he could to cheer her up. But his *conversation étonnante* was wasted on this occasion.

When they left the villa, he urged her to tell him what depressed her so much.

"How can you ask that question," she said, reproachfully.
"I have no home on earth. I do not belong anywhere; and
no one belongs to me. No one shares my lot, and bears prosperity and adversity with me. I am dying of the loneliness
of my heart."

She intended to bid him farewell, but he did not permit it.
Nothing, he said, could prevent him from accompanying her,
returning with her to Fossé, and spending there some time
with her. She accepted this offer without manifesting any joy,
and, in so doing, yielded only to his pressing supplication.

On the 23d of September she corrected the last proof-sheet
of her work on Germany. With heartfelt joy she added to it
the words, "The End;" so little did she anticipate the new
persecutions which it was to occasion to her. She cheerfully
drew up a list of one hundred persons to whom she intended
to send it, forwarded it to her publisher, and then went to the
estate of M. de Montmorency, situated five miles from Blois.
Overjoyed as she was to meet this dear friend of hers again,
she walked with him in the shade of the magnificent forest
surrounding his château, enjoyed the splendid weather, lingered at the vestiges of historical events, in which the place
abounded, owing to the battle of Fretteval, between Philip Augustus and Richard the Lion-hearted, and yielded to the gentle peace and tranquillity with which the scenery filled her
heart.

When they returned to the château, she went to her room
and wrote to Bonaparte:

"Sire: I take the liberty of sending my work on Germany
to your majesty. If you will take the trouble to read it, I believe you will find that it is the production of a thoughtful

mind, matured by time. Sire, twelve years have elapsed since
I have seen your majesty, and am in exile. Twelve years of
adversity chastens every character, and fate teaches resignation to those who suffer.

"On the eve of embarking for England, I beg your majesty
to grant me an interview of half an hour. I believe I am able
to communicate to you matters of interest to you, and for this
reason I pray you to grant me this favor previous to my departure.

"In this letter I shall confine myself to one point, namely,
a statement of the reasons which induce me to leave the continent in case your majesty should not permit me to live at a
villa so close to Paris that my children might remain with me
there.

"The displeasure of your majesty is so injurious to those
who incur it, that I cannot make a step in Europe without
feeling its effects. Some are fearful of compromising themselves by seeing me; others consider themselves Romans in
disregarding these fears. The simplest social relations become
services which a proud mind cannot accept.

"Among my friends are some who have shared my fate
with incredible magnanimity; but I have also seen the most
ardent affections recoil from the necessity of living with me in
the solitude; and for eight years past my life has been divided
between the fear of imposing sacrifices, and the grief to see
them made.

"It is, perhaps, silly of me to give the master of the world a
detailed account of my impressions; but that which subjected
the world to you, Sire, was your genius, which penetrates and
dominates everything. In your wonderful knowledge of human nature, your majesty understands both its highest and
most delicate strings.

"My sons have no prospects of a brilliant career; my daughter has reached her thirteenth year; in a few years she will preside over a household of her own; it would be selfish in me to compel her to pass her youth at the obscure places to which I am exiled. So I should have to part with her, too.

"Such a life, therefore, is intolerable, and I am unable to find any relief on the continent. What city could I select where the displeasure of your majesty would not be an insurmountable obstacle both to the success of my children, and to my personal tranquillity?

"Your majesty is, perhaps, not aware of the anxiety with which most of your functionaries look upon exiles. I could communicate to you in regard to this point details which must certainly be contrary to your instructions.

"Your majesty has been told that I long to return to Paris for the sake of the Museum and of Talma; this is a pleasant joke on exile—that is to say, the calamity which Cicero and Bolingbroke have pronounced the most intolerable of all; but if I love the masterpieces of art, for which France is indebted to the conquests of your majesty—if I love those beautiful tragedies in which the struggles of heroism are portrayed, can you find fault with me for it, Sire?

"The happiness of men depends on the character of their individual qualities; and if heaven has endowed me with talents, do I not possess an imagination which requires the enjoyment of the fine arts and of dramatic literature?

"So many persons ask of your majesty all sorts of real benefits, why should I blush to ask of you friendship, poesy, music, paintings, the whole ideal world, which I may enjoy without detracting from the reverence due to the sovereign of France?"

The Emperor Napoleon frequently read at the breakfast-table

novels or other literary productions of the day; and all books that displeased him, he instantly flung into the fire-place by his side; such was also the fate of the work on Germany, which Madame de Stael had sent him. * Scarcely had he read half an hour in it, when he threw it into the flames; and, as it blazed up, he ordered the police to hasten to the publisher and destroy the whole edition in the same manner; at the same time, the authoress was to be informed that she must leave France in the course of three days. Such was the answer to her mild and conciliatory letter.

Her friends hardly dared to inform her of the new blow that had befallen her. Finally, M. de Montmorency broke the dreadful news to her as delicately as possible. She burst into bitter tears.

Her last hope was gone. She gave way to her despair. What remained to her now?

She returned to Fossé, where gensd'armes had already surrounded her house. They were to seize even her manuscript, in order to destroy every vestige of her work. Vain endeavor! She gave them an imperfect copy, and saved the whole manuscript.

Whither was she now to wend her way but to America, the land of liberty? Ships were ready to set sail for the New World. But few days of preparation were necessary, and she asked permission to remain in France until she was ready to embark. The short delay was granted to her, but at the same time the ports where she would be permitted to embark were named to her, and thus the Government thwarted her intention to go to America by way of England. Without landing in England, and meeting her friends who lived there, she had not the courage to embark for the other hemisphere; and as

* "Memoirs of Constant, Napoleon's Valet-de-Chambre." Vol. IV.

20

she had to choose between America and Coppet, she finally decided in favor of the latter.

She passed the winter in a mournful state of mind. Even
literary employment was wanting to her, inasmuch as she had
not the heart to write anything after the fate which had befallen her last work. Her strength was paralyzed, the wings
of her mind drooped, her nights were sleepless, and the only
remedy by which she was able to alleviate her sufferings and
to give a seeming slumber to her tearful eyes, was the constant
use of opium. Blow after blow struck her now, and bowed
her deeper and deeper.

In the first place, Schlegel was ordered to leave Switzerland,
because the Emperor disapproved of his views on literature,
and was especially angry with him for having preferred the
Phædra of Euripides to that of Racine.

This was ridiculous; but what other reason could be alleged,
as long as the true one—his attachment to Madame de Stael's
family—had to be concealed? So she had to part with the
friend to whose presence she had been accustomed for eight
years past; she had to give him up at a moment when his loss
was doubly painful to her.

Next, it was Mathieu de Montmorency's turn. He was not
the man to desert his friend in the days of her adversity; he had
already repeatedly spent some time with her; he now hastened
again to Coppet, and was exiled in consequence. Madame de
Stael was in despair at the punishment inflicted on her generous friend. She uttered piercing cries of grief, and refused
to be comforted. She resorted again to strong doses of opium,
in order to allay the gnawing pain of her thoughts, and obtain
momentary forgetfulness.

When she awoke to consciousness, M. de Montmorency tried
to impart to her the tranquillity which he acquired by seeing

the hand of God in all events; but prayer proved ineffectual in healing the wounds of her heart. The thought that a friend had to suffer for her sake, was intolerable to her, and rendered life itself burdensome to her.

A letter from Madame Récamier, announcing her speedy arrival at Coppet, filled her, not with joy, but with terror. What if she should likewise incur the Emperor's displeasure by this act of friendship?

Upon her arrival, Madame de Stael implored her not to remain at Coppet. Vain endeavor! Her beautiful friend refused to pass her door, and she received Madame Récamier with streaming tears, and fearful of the consequences in which this step might involve the beautiful lady, in the walls of this château, where her arrival had so often been greeted with heartfelt joy.

Already, early next morning, Madame Récamier left Coppet again, but her speedy departure was of no avail; she was banished from Paris.

"Madame de Stael," said the Prefect of Geneva, "leads an agreeable life at her home; her friends and acquaintances come from distant points to visit her, and the Emperor is determined not to suffer this any longer."

She had never published a word of praise in regard to Napoleon; that was her crime. She would have even now restored liberty to herself and her friends by bestowing encomiums on the Emperor; but she refused to do so.

It was suggested to her to celebrate at least the birth of the King of Rome, but she declined acting upon this suggestion, too, saying she did not know what to say about it, except that she wished the little King, with all her heart, a good wet-nurse.

Napoleon was intent on forcing her to undergo this humilia-

tion, and her persistent refusals incited him to fresh persecutions. The world bowed to him, and this woman dared to bid
him defiance! More friends of hers were exiled, and all who
approached her incurred the displeasure of the Emperor. "He
who is not for me," he said, "is against me; he who visits
Madame de Stael is my enemy." Gensd'armes watched the
long alley leading to Coppet; they stopped all guests, and took
down their names. Finally no one could venture any longer
to go to her, and she looked forward to the time when she
would be entirely alone with her children—a prisoner in her
château. Her imagination depicted to her the most frightful
calamities. She fancied that her children, too, would be taken
from her, and that she would at last suffer the fate of Mary
Stuart. She felt that she must flee, and was determined to do
so; but whither?

At this trying time, the gloom of which was heightened by
her passionate temperament, which knew no resignation, there
remained to her but one source from which she drew consolation;
it was the passionate love of the pale, sick Rocca, who was
bent from the very first on compelling her, by the ardor of his
attachment, to bestow her affections on him. No dangers de-
terred him from staying with her; he was determined to remain, even though all should flee her; and he pledged himself
to share her lot, even though it should be the scaffold. Upon
hearing such protestations, she shook her head mournfully.

"You are determined to do what you cannot do," she said;
"you must succumb to force; every hour, every minute, can
bring you the order to leave me for ever; and what then?"

"Give me the right to stay with you," he cried, imploringly.
"Enable me to meet the tyrant's agents at the moment of dan
- ger, with the letter of a law which imposes on me the duty to
stand by your side as a protector in adversity and death."

She understood him, and, surprised at the proposal, was silent. But the anxiety caused by her perilous position, the sense of loneliness which had weighed her down for so many years, and the desire to be loved, which became more and more intense since she had been compelled to part with all her friends, finally induced her to yield to his pressing supplications. This led to new embarrassments and many unpleasant conflicts; but she had found a friend upon whom she could count in an emergency. This conviction did her good, and determined her to go to England, though by a circuitous route, passing through none of the States friendly to Napoleon.

Madame de Staël to Madame Récamier.

"I bid you farewell, dear angel of my life, with all the tenderness of which my heart is capable. I recommend Augustus to you; may he see you and meet me again! You are a heavenly creature. Had I lived near you, I should have been only too happy; but fate carries me away. Adieu."

With these lines, she took leave of her friend, whom she was not to meet again until during the Restoration.

CHAPTER XVI.

THE FLIGHT.

MADAME DE STAEL hastened from land to land, from city to city, without getting rid of her despondency. Her journey led her by way of Vienna to Moscow; she passed through regions entirely foreign to her, and almost impassable. She visited the ancient city of the Czars, and the brilliant St. Petersburg; everywhere she met with the most cordial reception, and her genius created here, too, a great sensation; but what escaped further and further from her, was tranquillity and happiness.

The exile and fugitive now bore in her breast a worm gnawing at her heart. For the first time of her life she kept something secret; she concealed her emotions and a step which she had taken. She had the utmost difficulty in doing so; and it was only the thought of the illustrious name she bore, that caused her to impose this sacrifice on her ambition.

She was accompanied by her full-grown daughter, from whom she wished to conceal her union with Rocca.

A son who had reached the age of manhood, sat opposite to her. How could she have confessed to him that her longing for love, for the happiness of a union with a beloved husband, had induced her to bestow her hand upon a young man who was not even on a footing of equality with her as far as rank and social position were concerned?

While she was thus compelled to carefully watch over her

words, nay, over the expression of her face, lest she should betray her secret, her eyes perceived in the distance the progress of the French armies, which almost followed in her footsteps, and filled her here, too, with uneasiness, so that she was at a loss to know whether she should go from Moscow to Constantinople, or to St. Petersburg.

Her solicitude for her daughter caused her to go to St. Petersburg, and she left behind the city of the Czars, which was about to be laid in ashes.

At St. Petersburg, too, she stayed but a short time. She could not gaze but mournfully upon this fast improving city; for her imagination depicted it to her devastated by French arms, and by the horrors of a war for which France paid by far too dearly with the lives of her sons.

Sweden, the native country of her husband, offered her a more tranquil and secure asylum; and so she hastened, after a two weeks' sojourn, from St. Petersburg to Stockholm, where she felt safe again for the first time in many months.

She was intimately acquainted with Bernadotte. She shared his love of France, and deplored with him the misfortunes which her country, under the usurper's scepter, had brought upon Europe. Her heart bled at the disasters of the French army, whose wretched remnants, a prey to the most horrible sufferings, were now fleeing back to their native country.

Here, in Stockholm, she wrote her essay on *Suicide*, which she dedicated to the Crown Prince of Sweden.

· In the spring of 1813 she went to England, just after the armistice had been concluded between Napoleon and the Allied Powers. The Emperor was in Dresden; he was still able to remain the sovereign of France, and rule over territories extending to the Rhine, and embracing the kingdom of Italy. It was doubtful, however, if England would accede to such a treaty.

Madame de Stael landed in June on the green shores of Albion. She rode from Harwich to London, a distance of seventy miles, as through a land of promise; gentle heights, alternated with fertile plains, in which were to be seen, along the whole road. villa after villa, surrounded by magnificent gardens and parks. Everything on which her eyes fell, indicated prosperity. Nowhere was to be seen a hovel of wretchedness, or a figure dressed in rags; the very cattle in the fields shared this general prosperity. And yet the French journals had asserted, again and again, that that country, weighed down as it was by its public debt, was destitute of the elements of vitality.

Madame de Stael had always been an ardent admirer of the English constitution, and, during her sojourn in that country, she learned to attach a still higher value to it. She familiarized herself with all public institutions; she attended the sessions of the courts; she listened to the proceedings of Parliament; and all that she heard and saw, added to her admiration of the country and its inhabitants. She called the English constitution *un beau monument de l'ordre social,* which Providence had vouchsafed to Great Britain, that other nations might not only admire, but also imitate it.

Public opinion is all-powerful in England; it is the real ruler of the country. Hence, popularity is the goal to which everybody aspires, and emulation often produces the most prodigious strength. The enthusiasm with which a whole people greeted the deed of an individual, the thundering applause of the multitudes, the cheers of thousands upon thousands, delighted Madame de Stael. The funeral of Nelson, and the reception of Wellington, seemed to her the ideal of popular applause bestowed upon glory.

"Ah! quelle enivrante jouissance que celle de la popularité!" she exclaimed, believing that there was no greater happiness

than that of receiving such applause. She met with a brilliant reception. Her genius was ardently admired, and no one here took umbrage at the interest which she took in politics. The women of England have always paid attention to that which engrossed the thoughts of the men, so that Madame de Stael was here in her proper element. She was distinguished by the women, esteemed by the men, and not a voice was raised to charge her with unfeminine conduct.

Even Schlegel had formerly often complained that too much attention was devoted to politics in her *salon*, while he took interest in nothing but literature. She therefore regretted that he had remained with Bernadotte, in Stockholm, and did not witness her triumph in England, which would have convinced him that he had been mistaken.

However, scarcely had her soul derived fresh elasticity and vitality from these cheering impressions, when a new and crushing blow befell her. Her second son, who had remained in Sweden, was killed there in a duel. She loved her children dearly, and the destruction of such a young and promising life, filled her with despair. As usual, she was unable to bear this cruel bereavement with fortitude; and to soothe her grief, she resorted again to opium.

On the 31st of March, the Allies had made their entry into Paris, the Emperor of Russia and the King of Prussia heading the columns of their troops. Madame de Stael was now at liberty to return to her native country, on whose soil she was to set foot in a mournful state of mind, and amidst sadly altered circumstances.

She had profited by her sojourn in England to publish her work on Germany, the manuscript of which she had taken with her from Coppet. Amidst the clang of arms, it could not attract the attention which was afterward bestowed upon it;

20*

and for the time being, she had to content herself with the satisfaction of having saved it.

She landed at Calais. For ten years she had been exiled from this soil—for ten long years. She joyfully set foot on the French shore, and her heart throbbed more rapidly at the thought that she was now again at home, and that she had spent, and might spend yet, so many happy days in this country. She was again animated with bright hopes.

But painful impressions were soon to lessen this first flush of joy.

Prussian uniforms met her eyes as soon as she had landed, and the town itself was occupied by foreign troops. She grieved deeply at this state of affairs. Although the invaders had humiliated her personal enemy, the disgrace of her country prevented her from gloating over his misfortunes. She deeply lamented the fate of France, and said that only a foreign tyrant could have exposed her to calamities to which her native rulers, no matter how deplorable their weakness might have been, would never have subjected her.

Her heart weighed down by such thoughts, she continued her journey. The nearer she came to Paris, the more painful grew her emotions at the sight of the vast masses of troops from all countries of Europe, which were assembled in the environs of the capital. They were encamped around the church of St. Denis, where the ashes of the French Kings reposed, and desecrated this hallowed soil by singing their native hymns on the grave of St. Louis.

At last she reached the gates of Paris. But was she awake, or had a dismal dream captivated her reason? Such was the question which she asked herself as she rode through the streets of the city, where she saw so many foreigners, as if France had ceased to exist. The Louvre and the Tuileries were occupied by Prussian soldiers, and she had to suffer the humiliation of submitting to the decrees and orders of foreigners.

"*J'ai un chagrin rongeur sur cette France, que j'aime plus que jamais,*" she had said in exile. "*Je sens distinctement que je ne puis vivre sans cette France.*"

And now she had returned to France and to Paris, and sighed at the thought that it did not offer her what she had expected to find there; for she was too ardent a patriot to be insensible to the humiliations which her country was compelled to undergo.

In St. Petersburg, Madame de Stael had repeatedly conversed with the Emperor Alexander. She was glad to meet him again in Paris, and, still engrossed as she was with admiration of the English constitution, she told him that she congratulated his subjects on being governed by him so well without such a fundamental law. He gave her the well-known answer:

"*Je ne suis qu'un accident heureux, Madame.*"

She now looked around for her old friends, the companions of better and happier days. What had become of all of them?

Benjamin Constant had quietly lived at Göttingen, while she had traveled through the world; he had collected there, materials for his great work on the religions of the nations. Since he had been unable to accompany Madame de Stael, whose wonderful genius attracted him again and again with magic force whenever he thought he had emancipated himself from her influence; since he had been compelled to part with her, the sweet joys of his domestic life had contented him, and he passed his days in cheerful intercourse with the distinguished men, such as Villers, Goerres, Kreutzer, and Heyne, whom he met in the small university town.

Here he wrote, in the midst of the remnants of the grand army of the poor mutilated soldiers who passed through the quiet town after the disasters of the Russian campaign, and amidst the booming of the cannon of Bautzen and Leipzig, his famous book, *L'Esprit de Conquête et de l'Usurpation*, which created the greatest sensation at that period.

Of Madame de Stael he had received no other news than such as the newspapers contained; for the governments did not respect the secrets of the mails; her letters were opened; and as she was well aware of it, she took good care not to write to her intimate friends.

Besides, her relations with Rocca had widened the gulf between her and Constant. She was unwilling to confess to the latter that she had adopted the obscure and sick young man as her protector and friend; she was clear-sighted enough to perceive the humiliating side of this union, and she was afraid lest Constant should discover in her letters what she wished to conceal from him.

No sooner had Benjamin Constant heard that she was about to return to Paris, than he left Göttingen, hastened to Coppet, where he joined her eldest son, Augustus, and went with him, in Bernadotte's suite, by way of Brussels to Paris.

A few days after his arrival, he published in the *Journal des Débats* of April 21, 1814, an article on the Restoration, whose leading idea was the neutrality of the royal power, and by which he laid the foundations of the new parliamentary opposition.

A new field now opened to his activity; a new life dawned upon him; his enthusiasm awoke, and his writings and speeches bore witness to the ardor with which he glowed for the glory and honor of France. In this frame of mind he arrived one morning, at the house of Madame de Stael, who was engaged in her toilet, and had her hair dressed at that moment.

She met him in deep emotion.

His appearance had undergone a marked change since they had last seen each other; nor had she remained the same. Although time had dealt more gently with her than with him, she had inwardly grown much older than he.

M. de Rebecque was now forty-seven years old; so he was at the height of his physical and intellectual strength. His head was bald, his hair gray; and his eyes, which had once looked so bright and hopeful, were deeply buried in their sockets. Only his enthusiasm had not left him, and with it he hopefully looked forward to the new era which he thought was dawning upon France; in this point he and Madame de Stael agreed once again before life parted them for evermore.

She now presented to him the pale, grave Rocca, of whose existence Benjamin Constant knew nothing. The sick young man cast on him a searching glance, which Constant met in the same spirit; but neither of them uttered his secret thoughts.

Madame de Stael met M. de Montmorency, too, in Paris, where he had lived for some time past under the surveillance of the police. Their friendship remained as cordial as ever, though their political views differed more and more. Montmorency shortly after went to Ghent, in order to lay the wishes of the Royalists before Louis the Eighteenth. Madame de Stael, on her part, was still an ardent lover of liberty, and advocated her political principles with as much zeal and eloquence as before.

Madame Récamier had traveled abroad since Napoleon had exiled her, and she had not yet returned to Paris. Madame de Stael wrote to her:

"PARIS, May 20, 1814.

"I am ashamed to be without you in Paris, dear angel of my life. Inform me of your plans. Shall I meet you at Coppet, where I intend to spend four months? After so many sufferings, I build my sweetest hopes on you."

Narbonne was the only intimate friend whom she was not to meet again. Having entered the service of Napoleon some time ago, he had first been appointed Governor of Raab, and in 1813 he had died of typhoid fever at Torgau.

The Restoration meanwhile progressed very rapidly, and Madame de Stael dreamed afresh of a constitutional kingdom. Although she was in feeble health, she yielded to these hopes with all her ardent zeal, while Benjamin Constant earnestly warned her against overtaxing her failing strength. His activity as a journalist was perfectly incredible, and his energy and perseverance increased with the obstacles which he had to surmount.

CHAPTER XVII

THE EAGLE AT THE TUILERIES.

MADAME DE STAEL had returned in autumn, after a brief sojourn at Coppet, to Paris, which the Allied Powers had left in the meantime. She hopefully looked forward to the winter, rented a fine house on Rue Royale, and opened her *salon* to the brilliant society of the capital. In spite of her feeble health, she would not and could not do without the enjoyments of social life; hence, she resisted her sufferings to the best of her power, and concealed from her friends her disease, which was not visible in her appearance.

Her friends had never seen her sick, and therefore believed that she was now, too, in good health. Heat and cold and the change of the seasons had never produced any injurious effect upon her. It had never been necessary for her to devote any attention to the preservation of her health, and her mental restlessness had even rendered it needless for her to take regular exercise. She never knew nervous weakness, and therefore did not believe in it. "*J'aurais pu être malade comme une autre,*" she said, "*si je n'avais pas vaincu la nature physique.*"

But, even though she had been able to overcome slight indispositions by the strength of her will, she could not stem in this manner the disease now preying upon her. No will is able to overcome sleepless nights.

She was now in the midst of a new world in that city of Paris, for which she had pined so long. A Bourbon sat on the throne, and slowly destroyed all her precious dreams.

Festivals were given in Paris. Madame de Stael had to introduce to the brilliant society of the capital her only daughter, to whom she wished to secure a home of her own. Albertine de Stael was to marry a man whom she loved, and she became Duchess de Broglie.

Her son Augustus, a grave young man of excellent character, did not stay a long time in Paris, inasmuch as the quiet life of Coppet was more agreeable to him.

Rocca lived with her, but never appeared by her side in public. He submitted to this incognito which she imposed on him, in order not to betray to her children the weakness of which she had been guilty. The pale, sickly man played the part of a faithful friend of the family; the world, however, contemplated him with a malicious smile. Madame de Stael did not take any notice of it. She was conscious of no wrong; and his love, whose warmth consoled her in all gloomy hours, and animated her with fresh hope and courage, was worth more to her than the sneers of the world.

Madame Récamier had now returned to Paris. She had always been a friend of the Bourbons, upon whom she looked, in her piety, as the rulers of France by the grace of God, and so her house became the rendezvous of the Royalists.

Madame de Stael differed with her friend on this point; but the respect which she always entertained for genuine convictions, prevented her from opposing her otherwise than with the warm words of her own convictions, and their friendship did not suffer in consequence.

It was, however, soon to be put to a new test. Benjamin Constant, hitherto an ardent adherent of the constitutional party, whose principles he had advocated for fifteen years past, suddenly kept away from the soirées of Madame de Stael, and society asked in surprise why he did so. He himself evaded in confusion all inquiries on this subject. But fame did not keep silent, and was not long in informing Madame de Stael of the cause of his desertion.

An ardent passion for her beautiful friend had suddenly seized him. The grave, bald-headed man loved her with the ardor of early youth, and basked only in the sunshine of her eyes. He had known her for many years past, without being enamored of her; and now, when earnest life had ripened his mind, and so many grave events counseled moderation to him, he suddenly forgot the whole world, and threw himself at her feet, and obeyed her slightest wishes. His attachment to Madame de Récamier silenced his hatred of the Bourbons, and it was her spirit which caused him to denounce Napoleon in unmeasured terms.

Madame de Stael regretted the course which her former protégé pursued. She was indifferent to his love, but she could not but resent his defection from his party. She punished him for it by instructing her banker not to make any more payments to him on her account. This step filled him with intense indignation.

Thus approached the year 1815.

Early in the morning of the 6th of March, Madame de Stael was informed that Bonaparte, her enemy, had landed on the shores of France. This intelligence threw her into the utmost consternation.

She knew what consequences would arise from this event; she thought the earth must open under her feet and swallow her up at his approach, so dreadful was the thought of his return to her. She tried to pray, but her lips refused to open. Her imagination conjured up before her all the terrors of hell, and filled her with boundless despair. She was unable to regain her composure; and the dreadful anguish which she suffered during these days, gave the death-blow to her health.

She hastened to Madame Récamier. The hour of danger and her terror made her forgetful of the obstacles which had lately arisen between them. The terror of Napoleon's name united the two friends again.

She found Madame Récamier engaged in reading a letter which she had just received from Benjamin Constant. It read as follows:

"Pardon me for embracing this opportunity to molest you; but it is only too agreeable to me. My fate will be decided in five or six days; for although, to conceal the interest you take in me, you refuse to believe it, I am convinced that Marmount, Chateaubriand, Lainé, and I, are the four men in France whose lives are in the most imminent danger. Hence, it is certain that, unless we defeat him, I shall in a week hence either be exiled, imprisoned, or shot. Grant me as much time as possible during these two or three days previous to the battle. In case I should die, it would do you good to have vouchsafed such kindness to me, and you would certainly regret having refused my last prayer. My attachment to you is such that a mark of indifference on your part would be more dreadful to me than my death-warrant four days hence. Did you like my article, and did you hear what was said about it?" *

"Poor Benjamin!" said Madame de Stael, as she returned the note to her beautiful friend. "His attachment to you, which is by no means inexplicable to me, *mon ange*, has caused him to lose his head. But what will become of us? Shall we stay here, or flee? *Mon Dieu! Mon Dieu!*"

Her beautiful friend tried to calm her. The Royalists did not believe in the possibility of Napoleon's return to Paris,

---

* Mémoires de Chateaubriand.

and she shared their opinion. Hence, she was indifferent to the apprehensions of Benjamin Constant, and she availed herself of her influence over him to cause him to attack the returning Emperor in more and more unmeasured terms.

But Madame de Stael refused to take the same hopeful view of the future. She passed three days in an agony of suspense. At last, on the 9th of March, when it was rumored that the telegraph had brought no news from Lyons, inasmuch as a cloud had obscured the view, she knew what kind of a cloud it was. Was she to flee the city?

On the same evening she went to the Tuileries to wait on Louis the Eighteenth. She found him seemingly in good spirits; but the uneasiness hidden under his calm air, did not escape her.

The walls of the Tuileries were still decorated with the eagles of Napoleon; they had led him to many a victory, and her forebodings told her that they would not yet be faithless to him.

From the Tuileries she drove to a soirée, in order to hear what the Parisians hoped and feared. Here she found the company engaged in the merriest conversation, and her anxiety was derided. One of the ladies said to her, sneeringly:

"*Quoi! Madame, pouvez-vous craindre que les Français ne se battent pas pour leur roi légitime contre un usurpateur?*"

These words seemed to her preposterous. Much as she hated Napoleon, she could not share the silly opinion that an army which he had led to so many victories, should forget the glory of these years, and suddenly be actuated by the principles of legitimacy.

No more did she believe in the possibility of a constitutional empire, and she smiled at Napoleon's efforts to mislead Paris by liberal measures.

" Quiconque est loup, agisse en loup,
C'est le plus certain de beaucoup,"

she said, shaking her head, when her friend proposed to her to join his party. She advised those who wished to serve him, to lend him their swords, in order to keep the foreign armies from the frontiers of France, and through their patriotism to regain the respect of Europe. She was too high-minded to consult her personal interests at this juncture, and looked with contempt on the men who now served a Bourbon, and now a Napoleon.

Benjamin Constant was to find out in a very unpleasant manner how little he could do without the advice of this lady. When he heard that Napoleon had reached Paris, he was panic-struck, and thought only of his personal safety; the courage on which he had prided himself before Madame Récamier had been a self-deception ; he trembled cowardly in the face of the danger; and to save his threatened life, he hastened to the American Embassador, Mr. Crawford, whom he implored to grant him an asylum. The Embassador helped him to make his escape; but no sooner had he left Paris, than he regretted what he had done; he had to return to the lady whom he loved; he could not bear a separation from her, and returned to his place of concealment.

General Sabastiani met him there, and persuaded him to support the new Government, and Benjamin Constant was weak enough to accept the position of Counselor of State under Napoleon.

No sooner had he taken this step, than he rued it; but he could not retrace it. He was ashamed to meet Madame de Stael; he was ashamed to look Madame Récamier in the face; and, to obtain forgetfulness, he became a gambler.

CHAPTER XVIII.

THE LAST DREAM OF LIFE.

THE Hundred Days were past. Napoleon had signed his abdication on the 5th of July, 1815, and sailed on the *Bellerophon* for St. Helena. Madame de Stael had witnessed these momentous events from afar. Despite her hatred of Napoleon, she could not forgive France for permitting the foreign troops to invade her, and she mourned over this new humiliation heaped upon her country.

Last year's events had taught her what might be expected of a Bourbon. The egotism of Louis the Eighteenth, who cared only for his own comfort, disgusted her. She built no hopes on the second Restoration, because the foreign powers had forced it upon France on their own terms; hence, the departure of her greatest enemy almost left her cold, and she sadly looked forward to the developments of the future.

At the beginning of the winter, she returned to her magnificent house in the Rue Royale. Benjamin Constant was no longer in Paris. Having performed the undignified task which the Chamber had intrusted to him, in commissioning him to implore the clemency of the foreign powers, he had, to escape from his remorse and confusion, gone to England, where he issued his novel *Adolphe* and his *Recollections of the Hundred Days*. Poor Constant! He had become the sport of circumstances, and had lost faith in himself.

Weighed down by the apprehension that he might never be

permitted again to set foot on the soil of France, he tried to write a justification of his conduct; and this paper, combined with Decazes' intercession, finally caused the Government to consent to his return to Paris.

Madame de Stael pitied him, although her compassion was not free from indignation. She saw how grievously she had mistaken his character; how few of the virtues with which her imagination had adorned him, he possessed in reality; how she alone had made a distinguished man of him; and how contemptible had been his course since he had emancipated himself from her influence.

Her sleepless nights gave her much time for reflection, and caused her to see many things in a new light. She prayed a great deal, not in words which she had learned by heart, but in thoughts full of faith in the immortality of those whom God had created. She had never dabbled with metaphysics, nor with subtle investigations into the objects and intentions of God in creating the world. "*J'aime mieux l'oraison dominicale que tout cela*," she said.

She loved life; she did not wish to give it up; she did not look forward to death with a heart full of resignation. Her breast heaved many a deep sigh as she felt the fatal progress of her disease. "Poor human nature!" she said. "Ah! What is life? What are we? Our existence resembles that gobelin tapestry whose front does not exhibit the woof, while the reverse shows all the threads. The secret of our life on earth consists in the connection of our faults with our sufferings. I never committed a wrong which did not result in suffering."

Rocco never left her now. He read to her, comforted her, cheered her up, and his love surrounded her with a tender solicitude which she constantly acknowledged with fervent gratitude. Her children, tenderly as they were attached to her, had before them the future with all its hopes and interests; but Rocco's life was bound up in hers.

She had renewed her social relations; she received a large circle of acquaintances; she was visited by all the distinguished foreigners who flocked to the French capital after the second Restoration, and no one suspected her intense sufferings, owing to the wonderful control which she exercised over herself.

After her sleepless nights, she rose at a late hour, and did not receive her friends until toward nightfall. In the morning she sat greatly exhausted in her room; the pale Rocca sat opposite to her; and she listened to him with eyes half closed as he read to her her letters and the papers.

"You are exhausted," she would say to him now and then. "Cease reading; it tires you too much."

"I do not feel tired as long as I am with you," he replied, with a glance of tenderness, which brought tears to her eyes.

"Oh, Rocca, if I should lose you!" she exclaimed, gazing at him with an air of tender anxiety.

He shook his head incredulously.

"What animates me, keeps death away from me," he said, serenely. "An immortal fire glows in my veins."

She sighed. "Would that I had met you at an earlier day!" she exclaimed, in a low voice.

A beautiful young lady entered the room.

"Pardon me for disturbing you, dear mamma," she said. "There is in the ante-room a gentleman whom you refused to admit because his name was not announced to you correctly. He complained to me about it, when I passed him, and I am sure you would regret not having seen him."

"Well, who is it?" asked Madame de Stael, impatiently.

"Ochlenschläger."

"Ah! Is it he? I shall certainly be glad to see him. Pray invite him for to-night, and excuse me for being unable to receive him immediately. Nine years ago, my friends could visit me at all hours; but now I have to try to find an hour when I may be able to receive them. Ah! Poor human nature!"

"You will get better," said Rocca, consolingly. "Next spring you will recover your strength."

"Say no more about it, Rocca. My daughter looks very well to-day, does she not? I hope she is happy. I have procured her another lot than that which fell to my share. I have warned her against the dangers of fame and politics; she was not to imitate in any manner the example I had set her. I did not want her to undergo the same sufferings which had befallen me. *J'ai assez de moi en moi, et je veux qu'on me renvoie autre chose que ma voix.* We must educate our children for life, and not try to deceive them. I always told them the truth, and never misled them. To become happy, they had to stand on firm ground, and look forward to their future with unclouded eyes. I never concealed my faults from them, but always pointed out to them the evil consequences arising therefrom. This produced the most salutary effects. My frankness touched them. ' *Si vous aviez des torts, non seulement j'en serais malheureuse, mais j'en aurais des remords,*' I said to them. I was unable to bear my exile. I did not set them an example of courage and resignation. Fortunately, I have to suffer for it. Ah, Rocca, how sad it is that our passions should darken our mind and mislead us so grievously. *Pauvre nature humaine!*"

"You could not help it," replied Rocca. "It was your nature."

He comforted her thus in her own words. But she replied:

"To yield to one's nature is weakness. I should have resisted it. It was Rousseau who misled me. Now it is too late. But I only was weak. I never was bad and vicious. I strove only for the good, and never injured anybody save myself; that is my consolation."

"Nature had endowed you with extraordinary gifts, and had therefore to exempt you from the ordinary rules. I should be loth to see you resemble other women."

She sighed.

When Oehlenschläger appeared in her *salon* in the evening, he found Madame de Stael surrounded by a brilliant circle of guests, and no one suspected the efforts which she had to make in order to play her part for a few hours. The Northern poet had to elbow his way through the crowd up to the sofa where she sat, her head covered with a turban.

"Ah, Oehlenschläger," she merrily exclaimed, holding out her hand to him. "I hope you have brought your youngest child with you? You do not appear here as a stepfather?"

The stiff Northerner could not adapt himself so suddenly to the *nonchalance* of her manner; she acted as if he had left her only yesterday, while he could not cross the long interval without a certain ceremoniousness. He looked at her in surprise.

"Speak! speak! I wish to hear if you have forgotten your French," exclaimed Madame de Stael. "We are going to perform some proverbs. *Il faut renouer la phrase interrompue.*"

She then introduced him to Alexander von Humboldt, whom he had seen in Berlin ten years ago, and now met here so unexpectedly. Augustus William Schlegel greeted him soon after. But, owing to the throng, no continued conversation was possible. Madame de Stael invited Oehlenschläger to dine with her on the following day. Our poet was unable to find his shoes on that day, and arrived, therefore, at seven, and not at six. Madame de Stael sat at a small round table with her

21

daughter, the Duchess de Broglie, and two elderly ladies. A seat had been reserved for Oehlenschläger. While the poet tried to make up for the time which he had lost, Madame de Stael congratulated him on the celebrity which he had obtained in the North.

"What is the North compared with the earth?" he replied, alluding to her fame.

She inquired about Werner, and chatted gayly about the past and present, the new productions of literature, and the successes of their common acquaintances, till the hour of his departure. Rocca and Schlegel did not make their appearance.

Madame de Stael now felt that her strength was fast ebbing away. Great as was her self-control, her will often was powerless, and she would then exclaim, "*Pauvre nature humaine!*" Her physicians were at a loss what to advise her. The balmy air of Pisa had not given her any relief, and she was soon unable to receive her friends in the evening; she had to keep her room, and often her bed.

Chateaubriand visited her one morning, and was surprised to hear that she could no longer leave her couch. Only a few days ago he had dined with her, and had not suspected that she was so very sick. She received him now in a dark room; supported by cushions, she sat in her bed, and held out to him her emaciated hand with her old cordiality.

It was so dark in the room that he was at first scarcely able to see her. When he had stepped close up to her, he perceived on her cheek the flush of the fatal fever which was preying upon her, and which could no longer be checked. Even in this gloom, a ray from her fine eyes met his face, and she said to him kindly:

"*Bon jour*, my dear Francis, I am sick; but that does not prevent me from loving you."

He took her hand and pressed it in deep emotion to his lips, for he felt that he would not often see her again.

When he looked up, he perceived on the other side of the bed a pale form resembling an apparition; and upon fixing his eyes on the figure, he discovered that it was Rocca. With hollow cheeks, dim eyes, and his features distorted with grief, the poor man gazed mournfully upon his sick friend, and seemed hardly to belong any longer to life. Not a syllable fell from his lips. He silently returned the greeting of the visitor by slightly nodding his head; he then arose and left the room noiselessly. He flitted past like a shade, casting a significant glance on the sick lady, who returned it. He probably wished to caution her against aggravating her fever by engaging in an animated conversation; at all events, Chateaubriand thought that this was his intention.

"You must husband your strength," he said to Madame de Stael. "You should do so for the sake of your friends."

She smiled gently.

"I cannot do so," she said; "I have always been true to myself, sincere, frank, and sad; *j'ai aimé Dieu, mon père et la liberté.*"

"God will preserve you to us for a long time; for he knows how little we can do without you," replied Chateaubriand.

"Ah, my dear Francis, it would be hard for me to die with such a wealth of love in my heart. I should not like to be separated from Albertine, neither here nor there. Ah, a daughter! You have no idea how dearly I love my daughter, my dear Francis!"

"But you do not think that you are in danger?" he asked, in surprise. "At your age? And with your strong constitution?"

"Why not? *Mon père m'attend sur l'autre bord.* Whenever I think of God, I must think of my father, too. I have asked Schlegel to write down all my sentiments on this sub· ject. I have tried to imagine the manner in which we shall pass from life to death, and I am convinced that God in His mercy will render it easy for us. Our ideas grow confused, our pains cease, and we are no more. That is my idea of death. With a last thought of all whom we love, we are there already. Is it not so?"

"Let us not think of it," said Chateaubriand, soothingly; and, in order not to weary her, he left her with the promise that he would soon repeat his visit.

A few days afterward, he received from her an invitation to dinner. He would scarcely trust his eyes. Could she have recovered so speedily? It was hardly possible.

When he arrived at her house, she was not in the *salon.* Like all patients in that state of decline, she was at times mistaken as to her condition, and believed herself to be quite well. None of her friends believed that her life was in danger. The lively interest which she took in everything that concerned them, whenever her fever abated, misled them. At the dinner-table, Madame Récamier asked M. de Chateaubriand what he thought of her friend's condition; he gave an evasive answer; for he himself did not suspect that he had already seen her for the last time.

Madame de Stael had removed to a house on the Rue Neuve des Mathurins; but the change had not done her any good. She could not sleep in the night time, and her strength declined more and more. Her hand was already unable to trace legible characters; her mind could no longer conceive clear thoughts; her life was fast ebbing away.

Her children were assembled round her bed; a grateful glance of love rewarded their faithful attachment. The pale

Rocca fixed his eyes on her as if unconsciously. She faintly wrung his hand yet, as if to console him for his loss, which, she knew full well, he would not survive.

Benjamin Constant, his arms folded on his breast, stood like a marble statue, at some distance from her couch. Since he had acquired the conviction that he would lose her for ever-more, both his love for Madame Récamier and his ambition had died away. He wrote no more books, he made no more speeches, he no longer took any interest in political affairs. Grief silenced all other emotions in his breast. The impending death of his friend aroused all his generous feelings. It was not until now that he felt what Madame de Stael had been to him, and he believed he could no longer achieve any-thing without her applause. He stood before her in somber silence, counting the years since he had known her, and since she had directed his steps with so much generosity and devotedness. And now he was to live without her for ever-more! He was scarcely able to restrain a loud outburst of his grief.

Madame Récamier sat in an arm-chair in a distant corner of the room, her face buried in her hands, and Benjamin Constant did not vouchsafe a glance to the beautiful lady.

Augustus William Schlegel appeared every now and then on tiptoe, and asked in a whisper how she was. This was the only interruption of the profound silence, amidst which the hands of the clock alone indicated the progress of time. Thus the still hour of midnight approached, and Madame de Stael ceased to breathe. She had passed away with de-vout faith, and in the hope that, by the side of her heavenly Father, she would meet her own father, and bask again in his love.

Her children looked after her, heart-broken and in despair.

The roses had just disappeared, when her remains arrived, in a carriage hung in black, and accompanied by Schlegel and Augustus de Stael, at Coppet, where they were to be interred in the mausoleum which she had erected to her father. It was built of black marble; and a bas-relief, the design of which she had drawn herself, surmounted the door. There she had knelt, weeping, at the coffins of her parents, who held out to her their hands from heaven. How often had she walked in the bosquet where it stood; how often had she sought there consolation in mournful hours; how often had she prayed there alone! Now she was to find repose there for evermore.

The members of the municipality of Coppet carried her coffin, as a proof of their love and respect for her; the whole council of Geneva attended her funeral. The Duke de Noailles had hastened from his neighboring estate of Rolle, to Coppet, and all her friends and relatives arrived from far and near, to pay the last honors to her. At her grave there was read a sermon written by Necker, and the thought that her own father thus took part in the funeral of his child, made a deep impression upon all mourners.

Her will was then read. It contained a request to her children to inform the world of her union with Rocca, and to treat the little boy, whom she had born to him, as a member of their family.

The bystanders heard this clause in surprise. Benjamin Constant turned deadly pale; his eyes shot fire, and he looked defiance at poor Rocca for a minute; but then his eyes fell on the coffin, and he left the room with a deep sigh, and disappeared for a long time.

Rocca, however, had remained perfectly apathetic. He had lost her; what were the affairs of this world now to him? He went to his brother in Provence, and died shortly afterward.

Augustus de Stael became proprietor of Coppet. Here he led a calm and grave life, devoted to the welfare of humanity, until his premature death, by which the name immortalized by his mother became extinct.

Natura la fece e poi ruppe la stampa.

THE END.

STEREOTYPED BY DENNIS BRO'S & CO., AUBURN, N. Y.